A
Woman
of Spirit

A Woman of Spirit

Herbert Tarr

DJF

DONALD I. FINE, INC.

NEW YORK

Library of Congress Cataloging-in-Publication Data

Tarr, Herbert.
    A woman of spirit / by Herbert Tarr.
        p. cm.
    ISBN: 1-55611-164-9
    I. Title
PS3570.A65W6 1989
813'.54—dc20   89-45441
                                                         CIP

Manufactured in the United States of America
        10 9 8 7 6 5 4 3 2 1

Designed by Irving Perkins Associates

For
ANNA TARGOVNIK
for a lifetime of lovingkindness
and joy

One

1

*I*F all life is change, I Hannah Brody must really be living! Once again my world is changing—this time for the good. The best. In a few more weeks, I leave my father's home to marry Rupert Trilling. A late age for marriage, twenty-five, but there were six good reasons: my six younger brothers and sisters. For them and future children of Rupert's and mine, I am setting down these recollections. How I wish Mother had left me such a keepsake.

At twenty-five, Mother already had her fourth child, me, and was again pregnant. What saved me from a similar fate was having the family and Papa to care for after she died in 1919 and our running away from Eastern Europe, where childbearing was regarded as the will of God, not of men. (As if all Jews, not just Jesus, were born with only nominal human participation.)

I was born on December 15, 1904, in Monaster in Galicia, which belonged to the Austro-Hungarian Empire before the Great War, those years when God reigned supreme and untested. Freud and Kafka and lots of other famous families also come from Galicia, but I don't suppose they boast about me. (What could they say about a

*plain Jewish farm girl who still misses her mother and tries her best
to help her family and bends God's ear on too many occasions? All
in all, He's behaved like a perfect gentleman: never has God told me
to shut up.)*

*My earliest memories—I was a child of five, maybe six—are of
Mother. She was very beautiful and very, very good. An extraordinary mensch. Really like an angel. I remember the way she washed
her babies. Testing the water, it shouldn't be too hot or cold. Picking
them up, cuddling them, kissing, before putting them in the tub, oh
so gently, all the while singing. The babies would coo back, gurgling
with pleasure. Bathed in love. She'd kill herself for each child,
Mother would.*

*I remember my father, a young man with deep-set black eyes,
heavy black eyebrows, moustache and beard. Handsome. He was
lovable to the children and the family. Also to goyim. Papa had been
married before, but his wife died in childbirth. He was about thirty
when he married Mother, she only sixteen.*

*Everyone said she was the most beautiful young lady in Monaster.
Bright, but quiet. Didn't like to show off. Immaculate. Always
dressed beautifully. Never sloppy. All the time wore an apron. (Me,
I can't go without an apron, either.) Hair reddish gold, like a sunrise.
When she married, it was all cut off for religious reasons. Mother
went with Father to ask a rabbi if they could make it a sheitel, a wig.
He said yes.*

*When not wearing it, Mother covered her head with a kerchief. I
was the one who would cut her hair. To the scalp I cut it. Foolish.
But that's the ultra-Orthodox custom. They believe a woman's hair
gets men all hot and bothered, so only her husband is entitled to see
her head uncovered. (Women, apparently, are incapable of getting
excited. Ultra-Orthodox men are forbidden to shave off any of their
hair.)*

*All of us children were close to Mother. But more than the others,
I listened. Out of rachmonus, compassion, she was so overworked.
I wanted to help. If Mother would say to my sister Miriam, two years
older, "Do this—" she wouldn't. She'd say, "Let Hannah do it." Me,
I wanted Miriam to do it. (You know, like children.) So Mother,
without another word, would start working herself, and then I'd run
over to spare her.*

But don't get me wrong—Miriam worked too. Only, she was a different type. Not domestic, like me. Afraid of nothing, livelier, a tomboy. More like Papa. Wasn't afraid to do things. To run like the wind, to climb a tree, to jump down. Me, I was a scaredy-cat.

Never were there birthday parties, only bar mitzvah celebrations for the boys. My parents made weddings in our house for poor girls. One was for an orphaned shiksa, a gentile. A big mitzvah, starting their married lives off happy. Father would make everybody to enjoy. He'd get up on top of the table to dance. Didn't dance with Mother, of course. That wouldn't have been proper. People liked Papa. The gentiles, too. They all made a living from him. A lumberman, he bought forests from them and cut lumber to build their houses. Never contracts, just a handshake.

Papa made a very nice living. I remember the presents he brought from the city. Blouses, skirts, shawls, exquisite jewelry. He took such great pleasure in bedecking Mother himself with necklaces and earrings and pins. (Once, though, he came back from shul on a Shabbas, without having eaten all morning, drank schnapps on an empty stomach, and because lunch wasn't ready, he slapped Mother. Oh, my! But maybe I just imagined that.)

Monaster was a small village, but our house was big. It had an attic, also a barn where we kept cows and horses. In the cellar was Papa's liquor store. And there was a large yard with grass and flowers. We grew our own oats, potatoes, corn, cabbage, other vegetables. People worked our fields.

Counting Papa's two married sisters and parents, there were only seven Jewish families there. Most of Galicia's Jews lived in cities—in some, were even the majority. But because he owned this big farm, Papa had settled among the goyim. There he built his own home, where he brought Mother. Her father was a well-to-do merchant, her step-mother a horrible woman.

(Mother didn't tell me that. She never said a bad word about anyone. But I myself saw that witch beat my young aunt with a broom handle. To this day it bothers me I did nothing about it. Of course, I was only a child, eight or so. Still, I should have done something.)

On Erev Shabbas Mother baked for the entire week. We had a stove you could creep inside—it was that big. The Sabbath was always holy at our house. Everything glistened. The dining room's big table was laid with a shimmering white linen cloth. A glittering candelabra on one side; on the other, gleaming silver candlesticks and two challahs covered with an embroidered shiny white satin coverlet, and at each setting, goblets of sparkling wine. After Mother lit a candle for each family member, Papa blessed every child and praised Mother by reciting the biblical chapter about eishes chayil, *the* woman of valor.

The Shabbas meal was always gefilte fish, soup with lukshen, a baked potato, carrot tzimmis, cucumber salad, fruit, a glass tea. Though we had a live-in maid, Mother always served. There was nothing she wouldn't do to please her husband. All through the meal we sang zmiros, afterwards the birchas ha-mazon, grace. A Sabbath musicale.

Every Shabbas morning Papa went to pray in shul in Lukavicz. Only men went to shul. We girls prayed at home. When they'd be blessing the new month, Mother went along. Papa led the service— he had a beautiful voice. Also read from the Torah, which not everyone could. After a lunch of cholent, my parents would take a nap. My cousins used to come over in the afternoon, and we'd read that week's Torah portion, then sing and dance and jump up and down in the attic in the straw till we looked like scarecrows, straw sticking from us everywhere.

I started school at six. My sister Miriam and a girl cousin were already there. The rest, goyim. But we went to learn, not to socialize. Studies were in Polish. (Until 1772 Galicia had belonged to Poland.) Also, because this was the western Ukraine, in Russian. To teach us girls Jewish subjects, a Hebrew teacher came to our house. During the week my brothers stayed over in the city of Linsk to study in a yeshiva, but for Shabbas returned home. To each other we spoke only Yiddish, to our goyishe neighbors, Russian. (German, we learned later in Bohemia, where we ran to during the Great War.)

Once a week the village priest would descend on our school like a plague. That was the terriblest time, hearing him call all Jews Christ-killers. He told my class Jews murdered Christian boys and girls to drain their blood for baking matzos!

Such a disgusting bilbul, *libel,* when the Torah prohibits the drinking of animal blood no less than five times. Well, I got up and told everyone how Mother spent hours salting meat to draw off the blood and soaking it in a pail of water to drain every drop. And that was from animals. Not only that, I said, Jewish children like Michalene Araten had been kidnapped and placed in convents, and their parents never able to get them out.

"What are you complaining about?" the priest answered me. "We save their souls." (Imagine!)

After that, after I opened up my mouth, the teacher sent us Jewish children to the yard whenever that big anti-Semite came to spread more poison. When I asked Mother to explain the behavior of a supposedly religious man, she said, "Hatred is curable—unless it rests on envy."

I have to write about Papa's mother, who lived with her husband a couple of miles from our house. Buba Bella was so clever, and she must have been very beautiful. Acted as a midwife for my mother and for other people. Not for money. Just to help. A mitzvah. She was a businesswoman too. Used to sell all kinds of things: schnapps and wine and tobacco, also cakes and bread which she baked. That woman was able to do everything! She supported her family because my grandfather—a very nice person, once an officer in Emperor Franz Josef's army—he got sick in the military. Something was the matter with his legs. I never saw him walk around. Bedridden. Oh, how he loved the grandchildren.

An extraordinary woman, Buba Bella. All the gentiles used to stop by for whiskey, and other things of hers too. One day this gentile comes in very drunk. Lots of gentiles there at the time. My grandfather was, as usual, in bed. Well, this here gentile went out from Buba's house into the yard, saw a ladder there and—who knows why?—decided to climb up to the attic. Being so drunk, he slipped off the ladder and fell down onto the woodpile underneath and was killed. Yes, killed.

The goyim ran out to see, made a big commotion. Grandfather screamed, "What happened?" When the police came, instead of telling the truth, the goyim said my grandfather had murdered that *drunk. My grandfather who was bedridden. So the police took him to court and sent him away to jail in Lemberg. And Buba Bella was left to look after five small children all by herself.*

Why did the gentiles say Grandfather murdered the drunk? Because they wanted to make a bilbul. No reason. Who needed a reason? Goyim made it up like they did in lots of places. Like all the blood libels. Or in France, that the Jewish Captain Dreyfus sold military secrets to Germany. It's happened in lots of places, they made up stories about Jews. But Austria-Hungary was different, because its Emperor Franz Josef was good to everybody, and especially to the Jews.

Not far from where Buba lived was the main highway. When she found out the Kaiser himself would be riding by there, she wrote everything down: how it happened, Grandfather's army service, her life, and all about the goy's accidental death from a fall, how many children she had, and how she supported the family because her husband was such a sick man and, yes, she went out to petition the Kaiser.

On the side of the highway was tall grass, and Buba lay there for hours until the Kaiser rode up in a carriage. Then she ran out and threw herself down in front of his horses. Luckily, he saw her in time to have them stopped. Soldiers came running over, grabbed her to throw her into a ditch.

But the Kaiser told them to bring Buba over to him. She bowed a couple of times, of course—this was the Kaiser—and, when he told her to speak, she handed him this long letter of hers. The Kaiser read it all, asked a lot of questions, then told her not to worry. She should go and take good care of herself and the children. After that—I don't know how long it took—the authorities let my grandfather go.

She was some personality, Buba Bella. Some people say I take after her. It's possible, I can't say. But I don't think I'm so quick like her. Nobody is.

1914. A month after my oldest sister went to America, war broke out. I remember Papa going to the train station all the time to find out what was going on. He talked a lot to Mother about the war.

Everyone was very frightened of the Russians, drawing closer and closer. Blaming the Jews for their military defeats, they were deporting entire Jewish communities deep inside Russia. Burning synagogues. Starting pogroms, which were a Russian invention. Looting. Murder. Rape.

Just at this time, Papa found a soldier lying almost dead in our fields. Papa picked him up and carried him into our house and worked on him, brought him to. The soldier hadn't eaten in days. So Papa gave him plenty of food and schnapps. I don't know if he was Polish or Russian. Didn't matter, Papa said, so long as he was a mensch, a decent person.

The next week the Russian soldiers came, or maybe they were Polish, and took whatever they wanted from our house. We were down in the cellar, hiding, everyone shivering when the soldiers broke in. My little brother started crying, and Mother covered his mouth, he shouldn't be heard. Two days later, afraid for our lives, we ran away from Monaster. Half the Jews of Galicia ran away at that time, hundreds of thousands. To Vienna, Prague, other places.

We settled in a town in Bohemia. Our whole family lived in one room. We went to school—Miriam, me and my five brothers. I was a good student, Miriam was better. She grabbed everything so fast. For the boys Papa hired a Hebrew teacher.

The Czechs and Germans very much admired my parents, invited them to town meetings and into their homes, when we observed holidays, asked them to explain Succos, Passover. Some people there were of Jewish ancestry, products of intermarriage, who wanted to learn about Judaism. One couple wanted to adopt a brother of mine (their own son had died). Another, childless, offered a lot of money for my new baby sister.

How terribly sad, my parents said, that these descendants of Jews were so completely assimilated. Whatever remained of their Judaism would die with them. Nothing to pass on to the next generation except money. End of the line.

Thirteen months later, Mother gave birth to still another girl. By that time, Papa had been drafted, with my oldest brother, Ben, into the army, leaving behind eight children to be looked after. I still don't know how Mother managed.

{9}

1919. When Papa returned after the war, nobody could recognize him. He'd refused all unkosher food. Shrunk. Papa decided to take us all back home, now under Polish rule after the collapse of the Hapsburg Empire. We walked all the way to Galicia. Trains were only for soldiers, being demobilized.

But Monaster was no longer home. Our house had been stripped bare by the goyim. Plundered. So Papa sold the house and lands and settled us in an apartment in the city of Linsk.

Miriam used to shop for the family. I did too, but I took more care of Mother and helped with the babies. In between the ten children there'd been a few miscarriages and twins who died days after being born. I often wondered how happy Mother was to have so many children. Even if she wasn't, I suppose she had to. Didn't talk about it. Mother used to keep everything to herself. Didn't have friends, always too busy caring for the family.

There was rationing then, and this Polish noble, a gentile, got us potatoes, cereal, other foods. He owed Papa a lot of money, and he was one of the few who paid up. Helped Papa sell the house in Monaster, too. Because he had dealt with Papa for years and liked him. A good man. But then—the greatest tragedy imaginable!

Mother came down with influenza. She was sick for three days. One bitter winter night Miriam and I were peeling potatoes for the next day, like always, in this terribly cold apartment. Mother had this big trunk filled with the girls' clothes and her own. In it a pink overblouse of hers, which she asked me to get. I looked and I looked, but couldn't find it. So I said, "Mama, why fuss so much about that one blouse?" Till this day it bothers me that I spoke to her like that. (Later on, I did find it, but I never should have been so fresh.)

That night Mother goes to bed in her pretty pink overblouse. After kissing the mezuzah and saying the Sh'ma, of course. The baby starts to cry, she tries to comfort her, but couldn't. Mama starts crying herself because she can't help the baby, being so weak from the influenza. So she asks me to take Tessie and give her something to eat, which I do, and everyone finally falls asleep.

When we wake up in the morning, Papa is calling Mother's name. She doesn't answer. "Sarah, Sarah," he calls. Still no answer. He goes over and shakes her, she doesn't move, and he sees she's dead.

Papa falls down, faints dead away. I can't remember what happened after that.

If my handwriting looks shaky, it's from tears. Because this didn't happen ten years ago. Before my eyes I see Mother dead right this minute. Only thirty-eight years old! Papa told me not to ask why. God, to His credit, has never offered an answer. There wasn't any I could accept.

Like my being barred from the funeral. To this day I resent their not letting the girls go. Even my baby sisters, who didn't have their periods yet and couldn't contaminate the men. No, they wouldn't let us girls into the cemetery. Stupid! My brothers went, said kaddish for mother. But not the girls. So I didn't see her any more. No more beautiful Mother, no more warmth.

Why did we come to America? The Poles and Russians were fighting each other again, and they wanted to draft my brothers. If it was hard to be Jews in civilian life, in the army it was impossible. Papa wouldn't give up his sons. A few years in the army, and my brothers would be Jews no more. They couldn't observe Sabbaths and holidays. They'd eat treif, marry gentile girls and forever be lost to the Jewish people.

Since there was no place better to remain Jews than Palestine, Papa went to the office of the Zionist organization to get visas. But Poles had libeled the Zionists, called them spies. Well, the police raided this office and arrested everyone there, Papa among them. A neighbor came running, saying Papa had been charged with spying. Spying! Could mean death. Miriam and I ran to the jail and we cried so, enough to bring heaven down to earth. The jailkeeper got hold of me and whipped me until somebody dragged me back to the apartment.

That's when my brothers and sisters came down with typhoid fever. Me, too. Miriam almost died. Her temperature shot up so high, the doctor shoved her into a bathtub of cold water, then wrapped her in wet sheets until the temperature dropped.

Weeks later, that fine Polish noble I've mentioned, he had pull with the authorities. He got to the mayor and showed the Zionists weren't doing anything bad. So Papa was finally released. And we were free to leave the country.

But England wouldn't let Jews into the Jewish National Home promised us by England and the League of Nations, not to mention God. So Papa worked to go to America instead. Cost him a fortune because he was taking along his sister and her six children. He went to Warsaw, to the American consulate. To get inside, where they gave out the visas, you had to lie on the sidewalk for entire days and nights.

Came time to leave, Papa's mother decided to stay behind. (Grandfather had died by then.) Said she was too old to go off to America. Have no idea how old she was then. In her seventies, I imagine, which was very old in those times. "I am the Jewish past, your children are the Jewish future," Buba Bella said. "You must go to America to save them."

When Papa returned with the visas from Warsaw, I had a relapse. This was shortly before Tisha B'Av, and Jews can't travel during the three weeks preceding that fast day. Papa started to cry, "What am I going to do? How can I leave? Hannah is so sick. I'm cursed!" But the doctor gave me medicine to take along on our voyage to the New World.

And so we left Galicia, where Jews had lived a thousand years. Left our homeland. Our home in Monaster. Aunts and uncles and cousins. And my beautiful Mother. (That such an angel lies in the earth! Isn't right, just isn't right.)

At the Polish border, the military were searching everyone. I was hardly breathing, so weak. They made us undress, even shoes and stockings. And all of Papa's money they took away from him— 100,000 guilden or kronen.

We were crying so, God Himself must have heard. From what was going on, my temperature shot up again. Everyone was so afraid of typhoid fever, they had me quarantined in a hospital on an island off Danzig. (The only time in my life I've had a room to myself.) I tried to doctor myself with my medicine and compresses, but my temperature wouldn't go down. Which meant I was holding up the family. I begged Papa to leave, I'd get to America later somehow by myself.

Poor Papa just cried. He was so depressed. Once after visiting me, it came into his mind to jump off the ferry into the water and drown himself. Somebody would then take pity on all his orphaned children and bring them to America. Then he realized, God in heaven, such a terrible sin it would be! And he felt a spirit restore him to sanity.

Back in Danzig, he was walking the streets. Didn't know what to do, where to turn. Suddenly he saw a sign outside a building with the name of that Polish noble Papa had done business with. This man, a lawyer, was his brother. Papa went inside, told him what happened at the border, how the Polish military took away all his money and passports.

The lawyer advised Papa to return to Warsaw. But at that time Warsaw was a dangerous place for religious Jews. The Poles ripped out their hair, tore off their beards. Papa was afraid to go. The lawyer, who was not Jewish, calmed him down. He wasn't a plain lawyer, this Pole. Knew influential people. Well, he made a party, got them drunk and bribed them. So we got back our passports and most of Papa's money. What Papa gave the lawyer I don't know, but a lot.

I was meanwhile getting stronger. But because I still ran a fever, the hospital wouldn't discharge me. Papa was frantic. The family would miss the boat to America. Then I got this idea. As soon as I heard the nurses in the corridor, I wrapped cold compresses around my thermometer before showing it to them.

"Goodbye, God," I said, "I'm going to America."

From Danzig we sailed to Rotterdam, where a big ship was to take us across the Atlantic Ocean. The ship to Rotterdam was very little and the voyage stormy. People having to go to the toilet went where they were lying or sitting. Miriam and I couldn't do such a thing, so we went up on deck to the toilet. Outside, it was terrible, with tall waves like mountains. Came one wave, sucked me to the railing, sweeping away barrels tied to posts. I tried to hold on, but was slipping into the ocean. Luckily, Miriam grabbed me. I grabbed her, she grabbed the doorknob. A huge wave knocked both of us inside a cabin onto the floor. Yes, Miriam saved me.

No, I don't remember seeing the Statue of Liberty from the boat. Too busy looking after my beautiful baby sister Tessie and all the others. But Ellis Island, who could forget? Thousands of people huddled there clutching their hopes to their hearts. This doctor examined us from head to toe. Put Papa on the side. You can imagine how scared we felt. Maybe he'd be sent back to Poland.

An official wanted to see if we could read and write. Polish, Russian, German, Yiddish, Hebrew we knew. But we were afraid they'd want to test English, which none of us could speak. We were so afraid they'd send us all back. But, thank God, they checked us off as literate.

That night—a Friday night, Erev Shabbas—there was a concert on Ellis Island. A great soprano from the Metropolitan Opera sang a Yiddish song Mother used to sing, Eili, Eili. Papa cried like a baby. Nobody could not cry watching him and listening to Lily Pons sing, "My God, my God, why have you forsaken us? . . ." But the song does end with the Sh'ma: "Hear O Israel, the Lord our God, the Lord is One." God in heaven, I'll never forget that.

I used to think all those pregnancies shortened Mother's life. But I may have been wrong. It was probably the housework and looking after all the children. Miriam, who disliked keeping house, took a job in a factory, which left me the house to look after. (My oldest sister and brother were married.) That, provided my two little sisters didn't wake me up during the night, took only from dawn to midnight. Of course, I wasn't the only one working. My brothers attended school and helped Papa in the grocery store he bought, while the two little ones ran me ragged at home. Miriam hoped Papa would marry again, but he said he loved Mother too much. (Who, except a complete lunatic or a woman with eight children of her own, would marry a father of eight?)

All week long I would dream of Shabbas, when there was no housework except feeding nine mouths three times that day and cleaning up afterwards. First, of course, I had to spend hours picking all the pinfeathers out of five chickens. (Miriam told me to wise up and discard all the skin. But that would have produced an un-Jewish soup: no fat.) There was also ten pounds of white fish, pike, carp and onions to chop for gefilte fish, and potatoes to grate for kugel, and noodles and fresh vegetables. (Those that came in cans and cardboard tasted as if they had crawled inside and died.)

At first, to keep shop people from taking advantage, I combed my hair into a bun to make me look older than sixteen. In six months' time, even without the bun, people thought me the mother of at least three. But they being so beautiful, I felt flattered.

I had no boyfriend for five years. Where did I go that boys went? To tell the truth, I didn't even look at boys. Who had boys in mind? My father and my motherless sisters and brothers needed me. So on that score I never had regrets. (Miriam says I have no regrets because I have no brains.)

Then, one day, I was coming home on the subway. It was crowded, every seat was taken, and this nice young man got up and gave me his. He took me home, and we made my first date ever. After night school he took me to a street fair. Later, to Broadway and lectures. A sportswriter for the New York Daily News. American-born, smart—handsome too. Mike.

He said I was pretty, a surprise. Never really paid attention to my appearance. But Mike kept insisting, and I didn't argue. I wasn't bad-looking, I suppose. But the pretty one in the family is Miriam.

Unfortunately, neither looks nor her intelligence helped. Papa matched Miriam up with someone from a very fine family in Galicia. But she didn't like him. Still, saying that love comes after marriage, as it did between Isaac and Rebecca, and Mother and him—also arranged matches—Papa pushed it. So Miriam went along.

I remember Ben, our oldest brother, pressuring her. "Who do you think you are, anyway? You should be grateful any man wants you." (What made big brother think he was smart enough to direct Miriam's life? Just because he could pee standing up?)

Mike and I went out together, I don't know how long, till he got serious. But I couldn't say yes, not with Miriam soon to marry. Who would look after the family? So I told Mike not to come around anymore. My little sister came into the apartment just as he was leaving. "What happened here? Why was that boy crying? Why are you crying?" she asked.

{15}

Such a fine young man, Mike. Once a week I continued to buy his paper, me who cared nothing for sports. Months later, his byline disappeared. The Daily News *told me he had moved to Chicago to write for the* Tribune. *Sure enough, there was Mike's name in a copy of the paper I got hold of. (Now that I'm getting married, I should throw it away, I suppose.)*

As maid of honor at Miriam's wedding, it was up to me to lift her veil when she was to sip from the cup of wine. When I did so—oh, my! Her eyes were filled with tears, but they didn't look like tears of happiness.

Remembering my aunt being beaten by her terrible stepmother, I wanted to cry out, to stop the ceremony. But I didn't do a thing. Couldn't make a scene, shame the family. Perhaps I had misinterpreted. After all, Miriam was the spirited one. Me, I was dutiful. Who was Hannah that she could see into another's heart?

Still, as the groom stamped on the emptied glass of wine, I ma le up my mind that nobody, but nobody, was going to interfere in r y life. I would choose my own husband.

Rereading that last sentence made me laugh out loud. Among who was I going to select a husband? It wasn't as if I was in great demand. Or even little demand. Except for that time with Mike. Mobs of boys were not breaking down my door. I didn't even have girlfriends. Miriam made friends at work. I had nobody. If a friend wanted to go somewhere, I couldn't make it. The family was always on my head. How was I to keep friends? And never having earned wages, I had no money to spend going out anyplace to meet people.

Thank America then for the public library. Every week I checked out a new load of books, which I could read now that my sisters were in school, and there was no chance of any more babies popping up. Books had so much to teach, all that wisdom distilled for years into a few hundred pages. "Live and learn"—that became my motto.

Often characters in fiction seemed more real than in life. Certainly more understandable. In real life only God knows what goes on inside of people, and I'm not sure even He can change them the way a novelist can—one, two, three.

Ben, for example. After the Great War, he got into a big fight over *something or other with Papa, who slapped his face. So what does his oldest son do? Runs away from home and Mother, who worries herself to death about him. Afterwards, when it was too late, Ben reconciled himself with Papa in America. God would have made Ben come back home in time, if He could have done so. Certainly any novelist with a heart would have seen to that.*

Funny, how things work out. If it weren't for Ben running away, I'd never be getting married now. He didn't have the money to get to America, but this stranger that he and his pregnant wife met on the train to Danzig loaned him the funds. That woman who took pity was Rupert's mother.

Only just before this, after years of near-starvation in Poland, she herself had received some money. Like tens of thousands of other men, her husband had gone to America before the war to earn enough to bring his family over. During the war, of course, no money got through, and Mrs. Trilling and her children were so poor, a single egg had to be shared six ways.

When Ben's wife gave birth to a boy, they invited their benefactors to the briss, where I was helping with the food. Mr. and Mrs. Trilling looked me up and down, examined my whole being till my cheeks burned with embarrassment. Then told their son Rupert to get in touch with me. (I think they liked the way I served.)

Rupert, who's in the textile business with his father and brothers, turned out to be tall, slender, dark, nice-looking. Big, sensitive brown eyes. Dressed very nicely. Only two or three suits, but immaculate. Always came shaved nicely, with a sky blue silk shirt, navy blue suit. The more I saw him, the more I liked him. He was very nice to me, in every way. Never coarse or vulgar. Spoke nicely. Intelligent.

An older sister who thought his original name, Reuben, wasn't American enough had renamed him. (His brothers had an even stranger story to tell. Their forged passports listed their birthdates as five months apart. And they aren't even twins.) Though I have more secular learning than Rupert, he's a lot smarter. He'd have made a good professional, a doctor or lawyer. But not a rabbi. The Great War's death and destruction, which he saw first-hand and refuses to talk about, made him question too much.

One of the wonderful things about Rupert: he can always make me laugh. *But his humor is never nasty or insulting, never at somebody else's expense. Reminds me of the Talmudic legend: Elijah pointed out two men in the marketplace as most deserving of guaranteed reservations in Paradise—clowns who cheered up unhappy people with their antics.*

We went out for a long time, and were engaged almost two years—the happiest of times for me—till my sisters were old enough for me to leave. Rupert is so good and patient. Very lovable. And the way he speaks. Shows respect to Papa, to the children, to everyone. I like his manner. Together we can make a life, I'm sure of it.

If the momzerim will let us. Just last week, with British soldiers looking on passively, the Arabs massacred sixty-seven Yeshiva students (including a dozen American boys) who were studying in Hebron, where Jews have lived since the days of Abraham, then expelled all the Jews, wounding sixty. Afterwards, Beatrice Webb, the British colonial secretary's wife, commented, "I can't understand why the Jews make such a fuss over a few dozen of their people killed in Palestine. As many are killed every week in London in traffic accidents, and no one pays any attention."

Nothing, I promise, will ever wipe that atrocity from my memory.

To go from the monstrous to the beautiful, with Rosh Hashonah coming up, weeks later Rupert wrote me a letter, which I immediately answered. May we be worthy for God to grant the wishes expressed in them.

September, 1929

My beloved, dearest Hannah,

Today we stand at the end of the old year and at the crest of the new one. This moment awakens in me entirely new feelings from those of years past. Before, at the coming of the new year, I always sent away the old year with the hope that the new year would bring me what the old year failed to bring. That's the way it used to be.

But now, things are altogether different. Whatever the future brings, my heart will always be full of longing for the year just past, which I will never forget. It remains imbedded in my memory forever. This has been the happiest time of my life, those sweet moments you have created for me. Many times, when we used to

{18}

dream of our future, I felt I had reached my highest happiness. This year has been a delicious appetizer of our life together.

As for me, I assure you I will do everything in my power to make you happy, you who are like my own everlasting glass of hot tea. My hands warm to your touch, my insides to your being.

I wish your beloved father a good year, and your sisters and brothers as well.

Gratefully yours forever,
Rupert

September, 1929

My beloved, my dearest Rupert,

Today more than ever I feel the seriousness of the coming new year, as I look forward to this great change in my life. I feel the responsibility, this great accountability life is now placing on me. But I believe with all my heart and with all my being and with all my might that you, only you, are the only one who understands me, and who will know how to lighten the burdens of life and how to make life pleasant and sweet under all circumstances.

My dearest, my greatest wish for the new year is to live happily with you. What a pity there are so few happy people in this world! How I would love us to be among them.

Yours, now and always,
Hannah

P.S. If I am tea, Rupert, you are a refreshing glass of cool seltzer. You make my heart fizzzzzzzzzzzzzzz!

Just realized! Next time I write in this notebook, it will be as a married woman.

2

SEEING her engagement drawing to a close, Hannah was almost sorry. This happiest of times had been her first vacation ever. Pouring out her heart as she had never done to anyone. Rupert's love had her thinking better of herself, his equal, just as in her company he spoke with more ease and confidence. Both, more poised now, stood taller in the company of others. Together they had created a shared loveworld that made them feel as superior to everyone else as religion made Christians and Jews feel to each other. No wonder everyone yearned to be in love. It was life's biggest bargain. Nourishment for the heart, as God was for the soul.

Hannah and Rupert chose a wedding band of white gold and platinum—perfectly smooth (customary, to invoke a marriage without rough spots. Not even quarrels; her parents never had any, valuing *shalom bayis*, household harmony, above all else). The diamond engagement ring reminded Hannah of all the times Papa had bedecked Mother with jewelry (most of which had been sold to start up the family grocery in Brooklyn).

Rupert told her to spare no cost in furnishing their future apartment. His father, having paid him a nominal salary for nine years, owed him. Fine people, though perhaps mismatched, Rupert's parents. Eight years by himself in America, Mr. Trilling had mastered English, become Americanized, while she had spent the war years in poverty in Poland and spoke only Yiddish. He was jolly, full of jokes, secular; she serious, almost somber, religious. Mr. Trilling on occasion even attended a burlesque show.

Which scandalized his wife.

Hannah too, having heard that women performers actually took off almost all their clothes on stage *in public.* "Can that be true?" she asked Rupert.

"You think people would pay to see women put *on* clothes?" Nevertheless, his father went to burlesque for the comics. "*That's* what's so funny."

Had Rupert himself ever gone to a burlesque show?

"Never in all my life to see a *comic.* Well, *one* of us shouldn't be taken completely by surprise on our wedding night."

Hannah turned a deeper shade of red than usual. (Before going to meet Mr. and Mrs. Trilling, she always scrubbed her rosy cheeks and powdered her face, lest they think her one of those girls who used rouge.)

"Marriage!" exclaimed Rupert. "It's like a rebirth. Only, better. You choose your own family."

The shocking crash of the stock market, which aborted their honeymoon plans, upset him terribly, called to mind his poverty-stricken teenage years. But for Hannah, love was theirs to stay, and Niagara Falls would wait for them.

Nor could the crash spoil the wedding. In addition to stocking her hope chest and buying a trousseau, Papa had hired a nice catering hall on New York's lower East Side.

The wedding gown was rented but, to hand down to future daughters, Hannah bought a headdress of exquisite Irish lace. For she treasured Mother's pearl necklace, the strand of freshwater pearls that had nestled against her lustrous skin, which she'd wear to the wedding. A touch of Mother in attendance.

Officiating at the ceremony would be a brilliant young modern Orthodox rabbi, from Galicia, who regularly came to the house to study Torah with Papa and talk out his heart. (To a Reform rabbi who asked why Rabbi Belzer wouldn't allow men and women to sit side by side in his shul as they did in Reform and Conservative temples, he replied, "To tell you the truth, I don't mind men and women *sitting* together. The trouble is, I give sermons—and I can't have them *sleeping* together.")

A fine speaker, who planned to study for a Ph.D in comparative literature, Rabbi Belzer preached in English as well as in Yiddish. One sermon criticized Jews who looked down on other Jews who came from lands different from their own. For the overwhelming majority of Eastern European Jewry—whether from Russia, Lithuania, Poland, Galicia, Hungary, Rumania, Germany—originated in the same country, Poland (before it was partitioned in 1772 among Russia, Austria and Prussia). Just as all peoples on earth—white and black, red and yellow, Jew, Christian and Moslem—share a common ancestry, Adam and Eve. But after the service, Hannah overheard one Lithuanian remark to another, "How do you like that Galician! Making himself out to be as good as *us*."

A week before the wedding Rabbi Belzer called Hannah and Rupert to his study to speak of the holiness of matrimony—in Hebrew *kiddushin*, sanctification. "In the ideal marriage each partner takes on the other's needs and desires. Indeed, it sets the standard for *all* human relationships. Marriage is an act of faith as much as love, believing in each other till the end. That's why the prophets described the Covenant between God and Israel as marital. In the words of Hosea: 'I will betroth you unto Me forever in righteousness, justice, lovingkindness, compassion, faithfulness.' "

Hannah said, "I've read that when souls are created in heaven, an angel cries out, 'This boy for that girl.' "

The rabbi's voice changed. "That's a pretty *legend*. Yes, marriage can indeed be wonderful, but only if your expectations aren't too extravagant. Don't expect miracles, and you'll never be disappointed."

Rupert smiled. "That's like telling someone to marry an ugly girl instead of a beauty. Because if an ugly wife runs off, who cares?"

"The trouble is, the ugly ones never run off," said the rabbi. "Anyway, remember this too: when the honeymoon ends, that's when the marriage, the true marriage, begins. A lifetime of mutual love punctuated on occasion—don't be shocked now—by recriminations, even outright anger."

"In that case, we'll never be married *officially*," Hannah declared. "Rupert and I intend to keep our honeymoon going forever."

Rabbi Belzer sighed. "From your mouth to God's ear. . . . Now, then." He showed Rupert the *ketuba*, the marriage contract, to be signed before witnesses during the ceremony.

"Where do *I* sign?" she asked.

"No need." The marriage contract details the groom's obligations to provide for the bride. Accepting, he takes a handkerchief from the rabbi. "To symbolize *kinyan*."

Hannah knew enough Hebrew to translate. "*Kinyan* means acquiring something. Isn't that word applied to *property*?"

He nodded. "But *kinyan* has another meaning as well: acknowledging obligations."

"The bride doesn't sign? She undertakes nothing?"

"Not that need be put in writing." The one whose interests have to be protected is the bride because the husband, after all, is the economic mainstay of the family.

"What *do* I do during the ceremony."

"You walk around Rupert seven times. That's to enchant him. A symbol of the bride's entering her groom's soul, whereupon they are admitted into heaven's higher spheres. . . . No, Hannah, the groom does not circle the bride."

"Why not? I'd love to be enchanted myself."

The rabbi smiled. "You will be, Hannah, you will be. When you take Rupert's ring as he says to you, *Harei aht* . . . The marriage isn't valid until the bride accepts something of value from the groom."

"Me, what do *I* say to *Rupert?*"

"Nothing."

But she didn't press the point. To devote her life to Rupert, she didn't have to say a word or affix her signature to a legal document or accept a rabbinical hankie. Hannah well knew where her duties lay, she always did. Mother had taught her: If each person sweeps in front of his own door, the whole street is clean.

Only afterwards did she remark to Rupert on the seeming one-sidedness. "No wonder Jacob never knew he'd married the wrong girl until the morning after. Laban could have stuck him with a sheep."

"I suppose it *is* one-sided—a man undertaking the care of a wife. In English that's called noblesse oblige."

"Maybe I'm just not used to being on the receiving end."

"Not having anything to do, you're *lucky*." When the moment arrived for Rupert's cousin to say to his bride, "Behold, you are consecrated to me . . ." he'd announced instead, "Behold, you are constipated . . ." Another cousin never lived down his failure to break the wine glass. Like a cannonball under his foot, it shot out into the congregation. "You can imagine how people kidded him before the honeymoon. That was two and a half years ago, they're *still* kidding him."

With the wedding fast approaching, Hannah's sisters, twelve-year-old Rachel and ten-year-old Tessie, took to creeping at night into her bed. Rachel would say, "We miss you terribly already." Tessie: "How will I ever manage? How dare you leave me!"

What kind of mother abandons young children to go off with a non-relative she's known only two years? Hannah felt her happiness was being purchased at her sisters' expense. "I'll be visiting a few times a week," she vowed, "and you both can stay over in my new apartment whenever."

Rachel wished her mazel tov, oceans of good luck. Not Tessie.

Which exasperated Rupert. "There are mama's boys and daddy's girls, but you're family slavey. Not even a cleaning girl once a week to help."

"*Everyone* in the family works hard, not just me."

"Have it your way, Hannah. Want us to postpone our wedding until Tessie herself gets married?"

"Rupert, I just want *everyone* to be happy, that's all."

"Admirable. So arrange that when *you* become God."

The night before the wedding Papa took Hannah aside to ask if she had any questions. Having set the date during the two weeks of her monthly cycle when marital relations were allowed, he now asked if Miriam had spoken to Hannah about what goes on between husband and wife in private.

(The look of relief that swept over his face when she nodded!) Repeating the rabbi's words, she said, "It didn't seem he was advising us on marriage so much as, well, issuing a warning."

Papa swore her to secrecy before replying. "Rabbi Belzer was talking about his *own* marriage, not marriage in general. I can't give details. Wouldn't be right, betraying a confidence. But you must know that our marriage, your mother's and mine, was very happy. So happy, that's the reason I've never married again."

Hannah always assumed her parents were happy together, but this was the first time either one had told her. Their ten children was an indication of *something*. (Buba Bella used to say, "Children are like glasses—you can never have enough." But she was *Papa's* mother.) Mother, she knew, always disliked living isolated on a farm, prosperous though it was, but Monaster was where Papa made his living. "Papa? Can a man so brilliant, a *rabbi*, be unhappily married?"

"It happens, it happens."

"How? Why?"

"It is as difficult to arrange a good marriage, the Talmud says, as it was to part the Red Sea. Individuals are so . . . *individual*. But maybe this will help." During the ceremony Hannah should step on the groom's foot. That could ensure her mastery over him and their household.

"Did Mother do that, step on your foot, Papa?"

"No. Her own mother wasn't alive to instruct her. And if she were, you think I'd allow any woman to step on *my* foot? Any more questions, Hannah?"

"Just one, Papa. Will you be dancing on the top of the tables?"

"At *my* age?"

True, Papa was over sixty. And who would look after him? One was such a lonely number, standing stark and alone, with no support. And Papa still hadn't learned English, probably never would, he who was fluent in five other languages. Must be terribly difficult, the change in status as well as culture, for one so well-off in Galicia, reduced in Brooklyn to being a grocer unable to communicate fully with Americans. "There's something else, Papa."

"Didn't you say Miriam talked things over with you?"

"Not that. I'd like to know if you're happy you brought us to America."

"Happy? My family is intact and still observant Jews. Our Covenant with God we're keeping, as commanded. So what I set out to do I've achieved. Forged still another link in the chain of generations."

Sleep wasn't easy to come by that night and, as was customary before one's wedding, Hannah fasted all of the next day. Rupert had tried to talk her out of it. "Makes no sense. To atone for past sins, Jews fast on Yom Kippur. So why on their wedding day? To atone for future pleasures?"

The intention of the fast was to focus on the seriousness of marriage, but by late afternoon all Hannah could think of was food: instead of nuptials, a bowl of chicken soup and a big *pulka*. The aromas emanating from the caterer's kitchen had her licking her dry lips and salivating at the thought of the glass of wine which she hoped, when sipped, wouldn't go straight to her light head during the ceremony.

In the bride's dressing room, Miriam helped Hannah into her gown and lace headdress, then stepped back to admire her. How beautiful, exclaimed all the wellwishers streaming in. That face! Those eyes! Such a smile! What a rented gown!

"In all of history, has there ever been a bride who was funny-looking?" asked Hannah, smiling.

The flower girl, Kitty-Kat, and page boy, Donny, each around four years old—cutie-pies, everyone declared—arrived within minutes of each other. But when their mothers—Hannah's oldest sister and Rupert's sister-in-law—took them into the bathroom to change, the darling couple started a fight that ended only when Donny shoved her outside and locked the door, refusing to undress in front of a girl.

Insulted, she demanded, "Why does *he* go first?"

"He's a boy. And older."

"I'm a girl and *taller*." Kitty-Kat tried to kick in the door.

Hannah called to her, "Come here, sweetheart, come to me."

"Don't tell me what to do. You're not my mother."

Nobody could restrain the flower girl from banging on the door until Donny emerged from the bathroom in an embroidered suit of silver satin like a baby toreador. "*I* got to change clothes *first*," he gloated. "Yah, yah, yah."

Kitty-Kat, acting the bull, rushed Donny. "His suit is prettier than my gown!" Snatching away his satin pillow, she pummeled him over the head with it.

Donny burst into tears as the two mothers, each blaming the other's child, almost came to blows.

Hannah intervened, as much as her billowy gown allowed. "Too much of a strain on the children, this page boy and flower girl business. Let's forget it. I won't mind, *really* I won't."

Both mothers turned as one on the bride. ("You know how much it *cost*. . . ?" "Not after I spent days on end *rehearsing* . . .")

Only when Miriam threatened to lock both children in the bathroom and flush the key did their mothers separate them and take them away.

"That's *another* thing that doesn't live up to all the propaganda fed us," said Miriam.

"What?"

"Children," she said.

"Their mothers wanted the kids to take part, and I thought, if it would please them—"

Miriam threw up her hands. "I give up on you!" But it wasn't so. Having almost fainted from hunger at her own wedding, she wanted Hannah to eat something. Just in case the rabbi, speaking on a full stomach, forgot when to stop.

But with duty there was no compromising. Hannah refused.

Finally, time for the ceremony. Wellwishers were asked to retire to the chapel, and the bride and matron of honor were ushered to the adjoining foyer. In front were all the other participants, and Donny was asking why Kitty-Kat had this great big basket of flowers to carry and he only an itty-bitty ring.

"It's a *gold* ring," said his mother. "Gold costs lots more money than a bunch of cut, dead flowers."

Hannah looked down at the bridal bouquet of white roses covering her Bible. *Dead flowers?*

Soon the rabbi and the cantor started down the aisle, chanting prayers. The best man following, after placing the wedding ring on Donny's satin pillow, reminded him to bring it forward when signaled.

"Just keep Kitty-Kat away. She scratches," the page boy replied.

Miriam embraced Hannah. "I want you to be happy, you hear me? I *command* you to be happy. Most of my happiness these last few years has come from you." And she was gone.

It was Kitty-Kat's turn then. But—suddenly shy—"Who are all those people? What are they doing here? Tell them to go home."

Everyone had come to see pretty Kitty-Kat in her beautiful gown, she was told several times, but that did not soothe the child. "Tell them, *go home*," she kept saying. Only when Hannah presented her with two white roses from the bridal bouquet, promising her the balance after the ceremony, did the child set foot inside the chapel.

A chorus of oohs and aahs. "A living doll!" Applause, too.

Pleased, Kitty-Kat curtsied, accidentally dropping the two white roses, which she immediately reclaimed. Down the aisle she inched, with no effort to discharge her function.

From both sides came whispers urging her to toss the petals in the air.

Instead, she hugged the basket to her chest, declaring, "Shut up. They're mine."

When hands reached inside to throw some petals for her, Kitty-Kat beat them off. "Stop that! Go home!" Those flower petals that fell out of the basket were immediately retrieved, and she reached the *chuppah* with more flowers than she had started out with, having been given a corsage along the way to placate her. There, Miriam patted her on the head, either to calm Kitty-Kat or to hold fast to her long blond hair lest she suddenly decide to scoot back up the aisle to recover any petals she might have overlooked.

"Oh, boy!" Papa said.

Taking Hannah by the arm, he led her into the chapel of 118 people. Thank God for the veil; without it, all her emotions would have been exposed and she'd have felt naked. Elated as she was, there was this void on her left where Mother should have been. Hannah's hand flew to the strand of freshwater pearls around her throat, and all at once she experienced a rush of warmth.

Midway to the *chuppah*, her father stopped short. Presently,

Rupert appeared to claim her, and Papa walked on alone. Pained to see him so solitary, Hannah wanted to call out, *Come back!* Why did he have to be excluded?

"Hold on tight to me," Rupert whispered as they ascended the steps. "So I don't fall down. I'll never forgive you for making me fast."

After Hannah walked around Rupert seven times, it felt as if the hall were circling *her*. (May she *should* have eaten.) Now there was nothing for her to do except keep an eye on Kitty-Kat, who was counting her flower petals. Who could tell what that living doll would do if any were missing?

Somewhere to the rear, Hannah's twenty-year-old cousin, Simon, a fine tenor preparing for a career in opera, burst into song.

> *I'll be loving you,*
> *Always.*
> *With a love that's true,*
> *Always.*
> *When the things you've planned*
> *Need a helping hand,*
> *I will understand*
> *Always.*

Hannah had always audited Simon's voice lessons. His teachers wanted to train her as well—her voice was of professional caliber, they said, and she possessed "presence." But she had no money to pay for lessons. Nor for art lessons, which she preferred. Pure foolishness. What need a housewife for such luxuries?

> *Days may not be fair,*
> *Always.*
> *That's when I'll be there,*
> *Always.*
> *Not for just an hour,*
> *Not for just a day,*
> *Not for just a year,*
> *But always.*

{29}

The rabbi recited the blessing over the wine and praised God for sanctifying His people Israel through marriage, then asked for the ring. As the best man signaled to the rear, Hannah held her breath. What if Donny and Kitty-Kat got into another brawl, which could knock over one of the four poles that held up the *chuppah*? Down would come the canopy on everyone's head, the lighted candles setting fire to the rented wedding gown.

But here, bearing the wedding ring atop his silver satin pillow, came Donny. He went to the *far* side of Kitty-Kat. To get at him she'd have to knock over the rabbi, and even she didn't have that much nerve. The best man grabbed the ring and handed it to Rupert, who took Hannah's finger.

"*Harei aht*—" he began.

But the ring would not go on. With prongs jutting out, definitely not smooth. And tinny. A ring from a box of *Crackerjacks*?

Hannah gestured to Miriam and wiggled her finger with the toy ring no further down than the tip of her fingernail. Miriam's wedding band could substitute. But strangely enough, her closest sister shook her head and wouldn't comply. "Not with *my* ring," she mouthed.

In one swift motion, Rupert took the toy ring and showed it to the best man who, aghast, whispered something to Donny who just stood there, mute, whereupon the best man rifled the page boy's pockets, and coming up with the band of gold and platinum, handed it to Rupert, who slipped it on Hannah's finger while reciting carefully, "Behold, you are *con-se-crated* to me with *this* ring according to the law of noses and of Israel."

Hannah exclaimed, "Thank God!" and many in the crowd chuckled.

After the reading of the *ketuba*, which Rupert and two witnesses signed, the cantor sang the Seven Benedictions, which ranged from Creation and Adam and Eve, fashioned in God's image, to the messianic hope of Zion restored in love and in peace, rejoicing with her children. "The time when there'd be heard once more in the cities of Judea and in the streets of Jerusalem voices of gaiety and gladness, the voices of bride and groom, the voices of young people reveling and singing. Praised are You, O Lord, who brings joy to groom and bride."

As the couple drank the glass of wine, Hannah worried anew. This time about Rupert's breaking the glass on the first try. With everything else going wrong, why shouldn't the glass just lay there beneath Rupert's foot and refuse to shatter?

The rabbi ducked down, and before he even straightened up, there was a sharp splintering sound and the assembled were cheering; Rupert was kissing Hannah *in public*, people applauding, the wedding party marching off, the newlyweds too, and hands from all sides grabbing amid cries of mazel tov.

In the foyer Rupert got hold of Donny and demanded why he handed over the practice ring instead of the gold wedding band.

"Kitty-Kat kept all her flowers," Donny sniffled.

Rabbi Belzer waved aside Hannah's apologies. "It was expected. I've never seen a wedding ceremony go smoothly. And don't worry about the mix-up with the rings. Nobody could see what happened. Everything was completely hidden from sight." He added, "And that's marriage."

"Is it valid, Rabbi? Instead of '. . . according to the law of *Moses*'—"

"English doesn't count. Rupert said it right in Hebrew."

In short order everyone was hugging everyone else, *kvelling*, and Hannah was crying, when Mr. Trilling swooned.

From *nachas*, he said, while being helped to a couch. "This is the happiest day of my life. Didn't think I'd live to see Rupert married." When Mrs. Trilling gave him a dirty look, he corrected himself. "I mean, the *second* happiest day."

Rupert and Hannah retired for several minutes to the bride's room by themselves which, according to custom, symbolized consummation. "Two wonderful things about our wedding night," he said as soon as they were alone. "Can't be mangled more than the ceremony. And at least there won't be 118 eyewitnesses."

3

*T*HE toughest is the first year of marriage, everyone had told Rupert. All those adjustments. Somebody else to take into account much of the time. Sharing the bathroom. Conjugal relations. "The position is ridiculous, the pleasure is momentary, and the expense is damnable," said Cousin Leo, which sounded so unlike him, he must have been quoting someone intelligent.

If who was boss wasn't determined during the first 365 days, male acquaintances stressed, nothing but trouble would reign ever after. For the wife as well. So strong discipline had to be exercised at the outset.

"Like the farmer who trained his new horse to eat less and less every day?" Rupert asked, chuckling. "Just when the horse had learned to live on practically no food at all, it died."

"You'll laugh out of the other side of your mouth," he was told, "once the battle of the sexes gets underway."

No such struggle developed, not even a jockeying for control. Having served ten years as housekeeper to an Old World father, Hannah always deferred. Actually, it was her nature to please one and all.

Pleasure to musicians and troubadours during the Depression—two pennies wrapped in a piece of newspaper and thrown into the backyard for the professionals; for the awful ones three because, she said, for them it must be so much harder to make a living. Pleasure even to dogs that she feared, since they had been set on "Christ-killers" in Galicia. Coming home from work one night, Rupert found a huge, snarling mongrel locked inside the kitchen and Hannah, at her wits' end, outside. That evening there had been a heaven-cracking thunderstorm, which had the dog yowling in terror in the street. Taking pity, she'd dashed outside and brought him in. Once the storm subsided, Hannah had to endure howling and attacks on the walls for hours, so scared was she to open the kitchen door to let the ungrateful dog out. It took them half the night to repair the damage.

"This should teach you a lesson," Rupert said.

"Yes. Wolves should be locked inside bathrooms. Less to break there."

Not that Hannah was an easy mark. She refused to attend any more family gatherings, when Rupert went along with his brothers in poking fun at their respective wives. "I will not be your fool or anybody else's. Eve *also* was created in the image of God."

Not from Adam's rib, as the Bible states?

"Exactly. Not from Adam's tongue, that she should be an object of ridicule. Nor from his head, that he should order her around. But from his side, that she should be nearest his heart. So says the Talmud."

And why *were* people put on earth?

"Men or women?"

There was a difference?

"Men seem to think so. The daily prayer book has one blessing for them: 'Thanks, God, for making me a man.' Another for women: 'Thanks, God, for making me according to Your will.' "

But the difficulties encountered that first year had nothing to do with each other and everything to do with the world outside. Stock market crash, the Depression, Rupert's father's illness, Hannah's pregnancy. Unable to manage his family without her there in charge, Mr. Brody broke up his home, farming his six children and himself out to his four married offspring. Rupert agreed to take in two brothers-in-law, which had Hannah thanking him daily. Surgery didn't help Rupert's father, who was pronounced terminal. End of Rupert's dream of going into business for himself; he'd have to stay on with his two younger brothers.

The baby, named Sandra—a modernization of Sarah—after Hannah's beloved mother, was born with a clubfoot. Hannah almost went mad. A *clubfoot*. But days after the funeral of Rupert's father, an orthopedist revealed that the obstetrician had lied! In order to hide his having broken the baby's foot during a breech birth. The foot, once set, healed properly, and Hannah never stopped thanking God for His mercy.

Through all this, she always made time for listening. People were always confiding in Hannah (often things she didn't want to know about) because she considered it a mitzvah, a commandment, to lend an ear. Maybe not one of the Big Ten, which got all the attention. But a commandment, nevertheless. Yet these troubles of other people would give rise to sleepless nights.

Even the news of the day could distress her. About people she didn't even know. Rising unemployment. A flood in California. A train crash in London. An unsuccessful experimental operation on a child somewhere. A bomb exploding in a Jerusalem marketplace. These would elicit a wince, a gasp, sometimes a moan, always *Hub rachmonus*, Have compassion.

"Keep this up, and I'm throwing out the radio," Rupert announced every once in a while. "And no more newspapers will I bring home. *Bed sheets* you'll have to spread on the floors after you wash them."

Hannah would ask, "You mean to tell me it doesn't hurt *you*, such terrible news?"

"Not like it wrecks you continually. Of course not. Certainly not."

"I don't believe you," she would retort. "You're *lying*."

Of her own problems, Hannah rarely breathed a word, sometimes not even to Rupert. Not that she didn't want to share herself. "What else is hearing people out," she said, "but intimacy with your clothes on? I just can't unload problems of mine. Wouldn't be right to make people lose sleep on account of me."

Knowing he was opposed to having another child during the Depression, Hannah didn't even tell Rupert about a false pregnancy.

And when found crying in the living room in the middle of one night, she claimed it was only that time of month. Even when that time of the month's weeping persisted for seven weeks, she refused to consult Cousin Leo the doctor.

Then, one night Leo stopped by after hospital rounds to announce joyously, "*Mr. Moskowitz* died today!" That the Trillings knew no Mr. Moskowitz did not diminish Leo's elation. "*Mr. Moskowitz*," he kept repeating, "*he* died." Finally, explained,"Not *you*, Rupert." Months before, Leo had informed Hannah that Rupert didn't have long to live. Only that very day, when Mr. Moskowitz was hospitalized with heart failure that turned permanent, did Leo discover Mr. Moskowitz's medical records had been accidentally switched with Rupert's.

Rupert was taken by surprise, though not as much as poor Mr. Moskowitz.

"Leo didn't tell you?" Hannah said at first with a straight face. Later on, when nagged: "And if I told you? Leo said the only constructive thing anyone could do was to buy a plot from his brother-in-law."

No question Rupert would have made a far less inept doctor then Leo. If Mr. Trilling had only taken Rupert to America with him in 1912. But a richer doctor than Leo, Rupert could never be. Leo probably made more money selling patients the free samples sent him by drug companies than from fees. Possibly made diagnoses on the basis of what medicines he had in stock. Or which family plots.

For bringing such swell news, that he had no reason whatsoever for nearly driving Hannah to the brink of a nervous breakdown, Leo asked her to fix him up with a wife just like her. "Only, *rich*."

"You think money makes everything good?"she asked.

"That's not the point," said Leo, eager to set up his own office instead of working for another physician. "The point is, *not* having money makes everything *bad*. Money helps people like reality. It's the soap that removes life's worst stains. The heavier the wallet, the lighter the heart."

"There are no pockets," she noted, "in shrouds."

"True. But I'll be wearing pants a lot longer than a shroud."

Though Rupert didn't side with Leo, he understood him. Didn't the Code of Jewish Laws, which never condones the pursuit of riches, observe that it was the nature of man to long for wealth? If you have money, Rupert himself had noticed, people think you wise, handsome, and able to sing like a bird. Surely, money had played an important part in his parents' marriage. His mother's regard for his father plummeted when, through no fault of his own, she was stranded without funds in Poland during the Great War. Then again, though also not his fault, when he lost their apartment house after the stock market crash. Man was the family provider, and if he failed at that, it didn't matter what else he succeeded at.

"What about your butcher's daughter?" Leo asked. "I see her father bought her a fur coat. He must be selling an awful lot of meat."

"But she needs expensive dental work," said Hannah, who couldn't in good conscience inflict Leo on any nice Jewish girl, nor on the worst shiksa. Not that her frequent tries at matchmaking had met with success greater than that of someone trying to mate two walls, and not even adjoining ones.

Rupert knew why. She, so full of illusions about those nearest and dearest to her, was always matching up not realities but dreams, not people but possibilities. "Hannah, you look at a man and a woman like some look at a used car or an old house. With a new engine under the hood, he'd be a real bargain; with two fresh coats of paint, she'd be a knockout. Another thing: those you're matching up have desires that are mutually exclusive. What does a man want? A woman. What does a woman want? A man. Result? Stalemate."

"Well, you could say the same about people and God."

"Exactly. You just proved my point, Hannah. Look how disappointed *they* are with each other."

"Not *me*. No, sir."

"That means you're not asking for enough."

But Rupert knew better. Every Friday evening Hannah took so long praying over the Sabbath candles for relatives, friends, the Jewish people, Palestine, America, good goyim, the unemployed, people in the news, that sometimes the chicken soup would cool off and the gefilte fish warm up, while Rupert would implore her to give God a rest.

Cut short her chats with Him? Impossible. As often as Hannah

{36}

asked for help for this one or that, she'd thank Him for the beauty of the sunrise, or for tasting the season's first peach, or for a neighbor's first bowel movement after a heart attack. And daily for Rupert's making a living at a time when America's unemployed numbered fifteen million and a full third of the nation had no income at all.

New York's one million jobless were everywhere in the city, dressed in rags, teeth rotting, ribs sticking out, bellies swollen, eyes dead. Newspapers under their clothes, burlap bags around their legs, cardboard for inner soles. On eighty bread lines. Making meals out of a cup of water and free ketchup on tables at the Automat. Searching through the garbage cans of restaurants for scraps of food. Leaving America, too: 100,000 lined up to apply for 6,000 skilled jobs advertised by a Russian trading agency. Brooklyn sweatshops paid as little as $2.40 for a fifty-hour week, the same as New York gave a family on relief. To get a job running elevators in department stores, a man had to be a college graduate. Women were offering themselves on the street for a quarter, but could be bargained down to twenty cents.

In 1932, 25,000 penniless World War veterans marched to Washington D.C. and camped there to petition the Government for early payment of their $500 bonuses. But President Hoover, the world's greatest food administrator, savior of millions of Belgians from starvation after the Great War, refused to meet with the bonus marchers. Help should come from private charities and local or state governments, not from Washington, he insisted, then ordered his chief of staff, General Douglas MacArthur, to drive the Bonus Expeditionary Force out of the center of the capital. Declaring the situation a revolution, the general had his troops attack those marching on Pennsylvania Avenue. On his own initiative, he also sent soldiers across city lines to destroy the bonus marchers' encampment in Anacostia, Maryland. Two babies died in a tear gas attack, and several veterans were shot to death.

Closer to home were the families being evicted from their apartments all over New York City. Rupert would see them out in the cold, huddled around their belongings in front of houses—dispossessed. Yet who had time to worry about those unfortunates when America's banking system was collapsing, and Rupert could have lost all his savings? He withdrew them, hiding them in a box in the broom closet, just before Governor Lehman closed all the banks and the Stock Exchange itself closed down. At his Inauguration President Roosevelt declared the only thing Americans had to fear was fear itself. But that fear was overwhelming, palpable, paralyzing.

All too reminiscent of the war years in Poland, when Rupert's mother baked a cake only when an egg dropped to the floor and broke, provided she had some flour. Malnutrition had given rise to what was diagnosed as tuberculosis, and Rupert was quarantined in a sanitarium too far away for his family to visit. Yet too close for its medical personnel, who left him in isolation for seven months, with meals at his door. He slowly recovered, and X-rays in America subsequently revealed no signs of tuberculosis. For that news Rupert would have thanked God if he had been a believer; for rescuing America from chaos or even revolution, he did continuously bless FDR.

Hannah's devout faith Rupert never challenged, though religious practices that impinged on his livelihood, he protested. When persuasion or cajolery failed, Hannah usually gave in for the sake of household harmony, *shalom bayis*, but never on observing the Sabbath, constant reminder of the divine origin of the world.

"Look," she said. "I could overlook your fooling around with another woman one night, maybe even two. (That's two nights, *not* two women.) People are weak, only flesh and more flesh. But never if you fooled around with that same woman every single week forever. Rupert, the Sabbath is what's kept the Jews Jews, me me."

So he stayed home on Shabbas and went to the family business Sundays, while his brothers worked Saturdays, which upset their mother. Fortunately, Hannah was no fanatic like her. When, after a debilitating illness of their two-year-old, the doctor prescribed jellied pig's feet to build up her strength, Hannah did not hesitate to buy pig's feet, which she cooked every day in a brand new pot and served on a brand new dish. (Never together with milk, of course, a violation of the laws of kashruth). Discarding the *treif* utensils two weeks later, Hannah even uttered a prayer of thanks for the help of pigs in restoring their Sandra.

Rupert's mother had grown maddeningly observant of religious minutiae since the untimely death of her husband. On the Sabbath she wouldn't let her daughters carry their babies in the street—it constituted work—or even tear toilet paper. Not too much met with the approval of the woman who often said people were not put on earth to be happy. (Conditioned perhaps by a nasty step-mother.) Certainly, being widowed did nothing to brighten her outlook. Then losing her small apartment house, sole source of income, during the Depression. Even so, the announcement in 1934 of her emigration to Palestine stunned everyone. Because her children in America weren't devout enough, she was settling in the Holy Land.

No doubt she was speeded on her way by Father Coughlin with his signed-up membership of eight million. The biggest thing on radio and in 2,000 churches which peddled his ravings, receiver of more fan mail every week than the President of the United States, the rabid priest was threatening to make America's Jews envious of those in Hitler's Germany. He called the New Deal the Jew Deal, Roosevelt Rosenfeld, Eleanor Roosevelt a negress, and publicized a patent issued for a "kike-killer," a club that came in two sizes, the smaller one for the fair sex. (Every once in a while Rupert would pick up a Coughlin tract just to read how the Jews control all the banks and the press and run the world.)

Rupert never expressed how he really felt about his mother. How could a grown man in his thirties, a husband and father, confess feelings of abandonment and, yes, betrayal? Though he sent money every month, he never went to see her in Palestine, unable to forgive her for never returning on a visit. Her fear of falling ill in America, which might end with her burial in alien soil, outweighed all desire to see her children and grandchildren. Equally galling, his mother always acted with more warmth and love toward Hannah than to her own children. Why, Rupert could never figure out.

Nor why Hannah mothered her entire family. Even with Hannah's two brothers moving in, and after they left to get married, a younger sister, Hannah wasn't completely happy until she arranged for her father to take an apartment, together with his four youngest children, around the corner so she could keep an eye on them all. Also in her charge across the street, an aged aunt and uncle, whose six children were otherwise occupied, and once a week she'd travel to

Bensonhurst to help her sickly sister Miriam prepare for Shabbas.

All this reminded Rupert of a sight he would never mention to Hannah: a sow with a dozen piglets hanging from her teats. But the sow looked impassive, whereas Hannah welcomed her lot, as if she possessed some secret nobody else did. Other husbands would have minded a wife's full-time social work, which didn't bring a penny into the house. Not Rupert. For Hannah was good to his family too, and always waiting with a hot meal, a smile and conversation when he got home close to midnight. For that reason, after investing in the stock market every month, he handed over the balance of his wages for her to deposit.

Leo was very critical, even when informed Hannah knew nothing about the Trilling nest egg, which Rupert would surprise her with someday. Having married fur-clad Laraine, daughter of Flatbush's biggest kosher butcher (but only after waiting for her father to pay her dental bills), Leo managed all of *her* finances, some of which he invested in a big house in Flatbush not far from Rupert. A devout believer in the dollar, Leo.

Hannah thought him foolish. "The greedy are prisoners for life," she said. "Leo married the right woman, but for precisely the wrong reason."

Just the place to live and bring up a child, Flatbush. A block away from the Trilling apartment on Parkside Avenue was beautiful Prospect Park; in the other direction tree-lined Ocean Parkway, both designed by Frederick Law Olmsted and Calvert Vaux, America's greatest landscape architects, whose work included Manhattan's Central Park and Eastern Parkway, Brooklyn's Champs Élysées with its very own Étoile at Grand Army Plaza.

The two parkways attracted families on outings, lovers, ambitious walkers, benchwarmers on the shady malls that paralleled the thoroughfares. At the south end of Eastern Parkway lay the world-famous Brooklyn Museum, the Botanical Garden and the Brooklyn Public Library, Hannah's personal trinity. Occasionally, she sketched a scene in the park or a painting in the museum, but she'd never show her doodling.

The Trilling three-and-a-half room apartment scarcely knew a time when stray relatives weren't staying over. Rupert's too, waiting for a parent to come home from the hospital or while convalescing from surgery. The double studio bed in the foyer rarely went unslept on, and sometimes Rupert would trip over someone sleeping on the living room floor. But Hannah never tired of thanking Rupert for his generosity.

The hospitality was Rupert's, but the extra work all hers. With a seventy-hour workweek and another dozen hours of subway travel, he was rarely home while guests were awake. Shabbas he slept late while she went to shul. That left them the rest of that day to play with Sandra—with her mother's dark beauty and laughing eyes and verve—and weeknight hours before dawn to get reacquainted. Scarcely enough time to fight like other couples.

Leo and Rupert's brothers and associates in business were always offering tips how to handle a wife, who, if a man wasn't alert, would end up ruling the roost. Not sweet Hannah, Rupert would say. "It's the *sweet* wives you *really* have to look out for," they would scoff. "With them, men let down their guards."

Marriage as a prizefight? Rupert had to laugh, envisioning himself and Hannah in boxing trunks.

Hannah, as if she didn't have enough dependents, had befriended a next-door neighbor her own age, Fanny Felcher. A lively, neat-looking bookkeeper who was especially attractive from behind, a real hip-swiveler, Fanny had a housebound father. Two broken legs never healed properly, and unable to afford a wheelchair, he got around by holding on to a chair with wheels. Hannah looked in on the father during the day, since the Felchers had no phone. Anytime he was ill, Hannah took care of him. In an emergency he'd bang on a shared bedroom wall to summon her.

"How do you get yourself into such a pickle?" Rupert wanted to know. "Nurse to a perfect stranger."

"Just being neighborly, that's all."

"But what do *you* get out of all this?"

Sometimes Rupert would awake at night to hear the two women in the kitchen. On more than one occasion Fanny was sobbing. Still unmarried while all her friends had husbands, children. Half her life already over, with no prospects. Nobody ever asked Fanny out for a second date. Time and again she wished she were dead.

{41}

Hannah would draw out the hurt like a warm compress does pus. Soothe like an ointment, point out Fanny's good qualities, gloss over her faults. Always end on an optimistic note: "You have no idea how good your life will turn out. Mark my words."

"You guarantee it?"

"Absolutely, positively. And if I'm wrong, you can get all your aggravation back."

One night, Hannah suggested Fanny be picked up on future dates at the Trillings', after still another beau failed to ask for a second date. The reason was obvious: no doubt Fanny's father was scaring off potential suitors. One needed great courage during the never-ending Great Depression to take a wife, and who'd dare the care of an invalid as well? Only someone who first fell in love with Fanny.

Soon the Trilling apartment turned into a salon for entertaining men Rupert would have taken pains to avoid in the steam room at the Turkish bath. Only a matter of time, he prayed, before she'd get a proposal and quit Rupert's living room. But then, Mr. Felcher died, and Fanny was back nights in the Trilling kitchen, sobbing—this time of her guilt for wishing her wonderful father dead for impeding a possible marriage.

Repeatedly, Hannah talked her out of it. Judaism credits good thoughts, never holds anyone to account for occasional bad ones. What matters is deeds.

"Hannah, you're the sweetest, smartest person in the whole world!" Fanny exclaimed on more than one occasion. "I'll never forget you as long as I live!"

Then Fanny lost her job, and Hannah was out canvassing, block by block, house by house, to find her employment. For Rupert's sake, Hannah said, when he commented that Fanny had become his wife's full-time occupation. With the poor girl facing eviction, they would have to invite Fanny to move in with them.

"You're not *serious*, Hannah."

"She has no place to go. I'll tell you something else, Rupert. With all your kvetching, you wouldn't object."

Like hell he wouldn't, but it never came to that. Through one of Hannah's leads, a job came through at a Manhattan jeweler. Rupert rejoiced—no more need to entertain Fanny's dates. Treating them like family, Hannah would serve coffee and homemade cake, which cost a pretty penny, while he had to make conversation. His wife, however, would ask questions and listen intently as if their replies mattered to anyone but themselves. "Talk about myself?" she said to several who queried her in turn. "What can I learn from that?"

Then one night, at long last, with all the jubilation exhibited over their own engagement, Hannah met Rupert at the door with: "Fanny's getting married! Fanny's getting married!" "Thank God," he exclaimed.

The lucky man was none other than the boss's son, whom Hannah had never met. How was that possible? Well, the engaged couple used to go out together after work, and it was always too late to stop by the Trillings' when he took Fanny home.

"*If* he took her home. And not to *his* home."

"Rupert!"

"Some couples today, you realize, do practice marriage without a license."

"Not Fanny!"

"Nice girls don't?"

"Only if they're kidnapped into white slavery."

As much as Fanny wanted her dearest friends to meet Maurice Ellenbogen, it never happened. He moved her out of Brooklyn and into a new apartment on the Bronx's Grand Concourse, where after the honeymoon he'd join her. The wedding itself would be a small one, in Chicago. Though he never said so to Hannah, Rupert assumed after a while that Fanny had robbed the cradle or her fiancé was a goy. How else explain so many obstacles in the way of their meeting? If only Rupert could find out for sure. For a mixed marriage even Hannah wouldn't send a wedding gift.

But she went right ahead and bought a crystal bowl, delivered personally, along with her headdress of Irish lace, to Fanny's office on West 47th Street. (Over the years half a dozen couples had borrowed the headdress and wedding ring, sympathetic magic to invoke a happy marriage like the Trillings'.)

Fanny wasn't at work, but the receptionist reported a change in plans. The wedding would be held in New York—in a hotel called the Plaza. Apparently, Maurice Ellenbogen's family had disapproved, and Fanny had been too embarrassed to tell Hannah.

Rupert suspected otherwise. Many a plan had been changed early

{43}

in 1938. With fifteen percent of the population on relief and the five million employed since 1933 once more jobless, there was scant interest in buying jewelry.

Fanny's feelings, however, troubled Hannah more than the economy. No family in attendance on either side, the wedding would be deserted, a dismal affair. All alone in a shabby hotel room. So when Hannah asked to go out to Radio City Music Hall that Saturday night, it wasn't hard to guess what was afoot. Once in Manhattan, she suggested stopping by the Plaza, whose address she had looked up in the telephone book, to wish the bridal couple mazel tov.

With the hotel only a few blocks north of the Music Hall, why not?

Whatever his looks, surely the groom could not be more of a surprise than the Plaza. The Fifth Avenue castle across the street from Central Park was a block-long, nineteen-story building of white glazed brick, topped by a great copper green sloping roof. Definitely not the place a jeweler on the skids could afford. Its ground floor housed a miniature city out of a fairy tale. Everywhere was marble, crystal, gilt, thick carpets. It beat Radio City Music Hall by a mile.

Hannah was relieved. "The rooms here must be big. I had visions of the rabbi having to stand on the bed while officiating."

The groom had invited a few guests, because when Rupert asked at the desk for him and Fanny, passers-by said to follow them. The woman's coat was a mink and even the man's sported a fur collar. Hannah, looking them up and down, whispered, "We should have gotten dressed up."

"In our *other* winter coats? Which we don't have?"

As they waited for the elevator, framed in marble and gilded grillwork, the woman remarked to her companion, "Can you imagine! Maurice getting married at *his* age."

"He's so young?" Hannah asked.

The man threw back his head and guffawed. "That's rich! In ten years Maurice will be getting social security. Too old to be getting married, I'd say, for the first time."

The year before, social security had gone into effect over the objections of people arguing it would encourage workers to quit their jobs and discourage children from supporting their parents. "What's your opinion of social security?" Rupert asked.

"A communist plot," the man replied. "What's more, it will take the romance out of life. The adventure."

So, Rupert realized, Fanny was marrying *money*.

On the second floor he and Hannah followed the other couple down a wide corridor with a high ceiling and ornamental moldings until they reached a foyer where someone asked for their coats. "We aren't staying," Hannah said.

By then Rupert was suspecting a wrong conclusion had been jumped at, and knew for sure upon entering the room where they were directed. Clearly not for sleeping, but for a bride. One was there in full regalia, with a train covering half the floor and a veil cascading over her face.

"Excuse us. We were—"

"*Hannah!*" The voice, a familiar one.

"*Fanny?!*"

The bride threw back her veil, and there was Hannah's headdress attached to an elaborate coiffure that nearly circled eyes bulging in astonishment.

"You look so *beautiful!*" Hannah exclaimed before realizing things were not quite as advertised. "This is a small wedding? In Chicago?"

"What are you doing here!"

"Just stopped by to wish you mazel tov, Fanny. We didn't think anybody else would be here."

"Is that what you thought? Well, there are over 215 guests, I'll have you know—"

Rupert spoke up. "And no room for your best friend Hannah?"

The color rose to Fanny's face.

"Thought we'd shame you in front of your swell new friends?"

Fanny faltered, then extended her hand. "Look . . . *afterwards*. I was going to have you both over later on. Even send a car to take you to the Grand Concourse. Well, say something, Hannah—"

Nostrils flaring, Hannah stepped forward, arm raised high as if to strike a blow, and in one swift motion plucked off the headdress. Anchored as it was with bobby pins and little combs, Fanny's hairdo followed in its wake, exploding in all directions like the Bride of Frankenstein's.

Fanny screamed, either in pain or outrage, possibly both, and

Hannah turned and fled, just as an attendant ran in from the bathroom and on to the bridal train. So when Fanny gave chase, her train was jerked out from under the feet of the attendant, who sprawled on her rump, while Fanny herself was dragged backwards by the dead weight. Staggering, she reached out for support to a table with a Tiffany lamp on it.

Not waiting around to see whether Fanny landed atop her attendant, and the lamp on top of both, Rupert dashed after Hannah, plowing her way outside. Grabbing her by the arm, he propelled her to an exit sign and down the stairs; at its foot she paused to rip her headdress into little pieces. "No daughter of ours will wear anything that touched a hair on *that* head," she exclaimed, discarding the scraps. "Why Rupert, *why* . . .?

"Like the Yiddish proverb says," he replied. " 'We anger God with our sins and people with our virtues.' It doesn't pay to be too good to the whole world."

"Which virtues? What pay? All I wanted was to see a friend happy."

All the way to Radio City and even inside the Music Hall, Rupert tried to soothe the hurt. To no avail. While the Rockettes kicked away during the stage show, Hannah sat there, biting her lips, face distorted. Finally, he whispered, "Did you know Mr. Felcher did not die a natural death?"

"What?"

"I'm sure Fanny knocked him off."

That was the night Rupert agreed to having a second child. They could afford it more than her foreign involvements. Despite the continuing Great Depression, he was making a nice living, and it made more sense for Hannah to mother a child of his than to busy herself eternally with everyone else's. Another child of theirs would mean less time spent on others outside the home.

Several days later a package arrived, postmarked the day before the wedding, from the ingrate bride. Inside was a nice note of thanks for the loan of the headdress, which was enclosed. Oh, boy! The one that Hannah had seized and shredded had been *Fanny's*. So perhaps God did indeed exist, moving in funny ways.

But not at that particular time in Europe, where Hitler was threatening all nations and tormenting the Jews. Such a remarkable talent calamity had for locating the Chosen People. Of course, it did have help from quarters like Rome's *Civiltà Cattolica*. Throughout the thirties the Jesuit publication contended that the Jews, guilty in every generation of engaging in ritual murder, using Christian blood in baking matzos, and repeating the Crucifixion, were to blame for the evils of both Communism and capitalism. At present, the Jews were trying to destroy the Catholic Church even as their international conspiracy sought to dominate the world.

Easier said than to have, a second child. He delayed so long in coming, Hannah spoke of resorting to adoption, setting 1940 as the deadline, for agencies didn't give babies to women over thirty-five. Fifteen months after the Second World War broke out, just three weeks before Hannah's thirty-sixth birthday, colicky Joshua joined the family. Hannah was overjoyed, which pleased Rupert.

In 1941, Congress renewed the Selective Service Act by a vote of 203 to 202. Four months later the Japanese attacked Pearl Harbor. Rupert was too old for the draft, but not two of Hannah's brothers, one of whom regarded the war as a conspiracy organized just to inconvenience him. Her cousin Simon lifted heavy objects to give himself a hernia and jumped down from kitchen tables to further flatten his already flat feet, all the while ignoring Rupert's advice to chop off a trigger finger. When Simon spoke enviously of the forty percent of America's young men rejected as physically unfit, having suffered malnutrition during the Depression, Hannah declared it a mitzvah to join the battle against Hitler.

Simon snapped at her: "Why don't you go take my place? You have my permission."

"If I only could! I'd give *anything* to fight the Nazis."

"A person can get *killed*. That's what wars are about, you know. Dying."

"There are things worse than death, Simon."

"Name one."

"After all America has done for you, for all Jews, for so many peoples—"

"Papa brought us to America to *escape* the draft."

"In Poland in 1920 Jews were being drafted *by* anti-Semites to fight *for* anti-Semites."

"War is war."

That wasn't the end of it. One night Rupert came home to an unusually subdued Hannah. She handed him a note from Leo to her: "Here's what you asked for." Attached was a letter to the draft board on official medical stationary claiming Simon had a bad back. Too bad to serve in the military.

"You asked Leo—?"

"Never! Simon lied."

"Smarter than I thought, simple Simon. He knows Leo would do *you* a favor."

As always, Hannah defended her cousin. She felt sorry for him. Simon's beautiful voice had taken him not to the Metropolitan Opera, where he belonged, but only as far as resorts in the Catskill Mountains.

"So what's the problem?"

"Whether or not to mail this letter. What do *you* think?"

"Me? I think someone exempt from the draft has no business offering an opinion."

It took till dawn for Hannah to decide. "If Simon doesn't go into the army, another boy will have to take his place. Some *other* mother's son."

"So?"

She tore up Leo's letter, eyes shiny with tears.

A few years into the war Rupert got caught up in a private war of his own, an internal one. All at once and for no discernible medical reason, food wouldn't stay down. Since he had no sense of taste or smell, Hannah always prepared meals that were pretty to look at. Vivid greens, deep purples, intense yellows—Van Goghs, she called them. But even after she switched to puréed pastels, French Impressionist meals, Rupert's evening sickness worsened. His time was up, like his father's before him.

Hannah reasoned with him. "You heard the doctors. They found nothing the matter."

"But my wallet they located with no trouble at all. And an excuse the angel of death can always find."

She spit three times to ward off the evil eye. "I won't let you die," she vowed. "There are *other* doctors."

Rupert had no faith in any of them. The Polish doctor put him in isolation for tuberculosis, which he never had. The obstetrician invented Sandra's clubfoot. Even Leo's premature prediction. And a doctor treated Josh for many expensive months for St. Vitus' Dance, which turned out to be a simple allergy to woollies.

Worst of all were surgeons like the one who closed his father up without doing anything at all, after which he died a horrible lingering death. When Rupert first fell ill, a surgeon removed his appendix, which was perfectly normal, but an allergic reaction to medication nearly killed him. His symptoms soon reoccurred, accompanied now by gnawing pains.

An internist recommended an exploratory operation, since he could find nothing amiss. Waving in the direction of Rupert's X-rays, the doctor said, "Normal stomach and intestines. So opening you up and going inside to take a look—"

"Excuse me, Doctor. What kind of stomach has four toes?"

Yes, the internist had been using foot X-rays to urge abdominal surgery. And not even of Rupert's foot.

"No wonder they call it the *practice* of medicine. Well, no more operations for me till it's *perfected*." Rupert made Hannah promise never to grant permission for any surgical wild-goose chase. Let surgeons hard-up for big fees go explore themselves.

Yet whatever was assaulting him would neither desist nor disappear. Unable to hold down food, Rupert was growing weaker by the day. He sought to lose himself in sleep, but the pain would start, then the retching, and Hannah would summon Leo for a shot to dispatch him to dreamland.

"What's the matter with Daddy?"

"Just something he ate, Josh."

"Will Daddy be all right?"

"Of course, Sandra. Certainly."

There would be Hannah hovering overhead. As if there were a mirror in the ceiling above their bed, Rupert could see himself being caressed as he floated up past her and sailed into the blueness, where cotton candy clouds dried the perspiration on his body and warm breezes tickled his toes. Born again! And *this* time, by God, he'd get it right.

{49}

Earthbound, Hannah remained below, smoothing his cheek and stroking his arm while importuning someone nearby.

"The shot takes effect right away. He should be feeling better . . ."

So fast had the years whizzed by. Like pages whipped by the wind before slamming a book shut. Every person on a deathbed must review his life as if it were a movie, trying to determine whether it was good or bad. Was Rupert's worth the price of having lived it?

Soon, very soon now, there would be nothing left to feel: Rupert would blow away. If it was cancer, he himself would make sure of that. Already he could visualize the inscription on his tombstone:

Son, Brother, Husband, Father, Businessman
1900–1944
He Could Have Done Better

Rupert should have died with more to show. Success. If only Hannah had encouraged him to leave his father's business and go in with his friend Manny, well on his way to becoming a millionaire. If only! The saddest two words in any language . . .

Dark man with black moustache and goatee at the foot of Rupert's bed. Did the angel of death smoke a pipe?

Bjdhye lkieg lotdgye retysd ghetysl hsyefg hjut lokps hjeyg hyarts hye hust.

"What?"

Rupert had come through very well indeed.

"Come through?"

Surgery.

"Surgery?"

What had been causing all Rupert's problems was an intestinal obstruction.

"Obstruction?"

No more. It had been remedied with a colostomy.

"Colos . . .?"

A section of his colon, the large intestine, had been removed.

"Removed?"

Elimination would take place temporarily through a hole cut into his abdominal wall.

"*My God!*" Rupert touched his belly swollen with bandages and swooned. Coming to, he heard Hannah chanting.

"It's temporary, temporary, *temporary.*"

He fixed her with a look of rage. "Broke your promise! You let them do this? Disembowel me?"

She gasped.

If not for his wife's consent, said the surgeon, Rupert would be dead by now.

There could be only one explanation for carving a hole into a belly. "I have . . ." He recalled his father's agonizing last months, when Rupert had put all the medications on his nightstand, hoping he'd take an overdose. ". . . *can* . . . *cer?*"

"God forbid!" Hannah spit three times in the air. "It was benign, the obstruction."

Yes. Rupert would be fine, just fine, the doctor said, and left the room.

Hannah took Rupert's hand. "Once you regain your strength, the surgeon will put you back all together again inside, then close that hole."

"And in the meantime?" Rupert touched his bandaged side. "Worse than a baby."

Gently, she stroked his brow. "Happens to lots of people, colostomies." She reeled off the names of several famous Jews, actors, politicians, athletes.

"Joe DiMaggio?"

She nodded.

How did Hannah know? She didn't read the sports section, nor pal around with the stars. Still, the surgeon had said. But just to be sure, Rupert asked to see his charts. Forbidden. Still, nurses and residents did confirm there had been no malignancy. He would live. Without pain? Yes, good as new. And be eating no more baby food.

Yet when a resident accidentally left the medical charts behind, Rupert retrieved them. He was leafing through the pages when Hannah walked in.

She couldn't have looked more shocked had he been licking his lips over dirty pictures.

He looked up. "I'm entitled. I'm paying for these records."

"Everyone's *told* you what's in them. A thousand times is not enough?"

"Once I see it in black and white . . ."

"Rupert, there's a name for people who don't believe anybody. It's a terrible sickness, paranoia."

"Paranoia?"

"I'm going to have to get you a psychiatrist. And a psychiatrist doesn't come cheap."

Rupert reconsidered. How vital was it anyway to know every single medical detail? What purpose would it serve? Was he or wasn't he in good hands, Dr. Litvak's and Hannah's? The doctor he didn't know, but she would kill herself for him and the children. "Okay, you win," he said, and surrendered the charts.

Softly, she said, "We *both* win, dear."

4

ON the way to the hospital Hannah was instructed by a barely conscious Rupert not to let him be operated on again, just so some surgeon's pockets could be lined with hard-earned Trilling money. Two hours later a hospital official handed her a consent form, and soon after she refused to sign, a swarthy man with a moustache and goatee and stabbing black eyes appeared. Dr. Litvak, furious surgeon. When she quoted Rupert's explicit orders, he swore.

"I have no time to waste. Or patience. Your husband's in such poor shape, he can't even be fully anesthetized."

"And if I sign?"

"At least he has a chance."

"Chance for what?" His father's lingering death?

"To correct whatever's killing him, possibly."

"And if you can't?"

"No problem. He'll never know you granted consent. He'll be dead."

Signing, Hannah prayed it was the right thing, and once having started praying, couldn't stop. Rupert and others often poked fun at her for bedeviling God with too many supplications in *good* times. Yet hers were never entreaties only. Often she expressed gratitude. Imagine if people knew that every once in a while she experienced a response to her "Go ahead, I'm listening." Just simple words like, "It'll be good, you'll see." Or, "I know it's hard, but you can do it." Or, "Be happy." And, "I love you so much. Pass it on."

That gave her strength after tragedies. At such times Hannah could feel God saying, "I'm so terribly sorry. Know, though, I did try. Next time will be better. You'll see. I'll try with My whole Being." Unlike those who believed God either all-powerful or non-existent, she considered Him if not always successful, ever accessible and always sympathetic. When people hurt, so did He. It lightened every burden, that feeling.

Especially during Rupert's operation, which dragged on. As she repeatedly wiped her eyes, her mother's words came to mind: "The gates of Heaven that are closed to prayer are always open to tears." Would that were so! Finally, after enough time had passed for every organ in Rupert's body to be replaced, Dr. Litvak emerged from the elevator and started across the hospital lobby. But Hannah's feet would not cooperate, transport her toward him. She felt herself sinking slowly, slowly into the floor. Was there something to pray for any more? Had Rupert survived the operation? Even if he did—

"Well," Dr. Litvak began, "it was cancer . . ."

Outside a distant siren wailed softly, an undulating, thin wail that chilled the blood. When Hannah sucked in her breath and the sound abruptly stopped, she realized it had issued from somewhere deep within herself.

". . . got it all out, Mrs. Trilling. So far as I can tell."

"You *did?* Then there's *hope?*"

Dr. Litvak nodded. "Once your husband gets through this week. I don't think the cancer spread." He went on to speak about something called a colostomy and the need for a second operation later on. ". . . in a few months . . . a normal life again."

"Normal? Really? You're not just *saying* that?"

"Lady, I never just *say* anything."

Speechless with gratitude, Hannah seized the surgeon's blessed hands and kissed them again and again.

They were jerked away so swiftly, his knuckles rapped her in the jaw. "Everyone is so damn grateful right after an operation! But when it comes to paying their bills, people always sing a different tune!" And off he stomped.

Hannah felt mortified. She should never have been so brazen. She had embarrassed the doctor. But there were enough other things to worry about first. *Cancer.* Nothing would be the same ever again. God, give my husband strength, she prayed on the way to him, and long years. Me too, to care for him.

From, the outside of his room three voices could be heard. Rupert's mumbled "Allergic," a young woman's giggling "*Stop* that!" and a young man's disingenuous "Stop *what?*" Inside, a nurse fiddled with an I.V. stand while a resident was fiddling with her.

"*Hold it!*" cried Hannah.

The two jumped apart, as if scalded by boiling hot water. The doctor tried to maintain his professional composure while extricating a hand caught in the nurse's blouse.

"My husband's appendectomy. An allergic reaction to some medication nearly killed him. Did you check?"

Red-faced, the two scurried away, returning some time later to substitute a different medicine. A miracle! Had Rupert been strong enough to be fully sedated, he'd never have been awake to speak up and save his life. And if the nurse and resident had injected him at once instead of fooling around, they'd have killed Rupert before Hannah had arrived.

She stayed with him until he fell into a deep sleep, then went downstairs to order round-the-clock private nurses, specifying middle-aged ones not likely to flirt or attract. After calling Dr. Litvak's secretary to ask the price of the operation, she hurried to the bank. The prospect of carrying a huge amount of cash on her person was unnerving, all the more so because of a greasy-looking, unshaven tough standing in line directly behind her. So when the teller demanded how she wanted the money, Hannah leaned over and whispered her reply.

"Can't hear you," the woman practically shouted. "Tens? Twenties? Fifties? Speak up!"

"*Anything*, so long as it's done *quietly*. I don't want the hoodlum behind me to hear. Doesn't look like he's up to any good."

{55}

The teller crooked a finger and beckoned Hannah close. "Sis," she hissed, "I'll have you know that hoodlum is my son."

"He *is?* Well, he certainly looks like a very *nice* hood—" Hannah buried the bundle of bills in her pocketbook and dashed away.

She arrived at Dr. Litvak's office breathless, dress stiff with a long day's dried perspiration. He was at his desk, head propped up by his hands and puffy eyelids drooping. No more the firebrand, he appeared a sallow, middle-aged man who might have a family and medical problems of his own. All those hours Hannah had been just praying, he had been battling to keep Rupert alive.

"I envy you, Doctor, and I don't," she blurted out to no one's surprise more than her own.

"How's that?"

"Saving lives every day. But holding the power of life and death in your hands . . ." She felt embarrassed, having talked so much.

Abruptly, Dr. Litvak said, "It was an exceedingly long operation. Needlessly so. Your husband's condition should have been diagnosed correctly a long time ago."

To carry out the first part of her mission, Hannah unwound the pocketbook strap from around her arm and took out a thick roll of bills, which she handed over. "It's all there. Count."

He looked surprised. "Nobody pays the day of the operation. Certainly not in full. They just thank me an awful lot. And all in *cash?*"

"The checking account is in my husband's name." Now for the hard part. "About his illness." His father's drawn-out death had horrified Rupert. "He's vowed to do away with himself if cancer ever struck him."

"Isn't always a death sentence, cancer. Many people do survive nowadays. Your husband could very well be one of the lucky ones."

"Not if he *knows.*" Unaccustomed to asking favors, she took a deep breath. "Suppose, Doctor, suppose you don't tell Rupert."

"Withhold information? That's not done."

"It's in the Bible. To save Abraham from being hurt, God never told him the whole truth, that his wife Sarah said he was too old to have children. Doctor, why have my Rupert live forever in fear? Everything medical he has to do will be done. I'll make certain."

"That's much too heavy a load to carry all alone."

"Oh, I'm not alone, Doctor. I'm never alone." (She refrained from again mentioning God. Some people had allergic reactions.)

Dr. Litvak stared hard at her until she lowered her gaze to those long, slender fingers, nails bitten to the quick. "Well . . ."

"Thank you, thank you, thank you!" She had to restrain herself from kissing the blessed lips that had not denied her request. "I'll tell the nurses—"

"I can enter it on his charts. That the patient be told he had an intestinal obstruction. A benign one." Dr. Litvak counted out five bills and pushed them across the desk at her. "There's a discount for cash," he said gruffly.

The number of private nursing shifts it would pay! "You're most kind, Doctor. I appreciate that even more than the money, kindness."

A look of wonder softened the doctor's steely expression. "Kind? After nearly knocking out your teeth? At the hospital they call me T.T. The terrible-tempered Litvak."

"Well, all the great artists are temperamental. But look what they accomplish."

"What I tell my staff. Thoroughbreds are high-strung." He almost smiled.

Rupert, after berating Hannah for having broken her word and consented to the operation that had saved his life, discharged the private nurses. "They cost a fortune, and for what?"

"Peace of mind."

"Waste of money!"

The peace of mind she meant was her own. Still flat on his back, Rupert was weak as an infant, unable at times even to summon help. Yet he grew agitated whenever the subject of private nurses was raised. "Only those who never worked for a living would be so extravagant. And who knows when I'll be able to return to work? If ever."

"Dr. Litvak assured me—"

"Don't ask the doctor. Ask the patient."

So most of the day Hannah stayed with Rupert, sneaking in through the basement because the guard in the lobby was strict about enforcing visitors' hours. For the night shift, when Hannah had to stay with the children, she did hire a nurse, who told Rupert she was attending the *other* patient in the room. Sometimes Hannah would fall asleep with the sleeves of one of Rupert's jackets folded around her, murmuring, "Soon, soon."

In a week, Rupert was sitting up and sipping liquids, which stayed down. The following week he was standing up and walking, and a week after that taking food, real food.

"Eating," he said, elated, "is believing."

A good sign, the return of Rupert's sense of humor. After his discharge from the hospital, it took several months for him to regain full strength. All during this time Hannah discarded Rupert's wastes several times a day, cleaned the rubber pouch, painted the skin around the hole in his side with zinc oxide to prevent it from ulcerating, after which she put on a fresh dressing. From the way she went about these tasks, one could only conclude here was a woman who reveled in excrement. Nobody else knew of the colostomy; whenever asked the whereabouts of Rupert's major operation, all Hannah would say was: "Inside." Only the children knew, because of the omnipresent dressings and deodorizers. But never about the cancer.

Four months after the colostomy, Rupert had gained thirteen pounds, which Dr. Litvak credited to wifely ministrations. He set the date of the follow-up surgery, one Rupert did not have to be talked into. Again, however, he railed against reckless expenditures and refused private nurses. With the money spent previously on night nurses still to account for, Hannah didn't press the matter.

Six weeks later Rupert was back at work, Humpty Dumpty no more, delighted not to be paying workers overtime to substitute for him. But discovering those private nurses had not been his neighbor's, he stopped handing over his paychecks and started depositing them himself. That was fine with Hannah, who had plenty of other things to look after.

Nor did it bother her that thanks was not as a rule part of Rupert's vocabulary. Neither expecting appreciation nor doling it out, he worked too hard, spent little money on himself, neither drank nor smoked nor ran around with other men, much less other women, and his wife was expected to do her share as helpmate. Since duty is what inspired Hannah, she never missed verbal acknowledgements. (As it was, whoever did thank her for anything, always received the same response: "For nothing" or "Don't be silly.")

Far more important was Rupert's waiting two years for her, and after the wedding, raising no objections to relatives moving in. And loaning money during the Great Depression to three of her brothers to go into businesses. Ben, the rich one Rupert helped to open a fancy kosher restaurant, refused his own bankrupt brother a loan. But not Rupert. Nor did he protest Hannah's daily visits to her family and weekly trips to Miriam, who had been diagnosed as having a heart murmur.

At least *those* people could be helped. For the war effort there was little to do other than give blood, knit for Britain, collect nylons for parachutes, buy and sell war bonds, serve at the USO, invite lonely soldiers over. For Europe's Jews not even that. All Hannah and Rupert could do was attend rally after rally at Madison Square Garden, begging for governmental intercession and assistance. For five decades before the rise of Hitler, Jews who were persecuted anywhere could at least find refuge in other lands. But in July, 1938 at a conference of delegates from thirty-two nations—convened in Evian, France, to discuss asylum for German and Austrian Jews whom Hitler wanted at that time only to expel—all unanimously agreed to accept *none*. Suicides among Viennese Jews jumped to two hundred a day. Four months later came Kristallnacht, the night of broken glass: 1,100 synagogues vandalized or demolished, 1,000 Jews killed, 30,000 shipped to concentration camps. The churches maintained official silence, the Western democracies opened no gates, extended no help to the victims. England and the U.S. actually asked Germany to halt a Jewish exodus to Shanghai, a remaining haven, to appease Japan. Such a tragedy there was only one God, when Jews had so many monstrous enemies!

In 1939 England refused to let 10,000 German Jewish children into Palestine, and Congress voted down Senator Robert Wagner's bill that would have admitted 20,000 German children into America.

Children! That same year in Haifa the British turned back boatloads of Jewish refugees, and America refused sanctuary to the thousand who reached Havana, which sent them all back to Germany's concentration camps. Seven hundred of them had U.S. immigration quota numbers—but for three years later.

Those few Jews who managed to reach the Jewish National Home of Palestine were fired upon. So the first casualty of the British in World War II was not a German enemy soldier, but an unarmed Polish Jew trying to land in Haifa. In France one-fourth of France's Jews were deported to Nazi concentration camps; most were arrested not by the Germans, but by the French police.

Not even the ensuing Holocaust persuaded the Allies either to bomb the factories of death and the railroads leading to them, as repeatedly requested, or allow Jews into Palestine or any other land. Inside Germany Himmler was saying, "To be able to kill thousands, yet remain decent, has made us Germans great"—while apparently no decent German civilian ever asked himself where the millions of used children's shoes were coming from. At war's end, England steadfastly refused to let 100,000 death camp survivors into the Jewish National Homeland while killing dozens who tried to gain entry.

After the Holocaust, many people asked, Where was God? Not Hannah. Where was *Man?* she wanted to know. God did not die at Auschwitz; Man who tortured and killed did, as well as those accomplices who stood idly by. Like the International Red Cross, that great humanitarian and hero of the Jewish people, President Franklin Delano Roosevelt, neither awakened the world to the mass extermination of the Jews, known since 1942, nor lifted a finger to save the Six Million. When his disinterest was fully revealed—"File no action," he had written on the bill to save 20,000 children—Hannah took down his picture, which hung above her sewing machine in the bedroom, and threw it into the incinerator. Fitting resting place for one who, despite U.S. intelligence reports, kept silent and inactive about Europe's crematoriums. The greater the man, said the Talmud, the greater his potential for evil. By doing nothing, FDR had let Hitler very nearly triumph posthumously. In FDR's place she put up a picture of his wife Eleanor.

Happily, the great majority of American boys came home from the war unwounded. Among them was Simon, who kvetched endlessly about his lost four years.

With newspapers reporting just then that for supposedly using Christian blood to bake matzos, scores of Jews returning from death camps had been killed in pogroms by Polish civilians and soldiers, Hannah lost patience. "If I were *you*, Simon, I'd *sing* everything," she said. "You do have a beautiful *voice*."

"But look where it's gotten me. A salesman."

"Simon is just unlucky," Rupert commented. "A person needs lots of luck to be born with brains."

Yet, luck did find Simon. He had married a charming young woman, so intelligent everyone wondered what she saw in Simon. But nobody said that to Hannah without getting an argument. "A man without faults," she'd say, "is possible only in a faultless world."

That was before Hannah received the check from the U.S. Government. Opening the envelope without realizing to whom it was addressed, she saw the word *disability*, and only then, blanching, Simon's name. So *that* was why he was always cursing his luck even after having married so well. Disabled! Remorse overwhelmed Hannah, then anxiety. All these years Simon had kept his secret. So dreadful, it had been kept from his wife.

By the time they next visited the Trillings, another disability check had arrived in care of Hannah, and she got Simon alone in the kitchen to say perhaps Dr. Litvak could be of assistance. (Every year he made Rupert against his will take a G.I. series, insisting so strenuously, Rupert was sure the radiologist gave Dr. Litvak a kickback.)

"What are you talking about?" Simon said. "There's no way to correct my condition."

She couldn't let Simon suffer alone, in silence. "You must tell me, Simon. I won't let you go till you do. I want to help."

"Help a bad back?"

"*What* bad back?"

He grinned.

"There's nothing wrong with your back."

"Says you."

{61}

"Leo told me so, Simon. He wished your good back on himself."

"Isn't it lucky then I applied to the army for disability and not to you?"

"The Government will be sending you monthly checks from now on for no reason?"

"No reason? Look how many years I gave to the army."

"And having these checks sent *here* instead of to your own apartment. What's the reason for *that?*"

"If you knew how my wife runs through dough. Hannah, don't tell me you don't have a secret hoard of your own."

From the cabinet under the sink she took out a jar containing cash. "Eighteen dollars. Never more than twenty-five. You're comparing this with the pile you'll be getting each and every month forever? Illegitimately?"

"Why all the fuss? I cleared this with Rupert. He okayed it."

Stealing money from the Government and hiding it from his wife was bad enough. But trying to involve Rupert in his lie. "Okay? Not in *my* book. This is *thievery.*"

Indignant, Simon waved the two blue checks at Hannah. "What gives you the right to call me names? Tell me that."

"You want an explanation? I'll give you an explanation." She seized both checks and in a flash showered him with confetti. "*Now,* you understand? Have I made myself clear?"

For weeks afterwards neighbors talked of the exquisite high C emitted by Simon, which rattled the Trilling windowpanes that Sunday afternoon. Indeed, many compared her cousin's voice to Caruso's.

Anyone surviving cancer five years was considered cured. So for the fifth anniversary Hannah planned a large party, which Rupert canceled. Maybe there was something else brewing. Six months later, X-rays of his large intestine showed what the radiologist called an apple core.

How to get someone to undergo major surgery without revealing the real reason? Adhesions from the previous operation, Dr. Litvak said. But Rupert, still feeling fine, suspected a plot against his bank account, and Hannah could not convince him otherwise.

Dr. Litvak grew testy, understandably. "This is ridiculous!" he told her. "I'm spending more time talking your husband into surgery than the procedure itself takes."

"I know, Doctor."

"So . . ."

"So can we try some more? Another chat—"

"More?! Give me one reason, Mrs. Trilling, just one."

"The honey cake I bring you every year before Rosh Hashonah. I've never tampered with the recipe. That's why it always turns out so well."

Once again the doctor summoned Rupert to his office. "Any more delay, Mr. Trilling, a colostomy, if there has to be one, will be irreversible. *Permanent.*"

That did it. Rupert submitted to surgery, which went smoothly. No complications whatsoever. The malignancy was removed in toto, and a month later he was back at work, but irritable. "Why should I pay anything at all? If Dr. Litvak had done it right the first time, he wouldn't have had to do a make-up."

To celebrate, Hannah suggested a trip to Israel. Despite repeated requests from the family to return to the U.S. in 1948, Rupert's mother had stayed on throughout the War of Independence, which saw over one percent of Israel's population killed and tens of thousands wounded after 50 million Arabs attacked the newborn state. Rupert, however, refused. Could he still be mad at his mother? Or was it the money?

"I don't have to go along," Hannah finally said, though a trip to the Holy Land was her heart's desire. "And if you stay with your mother instead of in a hotel—"

"Stop nagging," Rupert said.

Stop she did. Ever since that first operation Hannah considered her cancer-prone husband a sick man it was a sin to rile. Now to worry about, there was also Rupert's financial health. Anyone who couldn't afford a trip for one to Israel with no hotel accommodations must be strapped for funds. So Hannah looked around the neighborhood for a job.

Rupert was incensed when he heard. "People will think I can't support you."

Hannah dropped the matter, without regret. She preferred her own private social work, unpaid though it was. No way she could have continued that with a job plus the children, wonderful though Sandra and Josh were.

Such *nachas*. Pure pleasure from the day they were born, the kids. Well, aside from the usual childhood illnesses and stages of development—sometimes it was difficult to tell them apart. And the time Sandra ran through a plate glass door and the occasions Josh gave his sister bouquets of poison ivy. Or when Sandra shoplifted some gum from Woolworth's and Hannah had her take it back to the manager and apologize. Or when Josh received a score of 79 on his I.Q. exam, having been immobilized by the discovery of the answer sheet inside his test booklet. Sandra, good at nagging, got a bicycle out of Rupert, but Josh never the baseball mitt he wanted. Open school day was a treat with nothing but praise from their teachers. Pity Rupert could never take off from work to attend. Nevertheless, to his brothers he always boasted of the children's marks. (But why wouldn't he tell *them* how proud he was?)

They themselves lied about their grades, pretending they were lower. Sandra, believing boys didn't go for smart girls. Josh, for the same reason Hannah never wore her Persian lamb coat in the company of relatives and friends who had none. Both were good children, kind to others, amiable, considerate, helpful everywhere except around the house. Not that they were without faults. Neither was Rupert, for that matter. But she never mentioned them to anyone. Why spoil their reputations by divulging imperfections they'd surely outgrow? Didn't Hannah have shortcomings of her own?

Rupert was closer to Sandra than to Josh. The ten years' difference in age probably accounted for that. When she was born, Rupert couldn't get over having taken part in the creation of another living being. The only time in his life he ever used the word *miracle*. Josh's entry into the family didn't seem quite that miraculous, not during the Depression, when many regarded parenthood more of an accident or a chore than a delight. Nor did Josh's colicky first six months endear him to a man who needed sleep to work a seventy-hour week.

Strange, how two children in the same household can be raised by two different fathers. Hannah herself had no favorite. If forced to choose between Sandra and Josh, she told those witless enough to ask, she'd select exactly half of each. No less, no more.

And so the years were flying by, stayed every twelve months by still another G.I. series. Hannah every time apologized to the long-suffering Dr. Litvak for Rupert, who behaved as if he were doing the doctor a big favor. It became their private joke, the doctor and Hannah's, which objections of Rupert's to X-rays had to be overcome this time. Once he asked, if X-rays were so vital, why didn't Dr. Litvak ever undergo the nuisance himself?

"That's why I became a surgeon," he replied. "To *give* orders."

Presently, Sandra was going steady with an educated, polite, if humorless, young man, Charlie Heller, an idealistic assistant district attorney who put terrible people in jail. Rupert surprised everyone by hiring not a plain catering hall, but the ballroom of a New York hotel (not The Plaza). If he had gone into debt to do so, he wouldn't say. Just repeated what had become a litany of his over the years, that the landowner George Washington had to borrow money from a bank in Alexandria to go to his Inauguration.

During an intimate mother-daughter talk, Hannah urged the banning of flower girls. (Presumably, Kitty-Kat, now a successful actress under long-term contract to a major movie studio, no longer beat up page boys.) Sure enough, the day of the wedding the ballroom's air-conditioning system broke down, the flowers never arrived, and the groom's mother showed up in a white gown. Nothing could be done about the air-conditioning or the mother-in-law, but Hannah hurried to the nearest florist's shop, which was closed, then to a fruit store, where she filled four bridesmaids' baskets. The strawberries looked pretty but squishable, so Hannah took a knife and sculpted radishes into a bouquet of imitation tea roses. Just before walking down the aisle wearing her grandmother's pearls, Sandra had a fit of giggles.

"Imagine the surprise of the girl who catches this!"

The next wedding in the family threatened to be Kitty-Kat's. Neighbors called to Hannah's attention gossip column accounts of Kitty-Kat's warm relationship with a divorced former Illinois governor then running for the presidency, several decades her senior. Such a marriage would aggravate her observant parents to death because Adlai Stevenson, though brilliant and wealthy and a Democrat, would probably never get himself circumcised and convert. Happily, nothing came of that—saved, the family honor.

But then, Rupert had to undergo still another operation. For "polyps."

"Cancerous?" he asked, as he always did.

"Benign." Again, Dr. Litvak removed the entire malignancy and left plenty of healthy intestine to continue doing its job.

Even after a dozen years of office visits in his two-story brick house, Hannah knew nothing about Dr. Litvak's personal life. No family was ever in sight, even on his desk in photographs. Nor bicycles in the driveway or basketball hoops nailed to the top of a garage door. When the roses in the garden were in spectacular full bloom, Hannah had complimented his lovely home.

"Home," Dr. Litvak said, "is the wife." In a flat tone of voice that indicated neither a good wife nor a bad one.

If none were the case, Hannah would have loved to fix him up. But it wouldn't have been proper to pry. She couldn't even bring herself to use the strategem of asking if Mrs. Litvak would like the recipe for her honey cake.

Third in his graduating class of 532 and editor-in-chief of the literary magazine, Josh, now a senior in high school, was applying to college. Any city college was sure to accept him. He'd have preferred Columbia University, but who could afford the tuition, which could be covered only if Hannah took a job. Again, Rupert objected. One went to college for an education, not for a fancy brand name. And Josh had no profession in mind. Why waste money? It wasn't as if he planned a career in medicine.

"Medicine?" Josh made a face. "Why do Jewish fathers think a fetus is viable only after it graduates from medical school? And I do have a profession in mind. Writing."

"For that profession, a person needs one thing above all—a very small appetite." Rupert quoted from Isaac Bashevis Singer's many complaints in the Yiddish newspaper about the woeful living he and other writers were making after lifetimes of writing.

Hannah always retorted, "The world needs writers as much as doctors. Don't healthy people also need sustenance for the soul?"

Columbia accepted four of Josh's classmates, all with lesser qualifications than his. That disappointed Hannah more than Josh. It had been foolish of her to defer to Rupert. She should have gone to work, even if it would have caused their first fight. Their son had been shortchanged. Within the year, however, Hannah was thinking it a good thing, her not having vexed Rupert. For a call came from Dr. Litvak for her to stop by.

Indeed, the doctor's sloping features seemed to be sliding off his pale, drawn face, forecasting *tzuris*, big trouble. After all these years together she could read his expression almost as easily as Rupert's. But, thank God, her husband was fine. Dr. Litvak only wanted to tell Hannah in person of his retirement. Soon he'd be leaving the city.

"Oh, *no!*"

"Don't worry, Mrs. Trilling. I've spoken about your husband to a colleague. Fine surgeon, if the need arises. And a good liar too. It's worked so well all these years, we won't tamper with the recipe."

"It's not just that, Dr. Litvak."

"Yes, Mrs. Trilling? Something else?"

"I'll miss you, Doctor."

"Will you?"

"And how! You've been so good to me. To both of us. I don't have enough words to tell you."

"*You're* good, Mrs. Trilling. It shows even in your face."

"I'm just a housewife. I may have good *thoughts*. But you, Doctor, *do* good."

"Shielding your husband all these years. Quite remarkable."

"What *you've* done, Dr. Litvak. For complete strangers. Not very cooperative strangers, either. And I'm sure we're not the only ones. The remarkable one, Doctor, is *you*."

"You think so? Really?"

"Oh, I *know* so. With my whole being."

"That's . . . nice to hear. Very . . . nice. A person likes to think he's left something of a mark. Well, now . . . may I say, Mrs. Trilling, I've enjoyed our . . . I'm not quite sure what to call it."

"Association? No, *bond*."

"Yes, we have shared something all these years. Almost like parents jointly looking after their child."

"I don't know what we'd have done without you. Yes, I do know. But I'd rather not think of it."

"Then I have made a difference?"

"Are you serious, Dr. Litvak! I'll always remember you."

"You will? Remember me?"

"As long as I live! I'll never forget your lovingkindness. Never."

"Thank you, Mrs. Trilling. I think . . . I think that's what I wanted to . . ." Standing up, he held out his hand and when she took it, instead of shaking hers, he amazed her by putting it to his lips. "You've been a comfort. Now as ever. Goodbye, Mrs. Trilling. God bless you. Your husband is already blessed."

Only afterwards did it occur to Hannah that Dr. Litvak never mentioned where he was going. And she had neglected to ask. But two days later, while Hannah was going from store to store in search of the *perfect* going-away gift, she had word the doctor was dead. Reportedly from an overdose of pills. He had been gravely ill for some time, people said.

The childless widower left no immediate survivors. Only Hannah and all the other beneficiaries of his goodness.

Two

5

"IT'S amazing, really amazing," Hannah heard Rupert say one winter evening in 1973 to nobody in particular. "You look around and all of a sudden every young pisher today is at least seventy years old."

She spoke up. "That's a dirty lie. You know very well I'm a mere sixty-nine."

Not one of those who wondered where the years had flown, Hannah could pinpoint each and every month. Time does not flit by when arrested by the deaths of parents, the births of two grandchildren, weekly visits to Miriam in a chronic diseases hospital, a heart attack, two full months per year anticipating the verdict of Rupert's G.I. series. In between, two more operations for "intestinal obstructions."

Both had happy outcomes. Nevertheless, over the course of time Rupert had become withdrawn, as if trying to distance himself from the scalpel hanging over him. Perhaps also from Hannah, who, while surgeons came and went, remained the one constant, insisting on yearly X-rays and, when needed, surgery. That was pure guesswork, however—Rupert refused to discuss his feelings about the operations. Or much of anything. Her one-time intimate had grown increasingly detached—she could still make him laugh, but not talk—which Sandra attributed to the male's being uncommunicative by nature. "Something genetic activated by marital vows." (As if that could explain why Rupert, opening up two new accounts, selected as bank gifts two men's wrist watches, when Hannah had none.)

How she missed her ally, Dr. Litvak, for whom she recited the *kaddish* memorial prayer, each year in his name contributed that month's *knipple* to Jerusalem's Hadassah Hospital. That last encounter often came to mind. She still faulted herself for not having heard between the lines. Perhaps if the good doctor had had someone to shield *him*. Foolish to think so, though. Truth is not canceled just because it is hidden. Still, she should have done *something* to help. Exactly what, she had no idea. And did Dr. Litvak have another reason, aside from the one stated, for calling her in just before doing away with himself? A mystery.

Time also stood still during the Six-Day War of 1967 and the Yom Kippur War of 1973, and when Josh was drafted during the Vietnam War. To be sure, there would have been nothing to worry about if Hannah had run for Congress and gotten herself elected. Of the 234 draft-eligible sons of congressmen, forty-eight served during the war; of these, twenty-six were sent to Vietnam, of which eight saw combat and exactly one was wounded.

Yet, there were always blessings aplenty to count. Israel had survived as many invasions as Rupert had operations and the Vietnam War finally came to an end. All of Hannah's sisters and brothers were now married, with children, and the Trillings had two marvelous grandchildren, who did not take after their father Charlie, for which Sandra was grateful. Even worse than date-rape was date-deception, she said, because no woman ever married her rapist. Sandra's assistant D.A. groom was now in private practice, getting off the same lowlifes he used to prosecute and jail. The proceeds bought them a beautiful home in Westchester, which Hannah dubbed, "Who Says Crime Does Not Pay?"

Josh, thirty-three years of age, was still unmarried. Everyone knew about bachelors: they were people who came to work every morning from a different direction. Rupert blamed it on Josh's unrequited love for writing, and never having met an accountant who was poor, urged him to become one instead of a scribbler and editor.

Josh likened accountants to eunuchs in a harem, voyeurs of others' sources of satisfaction. And when nagged about marriage, "No great writer has ever married young. Look at the Author of the Bible." But his marital status, among other things, was sure to change with the publication in 1974 of Josh's first novel, *Captain O Captain*, which had been shopped around to every publisher in New York and half the literary agents. Hannah had just read the manuscript, which surprised her with its depictions of episodes drawn from her own weekly visits to Brooklyn's chronic diseases hospital.

Victim of a stroke since 1963, poor Miriam could neither communicate nor walk. Hannah she always recognized at once, welcoming her with shrill cries and kisses. The first few visits sent Hannah sobbing into the bathroom to throw up. Then, heeding the Yiddish proverb, "Before God, weep; before people, laugh," she forced all feelings aside and concentrated on cheering her darling sister. Inside the ward, the person Hannah did not exist except as a provider of comfort. Only after hurrying home to drop into bed, where she stayed for eighteen hours, did she allow herself to ponder Miriam's heartbreaking fate.

Rupert never questioned Hannah's constant visits, nor the long recuperation periods. But every so often he'd remark, "Such a huge family, all supposedly very religious. So how come you're the only one to visit Miriam religiously? Sandra and Josh go as often as your sisters, but your five brothers, never."

Always, she replied, "Not my business."

He would shake his head. "Hannah, it's going to be so awfully lonely for you up there in heaven all by yourself."

With a chuckle she'd respond, "Don't count on it. Me, I'm not going anywhere without you, Rupert."

"I'll tag along with you," he'd say, "only if heaven has a non-praying section."

But the children feared the hospital visits were making Hannah sick. Sandra and Josh wanted them stopped.

How could she keep away from Miriam, or the ward's eleven other incurables? According to the Talmud, each visitor takes away one-sixtieth of the illness. "I'm going, and that's that," Hannah just said, and her visits continued unabated, while she developed peculiar night cramps in her legs and a burning sensation in her crown.

On the sly she consulted Cousin Leo. "Something's not kosher from top to bottom," she said lightly. "What's cooking in my head?"

He prescribed an antidepressant and gave her a B-12 shot that had her walking on air. But much as she implored, he wouldn't give more than one shot every few weeks.

Little by little the night cramps and burning sensation subsided. They had almost vanished entirely by the time Hannah suffered a heart attack. "*Not,*" she insisted weakly in the cardiac care unit, "the result of visiting Miriam."

"What, then—?" said Josh. "*Ecstasy* transported you into intensive care?"

He had another grievance. Hannah, babysitting while Sandra and Charlie were in the Bahamas, had been experiencing severe chest pains when Josh phoned to say he was coming out for Shabbas. Not only didn't Hannah mention any discomfort, she told him to stay in the city because of an upcoming snowstorm. Notified on Sunday, he demanded to know why she had said nothing.

"I knew you had a date Saturday night," she replied, whereupon Josh yelled so loudly, the C.C.U. nurses ushered him out.

Calling the heart attack full-blown, the cardiologist suggested Sandra and Charlie be notified at once. But Hannah said absolutely not. Rupert was about to order Sandra home, nevertheless, when Josh stopped him. Much as his mother wanted her beloved daughter at hand, he knew it would affect her heart to ruin Sandra's vacation.

Never having spent a Friday night without lighting Sabbath candles, Hannah asked for some. With her on oxygen? But she persisted until a compromise was reached. The oxygen would be turned off so long as the candles burned, and instead of the regular large Sabbath ones, she lit tiny Hanukkah candles.

"I'm scared, I don't mind telling You," she told God right off. "But don't let Rupert and the children find out. They have enough to worry about without worrying about me worrying. I do, too. Who'll look after Rupert if something happens? He'd never move in with Sandra, inconvenience her, and Josh's still a bachelor. Oh, I'd give *anything* to see him married! And if it's not asking too much, my grandchildren too. Of course, that would take another ten years or so. But I wouldn't mind waiting around. Please see what you can do, dear God. Thank You so much."

Sandra, returning, came up with a grievance of her own. Rupert had canceled the private nurses. Hannah tried to mollify her. "Your father always cancels the nurses I order for *him*. So he's treating me as his equal."

What had precipitated the heart attack, said the cardiologist, had been Leo's antidepressants, which should have been discontinued long before. Leo, he indicated, didn't know a heart from any other part of anatomy.

"Well, at least my cousin didn't charge," said Hannah wanly. "I got me a bargain."

"And you're lucky not to have gotten hooked on his so-called B-12 shots. That was dope."

Having finally inherited his father-in-law's butcher store, Leo knew plenty about meat. But *dope?*

"I'm putting you on a blood-thinner to prevent clots."

So efficiently did the anticoagulant avert clots, it induced internal hemorrhaging, which extended Hannah's stay in the hospital. The cardiologist was very apologetic. "Totally unexpected, what happened, highly uncommon. The statistical chances are so remote—"

"Nice to have proof I'm one in a million, Doctor. And I'll forgive you if you do me a favor." Sandra and Josh had banned all future visits to the chronic diseases hospital. But Hannah could never abandon her sister. "Please tell my children that would do me more harm than good."

"Blackmail, Mrs. Trilling?"

"Heaven forbid! This neighbor of mine who has a heart condition. Her doctor lets her smoke a few cigarettes a day because, he says, for her stopping would be harmful. Of course, Doctor, I promise never again to let my emotions get the better of me. Visiting my sister in the future I'll exert more self-control."

"Bad idea, Mrs. Trilling. Your emotions must be given full play. That is, if I do grant permission to visit. This means, Mrs. Trilling, venting your feelings before each visit. Afterwards, as well. At length."

So that's just what Hannah did after being discharged and convalescing at Sandra and Charlie's for several weeks. On the way to the chronic diseases hospital and returning home, Hannah got off the bus a mile and a half before her destination and during each walk spoke of how she felt about going to see Miriam, then afterwards was debriefed. Only, because she would never burden a relative or friend, nor pour out her heart to a stranger, she spoke all the while to herself. Didn't patients talk for hours on end to psychiatrists who never uttered a word? At least Hannah always responded.

Those acquaintances she ran into on the street, who seemed shocked by such behavior, Hannah told at once, "I'm simply following doctor's orders. He wants me to talk to a clever person."

To ask for that wonderful new novel by the talented Joshua Trilling everyone was talking about, the week before *Captain O Captain* was shipped Sandra took her mother to half a dozen bookstores in the city. No copy being on hand—surprise, surprise—they asked the clerks to order several. One reported lots of requests for Josh's novel.

"Then you must be placing a large order," said Hannah.

"A first novel? Nah. I figure all the requests are coming from the author's relatives who'll never return to buy the book. Happens all the time.

They could have been written by Hannah herself, the prepublication reviews of *Captain O Captain* were so wonderful. Yet, it bothered her that the novel never alluded to all the *other* volunteers at the chronic diseases hospital; they might feel slighted. And why hadn't Josh highlighted Rosie, the black attendant for whose tender, loving care no amount of salary or tips could compensate?

"In case it's escaped your attention," Josh replied, "Rosie is not my mother."

"But Rosie is *somebody's* mother. *Four* somebodies."

"Nothing new, your reaction, just infuriating!" Hannah's first and only fur coat she'd rarely worn because Tante Miriam didn't have one. Whenever another sister babysat, Hannah couldn't enjoy the movie, thinking the sister at home deprived. To avoid hurting the feelings of the grocer across the street, whose dairy products were often sour, when shopping elsewhere she always made Josh walk around the block. "Maybe that will be the topic of my *next* novel: Moms Can Be a Real Pain in the Ass."

Hannah chuckled.

As much as the novel's publication also pleased Rupert, he still wanted to see a weekly paycheck. After all, how many novels could a novelist write per year? Josh had spent more years hawking *Captain O Captain* to scornful publishers than it took to write *Gone With the Wind*. "Worst of all, a writer's got *no inventory*."

"My novel's already in its second printing," Josh pointed out.

"So who do you think is buying it? But once you run out of friends—"

"The book's been sold to a paperback publisher."

"Even so. That woman who wrote *Gone With the Wind*. She never wrote another thing, did she?"

Hannah was astonished, and said so. If anyone needed encouragement, it was a writer, someone who dealt in intangibles, which had to contend with touchables for attention and sales.

But there was a reason, an internal one, for Rupert's negativity. X-rays soon showed he wasn't well. Never been worse. All these years Hannah had known one day it would come to this. Surgery was ruled out. Just as she'd always feared, the malignancy had spread. Rupert's only hope lay in chemotherapy.

Hannah invited Sandra and Charlie and Josh over to break the news, then stalled till after dinner. That wasn't the right time either: they were digesting. It wasn't until Charlie had gone for the car and Sandra and Josh were saying goodbye that Hannah, having escorted them to the lobby, blurted out, "It's about your father . . ." She couldn't continue.

"What *about* Dad?"

"Bad, very bad." Finally, "Can . . . cer."

Such news their mother had withheld for *three decades!* "Whywhy-why?"

Sandra screamed like a crazy woman, *"You didn't want us to aggravate?"*

"See what I mean?"

"Just hearing this now, Mom, thirty full years after the fact—"

"Josh, you wanted me to consult a *four*-year-old?"

"Mom, you are *impossible.*"

"Keeping it to yourself all these years. No wonder you had a heart attack—"

"And what good would it have done for the two of you *also* to live scared to death?"

She convinced them to go along with the deception. If the chemotherapy didn't work, Rupert would learn the truth soon enough. Till then, why shouldn't he enjoy whatever life remained?

The oncologist's aid was enlisted in describing Rupert's weekly injections as new miracle medication that would prevent future intestinal obstructions. No further surgery? Rupert couldn't believe his good fortune. It lasted several months, until the shots induced vomiting severe enough to make Rupert proclaim on occasion he was worried he might *not* die. Sometimes, the nausea would attack on the way home from the oncologist's office. Nevertheless, Rupert refused to take a taxi home—"a waste of money"—despite having to get off the bus to puke in the street.

"What kind of miracle is it makes a person retch for hours?" he demanded.

"An allergy to the shots," the oncologist said, and prescribed an oral cannabis constituent, which afforded some relief. In private he told Hannah that only smoking marijuana could stop the retching entirely. But since 1937 the use of marijuana in the U.S. was illegal.

Breaking a stupid law was of no concern to Hannah—imagine withholding relief from cancer patients! The problem was getting the stuff. Josh, with his literary connections, probably knew where to shop, but Hannah couldn't involve him. A grandmother picked up for buying marijuana would certainly fare better with the police than would an egghead. Everyone had a grandmother, few cops had eggheads.

Harlem was reputed to have drugs, but a white woman there would stand out—the police would realize she was up to something. Washington Heights, the home of Yeshiva University and where Henry Kissinger grew up. Newspapers called that former Jewish neighborhood the city's newest drug bazaar. That's where she had to go. In which dress? In her best one, a hand-me-up from Sandra, a drug dealer might mug Hannah for her supposed wealth; in her worst, he might spurn her as a charity case. She settled for one of Sandra's old suits.

Afraid to carry a pocketbook that could be snatched, Hannah wrapped a roll of bills in a handkerchief and pinned the bundle inside the top of her brassiere next to the keys to her apartment. In each pocket of her jacket and skirt went a card with her name and address and the children's phone numbers, just in case. Off she started without a hat, the better to display the snow-white hair of a sixty-nine-year-old. Then returned to don a black turban that concealed the white hair of a defenseless old woman, an easy mark. No simple thing, dressing for a drug buy.

There was still the subway to negotiate, which Hannah hadn't done in years. Now she remembered why. It was like traveling in an open garbage can, menaced by rodents. The litter. The disrepair. The graffiti. The deafening intercom. Some of the riders. During her last experience on the subway, a junior high school student actually set fire to a classmate's hair. After smothering the blaze with her scarf, Hannah asked the arsonist why.

"My friend dared me." Said with a snarl that frightened Hannah into responding, "Well, *that's* a good reason."

Outside the Washington Heights subway station were two cops, but she could hardly ask them for directions. On second thought, she did, claiming she wanted to move into the area.

"You're nuts, lady," advised one cop.

"Can't help it. Which drug-infested streets should I avoid?"

Though it was still working hours, Knox Place sported plenty of able-bodied males of all colors, a United Nations of hands in constant motion, giving, receiving. Cars drove up—many with out-of-state license plates—and the men went over to exchange things with the drivers. Several passersby were led inside apartment house lobbies or into alleyways, places Hannah would never go without a tank.

Now, what? Choosing a drug dealer was a lot different than selecting a doctor or a butcher; nobody on Knox Place came with a recommendation. And Hannah needed marijuana that was 100%

kosher. Slowly she walked up and down the street, eyeing its merchants for a friendly face, a sympathetic manner, perhaps a Star of David around someone's neck. But none were in evidence, only some crosses, a few horns and several razor blades, silver and gold.

One lithe black young man about the age of her grandson Zack flashed Hannah a broad smile the third time she passed him. "Hey, there, pretty mama," he said. "You picketing me?"

"B-b-browsing."

"No place for the likes of you. What you doing here?"

The words tumbled out all tangled. "Husband for my marijuana. Some I want to buy. He's a sick man, my husband."

"I bet he is."

"You don't understand. My husband is *really* sick."

The young man shrugged and reached into a pocket of his long leather coat. Fishing out a brown package, he thrust it toward her.

Hannah hesitated. "Is that the good stuff? No additives?"

He snorted. "Pretty mama, you think I be a health food store?"

"My husband has cancer. Real bad. He's going to—" Suddenly, tears were streaming down her face.

"Hey, pretty mama! What you want to do that for?" He pocketed the package. "Wait here. Be right back." And disappeared into an apartment house nearby. By the time she had dried her face and composed herself, he had returned with another package. "Acapulco Gold. Nothing purer." He held it out like a bouquet of flowers.

"Thank you so much." She turned away to unpin the bundle of money from her bra, difficult to do with one hand full of marijuana, and in her nervous haste ripped the bra without dislodging its treasure. House keys digging into her left breast, all of a sudden she felt a hand on her bosom. "*Oh!*"

"Forget it, pretty mama. Freebies. On the house."

"What? Why—"

"You remind me of my mama."

Gravely, she thanked him and hurried away. But at the corner, she turned and retraced her steps. "Young man," she said, "my husband's in textiles and I have five brothers. One of them should be able to line you up with a decent job. If you'll give me your name and address and phone number—"

"Hell, you *be* my mama!" The nice young man's face darkened. "*Scat!*"

Though it smelled like a hamper of dirty gym socks, the marijuana proved a blessing, once Hannah stopped giving Rupert an overdose, which prevented not only retching, but also getting off the bus. Twice they had to ride to the end of the line. Just a single joint smoked twenty minutes before chemotherapy kept the nausea in check. Now, Hannah didn't mind taking the bus home instead of a taxi, and Rupert headed straight for the refrigerator for something to eat. An honest-to-God miracle!

Still, how long could the malignancy be kept at bay? Eventually it would win out. Yes, of course, certainly. But not now. Hannah began praying, "Please God, let me go first." Life without Rupert was as inconceivable to Hannah as heaven without God, or Rupert without his textile firm.

But one day he astonished her by announcing its sale. Done under the influence? No, Japanese imports had killed his business. Should have sold out years before. Why hadn't he consulted his wife before selling out?

"This was a business decision," he replied. "What do women know about finance?"

The children, applauding the sale, wanted their parents to celebrate with a trip to Israel. Rupert rejected that, saying he wasn't sure whether he was just over an operation or before still one more. And when Sandra and Josh insisted their parents move from Parkside Avenue to Queens, Rupert waxed indignant.

"You want to break up my home?"

"This neighborhood's turned into a grade-A slum," said Josh. "Here, it isn't nuns who walk in pairs, but muggers."

"Well, it's *my* slum." Rupert left the room in a huff. His way of winning the argument, knowing Hannah wouldn't continue it after the children left. Ever since that first operation, she always let him have his way.

The visits to the oncologist continued, with Rupert his jolliest patient. The other patients, each with an escort, usually sat far apart in the waiting room, glum-faced, rarely speaking to anyone. That suited Hannah fine: she wanted no one there exchanging confidences with Rupert. ("I'm here for chemotherapy. And you? . . . *Vitamin* therapy?")

One afternoon everyone in the waiting room was cheered by the appearance of an adorable child with reddish golden curls, who was escorting her gaunt, hollow-eyed mother. Her heart going out to the two of them, Hannah engaged the child in conversation. Rupert, too, unable to resist the golden-haired child, wiggled his ears at her and moved his scalp up and down, the way he used to do with the grandchildren.

The child, laughing, pointed to his head. "Your hair looks so real, Mister."

He smiled. "Well, of course. Ever see a hairpiece with a bald spot on top?"

Nervously, Hannah glanced at the child's mother, but her wig was so expensive it looked just like normal hair.

"Mommy said *everybody* here wears a wig, just like me."

(Dear God, it was the *child* who was afflicted!)

Rupert laughed. "Your beautiful curls—a wig? A wig for eight-year-olds?"

"I'm nine," she said. "And this is the Shirley Temple. *Your* hair hasn't fallen out, Mister? How come?"

Once inside the oncologist's office, Rupert demanded to know all about his miracle medication and the waiting room full of wigs he had now noted. "No, don't tell me. I'll tell you. Cancer. Isn't that what you're treating me for?"

While the truth was at last revealed, Hannah wept softly, certain it would prove fatal. Nobody could survive hearing that dread word. In thirty years she had spoken it aloud only twice.

After his regular injection, Rupert stalked blindly out of the office, Hannah trailing behind, and hailed a taxi. They rode home in silence as deep as a grave, the only sound to be heard the minutes clicking away the minutes remaining in her husband's life. Hers, too.

Rupert vomited upon reaching their apartment. All night long he retched, lying in bed with his head over a pail on the floor, which Hannah emptied regularly. The next morning he was too weak to get out of bed. Hannah called the oncologist, who recommended an antinausea suppository, tea and toast, Jello and broth. But Rupert could keep nothing down. Desperate, Hannah gave him another joint to smoke and, on impulse, lit one up for herself.

It produced no discernible effect, puffed. Everything remained the same—Rupert was still retching, though in slow motion—except for the colors all around, which intensified till the pink in the living room carpet caught fire and turned into flames that seared Hannah's eyes, and the shine on the linoleum in the foyer blinded her with a diamondlike glitter. Otherwise, she felt no different until pigs' feet came dancing into mind, and she hurried off to buy some to save her husband's life.

Decades before, worried lest she be spotted by kosher friends, Hannah had traveled to an Italian neighborhood miles away. Now she walked over to Church Avenue, to Leo's late wife's butcher store, de-koshered after the influx of blacks and Puerto Ricans into the formerly Jewish neighborhood.

"*You*, Mrs. Trilling, in *my* store?" said the butcher in amazement. Then, when she placed her order, "*Whose* feet?"

This time Hannah used her own pot, dish and silverware (which she'd discard later, of course). As if to tell God, "See? I don't give a fig about anything but keeping my Rupert alive. In return, dear God . . ."

But the bargain didn't work. The jellied pigs' feet wouldn't stay down. Food had become Rupert's enemy, and he begged to be spared further invasions.

No longer could Hannah manage on her own. Only, now that she needed them, the children were away—Josh at Club Med, where she had encouraged him to vacation and bring home a bride, and Sandra in Chicago with Charlie at his law school reunion. Panicking, Hannah heard herself recite the *Sh'ma*, the prayer she said every night on retiring, the same prayer recited on a deathbed.

Suddenly, the phone rang. She snatched it up.

"How you doing, Grandma?" (Her grandson Zack. Thank God!) "Mother told me to check on you and Grandpa while she's away. You two behaving?"

"Oh, Zack! Come over! Please! *Hurry!*"

By the time he got there, Rupert had fallen asleep. She threw herself into her grandson's arms.

As was his practice, he kissed her on one cheek, then the other—"for balance"—then on her mouth—"it shouldn't get jealous."

How Hannah loved this nineteen-year-old. Such character, personality, warmth, intelligence, sense of humor, dark good looks. The very image of her father. Zack had been named after him, just as Papa had been named after his own grandfather. How comforting now to feel Rupert's immortality and hers hugging back.

"Hannah! . . . Hannah! . . . Hannah!"

They found him sprawled on the bedroom floor, one leg twisted beneath him. Rupert had fallen trying to get to the bathroom. "It's no good," he whispered hoarsely. "No good at all, no more."

Had Rupert's luck finally run out? Then so had Hannah's.

6

*T*HERE are few things more shameful to a six-year-old than soiling his bed after eating half a gallon of chocolate fudge caramel ice cream in one sitting and being called a big B-A-B-Y by his four-year-old sister, who threatens to tell the immediate world. Zack had loved his grandmother dearly ever since the time she'd shushed Debbie, cleaned up the mess, and tossed the linens in the washing machine, explaining to both of them that accidents were no cause for embarrassment.

"The only thing to be ashamed of in this world is hurting someone's feelings. Sheets can be laundered. But not feelings, and never hearts."

Several years later, Grandma had suffered a heart attack while baby-sitting, which Zack felt was his fault. That entire week he'd been battling her veto of his going along with fellow twelve-year-olds to see a slice-and-dice movie. Instead, she wanted them to sit down and write all the parents of the movie's director, producer, writer and actors to ask if they knew what their children were doing. The day she came home from the hospital, Zack begged forgiveness for nearly killing her with his obnoxious behavior.

Grandma had taken him in her arms. "Don't be silly, Zack. If obnoxious behavior could kill, half the children in this world would be orphans." She added, "And the other half, murder victims."

Her radiant face, which seemed lit from within, was rarely without a smile. So integral a part of her appearance was it, when Zack encountered her the night of Grandpa's collapse with face drawn, eyes dulled, lips turned down, it was as if he had happened upon Grandma without dentures or a glass eye in place, and his first impulse was to turn away to avoid embarrassing her.

She embraced him, exclaiming over and over again, "I've never been so happy to see anyone in all my life!" Words she rarely used, though her demeanor always conveyed that message. Grandma had a way of making people feel appreciated, unique. A girl his own age with that knack, Zack would marry in a flash, provided she was built like the proverbial brick outhouse.

One look at Grandpa sprawled on the floor told Zack things were as bad as Grandma feared. Getting him back in bed was easy, the hard part was knowing what to say. In the best of health, Grandpa was a taciturn man, who occasionally illuminated his protracted silences with flashes of humor. From the look of him that night he would never be up to it again.

Back in the kitchen, Grandma was wringing her hands. "All these years I've been praying for my mother to intercede with God on behalf of Grandpa. Seeing that beautiful golden hair, just like Mother's, in the doctor's office. An *omen*, I thought."

It became clear over the next few hours that home was not the place for Grandpa. Professional help was needed, lots of it.

Grandma wouldn't hear of it. "Never. That's *my* job. I've always done it, I always will."

Rather than argue, Zack phoned the oncologist who concurred. Reluctantly, Grandma gave in, then objected to calling 911 or even a private ambulance. It had to be a *Jewish* ambulance service.

"A *Jewish* ambulance?" (One with a tailpipe foreshortened?)

"Hatzolah is run by volunteers. People who don't do it just for the money. And they speak Yiddish and wear yarmulkes and—I suppose you think me a silly woman, Zack. But when a person is sick and frightened, little things count."

Whenever his grandparents visited Westchester, Zack or his

mother had to pick them up at the end of the subway line in the crime-ridden Bronx, because they would never take the commuter train from Grand Central Station, which cost a few dollars. How sad that even now, with Grandpa terminally ill, to be still fixated on money.

"Okay, Grandma. We'll ride Jewish, go gratis."

A pretty good idea, as it turned out. The two bearded, skullcapped volunteers, in dark business suits and ties, treated Grandpa with respect and solicitousness. Their kibitzing even brought a wan smile to Grandpa's waxen face.

"You taking me to a Jewish summer camp?" he joked. "Called, maybe, Trail's End?"

Grandma spit three times in the air. "God forbid! Bite your tongue, Rupert!"

While she accompanied Grandpa, Zack went for his car. On the driver's side someone had smashed the window. Amid the debris lay his "No Radio" sign with one line added: "Just Checking." What a neighborhood!

At the hospital the Orthodox volunteers refused the tip Zack offered. They were performing a mitzvah, and wished Grandpa a complete and speedy recovery, with God's help.

"What if," said Grandpa, "He's otherwise engaged?"

The emergency room's waiting area was familiar to any rider of the subway during rush hour. All seats occupied. Papers on the floor. People milling about, some in distress. Nobody offered Grandma a seat. Not even graffiti was missing. On the men's room wall: *Life's a bitch—and then you die.*

Tires screeching, a car drove up at full speed into the driveway, where Zack stepped for a breath of fresh air. A man jumped out, ultra-Orthodox sidecurls flying, shouting, "He's *here!* He's *here!* He's *here!*" as if heralding the Second Coming.

Zack, opening the car's back door, was startled to see the top of an infant's head protruding from between a woman's spread legs. No time to waste! With nobody else in sight, Zack grabbed the taxi driver's arm. "Come, let's get her inside quick!"

"Not allowed!" The driver recoiled and struck away his hand. "*Blood!*"

Unable to extricate the mother by himself, Zack dashed for help.

{87}

Two attendants came running with a stretcher and carried her off. Behind followed the uncooperative driver, giving them a hard time.

Zack wanted to punch out the s.o.b. "Is that cab driver asking for a tip? You saw. He wouldn't even touch the poor woman."

"What cab driver? That's her husband."

Zack bounded over to the driver-father. "Hey, fella!" he said, and spit full in the man's face.

"Did you just spit on me?" he cried. "Is this actual *spit?*"

"Consider that," said Zack, "the afterbirth."

"Stop me before I kill the *momzer!*" shouted the new father whom nobody was restraining. "Stop me! Someone stop me!"

"Generally, it's better to let God do the punishing," Grandma said when Zack rejoined her. "But in *this* case . . ."

Waiting an hour for Grandpa to be admitted was no picnic. And then only to the emergency room, no hospital beds available. Grandpa kept quiet while she held his hand and gave him liquids. Periodically, she ask if there was anything else she could do.

"Yes," he finally replied. "Nothing."

Inside the emergency room, Grandpa's medical history was taken time after time. Evidently, that's how the residents learned their profession, by torturing patients and family with the same questions over and over. The eyes of one resident welled up with tears. "That many operations?"

"Put this down in the chart, please," Grandma told her. "All these operations, and even now, my husband has never complained. He's a very brave man, my Rupert."

Surprising, the way Grandma conducted herself and gently took charge. Here was Zack in his Yves Saint Laurent and of the same generation as the residents. Yet they all directed their questions only to the little old lady in a worn housedress. One resident actually shushed Zack when he interrupted, another offered her his own cup of coffee.

In a way, she did stand out. A naturally pretty woman who shunned beauty parlors and make-up, except for lipstick, she carried herself with the dignity of an aristocrat and sincerely wished everyone not merely well, but the very best with her whole being. Whereas the faces of most people were masks, heres was as diaphanous as a negligee. One could read her thoughts through the bright, warm brown eyes and facial expressions. On more than one walk in Westchester, a handicapped passerby said to Grandma, who hadn't spoken a word, "Don't feel so bad, lady." And once a couple, "How'd you guess we're expecting?"

Zack felt for Grandma, who kept up a one-sided patter of good cheer with Grandpa, which must have been enervating. When he was finally taken to a room, she disappeared into a toilet, emerging after ten minutes with puffy eyes. On the ride back to the apartment, Grandma said nothing; once inside, she led Zack to a hutch which displayed her sterling silver candlesticks, kiddush cups, seder plates, porcelain figurines, china pieces. "Take, Zack," she urged, "whatever you want."

He was accustomed to her shoveling food at him, but not her treasures accumulated over a lifetime. "I can't."

"You'll be doing me a favor."

He selected a porcelain figurine of a topless young woman with arms outstretched in supplication, to appease her.

"Rosenthal," Grandma said. "From *pre*war Germany. After the thirties, I scrubbed their language right out of my mind."

She was fluent in German?

"Used to be, sure. Since Hitler, just hearing German—There's suffering in every syllable, torment in every word."

"That was all so long ago, over a third of a century."

"Not for someone with a memory, not for anyone with a heart. The German company that built crematoriums during the war still makes them. Never even bothered to change its name! Only, now those crematoriums are used to burn people who are *dead*." She added, "Isn't memory what separates human beings from animals? Without memory, without a heart, they win."

"Know what time it is, Grandma? Let's go to sleep."

"*You* go. I have to write my ethical will."

"What kind of will?"

"Ethical. Grandpa and I having no estate, that's all we have to leave. Our best wishes, a few thoughts, lots of hopes."

"Not *now*, Grandma."

"Oh, yes. While there's still time."

{89}

Zack didn't argue. Couldn't hurt, letting it all hang out on paper. The emotional release would be good for her. But morning found Grandma in the same housedress.

Zack called the hospital, which reported Grandpa was resting comfortably, and he was taking liquids. The prognosis? Nobody would hazard a guess.

"This is one time I regret being prelaw, instead of premedicine."

"Yes, who knows? You could have been the one to discover a cure for cancer. Don't misunderstand, my dear. I'm sure lawyers *also* do a lot of good. I just don't know exactly what, that's all." Then, as if there was nothing else on her mind, she asked about his future.

"Some form of public service. Maybe legal aid work for the poor. The greatest good for the greatest number. That's what I believe in, Grandma."

Her eyes shone. "That's a big mitzvah, nothing greater."

Nor was it in Zack alone that Grandma took an interest. On the way downstairs, she asked several neighbors about their entire families, many of them Puerto Rican and Oriental with names that were unpronounceable. All questions about Grandpa were deflected, however. Only good news did Grandma report.

At the hospital neither grandparent voiced his true concerns. Instead, she fussed with pillows and blankets and brought him ice cream, and he spoke of current events and doctors' bills and Medicare. No, he didn't want the family notified; visitors would tire him out. Yes, tea and toast would be nice, but he would do without a TV rental. Too expensive. His regular gifts of money to his widowed sister, he wanted continued. Grandpa's parting words at the end of the visiting hours: "Now, you'll have it all, Hannah."

What did that mean?

"He's given up," Grandma said, eyes filling with tears. "This is it. The end. For me, too."

Not melodramatic, really. In new widows the rate of death from heart disease more than tripled that first week. What could Zack do about that? How, to start off, to get Grandma through the rest of that day?

Back on Parkside Avenue, Zack took from his car trunk a recorder. "This, Grandma, is a travel ticket."

"Travel ticket?"

"That's right. I have your reservation right here. You're taking a trip."

"For the next world, no reservation is required. You just show up, and they take you in without any questions."

"It's to your past, this trip." In the apartment he inserted a fresh tape in the recorder. "Just say whatever comes to mind."

"I'm a listener. What can a person learn talking about herself?"

(There went the entire science of psychoanalysis right down the toilet.) "Grandma, don't you want *me* to learn?"

"What? Me, you already know."

"What about your mother and your father and—Come on now. Memory, Grandma, memory."

Face relaxing, she walked to the living room window and looked out at the magnolia tree, then up at the sky. "A visit to my parents, may their memories be for blessings. I *should* tell you about them. Because when *I* go, well, *they* go." She spun around on her heels. "Wait. Just remembered. I've written down some reminiscences. I'll get them—"

"Uh-uh. Not good enough. Lots of questions I want to ask." Zack made a pot of coffee, poured out two cups, and sat Grandma down at the kitchen table, then switched on the recorder. "Ready, Grandma?"

"No," she said. "Go ahead."

Exhausted from a night without rest and an afternoon of talk, Grandma had fallen asleep in the foyer. With her head thrown back, eyes set wide apart, straight, delicate nose (which Grandpa always joked should be enlarged), opaline unlined skin, high cheekbones accentuated by rosy apple cheeks, she looked like a young woman with prematurely white hair. Hers was the luminousness of the old-time movie stars who were bathed in back lights till they fairly glowed with a halo effect. But which director was lighting Grandma from above now as she slept?

The interview, meant to distract Grandma, shook Zack up. He'd always taken his grandparents for granted, adjuncts of Mother. Now to learn of Grandma's childhood, her adventures during World War I, immigration to America, sportswriter boyfriend, the Depression. The taping reminded Zack that Grandma had a full-fledged life of her own. Was a world unto herself.

Suddenly, she awoke with a start. "Oh!" Looked at her wristwatch. "Maybe you have someplace to go tonight. Do you?"

He hesitated.

"You don't have to keep me company anymore, Zack. I'm all right."

"I have this date, Grandma, and I can't contact Sophia anywhere now to cancel. Sure you don't mind?"

"Am I a baby? I've been taking care of myself all my life, haven't I? What kind of name is Sophia?"

"Grandma, did it ever occur to you that, well, you may be anti-goy?"

"Heaven forbid! You just heard part of my life story. Without some good goyim in the world, the Jewish people never would have survived. That goes for the state of Israel too. Such a tiny minority, us Jews. But you never did say, Zack. Is this Sophia Jewish?"

That one-track mind of hers made him laugh. "Of course, Sophia is Jewish."

She heaved a sigh.

He kissed her on each cheek and on the mouth.

Blessing him profusely, she saw him to the elevator and accompanied him all the way down to ensure his safe journey to the lobby.

So what if he had lied about Sophia? The last thing Zack had in mind was a hot night of marriage.

7

*I*T took Josh years to figure out he had but one sister and no brothers. Not infrequently, he'd awaken to find a family member, sometimes a stranger, lying beside him on the studio bed in the foyer. To such guests Mom instructed Josh never to say, "Who the hell are you?" (A lesson that came in handy during the sexual revolution.)

This demeanor, of the lady in New York harbor lifting her lamp beside the golden door, Josh deemed a windfall for relatives who never reciprocated. When he said so, often, Mom always replied, "Thank God I don't *need* them to do anything for me." What about when Josh needed? Mom had moved her newly divorced youngest sister out of a boarding house and in with the Trillings, where she stayed two years in the room Josh inherited after Sandra's wedding. Later on, when Aunt Tessie married a well-to-do businessman with a country home, Josh asked to stay the summer in her empty city apartment, to embark on his first novel. Agreeing reluctantly, Aunt Tessie gave Josh a house key, then had the electricity, gas, and phone turned off.

When Mom's father died, her three middle brothers asked Josh to help out in their clothing store during *shiva*. After six ten-hour days, he received not a penny in wages he planned to use for down payment on a typewriter. "That's what families are for," they advised him. "To help each other."

"Terrific! I get credit for a mitzvah, while your brothers got a week's vacation and cold cash."

His mother replied, predictably, "Josh, with those you love, you don't keep score."

Good old Mom! She was a free pass made flesh.

Those she helped least appreciated her most. Returning to college after a bout with pneumonia once, Josh was called out of class by the dean, who, as a blizzard blanketed New York, reported a phone call from Mom, urging Josh to pass up that night's rock concert in the city and come home right after class, lest he suffer a relapse.

Josh cringed and turned red. "Called *you*? To say *that*? Well, you *see*—"

He was cut off, sharply. "I am the *dean*. No need for me to deliver messages. A secretary and office boy do my chores. But your mother sounded so charming over the phone, I wanted to see for myself what kind of son she'd produced. Well, evidently nothing like her."

Years later, a nurse showed Josh a notation she, in twenty-three years of nursing, had never seen on a medical chart. Mom's cardiologist had written: "Her reaction to heparin is not all that's rare about Mrs. Trilling. She is the kindest, most gentle person I have ever met."

Gentle even with a retort. One bitterly cold winter, when an ultra-Orthodox Jew scolded her for wearing gloves on the Sabbath— "a sin"—Mom replied, sweetly, "I'll be happy to remove my gloves, just a soon as you take off your pants."

And ever encouraging. During the four years Josh's novel was making the rounds of publishers and agents, Mom assured him time and again it was a marvelous book that would be an enormous success. This, without having read a word of it. And after reading the manuscript, "Why, it's even better than I knew! That morning I first laid eyes on you, Josh. Didn't I tell you I saw this gorgeous rainbow up in the sky?"

What about the morning of Sandra's birth? "*Another* gorgeous rainbow. A remarkable coincidence."

Dad was more restrained. What would novelist Josh do for an encore? "No accountant," Dad pointed out, infuriatingly, "has to come up every year with *new* numerals."

Since taking an apartment in Manhattan, only on occasional Friday evenings did Josh venture to Parkside Avenue. Visiting now every Sunday afternoon for a month, to see how the area had deteriorated jolted him.

Unlike the Italians who, even after coming into money, rarely left their old neighborhoods, thereby remaining the city's largest national group, the Jews had taken pride in their progeny's relocating to the suburbs. Vicarious success, the American Dream realized in real estate. Overlooked at the time was the abandonment of parents to decaying environs, which didn't strike home till they had grown old, infirm, with insufficient funds to relocate. Now these aged Jews found themselves trapped in neighborhoods they no longer recognized—worse, feared. But Dad wouldn't go to heaven if it wasn't rent-controlled.

That afternoon Josh sought out a cop on the beat to determine how unsafe Parkside Avenue was for a woman living alone. "First of all," said the policeman, judging by his nameplate, an Italian, "I wouldn't let no mother of mine live by herself in *any* neighborhood."

Josh hurried away without waiting for second-of-all.

Not that there was reason to feel guilt. He had always offered his parents financial aid. But neither one would take so much as a dollar from him. Nor even presents. Mother's Day and Father's Day were always hassles. "Who asked for this?" Or, "Don't need it" or "Too expensive." And always, "Take it back." There were two ties and a shirt that Josh brought over each year in their original box for Dad to spurn. Another year, they'd be back in style.

Captain O Captain, however, contained an offering that couldn't be returned. Amazing that a woman unable to pass a handicapped person on the street without a sharp intake of breath and either "Such a pity!" or "God have compassion!" could tend smilingly to the paralyzed, deformed, amputated at the chronic diseases hospital. Ending up each morning-after sick in bed from the strain never deterred Mom from returning the following week. Not even a heart attack kept her away.

All this Josh had put in *Captain O Captain* to explain in part the behavior of his young hero. Otherwise, Josh didn't have much of a usable past to write about. No harpy mother, no abusive father, no sluttish sister, and plenty of no sex. To top it off, Josh himself was no alcoholic, which Random House's publisher said was the lot of every great writer he knew.

Graduate school and the academic life it was leading to could produce no saleable novel. Then came the draft, but army duty stateside was the basis for another *From Here to Eternity* only if the North Vietnamese had bombed San Francisco in a sneak attack. The novel Josh eventually wrote was rejected by thirty-two publishers and seventeen literary agents. Said one editor: "You've made poor artistic choices. Why is your hero, who's always in the doghouse, never inside a cathouse? Un-army, if not un-American. True what they say about sex, you know. It sells." So Josh ended up a magazine editor.

At the hospital Mom sat huddled beside a dozing Dad in the four-bed room, stroking his hand. Strange. He had been doing so well on chemotherapy. But just as soon as Dad had learned of the cancer—

"His color is better. Don't you think so, Josh?"

(No.) "Yes, Mom."

"He'll pull through. You'll see."

That was far more likely than Dad's ever explaining something Josh could never understand. Why all these years he had felt they were related only by marriage.

Any such criticism always had Mom leaping to Dad's defense. Life wasn't easy for an immigrant who had none of the advantages and opportunities he had afforded Josh. And how much time did twelve-hour workdays leave for cultivating human relationships? Once, she exclaimed, "If only you could have known your father when he was young, in his beautiful navy blue suit and silk shirt, and we were engaged. What a pity children only know their parents as oldsters."

Now, at Dad's bedside Mom was whispering, "Rupert, don't ever leave me."

Josh swallowed hard.

Just then, Sandra entered unexpectedly with her seventeen-year-old, sweet Debbie. Both tall, slender brunettes, with bright, dark eyes and very attractive.

"What are *you* doing here, Sandra?" Josh asked. "This isn't the high seas."

"Had to get in one last visit before—" She fidgeted with her pocketbook. "I did try to cancel. But when the Cunard Line wouldn't refund our $4000, Charlie pressured me. I feel simply *awful*—"

Mom hugged them. "Don't be silly, Sandra. The cruise was booked months before Dad took sick. He knows that. And it's only for two weeks."

"Leaving at such a time. And when you had your heart attack, Mom—"

"Nonsense. We'll be fine."

Josh worried about his mother. All she knew was doing good. Not much future in that.

When a nurse objected to the number of visitors in the room, Josh and Sandra left to shop. Lately, Mom seemed to have stopped eating; her clothes hung on her. They drove by the Gothic towers of their alma mater, the second oldest high school in the United States, once famous for the high caliber of its students. Now it sported broken windows and littered walkways and dropout and attendance rates that rivaled the city's worst.

At a liquor store that admitted no customers—the owner possibly emerged once a month to deposit his proceeds in a bank and stock up on food and toilet tissue—they stopped for a bottle of kiddush wine. He sat behind bulletproof glass in the window, like the fabled prostitutes of Hamburg, asking your pleasure through an intercom. Collecting the money, he slipped purchases through a slot and said, "Have a safe day."

"Mom and Dad are leaving this neighborhood," Sandra vowed. "Even if I have to hijack the two of them."

"Right." Josh felt relieved, grateful. Big sisters did come in handy, for teaching kid brothers how to dance, to dress, to approach adolescent girls without falling all over one's tongue. Now too, freeing Josh from worry about Mom.

At the apartment house he unloaded the car and toted the groceries inside while Sandra carried the new dresses. The dilapidated lobby had him swearing. "Used to be so grand, this building."

In a moment they were playing the game of remember. When the lobby boasted a new marble floor, wood-carved walls, a sofa and chairs, tables and lamps, a fireplace glowing with artificial logs, a live doorman. When the now boarded-up Loew's Kings nearby—with its statuary, sweeping staircase, gilded ceiling and twinkling lights, uniformed ushers, fountains—was their idea of the palace at Versailles, and elegant stores on Flatbush Avenue were magnets for the rich and the tasteful. When no store there sported steel shutters to prevent break-ins and looting. When nobody was afraid to enter nearby Prospect Park in the daytime or even sleep there at night. When the elevator in the house always worked.

Josh proceeded into the living room. It had been off-limits during his childhood, when family life centered around the kitchen table. In an instant the ancient sofa and chairs and tables and lamps and drapes, which still looked eerily new, transported him back to the late forties and fifties. Even the carpet seemed untouched by feet. Once a velvet rope hung across the entrance to the living room, cordoning it off like masterpieces at the Metropolitan Museum of Art. Now, Josh plopped down on the couch, whose plastic covers crackled as if roused unwillingly from a deep slumber, and put his feet up.

Sandra appeared. "Josh! What are you *doing?*"

"What's it *look* like I'm doing?"

"In the living room? On the sofa?"

"Sandra, I haven't lived here for years. That makes me company." Leaning over, Josh switched on a lamp whose shade was also swathed in plastic. "Mom and Dad bought this furniture *ages* ago. You'd think they'd have unwrapped it by now."

Sandra gestured. "And those drapes."

"Know how old I was before Dad let me sit on this couch? I'd had sex three years before. Wasn't much fun. Of course, I was alone at the time."

"Well, you don't need Dad's permission to get *married*."

"Don't you think I want to? Long overdue. Most of my friends are already divorced. *Need* to marry. I can't cook. My smoke alarm doubles as a timer."

"So what's stopping you?"

Death by starvation was the lot of the proverbial jackass who couldn't choose between equidistant bales of hay. But hay could be consumed in one session without a lifelong commitment; with a wife, consummation was only the start. What if one's tastes changed? It did with other appetites. Stuck with yesterday's passion grown cold. "Ever eat day-old lox and eggs, Sandra?"

"Poor Josh. All those meals and still not full."

"You think it's one long orgy, the single life? Living up to the image of the swinging bachelor—"

"Who says you have to live up to other people's expectations?"

"I'm talking about my *own* expectations. I listen to guys all the time, scores of scorers, and I read those letters to *Playboy* and *Penthouse*—at the barbershop. All those encounters related at such enormous length. They never happen to *me* in *brief*."

"Josh, you can be sure of one thing. Whoever's writing all those letters is lying through his teeth."

"Oh, no. No, no, no. Why, there are men in prisons all over the United States who are getting more action than me. I mean, than I." Josh shook his head. "One thing puzzles me. No guy has ever bragged to me of his great *love* for somebody or other. Always great *sex*. Friends, strangers too, will reveal every clinical detail. But about love, not a whisper."

Sandra sighed. "Sex being the icing, people are generous with licks. But the cake—"

"Never had myself a piece of that. Intimacy."

"It'll happen to you, Josh, it will."

"What makes you so sure?"

She turned away and spoke so softly. ". . . this theory. People usually fall in love when they are the most miserable."

(If this wasn't the most absurd conversation, with their father so sick.) "About Dad—"

"A great regret of his. You know that, Josh? Not seeing you settled."

"Dad spoke of that? About me? Honest?"

"Last week, and the week before. Probably today also if—Josh? How long can this go on, do you think?"

"Well, if the chemo works again, maybe years, the doctor said."

"That makes me feel better. Well, not *better*. This damn cruise! I'd pay $4000 *not* to go. But Mom and Dad wouldn't let me back out. And you know my Charlie."

(A humorless publicity hound and obsessive-compulsive careerist. Josh fantasized shooting Charlie, then hiring him as defense lawyer. Just to see whether he'd adhere to his standard operating procedure of blaming the victim—in this case, himself.) "Why on earth did you ever marry the guy?"

"Who remembers? But the man I married was an idealist—"

"Crimebuster turned moneymaking crimebooster.

"Charlie does have his good point . . . s."

Josh walked to the window brushed by the magnolia tree's branches. Mom looked forward to each springtime's pink and white blossoms, which Dad called pretty eyesores that kept the light from the apartment. "Dad also started out very much the hero. So admired. A scrupulously ethical businessman, if that isn't a contradiction in terms. Yet—"

"Josh, just because Dad is undemonstrative. The style he was raised in. Doesn't mean he doesn't care."

"Never a birthday present. That, I can understand. There'd be three presents per year to shell out money for. But why no anniversary present? Dad has only one wife."

"Sent us both to college, didn't he? And me a female."

"*City* colleges. No tuition."

"Enough already. Therapy session over. More important now. What do we do if . . . Mom can't stay on here alone."

"But I thought, with Debbie going off to college—"

"Don't you think I thought of that myself! I'd *love* to take Mom in. Did try. But Charlie. He won't hear of it."

"He banned the Mom?"

"For one thing, instead of calling Charlie a criminal lawyer, she accidentally calls him a lawyer criminal. Or her saying every April when he's whining about taxes, that he should feel grateful for being able to repay the Government in part. For another thing, I refused to take in Charlie's father, that creep."

Josh hurried to the liquor cabinet and poured himself a shot of something. What adults in plays and movies always did when confronted by giant problems. Mom, when widowed, with no place to go!

"As I see it, there are two alternatives. An apartment in Queens or in Florida."

"Florida? We'd never get to see her!" All those widows in Miami Beach. Adult foundlings.

"Well, in *that* case, brother."

"Sandra! You don't mean—"

"I seem to recall she's your mother too."

"How would it look for a man my age to be living with his Mommy? People would think I'm . . . funny."

"So get married, Josh. *Then* invite Mom in."

"But I can't get married until, well, until I explore different possibilities. To me *women* are the Dark Continent. And how can . . . explorations . . . be conducted . . . with Mom there?"

"There's a new invention, Josh. It's called The Motel."

"I should pack Mom off to a motel every time I get the urge?"

"No, brother dear. Hie yourself and your tootsies there."

Then girls would think him a married man. And bachelorhood was the ultimate aphrodisiac. The best thing a lowly paid editor and author unpublished till now with a heavy-metal mouth had going for him. Because Dad had refused Josh orthodontia as a kid, Josh at thirty-four was stuck with braces for two years. Grilled cheese bonded to them; vegetables, when chewed, set up housekeeping; lips got impaled on the wires, like prisoners caught escaping from a P.O.W. camp. Last time Josh soul-kissed, a rubber band broke and nearly snapped off the girl's tongue. "What about a nice apartment in Queens? With a companion."

"*Pay* someone to keep Mom company? She'd feel demeaned."

"Mom's brothers? sisters?"

"I've already checked. Only Aunt Rachel in California would take her—and just for a few weeks.

Alarmed, Josh drank up. "What *are* we going to do?"

The doorbell drowned out Sandra's reply. He went to answer the door, only to be confronted with something worse.

In his hand a stained brown paper bag from school lunches of decades past, Leo, Dad's pesky second cousin. With a face like an Idaho potato, a Silly Putty body, and an abiding interest in his own creature comforts, the septuagenarian spoke as if stringing words one by one on sentences. The verbal equivalent of the Chinese water torture.

"Oh, it's you, Leo."

"Of course it's me. Who else looks like this? Not Cary Grant, not any more." Entering, Leo expressed surprise in slow motion. "Sandra! *Also*. Is your poor, dear father kaput?"

"Bite your tongue!" said Sandra. "I wanted to see my folks before I left . . ."

"Going away?" said Leo. "Where to?"

When Sandra hesitated, Josh filled in. "Jamaica, St. Croix, Aruba, Caracas—"

"What's that? A cruise? With your father on his last leg, a *cruise?*"

"It's in Dad's memory," Josh volunteered. "Charlie is dedicating the cruise to Dad."

Leo shrugged. "Your mother, it's safe to guess, is not joining you. How's she holding up?" Josh and Sandra looked at each other. "Not so hot, huh? I know, I know. Been visiting every night, just about."

"Strange. Dad's mentioned only a couple of visits."

"Well, not that often to the *hospital*. Your father and I are just like brothers. For two years I even loaned him my Medicare card to ride the bus for half fare. Just can't bear seeing Rupert suffer. So I keep tabs on him by stopping here regular."

"At suppertime?" Sandra asked.

"Without me, your mother would never make herself supper." Opening the brown paper bag, he unwrapped the package inside that held raw meat. "Kosher, which my store doesn't even sell."

"You never take Mom *out?*" Josh asked.

"Since my wife died, God rest her soul, I eat out all the time." Leo looked around. "Your mother all right?" Told she was still in the hospital, he headed into the kitchen. "I'll start things. Save time. I'm starved."

"Hmmmmm." Sandra looked pensive. "Josh, I've been thinking . . ."

"Well, strike up the band!"

"We agree Mom can't be left alone in case . . . Right? After all, she is sixty-nine years old."

"So?"

"So . . . Leo is also alone."

Josh choked.

"The man's a doctor. Retired now, but he could look after her."

"A doctor who specializes in causing heart attacks."

"Who *else* is there?"

It hadn't occurred to Josh, for Mom to remarry. Later on, some year. But *Leo?* "The man has no redeeming social *anything*." He had hoped to strike it rich by marrying the daughter of Brooklyn's most successful invalid butcher. So all during the twenty-one years his father-in-law refused to die, Leo went around griping of being swindled out of his rightful inheritance.

"You got a better idea?"

"Yes. Sandra, you, me and Aunt Rachel. Suppose we *share* Mom . . . even steven."

"Four months apiece? But Josh dear, could you do without for so long? You might forget what goes where."

"*Two* months." He darted to the calendar. "Winters we can send Mom to Florida. *Movie stars* send their mothers to Florida. Summers to the mountains. Who wouldn't give a right arm to escape New York's heat? That would leave only—"

"Sounds great, Josh, really does. If only *Mom* thinks so!"

"Of course, she'll think so."

"God knows we want to do what's best for her. But it isn't easy when you're married." Sandra sighed. "When you're married, nothing is."

Josh formed a mental picture of marriage as a great big, beautiful cage. Those outside wanted in, those inside wanted out.

Dinner would be ready in twenty minutes, announced Leo, returning. Instead, Sandra suggested a rain check. There were many important personal matters to discuss with Mom. "I'm sure you understand, Leo."

"Of course." He took off his apron and folded it methodically into small rectangles. "Leos have understanding." After another sojourn in the kitchen, he soon returned minus the apron but with his brown paper bag, bulging once more. "You two *are* taking your mother *out*, aren't you?" At the door, he paused. "If I were you, I'd try Katznelson's. They give value for the money."

The new restaurant on Kings Highway?

"What restaurant? Katznelson, the funeral parlor on Coney Island Avenue." He left.

Josh insisted, "Dad's going to make it."

"Will he? Leo *is* a doctor."

All of a sudden Josh felt finally, hopelessly grown-up. Only adults, or pathetic waifs, were orphans. And nothing like losing a parent to make one feel where the buck stops next. "Mom will pull Dad through. She's done it before, she'll do it again."

"Josh, something tells me Leo knows something Mom doesn't want us to know yet." Sandra strode to the telephone and picked it up. "That settles it. Charlie sails away by himself on the QE2."

8

WHEN no one picked up, Sandra left a message on the answering machine, then set out with Josh for the hospital. On the way she bought some ice cream for Dad. "I scream, you scream, we all scream for ice cream," he used to recite whenever presenting the child Sandra with a vanilla Mello-roll. Even now, gliding a middle-aged tongue around ice cream and sliding it down her throat instantly triggered pigtailed memories of sunbathing on Tar Beach on the roof, swimming at Coney Island, rides at Stee-plechase Park, rowing in Prospect Park lake, playing potsi on the sidewalk.

One New Year's Eve Dad brought home a quart of ice cream, which could be divided, and but a single horn. When adolescent Sandra insisted on her fair share of tooting, five-year-old Josh said, "You want it? You got it!" and hurled the horn, which split her lower left cheek. She could still hear Mom's wail—"What boy will marry a girl with a crippled face?"—as Dad rushed Sandra to Cousin Leo, who had trouble sewing up the cut because Dad, watching in horror, kept swooning.

Whenever she went to play on Shabbas with friends on the other side of Ocean Parkway, Dad would escort Sandra. On the way back home he'd offer advice, like before her going away to camp for a week: "Don't ever talk with strangers." (A stranger herself at the new camp, that would have left Sandra mute.) Every few days Dad wrote her a letter titled My Day, after Eleanor Roosevelt's newspaper column, ending with: "So how's your day been? Nice, I hope."

Josh asked suddenly, "Remember the anniversary party?"

No need to specify. There had been only the twenty-fifth. All the preparations that had gone into it. Josh, annoyed at being asked to chop fish in a wooden bowl and beat egg whites with a whisk and stretch out thin sheets of noodle dough on bedspreads, demanded to know why the party wasn't being held at a restaurant.

"Better yet," Dad replied, "why not on the Queen Mary?"

Mom said, "For what the tips alone would cost, I'm making this entire party myself." Everything there she cooked and baked, and the day before, she scrubbed the kitchen and bathroom floors and foyer linoleum on her hands and knees. (No mop for one who always distrusted what was easiest.) Each window she washed too, sitting on the ledge of their third floor apartment and getting trapped half outside for forty-five minutes till Sandra, coming home from school, pried the window open. The party's highlight was Dad's speech, which stunned Mom even more than the company. Sandra rarely saw her parents kiss. But lo, there was Dad, carrying in a cake ablaze with twenty-five candles, shushing everyone, taking the floor and calling Mom the captain of her family's ship, forever helping everyone steer the proper course in life. Mom's cheeks turned a brighter shade of rosy pink then usual and she rushed out of the living room. Compliments made her uncomfortable, she explained later. She just wasn't used to hearing them. Maybe if she'd had more practice . . .

"I remember, Josh. Beautiful party, just beautiful." Now the only anniversary candle in Mom's future was likely to be a solitary annual *yahrzeit* memorial.

At the hospital was a lovely surprise: Zack. For five weeks straight Mom hadn't stopped blessing him for accompanying Dad in the ambulance and staying with her that terrible night.

Sandra would break in. "Enough, Mom. You'll give Zack the evil eye." No human being was as wonderful as Mom liked to believe and, of course, she knew nothing of her grandson's shortcomings which surfaced at close quarters. Like his short fuse, which blew whenever he didn't instantly get his own way. This was now on display to a hospital guard, who had refused to let Zack by, the two passes already taken by Mom and Debbie. He had stormed upstairs and, troubled by Dad's appearance and with no resident available for questioning, insisted on inspecting the medical charts.

Sandra and Josh arrived just as a security officer was ordering Zack to leave. Enraged, he quoted from the Freedom of Information Act, impressive-sounding as it was irrelevant.

Was he acquainted, a guard asked, with the bum's rush?

Zack would not desist. It had become a matter of honor to badger the nurses for charts that, they explained, were not made available even to outside physicians, much less to laymen.

"What layman? I am a *lawman*. And I hereby demand full patients' rights." He pushed his way into the nurses' station.

An intern barred Zack's way, guards seized him, while Josh shouted something and Sandra nearly had a fit over her nineteen-year-old's temper tantrum, so like his father's.

From all sides people came hurrying—nurses, porters, residents, visitors, even patients.

"What's going on?" Mom cried.

"Nothing," Sandra said. "Zack stopped by to see you and Dad—isn't that nice?—and now he's leaving. Isn't *that* nice?" To the guards: "*All* of us are leaving. Thank you very much."

"That's right, Mother, take *their* side!"

Josh asked, "What's with Zack?" as Zack, swearing, stalked off.

Go tell him, and Josh would never procreate. As impossible as marriage was, raising children to be normal human beings was worse. "Zack's just upset, like everyone else—"

An alarm sounded suddenly, sending nurses and residents running. This time they converged on Dad's room. Sandra, restraining Mom, found her shivering uncontrollably. They heeded a nurse's suggestion to retire to the visitors' lounge. There Josh reminded Mom that Dad's room contained *four* beds.

Mom shook her head. "Terrible! Don't know what to pray for. That it not be Dad? Then somebody *else* would be at risk."

Inexplicably, Sandra found herself reminiscing of the time Dad took her to Coney Island, where she got lost. Crawling under the boardwalk, the five-year-old covered herself with newspapers, then waited to be rescued. Not at all scared, for she knew that sooner or later her father would find her. He did after almost three hours, with the aid of half a dozen relatives he had phoned. For that reason alone, Dad himself would be rescued now.

The container of ice cream had turned soft by the time a resident appeared to ask for the Trilling family. Too fearful of what he might say, nobody responded at first.

"I'm sorry. Mr. Trilling. He's gone."

A sharp intake of Mom's breath. No crying, though. The past weeks had wrung every tear from her. "I have to see him, my Rupert," she said matter-of-factly. Disengaging herself from Sandra, she left the lounge, carriage erect as ever, and hurried into Dad's room, where she addressed him as if he were able to listen. Passionately, she thanked him for all their many good years together, years of happiness, their two wonderful children, and much more, continuing at a clip too fast for Sandra to absorb it all. Where did Mom get the strength? Or the presence that didn't flinch in the face of death? On she went, granting Dad forgiveness for the deathbed confession of sins he'd have made if conscious, then asking his forgiveness for her own transgressions against him. More expressions of gratitude and love before concluding with the *Sh'ma*. Then she kissed Dad full on the lips and said, "I love you so much, Rupert, I always will."

Sandra turned away in tears. Debbie, sobbing, put her arms around Mom. Josh kept clearing his throat, as if words had lodged there that could never be disgorged.

"No more Rupert. I'll never see him again. Dear God!"

It was a long ride back to Parkside Avenue. So in the end it all came down to this: a shopping bag with some clothing, toilet articles, transistor radio, wristwatch. And a leaking container of ice cream.

Mom looked around her apartment as if she'd never been there before, seeing now with one pair of eyes what she'd always viewed with two. "Rupert, why did you leave me?" she whispered, then went to the hutch and took out all her treasures and began distributing them. Everything reminded her of Dad, and it hurt to think of him, just as it hurt *not* to think of him. She allowed herself to be led to the couch. But when Sandra put her legs up, force of habit made her sit upright and wipe the plastic covers with her hand.

"Silly!" she said. "What am I cleaning for? For who?"

"You always taught that a person should take pride in whatever she does," Sandra said.

"I said that? Well, that was *before*. My life is over now."

"Don't say that, Mom!" Josh cried. "Never say that. It's a—a—a sin."

"It's the truth, children."

Debbie threw herself into Mom's arms.

Sandra tried reasoning. "Mom, think of all the *other* widows in the world."

"That's supposed to cheer me up? That there are lots more unfortunates everywhere? I should cry for them too."

A telephone call, though a wrong number, came as a welcome distraction, even as the caller insisted Mom's number was wrong. And he called back to say so, and would have phoned a third time if Charlie hadn't phoned just then.

Sandra reported Dad's passing, which Charlie accepted as if it were that of a client who hadn't paid his bills. Barely missing a beat, he mentioned something about a cruise. "*What* cruise, Charlie? . . . Don't be silly, Dad *can't* be buried before midnight." Embarrassed that Debbie was hearing this, Sandra sent her for a glass of water. "What was that, Charlie? . . . I inquired two weeks ago. It was too late *then* for a refund."

Arms hugging her chest, Mom was rocking herself back and forth, as if she were her own baby.

". . . Contact the Cunard Line yourself." Sandra took the tickets from her purse and read off the numbers, then slammed down the phone.

Josh couldn't resist saying, "I'm surprised Charlie didn't suggest burying Dad at sea."

Mom excused herself.

All things considered, she was holding up pretty well, everyone concluded, hearing the shower go on in the bathroom. It would calm her, hydrotherapy. But when the shower showed no sign of stopping after twenty minutes, Sandra went to investigate

Mom was sitting fully clothed on the edge of the tub, weeping softly, face contorted, wavy white hair damp and stringy from the steam. Sandra cradled Mom in her arms. If only they could get past the funeral, speed through the week, skip ahead to the following month.

"I know, Mom, I know. It hurts. I know."

"You know how it feels? Never to see someone you love ever again?"

The phone rang. It was Charlie calling back to rattle on to Josh about the cruise. Nothing, absolutely nothing, ever derailed Charlie's train of thought. If Sandra hadn't stopped him, he'd have used his tickets to *Hello, Dolly!* the night before his own father's funeral.

"Poor Charlie." Mom took a towel and wiped her face. "His vacation ruined." She asked Sandra to accompany her into the bedroom, whose walls bore photographs of the early days. Dad a tall, slender, swarthy man with an impassive face, she a curly-haired, dark-eyed beauty in an off-the-shoulder silk dress with a fur boa. Their wedding portrait showed a painfully earnest, young couple peering intently into the camera as if trying to discern their future.

Mom went to the chest of drawers, opened the bottom one and took out a box which held two little cloth sacks. "My father was buried with a bag of earth from Israel under his head." She picked up a bag, kissed it and placed it inside her bodice. "This goes under your father's head tomorrow. You won't forget where this second bag is, will you?"

All her life Mom had dreamed of visiting Israel, her father's original destination. Papa wanted to be buried in the Holy Land, but chose instead to leave the transportation costs to charity, settling for a little bag of Israeli soil.

In the living room was a tray of sandwiches and fruit, prepared by Debbie. Mom wouldn't touch a thing.

Josh sought to reassure her. "You won't be alone. Ever. Once you move from Parkside Avenue—"

"What's that? Move? I can't afford that. It's rent-controlled, this apartment."

"But not crime-controlled," Josh said. "No place for a woman living alone. For a man, either. Maybe for a S.W.A.T. team."

"Where can I go?"

Sandra said, "To us, of course. To your children who love you and to your sister in California."

Josh added, "And to Miami and the mountains upstate."

Mom looked from one to the other. "The three of you? And where else, did you say?"

"Miami and the mountains."

"But—but—but—"

"But what, Mom?"

"How can one person live in three—no, *five* different places?"

Josh smiled and took her hand. "She can when she's a sweetheart everyone wants."

Disengaging her hand from Josh's, Mom rubbed her eyes. "I'm so confused, so confused. Five homes?"

"It's simple, Mom. Stay a couple of months with me, a couple with Josh, a couple with Aunt Rachel—"

"Children, I still don't understand, I really don't."

"What's not to understand?" said Josh. "You're a very popular lady, Mom. We all fought for the privilege of having you *exclusively*. Finally, we agreed to compromise."

"You mentioned Miami and the mountains? They fought over me too?"

"That's for the winter and summer months, Mom. Breathers, you might say."

"Breathers? For who? Or is it *from* who?"

"Nobody loves New York in the winter and summer, Mom."

"*Now* I see." Mom got up from the couch and walked to the window and looked out at her magnolia.

"Good!" Josh said. "Then it's all settled."

"So that's what this boils down to," Mom said quietly. "Joint custody."

"Mom! What a thing to say!"

"Joint custody," Debbie repeated. "Isn't that for *children?*"

"Yes, it is," Mom replied.

Josh hurried to Mom. "It's for anyone in contention who lots of concerned parties want very, very much."

She looked him in the eye. "Or for somebody *nobody* wants very much at all . . ."

As Sandra and Josh expressed dismay, Debbie jumped up and rushed to Mom. "Oh, Grandma, *I* want you. So does *everyone*."

". . . So she's split up into little pieces. A little bit here, a little bit there, a little bit everywhere."

"*No, Mom!*"

"*That's not so, Mom!*"

"Okay, it's not so, children. Then don't evict me from my home, make me a gypsy. Whatever you've decided, just undecide. I won't be a Wandering Jew, you hear?"

"Mom, we'll work something out. You'll see. Something each of us can live with happily."

"What's this, some kind of peace treaty? I've lost a husband, not a war."

Josh reached out to hug Mom, who held herself stiffly. "You decide what you want to do. Then *tell* us. Okay?"

Mom wilted. "That's just it!" She said wistfully, "*If I only knew* . . ."

A good time to stop talking, for Mom was becoming increasingly agitated. God knew Sandra wanted to do the right thing, but that wasn't the same as knowing what that was. Not with Charlie around to gum up the works.

A phone call from Katznelson to set a time for the funeral. Did the Trilling family have a plot?

Yes, Mom said, and directed them to the broom closet in the kitchen. Inside was a gray metal box in which Dad kept all his important papers. What, no safety deposit box in a *bank?* Well, after Mom's heart attack, or maybe during, Dad had discontinued it. As for the key to the gray metal box, it was someplace in the china closet. She didn't know where. Dad kept switching it around.

"Just what we need now," Josh muttered to Sandra on their way to the kitchen. "A treasure hunt."

The gray metal box was found under balls of string and scores of plastic shopping bags—each carefully rolled into a little ball. When-ever Sandra threatened to clean out the broom closet, which con-tained enough plastic and string to bag Brooklyn, Mom would vow to go to Westchester and discard all the junk in *Sandra's* house.

To find the key, they had to rummage through six sets of dishes—everyday dairy and meat, the good ones for Shabbas and holidays, and the Passover ones. Then there were the *chachkes:* wedding pres-ents from forty-five years before. Eggcups shaped like bluebirds, the porcelain juicer with the head of a winsome girl from whose ear orange juice flowed, and more.

Inside an empty tin of bicarbonate of soda they came across dollar bills wrapped in a handkerchief. The *knipple* of every Jewish house-wife, savings from her weekly household allowance so she needn't ask her husband for extra money.

"So quiet in the living room," Josh noted. "I'll check."

Sandra stopped him. Debbie was good for Mom. Theirs was a special relationship.

With the search for the missing key looming as an all-night affair, the silence in the adjoining living room was finally broken.

"Grandma?" Debbie asked. "Well . . . I don't know what to say."

"You don't have to say anything, Debbie. You are."

"I *am?* . . . *What* am I, Grandma?"

"With me. Back in the hospital for a moment I felt you *were* me. They way you grabbed hold of my hand and squeezed so hard when we went to Grandpa. Never letting go till we got back here."

"Grandma, what you said to Grandpa. I'll never forget it."

"Me? I spoke? What did I say? My mind's a sieve."

"Can't remember the words. But the *music.* It poured out for maybe ten minutes. Like an aria."

"Ten minutes! What could I have said?"

"My drama teacher teaches us, Always play the feelings, not the words. You loved Grandpa very much, didn't you?"

"Rupert was my life." Her voice broke. But a moment later, "Is that what you want to become, my darling? An actress?"

Mom would now do what she'd always done at the chronic diseases hospital, a place so horrifying Sandra would have bombed it to smithereens. There, Mom entertained like a gracious hostess at a garden party, focusing all attention outward. At least, concentrating on Debbie's future would blot out, if only temporarily, thoughts of Mom's own bleak prospects. So goodness did pay. Once in a blue moon.

". . . go to drama school in the fall."

If only Mom could change Debbie's mind. She had spurned Sandra's advice to postpone drama school.

"What about college, Debbie?"

"Barbra Streisand never went to college after graduating Erasmus High."

"Well, don't you think she regrets it?"

"Somebody going into the theater has to get an early start. Look at Kitty-Kat, a radio actress at *eleven*. Grandma, I never feel so alive as when I'm acting. There are such great plays, such great roles, such great lines!"

"Yes, of course. But whose are they? Some college graduate's. A person has to bring something of her *own* to all that. Then, there's also a life to live after the curtain goes down. Marriage. A woman needs to contribute something more than playacting."

"Well, what do men contribute beside salaries? Why should it be up to us women to make all the sacrifices?"

"For me, Debbie, the only us was Grandpa and myself."

"That's so antediluvian, Grandma. Let some *other* sex be subservient, for a change."

"How can I make you understand, Debbie? Marriage can be a profession. It certainly is mine. Was."

"Not a job with the most independence in the world, is it?"

"An actress doesn't cater? To producers, directors, critics?"

"At least all my eggs won't be in one basket—a husband."

"Husband or no husband, Debbie, remember this: A person with learning always has company."

"Oh, Grandma, you'll always have *me*."

"My darling!"

With a cry of jubilation, Josh dug out a key from a salt cellar. Why all that bother to hide it? Any burglar would have forced the metal box open or taken it home. Sandra brought the box into the living room, placed it on the coffee table and opened it. Inside, piled two inches deep at the top, were dozens of smelly cigar butts.

"Phew!"

"Oh!" Debbie exclaimed. "I thought those were turds."

"Mom, you did say Dad kept his papers in here."

She wasn't sure. "I never opened that box, of course."

Josh dug into the contents and unearthed lots of papers. "Just camouflage, these butts. To throw burglars off the scent, so to speak. What does the deed to the cemetery plot look like?"

Mom had no idea.

"Weren't you at all curious?"

"As much as Dad was about my housekeeping."

"What a mess!" Sandra leafed through batches of papers and clippings. "Didn't Dad ever throw anything away?"

"Your father was a great believer in Who knows? and Maybe. Who knows? Maybe this'll come in handy one day."

Debbie suggested divvying up the papers among the four of them.

"Yes," said Mom, "*Papers* can be easily divided."

Sandra bit her lip.

Plowing through the pile, each periodically announced a finding. Old gas bills. Electricity bills. Phone bills. Cancelled checks. Bank statements. Receipts. Store coupons. Fifteen cents off Dial soap, twenty-five cents off Grape-nuts. Report cards?

Mom looked those over. "*I* saved your report cards. What are they doing *here?* Evidently, Dad didn't tell me *everything*."

Debbie held up a large certificate. "Hey, look at this!" A bearer bond worth $10,000. Clipped to it was a note that read: "This is for Debbie if she marries a doctor. To help them open up an office."

"*Ten thousand dollars!*" exclaimed Sandra.

"For *Debbie?*" said Josh.

Mom couldn't believe it even when she held the certificate in her hand. "Where'd the money come from?"

Debbie held up another piece of paper. "This what we're looking for? Uh-uh, no. Says here International Business—"

Josh grabbed the certificate and examined it. "Mom, I didn't know you and Dad owned 300 shares of IBM."

"What's IBM?"

Debbie picked up still another certificate: "General Electric Corporation, 500 shares."

Sandra corrected her, "You mean a hundred."

"It says *five* hundred."

Sandra seized the certificate. "Good heavens!"

By then, Debbie had struck gold again. "Mobil Oil, 600 shares."

Sandra and Josh dove at the box and pulled out certificate after certificate, each looking perfectly genuine.

Mom was unable to absorb all this. "I don't understand. Is this some kind of *joke?*"

In a moment everyone was reading off the names of companies and the number of shares. United Airlines. Bethlehem Steel. Penn-Central stock, which was only twelve shares, Josh tossed aside.

"Josh, Sandra, *somebody*," Mom pleaded, "What's going on here?"

"U. S. Treasury bills, by the dozen . . ."

"Chase Manhattan Bank . . ."

"Philip Morris . . ."

The gray metal box held stocks and bonds worth *hundreds of thousands of dollars.* And Sandra knew exactly what she was going to do with her share. "Mom, we are *rich!*"

"*Filthy* rich," Josh cried. "*Stinking* rich!"

Debbie asked, "*Who* is rich?"

"What?

"Wait a minute, children, wait just a minute."

"Yes, Mom?"

Mom stood up. "Good question, Debbie's. Who does all this belong to?"

"Why, to you, Mom, and to—"

Josh cut in. "Sandra, there is no *and*. It's all Mom's now."

Mom fell into the club chair, dazed. "*Nothing* makes sense any more!"

"Mom? You have any explanation?"

"My God! You think your father robbed a bank?"

"If Grandpa did," Debbie noted, "It must have been more than one."

Josh held up a batch of receipts from brokers and results of stock splits and dividends that had been automatically reinvested. Since the Depression, when stocks were so depressed, Dad had plowed all his savings into the market. "Sonofabitch! Why didn't Dad ever give *me* a tip or two?"

Mom sat there, shaking her head from side to side. "The man would yell at me for buying a jar of Sanka when it wasn't on special. Always had to use those money-off coupons. And when the thirty-one-year-old Hoover broke down, he wanted to buy a generic brand."

"Maybe," Debbie suggested, "Grandpa wanted to surprise you with this bonanza."

"When? At *my* funeral?"

"Let's face it," Josh said. "Dad was a miser. A very *successful* miser."

"Mom, when you signed your joint tax returns—"

"Your father had me sign *before* he filled them out. Clever, wasn't he?"

"What about later? When you checked them afterwards?"

"What afterwards? Who checked? You don't understand, children, either of you. I *trusted* your father. Even after he cut my household allowance by twenty-five percent when Josh was drafted. Oh, they ought to change those words in the wedding ceremony to: Love, honor—and *look out*."

Was the father who bought Sandra a fur coat for her eighteenth birthday a man who would keep this hoard a secret from his wife? "It's a sickness, miserliness. Dad must have been *sick*, Mom."

"Was he, my dear? Your father was well enough to hide this treasure from me year after year. But for who? For *when?* The World-to-Come? I'm sorry, children. Excuses do *not* excuse."

"Well, what do *you* think were Dad's reasons?"

"Who cares! I'm sure Jack the Ripper had *his* reasons. All these great minds always *explaining*. Gives people the idea anything goes so long as they can come up with *reasons*. Or remorse. Well, to *hell* with reasons. And remorse is for the birds."

"Try to look at the *bright* side," Josh suggested. "You have all this wealth to enjoy *now*. You can move anywhere, Mom, do anything. Live it up!"

"At *my* age? Too late, too late. You think I've enjoyed accepting your hand-me-downs, Sandra? Going years without a show, a movie? Keeping the same furniture and drapes for forty-five years? Living the constricted life *Rupert* wanted to live. A sacrifice is no sacrifice when it's a necessity. But when it's a waste, a total waste . . ." Mom hurried over to the secretary in the foyer and took out a large pair of shears, which she raised high over her head.

"*Stop her!*"

"*Grandma, don't!*"

"*He isn't worth it, Mom!*"

They rushed toward her.

Evading them all, she dashed to the couch and, with one swift motion, stabbed it. "Sticky little plastics." Then, again.

As Josh took away the shears, Sandra, embarrassed, turned to Debbie. "Suppose you go downstairs and get me a—"

Debbie stood fast. "I'm staying, Mother. Have to. This is theater. On the grand scale."

Mom backed her up. "That's right, my darling. Stay and learn. Now, Debbie, watch carefully." Mom went to the shopping bag she had brought back from the hospital and emptied it. Taking the gray metal box and its contents, she dumped everything into the bag. Proceeding to the hall closet, she took out a suit and a few dresses and stuffed them into another shopping bag.

"What are you doing, Mom?"

"You're staying for the funeral, aren't you, Sandra?"

"What?"

"Children, I am on my way."

"*Where* are you going, Mom?"

She marched over to the end table and scooped up the cruise tickets lying there. "The Caribbean."

"*WHAT?!*"

"*Grandma!*"

Digging into her shopping bag, Mom took out a certificate, which she handed to Sandra. "Charlie should be delighted. Now he has his refund."

"But—but—but—but—the *funeral!*"

"I'm sure Rupert will understand."

"Mom, you can't play hooky from Dad's funeral!"

"What I can't do is let $4000 go to waste. Rupert would never forgive me." She headed for the door.

"What'll we *tell* everyone?"

She paused at the door and drew herself up to her full height. "Tell everyone I am Mrs. Rupert Trilling *not any more.*" The door slammed behind her with such force, the secretary's doors flew open and a hand-painted dish fell off the foyer wall.

Sandra and Josh looked after her, mouths agape.

Debbie clapped her hands. "Bravo! I mean, brav*a*!"

Josh started after Mom, but Sandra restrained him. "Let *me.*" She left the apartment and hurried down the stairs; spying Mom in the courtyard, she slowed her gait. The woman needed to be alone for awhile to let off steam. Afterwards, Sandra would be there to bring her back home. Entirely understandable, Mom's initial reaction. She had been royally screwed. Nevertheless, who ever heard of any wife absenting herself from a husband's last rites?

Certainly, Mom wouldn't follow through on the cruise, if only because she hated the subway that would take her to Manhattan. Indeed, she headed in the opposite direction, toward Ocean Parkway, where she and Dad often took their children for a stroll.

But who knew how long the cooling-off process would take? So Sandra ran to her car, got in and followed after Mom, lugging the matching shopping bags. Sandra herself needed time for reflection, unable to fathom Dad's secret life.

At the parkway, Mom paused, placed the shopping bags on the pavement and looked around. Minutes later, she waved one hand, then the other. At whom?

A taxi drove by, its off-duty light on. Mom, who had probably taken only two cabs in her life, each time while contractions were coming ten minutes apart, was trying now to hail her third.

There would be plenty of time for Mom to think things over, however. Cabs on Ocean Parkway were few and far between, and those available would hesitate to pick up someone resembling a bag lady.

But all of a sudden a cab driver going toward the ocean made an illegal U-turn and headed toward Mom. Stepping on the gas, Sandra beat him there. She opened the car door on the passenger's side and called to Mom to get inside.

Mom stood her ground. "Rupert *owes* me," she said.

Even after Mom's heart attack, Dad refused to hire a cleaning lady. What upset Sandra, who cleaned their apartment regularly for years, was not the work, but seeing Mom so upset. Many times she did all the heavy cleaning herself to spare her daughter. And with the money saved Dad bought yet another piece of paper to hide in his gray metal box.

"Come on Mom. *I'll* take you to the ship."

Worth doing if only to see the expression on Charlie's face at the funeral, when he found himself in attendance and no widowed mother-in-law there.

9

WHENEVER Hannah hit a finger with a hammer, she never experienced instantaneous pain. Instead, all feeling within shut down completely to alert her a big hurt was imminent. *Ready, set, withstand.* So she now felt on her way to the city. Numb.

"Want to talk, Mom?"

That was the *last* thing Hannah wanted. Answers were what she craved. Actions should make some sort of sense. Why so cuckoo, Rupert? All her life she had believed an inch is an inch, a promise is a promise, a spouse is a spouse. All of a sudden, in the twinkling of an eye, in the opening of a gray metal box, it turned out that nothing was what it was supposed to be. Words didn't mean what they said, marital vows and devotion signified nothing. Hannah's well-ordered world had turned topsy-turvy, she with it. And how did one live inside chaos?

Poor, distracted Sandra. Instead of driving to the Manhattan Bridge, she turned into the Brooklyn-Battery Tunnel, which claustrophobia always had her shun. Concerned, Hannah touched her on the hand, which was sweating and fixed like a vise to the steering wheel.

"Don't worry, dear. Nobody ever drowned in this tunnel."

At the Hudson River pier, Hannah got out of the car with her shopping bags, but was told to leave them. On the way to the hospital that morning Sandra had checked her luggage at the QE2. Hannah could use that wardrobe. There was nothing unusual about her wearing secondhand clothes. ("Not used, just pre-owned," Rupert always told her. "Well, don't *shoes* feel better for having been broken in?")

Only after reaching the gate did Hannah recall what had been inadvertently left behind. She stood rooted to the spot. Asking for the metal box would indicate distrust, hurt Sandra's feelings. Yet, inside were papers Hannah did not want either of her children to see just then, if ever. Too bad she couldn't have kept those papers a secret even from Rupert too. Might have made a big difference to him as well as to their son.

"What's the matter, Mom? Second thoughts?"

"Well . . ." She turned and took a step toward the car, turned around again, started for the ship, then stopped short.

"Oh! Wait here, Mom. Forgot to turn off the headlights. My battery will run down."

Before Hannah could ask for the gray metal box, Sandra was gone. Soon she reappeared with one shopping bag, telling her much relieved mother to record the contents of the metal box and deposit it for safekeeping with the purser's office.

As soon as they got to the stateroom, which took almost as long as climbing to the top of an Empire State Building that had toppled over onto its side, Sandra called Josh. He had been wondering by then whether he was the sole surviving member of the Trilling family. His voice resounded through the phone.

"What the hell happened, Sandra! You went downstairs for *five minutes*. That was over an *hour ago* . . . You're *where?* . . . You're *kidding!* Next, you'll be telling me you're running off *together*. You *aren't*, are you?" He demanded to speak to Hannah.

"Mom, I just want to tell you one thing. Get it off my chest . . ."

"Yes, Josh?"

A long silence. ". . . We love you, Mom. Bon voyage."

After having Charlie's bags sent to the gate, the two of them unpacked Sandra's. Good therapy, doing instead of thinking. If only Hannah could work her way down to the Equator and back, then sideways around the world. Finally taking her leave—there were funeral arrangements to make, she was at great pains to avoid saying—dismissing all protests, Sandra handed over her pocketbook, which contained hundreds of dollars and several credit cards.

"Don't worry, Mom. I expect to be fully reimbursed." At the door she cradled Hannah's face in her hands. "Why do I feel as if I'm sending you off to camp for the very first time? Well, take good care."

"The family, Sandra. What will you tell them?"

"Don't know yet."

She thought for a long time. "Anything but the truth will be just fine."

Then, for the first time in her life since being quarantined in Danzig fifty-four years before, Hannah was left alone. Ahead lay another ocean voyage, this time with nobody around to save her but herself. She called to mind God's charge to Joshua on his way to the Land of Israel: "Be strong and of good courage." For further support she looked inside the gray metal box. But it contained nothing more personal than Rupert's naturalization papers and her own. No ethical will like the one left by her father and grandfather or herself. Just a *knipple* of stocks and bonds worth more money than in a game of Monopoly. Boyoboyoboy! And Hannah thought *she* could keep a secret.

The years of senseless scrimping and saving, drudgery, doing without, Sandra's hand-me-downs, when Rupert and Hannah could have been living it up. Contributing to charities, visiting Israel, having a cleaning lady in. Nor was money the only thing her husband had hoarded. Feeling, encouragement, sympathy, affection were doled out in teaspoons.

Often, he would ask, "Have you figured it out? Life, I mean." And among his last words to her, "Now you have it all." Whatever. So foolish, depriving himself as well as her. Like the dragons in fairy tales that guarded caves full of gold and virgins to prevent them from being enjoyed.

At Sandra's eighth birthday party, all the children had gone into a frenzy over amassing jelly beans. When Hannah asked a boy who had piled up over a hundred what he would do with so many, he stared blankly. "Do? I *have* them."

Yet, when the QE2 set sail, remorse came washing over Hannah in great waves. One of the biggest mitzvahs of all was attending a funeral, for it was something done without any thought of reciprocity. And here she was boycotting Rupert's and observing a floating *shiva*.

The finest of husbands at first, that good man had changed so gradually later on, she couldn't pinpoint its beginnings. His growing miserliness, the discontent with his lot, the envy of a millionaire friend, the withholding of conversation. Something's terribly wrong, she said; consult a doctor, she begged. But he wouldn't spend the money.

Perhaps all the operations had warped his thinking. And in their aftermath feeling too dependent on his wife. There was the baleful influence of friends whose male bonding often degenerated into female shredding. The two things some men boasted about most were their children's achievements and wives' inadequacies. Unhappy with yourself? Try scapegoating. Spread the misery around, you'll feel better.

Once, Hannah overheard a man telling a friend standing in line at a bank, that if he died that day, his idiot wife would be thrown for a complete loss, never having been allowed to write a check in her life. Chortling, his friend said, "Same with mine." In supermarkets Hannah noted retirees ordering wives around, deprecating them. "Too expensive!" "Who needs it!" "Wait for a sale!" "*I'll* do the shopping!" That put the men back in business, their wives in the toilet. And now to discover *herself* in that company.

There were no answers forthcoming that night, only scores of questions. *Why, Rupert, why . . . ?* At dawn she hung the *Do Not Disturb* sign on the doorknob and finally drifted off to sleep. To dream of Rupert, so young and good-looking. They were strolling through the park. Sunny day, flowers everywhere, birds chirping, future bright. All of a sudden from out of nowhere sprang a big, nasty, filthy black dog. She cried out for Rupert, but he was nowhere to be seen . . .

Worn out from restless nights and having no wish to see anyone or be seen, Hannah kept to her room. In the flickering light of a candle lit as a memorial, she kept posing the same questions to the same profound silences. The first time a steward entered in the middle of a conversation with herself, he apologized for having brought "them" only one dinner. It was at dawn that sleep came to her rescue. Afternoons she read Psalms from the Gideon Bible, between soaks in a warm tub. The stewardess she never let inside until the day Sinead said she'd be fired if she wasn't allowed to do her job.

A thin, pert girl with big green eyes, light brown hair and freckles, she offered to bring Hannah some medicine for seasickness.

"That's not the problem. I think—well, maybe my body has traveled too far and too fast for my soul."

"I understand, Ma'am, I do. Have out-of-body experiences myself. Dream I'm rich." She was amazed that Hannah tried to help her change the linens.

Such a charming lilt to the girl's voice. "You speak so beautifully. You must be English."

Sinead bristled. "*Irish.*"

"Oh. I thought, this being a British ship—"

"You're aboard too, aren't you, Ma'am? *You* British?" In a moment the skinny girl was acquainting Hannah with details of the Irish-English conflict. ("The troubles" made Hannah's pale in comparison.)

No sleep again that night; at dawn the *Do Not Disturb*. In late afternoon Sinead came not only to straighten up, but to urge Hannah to rise and get ready.

"Fire drill?"

"The Captain's Welcome Aboard."

Well, Hannah had to leave the room *one* day, face the world alone *some*time. What better surroundings for a coming-out party from anger, recriminations, self-pity, Brooklyn? Sinead said to wear an evening gown, but under the circumstances, Sandra's were far too festive. A simple long black cotton dress with a white ruffle at the neck seemed suitable.

The hour being late, Hannah went to have her hair washed in the beauty parlor. Bushed, she dozed off as soon as she stretched out on the chair. Every once in a while she roused herself to ask if the operator had finished though, relaxing for the first time in weeks, Hannah didn't much care if she never did.

". . . And now, how about eyelashes?"

"What happened to mine?"

"*False* eyelashes. Make your eyes look ever so much bigger . . . No?"

A mirror held up to Hannah showed no more French twist; her naturally wavy hair cascaded in ringlets down the nape of her neck with curls bordering her face, freshly made up and over. Groggy, she asked, "Who am I?" and was told the Empress Josephine.

Since Hannah was in no need of a coronation, once back in her stateroom, she scrubbed off all the make-up before putting on the long black dress. Uh-oh, it was cut much too low. The gaping bodice she closed with a diaper pin, camouflaged it with a pink rose (from an uncollected luncheon tray) wrapped in a piece of water-soaked cotton (from the top of a bottle of aspirin) swaddled in a piece of plastic (cut from the shower cap in the bathroom). It wouldn't do for anything to die in her cleavage during the Captain's Welcome Aboard.

The reflection in the QE2 mirror was decidedly not what had been foreseen all those past weeks in the hospital. Then, she had pictured a black dress being slashed by the rabbi while she recited, "God has given, God has taken, blessed be the name of the Lord . . ." Fighting back tears during the eulogy so as not to distress the children and embarrass the grandchildren. The long ride to the cemetery plot, which Rupert called their low-rise condominium. Battling the impulse to join him in the grave. Sitting *shiva* and making small talk while hoping people would go away and leave her alone to die.

Instead, here was Hannah stepping out that night like Ginger Rogers off to meet Fred Astaire. The ship's carpeted corridors were swarming with handsomely dressed goyim out on the town as if they had nothing better to do for the rest of their lives. Was this how people really lived?

After days at sea, everyone lined up outside the Grand Lounge knew others. Hannah not a soul. No matter. Who wasn't a stranger to everyone else? Look at Rupert. Probably a stranger to himself as well. But the longer she waited, the more time there was to think of no good reason why the ship's captain would want to meet *her*. It would be a mitzvah to spare him another handshake and more small talk. Besides, for her first time out Hannah had ventured far enough. So back to her stateroom to reflect. Running away from New York on impulse was all well and good. But where on earth was she running *to?* When the Children of Israel fled Egypt, they didn't head for a junket to the tropics.

A knock on the door. It was Sinead, and Hannah was too embarrassed to confess having already beaten a hasty retreat.

Inside the room, one look had the girl exclaiming, "Mother of God!"

"Diaper pin open?"

"It's *you*, Ma'am. A real beauty you are. Go on now, Ma'am, and knock 'em all for a loop. I pray tonight's the night your soul and your body catch up with each other."

Hannah allowed herself to be led out of the stateroom to a shortcut where there was no waiting line, the Grand Lounge's second tier. It was full of shops with foreign names—Gucci, Harrods, Acquascutum, Alfred Dunhill; below was the captain's reception line, surrounded by those who had already passed through. Afraid of tripping over her long dress, Hannah proceeded slowly down the semicircular stairway. Looking up once, she almost took a tumble, on finding herself the center of all eyes. Had the plastic shower cap container sprung a leak? She looked down to check. No, the pink rose was alive, her bosom dry.

Jumping the line did pay, for in short order a uniformed officer asked Hannah's name and introduced her to the ship's towering, dark-haired captain, who looked exhausted. The first word to roll off Hannah's tongue was: "Arthritis. A person could get it from shaking two thousand hands at a time."

The captain chuckled. "And that's not all."

"Must also be hard on you and your family, separations as long as three months at a time."

He heaved a sigh. "Yes, it is. Not something one ever gets used to—Mrs. Trilling, is it? Now, in *my* case . . ."

Dinner was announced. On the way through the dining room she was again conscious of stares. Probably from those wondering why they had never seen her before, thinking she had boarded the QE2 in mid-ocean. Everyone at the table was complimentary, friendly. After introducing themselves—too many names to catch anyone's— they asked about her seasickness and—with a nod toward the empty chair nearby—husband.

". . . died," she said.

Expressions of regret. "When . . .?"

Too quickly, "Sunday."

Who could blame them for looking startled? Until this man with Paul Newman blue eyes and Kirk Douglas cleft chin laughed. "Anyone here think Mrs. Heller meant this *past* Sunday? In *port?*"

Chuckles all around.

She corrected him. "I'm Mrs. Trilling. My daughter, Mrs. Heller, and her husband couldn't make it. I'm their replacement."

"Me," said a middle-aged ash blonde in a gown cut all the way down to well below table level, "I'd never take a cruise all by *myself.*"

"Me neither," said another middle-aged, low-cut ash blonde. "Wouldn't have the *courage.*"

(Go tell them it would have taken more fortitude to stay home and keep quiet about Rupert without busting a gut.) Oh, why couldn't a waiter drop a tray or something? Hannah hated being the center of attention as much as she disliked those who thought that wherever they sat was the center. Food provided a welcome diversion. The broiled salmon was so delicious, Hannah made a mental note to order some for Sinead. During dessert, a band began to play, and the blue-eyed clefted chin asked for a dance. So did two men from nearby tables. Hannah declined with wonder. At family affairs she always had many invitations to dance, all from women whose husbands didn't. Several more invitations had Hannah feeling distinctly uncomfortable; inappropriate for her to cavort. It was time to call quits to this first step in the uncharted voyage of widowhood.

Newman-Douglas insisted on escorting Hannah to the door, speaking, on the way there, of her previous cruise on the QE2. Told this was her first, he asked why then the ship's captain granted her more time than to other passengers. "What did you two talk about for so long?"

"Well, we started with arthritis—"

He gave her a hard look, then a smile. He offered to escort her back to the stateroom, but for forty-five years Hannah had never taken a walk with a man other than Rupert.

"See you at breakfast, Mrs. Trilling?"

"I don't eat breakfast." (Still asleep.)

"Lunch, then."

"Well, I'm not much of an eater these days."

In bed, Hannah reviewed still again all of Rupert's many virtues and good deeds. Let *that* memory be for blessing. But rest still eluded her. When would this stop! Dawn provided a respite.

The breakfast at her door Hannah left for Sinead when she went out for an early lunch. Only the two ash blondes were at the table, this time steely-eyed and cold. When she wished them a good morning, one snapped, "You put out for him, didn't you?"

"For *who?* Put out *what?*"

"Miss Innocence! As if Sheldon didn't *also* miss breakfast this morning."

Hannah, whose policy was never to quarrel with someone loud, excused herself and left the table. At the door she ran into Newman-Douglas.

"You can't have finished lunch so soon, Mrs. Trilling. Why, what's the matter?"

A gesture toward the two women at their table. "I don't understand. Last night they were so nice. But—"

"Nice?" He chuckled. "You didn't catch their drift?"

"Why so *openly* nasty now? Something about a Sheldon . . . You?"

"With all due modesty, Mrs. Trilling"—he bowed his head—"those two woman have been hitting on me."

"No! *Hitting* you?"

"Hitting *on* me. They've come on to me. Mighty strong."

Put out? Hitting on? Come on mighty strong? "So . . .?"

"So, Mrs. Trilling, we can do each other a favor. Men and women will keep pestering you and me. That's what cruises are for, making out. Unless we do something."

"Making out?"

"I propose we join forces."

"What does it involve, joint forces?"

"Just keep each other company, that's all. Make believe we're together."

"I'm not up to company right now."

"Just give the *appearance* of being together. Here, let me show you." Taking her by the arm, he guided her to a table for two at the far end of the room. "First person to speak is a rotten egg."

Hannah could not help smiling.

"I have my moods too, Mrs. Trilling. There's no reason for you ever to respond if you don't feel like it. Agree?"

She did not respond.

After lunch, he escorted her to the One Deck Lido, where the sun dazzled and the colors all around made her gasp. Coney Island's gray green waters were sludge compared to the intermingling vivid greens and intense blues of the sea swirling beneath a sky of the bluest brilliance. Automatically, Hannah reached out, as she did whenever admiring flowers. Colors always acted like a magnet, drawing her out of herself.

"A million miles away? Left me high and dry," he said. "Well, tomorrow, we can leave together. The ship docks at one of the islands for a few hours."

"Can't. Not this week."

After a long stroll in the invigorating sea air, they stretched out on deck chairs. Sheldon had changed into a bathing suit that revealed the trim, athletic build of a swimmer, while Hannah hid behind long sleeves, sunglasses and sunscreen. They spent the afternoon in and out of the sun. A satisfactory arrangement for her, having someone nearby who made no demands and whose presence kept others from intruding. But what did *he* get out of it?

Ordinarily, Hannah would have asked all about him during dinner, but she held back for fear of provoking queries in turn. Ordinarily, even without being asked, everyone was only too eager to spill his life story, but Sheldon showed the restraint of someone who might also be observing an unorthodox *shiva*. By the time coffee was served, Hannah felt her reticence being worn away by his.

Suddenly, he said, "I'm ready any time you are, Mrs. Trilling.

"Ready for what?"

"For whatever you want to say. Looks to me like it's burning a hole in your skull."

Well, why not? It wasn't as if Sheldon was a relative or friend who would take her *tzuris* to heart. Or blab it to the whole world. After the cruise they'd part company, never to meet again. To a complete stranger she could divulge Rupert's preference for inanimate assets over her without feeling embarrassed to death for herself or Rupert.

"Well, after my husband passed away, we were looking through his papers, my children and I, for the cemetery plot . . ." Everything came pouring out, as it had been doing nightly; the only changes were from questions to statements—in pronouns from *you* to *he*.

Sheldon never interrupted, not even to exclaim, "*My God! Last Sunday?*" Every once in a while he'd just say, "Uh-huh" or "I understand." At the end, simply, "Good for you, Mrs. Trilling."

To be fair to Rupert, Hannah then recounted all the many good things he had done for her family as well as for her.

"A man is what he is," Sheldon responded, "not what he used to be."

Hannah asked his surname.

The following morning she awoke refreshed. The burden was still there, would be always. But for having been openly acknowledged, it felt lighter. To show her gratitude that morning, she took a personal interest in Sheldon Wilson.

He spoke only briefly about himself. Beloved wife had died the year before after a long illness. Father of a terrific daughter with three wonderful children and a supercilious husband. Bank officer. Despite his youthful looks and physique, on Medicare for almost a year. Jewish.

Hannah's response was to repeat her monologue of the night before. She just couldn't stop herself. It was something that needed doing, again and again, like an infection that had to be purged continually. Mr. Wilson never called a halt that day or following. The result was that by week's end Hannah was at last able to shift her attention to Sandra and Josh. How worried they must be. What a predicament she had placed them in. How many lies they must have told everyone!

For fear the QE2 stationery would give Charlie a fit ("My mother-in-law's sleeping in *my* berth?"), Hannah dropped a line only to Josh. And just in case it was spotted by a family member, she signed it "Henrietta Szold."

That prompted a much needed change of subject, one she was pleased to elaborate on, Henrietta Szold being one of Hannah's two favorite heroines. After the man she loved married another woman, Henrietta Szold didn't crawl into a shell in 1912, but founded the Hadassah Women's Organization, which now numbered 350,000 members. "Dare to dream," she had written, "and when you dream, dream *big*." One reason Hannah wanted to visit Israel was to see the Hadassah Hospital, one of the world's leading teaching and research centers, for which she had raised money for four decades.

Mr. Wilson broke in. "Why don't you do it, Mrs. Trilling?"

"Do what?"

"Visit Israel."

"I certainly plan to. Sometime next year."

"Why wait? Dare to dream big *now*."

"*Now?* Bad enough, shipping out like I'd been shanghaied. But to continue on to Israel. My children—"

"Ready to face family and friends a week from now? Couldn't you use an intermezzo? Recharge your batteries the way Henrietta Szold did after being dumped?"

"Dumped? I've never thought of the great Henrietta Szold as being *dumped*."

"That's probably what made her great, the dumping. I bet your other heroine was also, Mrs. Trilling. Dumped."

"*Eleanor Roosevelt?*"

"Proves my point. Did Eleanor stay home in the White House after discovering her husband fooling around? Of course not. She roamed the world far and wide."

What a gentleman, to take an interest in her plight. But she had repaid Mr. Wilson's kindness by monopolizing his time. Such a mensch deserved a lovely wife. Hannah had to see to that.

None of the women passengers were known to her, however, nor which were Jewish, and he was probably shy. Why else attach himself to an older woman? So the next day, she insisted on his disembarking. And for dinner Hannah arranged to join a table of eight. Well, it was a start.

To while away the day, Hannah explored the ship, a veritable city at sea with a world of activities and no fear of muggers. The last word in materialism, it contained a spa with exercise machines, aerobics classes, Jacuzzi whirlpool baths. Sports area with paddle tennis, electronic golf course, tetherball. Casino gambling and slot machines. Even a kennel for those unwilling to be parted from their pets, as well as a hospital for humans. Arts and crafts, whose instructor gave Hannah some drawings to copy.

With the instructor's encouragement, she sketched in charcoal the Western Wall of the Temple in Jerusalem's Old City, so familiar from television, picture books of Israel and postcards.

"Suppose you touch it up with these," said the instructor, handing over coloring sticks.

The huge blocks of stone that made up the Wall came out authentic as well as pretty in a dusky rose. For contrast Hannah chalked in tiny spots of greenery in the crannies, where pilgrims from the world over left *kvitlach*, written petitions to God.

She faked men by chalking white and blue prayer shawls which, except for the bottoms of their trousers, completely enveloped those at prayer. For women, she chalked in a segregated section of assorted hues, which gave the impression of dresses and scarves.

The instructor said approvingly, "How long have you been taking art classes?" when she finished.

The sketch delighted Mr. Wilson, but he was annoyed to learn of their dining with others. Since her motive could be misinterpreted ("You think me incompetent to marry myself off, Mommy?"), Hannah spoke of the need to get her sea legs as a widow by mingling with as many people as possible.

Mr. Wilson conceded.

Unfortunately, their dinner companions took them for a twosome. And Hannah could think of no gracious way to deny it to the unattached women at the table who asked on the sly, "Well, how *is* he?"

{133}

"Why ask *me?* Ask *him*," she answered each time, only to get a dirty look in return.

Afterwards, on their strolls around the deck, Hannah made a point of pausing to chat with suitable-looking women. They showed considerable interest, Mr. Wilson none. And when she urged him ever so diplomatically to pursue one particular woman, he took offense.

"Mrs. Trilling, are you trying to *dump* me?"

"Mr. Wilson!"

"You want to meet other men? Is that it?"

"Don't be silly. What on earth would I do with *other* men that I can't do with *you?*"

Those men Hannah did converse with were all married. She made sure of that. And recalling the behavior of the two ash blondes who didn't even have a claim on Mr. Wilson, only in the presence of wives. Thanks to Sinead, she now knew the meaning of "put out."

The next tropical port of call Hannah finally went ashore. Along with the others, she was immediately besieged by hordes of ill-clad native children, all barefoot and begging for money instead of attending school, where they belonged. Disturbed, she handed out all her dollar bills and change.

In one of the dozens of picturesque shops that lined the port, Hannah bought for Mr. Wilson a hand-carved wooden figurine with oversized ears. (Presenting it with thanks and appreciation, she requested nothing symbolic in return, envisioning a figurine with a mouth in perpetual motion.)

Her fellow tourists, reverse images of Rupert, went on a rampage of spending, while beggars dogged their footsteps. After breaking two hundred-dollar bills to disburse, Hannah, unnerved by the poor children, slipped away and returned to the ship without touring the port.

In the evening Mr. Wilson came back with a hand-carved wooden figurine of astonishing dimensions on top. Did Hannah really appear *that* big?

He insisted on its accuracy. "Nobody's heart is bigger, Mrs. Trilling."

"Oh . . ." *Heart.*

Before long, the QE2 made a U-turn somewhere in the Caribbean and headed home. Presently, Hannah would be returned to New York City, not the ideal refuge for widowhood, which was as foreign a state as old age and equally forbidding. Both the widowed and the elderly had little idea of what lay in wait for them, and no experience whatsoever. A double whammy. How could Hannah give it the slip?

That night, after drifting off to sleep facing her sketch of the Wall, she dreamed of the time she had traveled to New York to hear Eleanor Roosevelt address a Hadassah convention. Remarkable woman with a heart encompassing all humanity. Look what she had accomplished with her life despite an alcoholic father, domineering mother-in-law, unfaithful husband, exasperating children. So plain-looking when young, she was called "Granny" by her own tart-tongued mother, Mrs. Roosevelt had grown prettier with the years, until her character shone through and made her a beauty. Hannah had pushed her way through the crowd to Mrs. Roosevelt but, once in her presence, was struck dumb. All that came out of a tongue-tied mouth was: "I just want to shake your hand." The First Lady and the farm girl had grasped hands. Reminiscent of the Emperor Franz Josef and Buba Bella.

In the morning Hannah could hardly wait for breakfast to end, so she could consult Mr. Wilson in private. Taking him aside, she began, "Have to talk to you."

"Fine. What about?"

"Mrs. Roosevelt."

"Mrs. Roosevelt?"

"Yes. If she had been just widowed. And was Jewish. You think maybe she'd proceed to Israel right now?"

"Mrs. Trilling," he replied, "if Eleanor Roosevelt came back today as a nice Jewish widow, I think there's a good chance she'd be Golda Meir."

10

*D*EBBIE considered Grandpa's funeral altogether weird—the co-star of his life had breezed off before the reviews were in. Not that Debbie faulted Grandma. Grandpa had played her for a sucker. Or worse: a martyr.

The cover story given out was that Grandma was incommunicado in a rest home, which was entirely in character. "Isn't that just like Hannah!" Three relatives expressed relief, one surprise, that she hadn't taken her life. It occurred to no one that, were the situation reversed, Grandpa would have canceled himself out over *her* passing. Evidence that the traits that made women so lovable—sensitivity, compassion, expressiveness, flexibility—were not inborn, biologically determined, but products of women's powerlessness. Well, if men wanted that better world of sweetness and light, let *them* sacrifice for it.

Take Cousin Leo, who hailed Grandma for having cracked up and gone all to pieces. When his nephew Roger died in the middle of a mambo contest, his wife Lena had him shipped off to the Miami morgue until the two weeks' vacation were up, *then* had him flown him back to New York for burial, claiming that's the way Roger would have wanted it.

"Today's wives!" Cousin Leo concluded disdainfully.

"Yesterdays' husbands!" countered Debbie, who had been sworn to secrecy about Grandpa's secret hoard and Grandma's dropping out.

Poor Dad kept fretting he would inherit Grandma, while Mother let him scheme to avoid it, just to make him feel all the more swinish when Grandma moved into a glamorous new Manhattan apartment. What did Dad have against her? The same thing he had against the world in general, and he didn't have a clue what that was either. How he treasured the chip on his shoulder. To feel good Dad craved praise—no, adulation. Brash, self-assured and successful in his chosen profession, at home he required constant reassurance, even while lambasting one and all. On the way from the funeral service to the cemetery—shades of Narcissus—Dad stopped off at his office. Debbie could hardly wait to move away from home.

The week of mourning was catered like an elaborate bar mitzvah, the only difference being everybody brought condolences, which lasted until the very minute callers took their seats. Then, endless cocktail party chatter about the stock market, vacation spots, restaurants, business, condos, maids: the usual. As if any mention of death would have detracted from the festivities. Grandma, on the other hand, always talked at such length about the departed during a condolence call; some called her a wet blanket. Never the mourners, however.

Now, at long last, she was returning home after having jumped ship in Miami to fly off to Israel. Imagine a woman her age skipping off alone *twice*, via sea, then air, when she wouldn't travel solo via subway. Proving life was a bouquet of options. How terrific! But scary. Suppose you picked the wrong one. Could you just return it, none the worse for thorn pricks?

"Outlive long enough, everything is possible," Grandma had written Uncle Josh, signing the postcard "Eleanor R."

Debbie received a post card, saying, "You want drama, you want poetry, you want beauty? It's all here in Israel. Wish you were, my darling Sarah Bernhardt."

The walls of Debbie's room were plastered with photos of Kitty-Kat on the covers of *Life*, *Look*, other publications. Was it true she had dated Frank Sinatra and Cary Grant and some guy running for presidency of the U.S. way back in the fifties?

Kitty-Kat tried to talk Debbie out of acting, unless she had a genuine commitment to a life of rejection. "In acting, unlike other professions, success is more a matter of luck than hard work. There are just as many talented actors still unknown."

At the end, Debbie put just one question to her. "What profession have your two sons decided on?"

"Acting."

One's limitations could be transcended through acting. Lovely refuge for someone shy and unsure of her unscripted self. Grandma said shyness could be overcome by concentrating on others. But how did one *do* that? It was as difficult as acting natural in a play. Or in life.

"Just *look* at this room!" Mother's wake-up call that morning, like every other one.

Debbie opened her eyes to see clothing flying around, some headed for the hamper, others into the closet. Why were mothers so anal retentive? "You realize," Debbie said with mock grandeur, "every Broadway star has a personal dresser."

"You, honey, will need the services of the entire union."

"*All* creative people are sloppy."

"Why, you must be a positive *genius*, then." A bath towel was whipped off the torchier, where it had been hung to dry two days before.

"They are never appreciated before middle age."

"Geniuses?"

"Teenagers."

Mother swept a pair of sweat socks out from under the bed. "It's the same with mothers. No appreciation till middle age. Their *children's* middle age. Why Mother's Day was invented. To honor mothers who fell in battle."

"Well, there's a reason. Mothers are always *after* children for something. Grandmothers, on the other hand, are *for* them. In everything."

{138}

"I see."

"What I mean is, well, if I were a play, Mother, you'd be criticizing my plot and language and direction, whereas Grandma would focus on my *concept*. Understand?"

"Not a word."

Mischievously, Debbie said, "*Grandma* would understand."

Two large potted plants had to be transported to Parkside Avenue, as well as some new flowered drapes, which were on loan from Bloomingdale's. (The day Grandma moved out, back would go the drapes. Much more hygienic, Mother rationalized, then those who return the laying-out clothes from a wake.) Debbie, having read that stroking pets lowered the blood pressure and heart attack rate of older people, had bought Grandma a pet for a coming-home present. A panda bear of acrylic, named Buba Bear. Would Grandma like it, not think her silly or childish? Debbie so wanted to please her.

A guardian angel, Grandma. She knew the difference between listening and talking, never jumped in with advice. Instead of trying to lead the conversation, she'd first listen, after repeating Debbie's sometimes overwrought remarks. This would get her back on track, spur a continuous flow that Mother would shut off with comments and premature recommendations. And Grandma was constantly pointing out virtues in Debbie discernible to nobody else, least of all to herself, while carefully overlooking obvious failings like compulsive overeating and tanning. Mother often said she couldn't tell Debbie apart from the leather couch in the den, but Grandma: "You're so nice and chocolaty now, my darling, your brown eyes look a lovely shade of beige." And, "When I was a girl on the farm, all the cowhands loved *zoftig* girls. Especially those cowhands who were themselves *zoftig*." When Cousin Leo started calling his sweet wife Stupid instead of Laraine, Grandma kept asking him in public, "And how smart do you suppose is a man who marries a stupid woman?" until he stopped.

Even the subject of sex, which was giving Debbie periodic outbreaks of postmenstrual syndrome, Grandma made less pesky. Everyone was doing it, Debbie's friends said, why was she alone holding back? Friends talked of little else, taking time out only to do it themselves. What was the matter with *her*?

"Baloney!" Mother exclaimed. "Everyone *isn't* doing it."

(That's how much *she* knew, hers being the presex generation.)

Grandma said, "Suppose everyone *is* doing it. Well, some of the most heavily-traveled roads lead nowhere. And is everyone Jewish? No? You mean to tell me there are billions of gentiles in the world and only twelve or so million Jews? Does *different* mean *worse?* Can it be equal; just as good? Sometimes, maybe, even a little bit better?"

But what was Debbie saving it for? Why make sex such a big deal anyway?

"If it's no bigger a deal than blowing a nose," Grandma said, "why *potchke* around? The only things worth doing are the big deals. If it's no big deal, it should be no deal at all at your age. Why not wait till it *signifies?*"

At noon Debbie drove with her mother to Brooklyn to get Grandma's apartment in shape. Her mailbox was stuffed with cards, letters and certificates in Grandpa's memory from Hadassah, Trees for Israel, UNICEF, as well as dinner invitations. Hadn't that made Mother jealous as a youngster, Grandma's devotion to so many others?

"No, because I grew up thinking *all* mothers behaved like her. The jealous one, Debbie, is your father. He resents my modeling myself after Mom—not that I succeed very often. Anything bestowed on outsiders are goods stolen from him. And everyone but himself he considers an outsider. His idea of family is a group of people gathered together under one roof to divine his needs and take dictation."

Did *all* men turn into frogs after the wedding?

"No, of course not, Debbie. Lots of men are frogs to *begin* with. But there are good and bad in *every* species. And you are living proof, honey, that we can at least *mate* with them." She patted Debbie's cheek. "With results that make it all worthwhile. Much of the time."

After filling up the refrigerator, they cleaned the apartment, did the laundry. Debbie removed the slashed plastic covers from the couch and turned over the cushions. Mother unpacked the drapes and Debbie took down the antiques, which she carried to the incinerator room, and hung the new ones. By then it was time to head for the airport.

"We have to be very considerate of Grandma's feelings. Psychologists say it takes between one and two years to recoup after the death of a spouse."

"Regardless of merit?" asked Debbie. "Affirmative action for the dead?"

"People die. Long-term meaningful relationships never do. For better or worse."

It was one huge disco, Kennedy's International Arrivals Building. All that was missing were strobe lights and musical amps, but definitely not the weirdos. Saffron robed cultists with their flowers and snotty foreheads. Ban-the-Bomb-ers and Down-with-Jane-Fonda-ers and Ban-the-Ban-the-Bomb-ers.

Mother had Debbie go to the bookstore to ask for Uncle Josh's novel. It had just arrived, so Debbie told the clerk, "No, I don't want to buy. My uncle wrote the book."

"Congratulations," he said, "for wasting my time."

Back outside, she found the horde had swallowed up Mother. Terrific! Debbie had no money with her. Not even coins for a phone.

"What's wrong? You look worried. "A tall young man in a three-piece suit tapped Debbie on the shoulder. A neat fellow with lanky blond hair, cat's eyes, a square jaw with shoulders to match, and the warmest smile. "Can I help you?"

In her entire life Debbie had never been picked up. Dates were either classmates, a friend's brother or somebody's terminally obnoxious buddy. And here was this great looker culling her out of the crowd to talk about the din and confusion at the airport, the frantic pace of modern life, the loneliness of crowds. He sounded like a term paper, but an A-plus one, and ever so simpático. "Don't you feel the world is much too much with us?"

"Yeah, exactly," she said, though her thoughts ran more to boys then to worlds.

The fellow—Tom was his name—even stroked Buba Bear with long, sensitive fingers, while locking eyes with her. Debbie felt caressed by his thick brown lashes, invaded by his piercing pupils.

"Too much of that alienation around," she concurred. "Makes a person feel, well, alienated. A lot."

As a lock of blond hair fell over his forehead, she couldn't restrain herself from reaching out to brush it upward. "Excuse me!" She felt herself blushing. "I didn't mean to."

Tom's smile widened. "Of course, Debbie. Friends do that for each other, Debbie. Matter of fact . . ." There was this weekend retreat in Connecticut he wanted her to attend. "Not with me alone, of course. Lots of people will be there. Friends, Debbie. *You*, Debbie, can be one of us."

She felt honored.

Opening his attaché case, Tom took out a few pamphlets, which he handed over. "For you, Debbie." One was entitled, *When a Person Needs a Friend*.

So hypnotic, Tom's repetition of her name, which she'd never liked till then. And so intimate, like those exchanges of first names on TV talk and news shows (you just knew everyone went out for drinks afterwards and a little sex). Involuntarily, she rubbed her fingers together. Something had registered as strange. What? Tom's hair. It felt like Buba Bear's.

"Tom? Are you wearing a *wig?*"

His smile wavered. "No, Debbie. It's a hairpiece."

"But you're—what? Twenty-two?"

"Twenty-five, Debbie."

"Why—"

"Debbie, let's not get sidetracked—"

"Oh! You have *cancer?*"

"What? My head's shaved, Debbie, that's all. All my friends shave their heads—Well, not girls. Anyway, people being so bigoted, Debbie, they wouldn't talk to baldies. So . . ."

Debbie looked at the other pamphlets: *God, the Force of The Source* and *God Loves You, You Sinner You*. So! This hunk was pimping for God. And not even for Debbie's. "I'm Jewish," she declared.

"Hey, Debbie, we dig that. Jews are just as lost these days as straight people. Even more so. You'll meet lots of them in Connecticut. Some of our best recruits. Come, see for yourself."

"*Look*, Tom." Fishing out the Star of David on the gold necklace under her sweater, she held it up as if it were a cross and he a vampire. But not trusting completely in the power of the star to vanquish her attraction, she turned and fled. Damn! The first proposition she'd decided to embrace, and it had to come from someone wanting only her mind. And that to brainwash.

Uncle Josh, carrying a beautiful bouquet of flowers, stopped her. Nice guy, Uncle Josh, always asking her opinion about movies, books, people, everything, which annoyed her, because she just didn't have any. "What we're trying for here," Uncle Josh would say, "is what's been called conversation. Helps pass the time, connects people. Can stimulate, even teach." But what did Debbie have to teach anyone? And learning was reserved for school.

Now, she reported *Captain O Captain*'s arrival at the airport bookstore. To deter his asking her opinion, Debbie got in the first question. "How does it feel to be published?"

"Like any proud parent, I'll be boasting about the new edition. On all the brainless talk shows I've always denounced."

"Why denounce them?"

"They never had me on before."

Together, they went looking for Mother and found her emerging from the ladies room. Each was anxious about Grandma's homecoming after five weeks away, not to mention what had propelled her departure. Mother was inviting Grandma to spend the weekend in Westchester. Josh wanted her surrendered on Monday for a week's stay at his place.

The arrivals board flashed the landing of Grandma's plane. In an hour or so, the time it took to retrieve her baggage and clear customs, she'd be joining them. But no, before long there she was, materializing before their eyes with her shopping bag, wearing a new royal blue suit and jungle green silk blouse with alligator pumps and matching handbag. How come she was the first person off?

"I've discovered the wonderful world of tipping. Shmear, and you slide right through." Grandma's repackaging required a lengthier explanation. Always sparkling-eyed and pretty, if chubby, she was svelte now and, in her chic new outfit and stylishly short hairstyle, a total knockout.

Debbie ran up for a hug. "Grandma, you're *dynamite!*"

"So are you, my darling."

Uncle Josh exclaimed, "Mom, you are a regular Sleeping Beauty up and about."

She looked rueful. "So why did it have to take a funeral to wake me up?"

Mother took Grandma's face in her hands and kissed her several times. "It's true, Mom. You're gorgeous. Look like a million dollars."

Everyone froze for a moment, as people do whenever rope is mentioned to the family of someone who's been hanged.

"You're only a quarter-right," Mom said. "Too bad."

Mother tried to clear the air. "That awful day, Mom. The way we reacted—at *first*. It was on account of . . . *circumstances*."

"I see. Circumstances."

"We did offer you money time and again, me and Sandra. But you always refused."

"True, true. Nobody has more pride than the poor. Because that's all they have."

"Years ago parents didn't live so long," Mother began.

"Well, excuse me for surviving, my dears."

Mother's face turned red. "What I *mean* is, there are no guidelines. Please, Mom. Try to understand. I'm caught in this big squeeze between caring for my kids and husband and caring for you, while working full-time, with Charlie off on the side kvetching I'm not paying enough attention to his highness. If I paid any more attention, really concentrated on that nudnik, I think I'd junk him."

Grandma sighed. "You'll have to forgive me, children, I *am* overly sensitive. Widowhood does that. Skins a person alive. Exposes nerve endings you never knew you had."

"How can we make it up to you, Mom? Tell us, just tell us."

Grandma's usual smile lit up that pretty face once more. "Actually, Josh, there *is* a way. Yes, there is."

"We'll do it, Mom. Gladly. What is it?"

"Well . . ."

"Yes? yes? yes?"

Grandma brushed away dust that wasn't on the lapel of her jacket and fiddled with the collar of her blouse. "Let's go out for dinner. My treat."

What about her luggage? They had to wait for the porter to bring it over. No, someone was delivering it to Parkside Avenue; Grandma had given him the key to her apartment. Was that wise? Of course, nothing there was worth stealing. Everything precious she now carried in her heart and the gray metal box.

On their way outside, Debbie couldn't help noticing the admiring glances cast Grandma's way. People were always complimenting her appearance; Grandma rarely thanked them, so busy saying, "So are you" to the women, and "You're so nice looking" to the men. Clearly, Grandma had sexagenarian appeal.

In the car Uncle Josh announced their destination, Tavern on the Green in Central Park. It had been recommended by a friend Grandma made on the QE2, a real maven. Who hadn't reacted with shock and dismay to her floating *shiva*.

No need to explain her absence from the funeral. "As far as anyone knows, Mom, you've been recuperating in a rest home."

"I bet that astonished exactly nobody."

"Right," said Debbie. "Everyone called you the perfect wife."

"Of course I was. The years Rupert gave me shit, and I took it. The perfect marriage"

"Oh, Mom," said Mother. "Bitterness doesn't become you. Not you."

Grandma burst out: "A saint forgives, a fool forgets. Me, I'm neither. All my life I lived strictly according to the Golden Rule. Despite what people thought. 'Good old Hannah, very sweet but ever so simple-minded.' Never bothered me until now. *Now!* People were right all along. I was the perfect *patsy*. Yes, I am bitter." She turned to look out the car window. "I don't know, children. Maybe I should have stayed away, a dozen more cruises. The Flying Dutchwoman."

"Never see you again, ever?" Debbie flung herself into Grandma's arms. "Bite your tongue!"

Nothing more was said till the car double-parked at Broadway and Sixty-fourth Street. There, in a block-long high-rise, Uncle Josh had placed a deposit on an apartment for Grandma.

But she was glancing in the opposite direction. "Lincoln Center! I have to take a look." She jumped out of the car. When Debbie and Uncle Josh caught up with her, she said, "If a person only lives long enough . . ." An ardent fan of televised opera, concerts and ballet, she'd never attended any, because Grandpa would neither take her nor let her go. Now she wanted to see the Met, and its Chagall murals in particular. A must-see, said a friend in Israel who had accompanied her to the Hadassah Hospital synagogue, which contained Chagall's glorious twelve stained-glass windows. Hanging in the Knesset were tapestries by Chagall, and in the Israel Museum still more masterpieces.

"Such artistry! Such *feeling!* Scenes and people so like my Monaster. Imagine someone from a tiny village in Russia creating beauty to thrill the entire world."

Curiously, the news about her new apartment, just across the way from Lincoln Center, ready in six weeks, failed to excite her. The view from the well-appointed one-bedroom apartment was spectacular, and all the lovely furnishings for sale. Grandma's reaction?

"What do you children think of Lawrence?"

"Lawrence who? Welk?"

"Lawrence, Long Island."

Where had she heard about that fancy town on Long Island's south shore? On the QE2, from a friend. Did the friend mention Lawrence had no apartments, just private homes? Yes, so a friend in Israel had said. (Grandma sure did make a lot of friends in just five weeks.)

"Children, how about a walk?"

"What about dinner?"

"Not hungry yet. El Al stuffs its passengers with so much food, one passenger who napped during lunch swore the stewardess had fed him intravenously." A report followed on the QE2's Scotch salmon, Golden Door, sports facilities, theater-in-the-round, arts and crafts. In all her life Grandma had never chattered that much. Repeated glances at her wristwatch suggested, however, a filibuster. After stopping to make a call from a street phone, she announced her luggage had just reached Parkside Avenue.

"Grandma's changed," Debbie whispered.

Mother nodded. "I'm going to check her fingerprints."

Uncle Josh said, "She's only become what she always was. The way she used to be those years I was living at home. Before Dad got really sick."

Tavern on the Green, originally a sheepfold, had Grandma exclaiming over its woodwork, brass candle sconces, copper animal heads, stained-glass lamps and stained-glass window. Mother asked for a table in the Crystal Room, a glass pavilion which looked out on a landscaped terrace garden.

Grandma said, "Such a pity! Rupert could have enjoyed all this too."

After the waiter took their orders, they asked about her passport, and sure enough, "My friend from the QE2 made all the arrangements."

Uncle Josh said, "Certainly was solicitous."

"Oh, yes. And being in banking, he was able to help out in lots of other ways too."

"He?" said Mother.

"Withdrew money for me from a bankbook I found. Not much there, really. Less than $14,000."

"You liked this friend, Mom?"

"Very much, Sandra."

"You didn't show him your portfolio, did you?"

"*Josh!* I did no such thing!"

"Mom, Josh means the stocks and bonds."

"Oh, them. Well, I had to talk to *somebody*."

Grandma's pretty blue suit and blouse and matching alligators. Debbie asked where she got them.

"The QE2 has lots of boutiques, which in Brooklyn we call shops. Sheldon helped me pick these out. Doesn't he have beautiful taste? The rest of my new wardrobe I got in Israel. Jewelry, too." She opened her pocketbook and took out three boxes, which she handed over. "Hope you like these."

"Mom? Is that a pack of *cigarettes* I saw inside?"

"Israeli memento. Every evening after dinner, Sheldon would light—"

"He's Israeli?"

"Who's Israeli?"

"But, Grandma, you've never smoked."

She smiled. "After dinner at the King David Hotel, Sheldon would light two cigarettes at a time, then hand me one. I'd just hold mine, of course—"

"I thought this Sheldon was on the *cruise*."

"Mom, that cigarette routine is from a Bette Davis movie that's older than me. I mean, than I."

"And how original are *you*, Josh? If you tried something new with each romance, you'd be locked up by now."

"Romance?" said Debbie.

"Mom! You're not *involved* with this man, are you?"

"What a thing to say! *Involved?* I should say not! Just because we flew to Israel together, Sheldon and me, doesn't mean *involved*."

"Together? You and this man? *Alone?*"

"What alone? The plane had 400 *other* passengers. And you know how many guests the King David Hotel holds?"

"Nevertheless—"

"Anyway, we're engaged."

The breadstick in Mother's hand crumbled. "You're *what?*"

With a nervous laugh, "And don't tell me you're stupefied, children, because what do you think I am myself?"

"*Engaged?* As in, to be *married?* Josh, did she say—"

"Mom! You just told us you are *not* involved."

"Sheldon and I are not putting out. Not one bit. That *is* what you meant, isn't it?"

"No! Yes! Oh, who knows *what* I meant!"

"Well, children? Did I hear someone here say, mazel tov?"

Debbie jumped to her feet. "Mazel tov mazel tov mazel tov! *Everything* tov, Grandma!" But flabbergasted, the others just sat there.

"Cat got your tongues? Sandra? Josh?"

"Mom," Mother said finally, "Dad gone only five weeks, and *already*—?"

"Well, don't you think *I* was surprised? But the other widows I've been meeting *explained* it all to me. Remarrying is the highest tribute a widow can pay the deceased."

"*Mom!*"

"People will *talk*."

"My dear children, people can *lump* it."

"Hurray for Grandma!"

"Debbie, be quiet."

"Is that what you want now, Mom? To play nursemaid to another sick old man?"

"Sheldon is fit as a fiddle and ready for—well, never mind."

"But what do you know about—this stranger?"

"Your father *wasn't* a stranger? But Sheldon. You should see how he *caters* to me."

"Mom, caterers don't cater for nothing."

"What are you saying, Sandra? That Sheldon is after my money? Well, *this* time I know where it's at. In *my* name."

"And if you change your name to Sheldon's? What, then?"

"Okay, children, ask to see *his* bankbook. He's waiting for us now at my apartment. I wanted this time alone with you to break the news, soften the blow."

"It's great news, Grandma! Terrific blow! The blowiest! Can I be your maid of honor?"

Grandma laughed with delight and squeezed Debbie's hand, then turned to Mother and Uncle Josh, who were having a tough time reconciling themselves to becoming step-children. "Okay, shoot. Wouldn't want the two of you to explode."

Harumphing, Uncle Josh addressed Grandma as if she were a jury. (But who was on trial here?) "Mom, every week of the year somebody wins the lottery. However, the chances of doing so are seven million to one. Higher, I suspect, for a brand new heiress who hasn't dated in almost half a century."

"We only want to protect you, Mom. As you used to protect us."

"*Children* I protected. Me, I am a grown woman."

"We're not getting anywhere, are we!" Mother had lost her cool. "Okay, Mom, okay. Suppose we take a different tack. Nowadays, there is an alternative to marriage."

"Go steady? At *my* age?"

"What I mean is, well, nowadays lots of couples simply . . . you know."

"I know what?"

"Live . . ."

"Live?"

". . . together."

"Together live? *Oh!* Sandra!"

"Mother!"

"Mom *shack up?*"

"I suppose *you've* never shacked up, brother dear?"

"Never," Uncle Josh declared, "with a *grandmother*."

"Sandra, how could you!"

"*This* time, Mom, be smart. Play it safe."

Grandma bit her lower lip. "Why," she said softly, "are both of you so determined to convince me—"

"That this Sheldon is a gold digger?"

"—that I am not the least bit desirable?"

Tears sprang to Mother's eyes. "Oh, Mom!"

"You are a *treasure*, Mom. But a guileless rich widow landing a sincere gentleman interested in herself alone her first time up at bat. That happens only in the movies Hollywood no longer makes."

"Josh? I'm not entitled to a happy ending?"

He winced. "Nobody more than you, Mom. We just don't want to see you get hurt again. You must admit this romance has been so sudden."

"At this stage of life, what have I got left *but* sudden?"

"Well, how long did you go with Dad?"

"*Two years?!* Even then, I never really knew the man till I saw his effects."

"Hold it, everybody! Just thought of something!" In his excitement Uncle Josh stabbed the air with his fork. "Children. Does this Sheldon have children?"

"A married daughter. Why?"

"Does she approve?"

"There are children in their world, you know, who want their parents to be happy."

"Mom, if Sheldon has plenty of assets of his own, his daughter will want them protected too. She'll insist on the prenuptial agreement."

"The prenuptial agreement? Sounds like a spy thriller."

"It's a legal arrangement drawn up before weddings, Mom. Whereby the couple for'swears all claims on each other's assets."

Mother congratulated Uncle Josh: "Great idea! *Perfect*."

Grandma, however, was appalled. "Downright rude to ask that. *Insulting*."

"Mom, it's done all the time. Jackie Kennedy did it to Aristotle Onassis."

"She renounced all rights to his billions?"

"Well, Jackie demanded them. Still, the principle does hold."

Grandma scratched her head. "If Sheldon's daughter welcomes me with open arms—"

"Clearly, Sheldon is a fortune hunter."

"And if she fights his remarriage tooth and claw, like you?"

"She's a devoted daughter. No question."

"It means Sheldon is a man of means himself—"

Grandma interrupted. "I do see. So you need have no worry Sheldon will steal all my money—"

"Exactly."

"—from the two of you."

"*Mom!*"

Grandma, relenting, opened her mouth wide. "Look, I'm biting my tongue. *Bad* tongue." She slapped it, lightly.

Uncle Josh called over the waiter, seized his menu and pen, and scrawled something on the back of the menu. Signing it, he had Mother sign too, and the waiter and Debbie witness the statement, which read:

> WE THE UNDERSIGNED HEREBY RELINQUISH FOREVER
> ALL RIGHTS AND CLAIMS TO THE PRESENT MONIES AND
> FUTURE ESTATE OF OUR BELOVED MOTHER, HANNAH BRODY
> TRILLING. ALL WE WANT, NOW AND FOREVER, IS HER
> SAFETY AND HAPPINESS. AMEN.

"How exciting," said the waiter. "This is a first for me, signing a will."

Debbie picked up a goblet of water and offered a toast. "*L'chayim*, you all. To life! And to love ever after!"

11

*T*HE children were really upset. Hannah could tell. Asked about his book, Josh replied, "Book?" And claustrophobic Sandra again drove into the Brooklyn-Battery Tunnel. So disconcerted this time, she forgot to break out in a sweat.

Don't worry, children, I still have most of my marbles, Hannah wanted to assure them. Sheldon is a whole lot nicer than your cantankerous Charlie, Sandra.

"Mom? Have you thought this through?' Josh asked. "Sheldon may be your way of getting back at Dad."

Hannah heaved a sigh. "When your best friend Michael wouldn't let you play with any of his toys. What did I suggest you do to to get even with him?"

"I remember. You said the next time Michael came over, I should give him *all* my toys to play with—*that* would fix him. Still, Mom. You wouldn't be the first person driven by unconscious motives."

"And you wouldn't be the first novelist, Josh, to turn a mother into fiction."

Getting even, indeed. Who *wouldn't* appreciate Sheldon's kindness? Renting a car in Fort Lauderdale to drive Hannah to Miami to pick up her passport, then dropping her off at the airport, saying goodbye. But after her emergence from the cockpit, where she'd gone to wish the crew all the good luck (this being her very first flight), there he was in the seat next to hers, grinning like a little boy who had pulled a fast one on teacher. Well, sharing Israel could only heighten the pleasure. And perhaps there she'd yet find someone nice for Sheldon.

Sharing, however, didn't mean agreeing. He wasn't keen on starting off sightseeing at Yad Vashem, the Holocaust Memorial and Museum, a stark building of massive, uncut boulders, with heavy iron doors that suggested barbed wire. Inside, names of a dozen Nazi death factories were inscribed in the bare, cavernous antechamber's mosaic floor in front of the Eternal Light, flickering over the ashes of human remains from one of the Nazi crematoriums. And to think of their descendants who would never be! One look at photographs of wagons full of murdered children, being pulled by children soon to be murdered themselves, put Hannah to flight.

Imagine men getting up every morning, kissing their wives and children, going off to work each day to slaughter thousands of men, women and children. Taking time out for lunch with friends before devoting the afternoon to the butchery of additional men, women and children. Then returning to the bosom of their families each evening. And in between, attending Christian chapels built on the death camp grounds. What did those husbands, fathers, sons pray for? That they meet their daily quotas? And why in God's name had none of these killers been excommunicated—*not even Hitler!*—as they surely would have been for remarriage after divorce?

Retreating outside to the Hill of Remembrance, Hannah found herself on the Avenue of the Righteous Gentiles, lined with trees planted in honor of individuals who risked their lives to rescue Jews during the Holocaust. No, she reminded herself, not *all* people were sadistic fiends. There *was* a saving remnant.

When Sheldon finally exited, face gray and sweaty, Hannah insisted on going straight to the Hadassah Hospital.

He rolled his eyes. "Gee, that sounds like fun."

"If I could have a hand in founding such a hospital, I wouldn't mind a bit being dumped myself."

"Ah, but the best medicine of all, it's said, is love."

"Really, Mr. Wilson? How many broken bones has love set?"

That night they didn't go anywhere—too emotionally drained. From the terrace of the King David Hotel they watched the sun, in a hurry to set as if late for a previous appointment, change the walls of the Old City in swift succession from a golden yellow to bronze to pink to scarlet to purple to mauve to a chilly black. In the morning Jerusalem, all its buildings a dusty rose colored stone that glowed in the sunlight, enveloped them once more in warmth, while a tour saturated them with the history of a city conquered by Egypt, Babylonia, Persia, Greece; by Romans, barbarians, Arabs, Crusaders, Turks. Yet inhabited continuously for well over three thousand years by Jews, each one a link in an unbroken chain dating to the Covenant struck with God at Mount Sinai.

After ten days of touring the country, back it was to the City of Gold. In the Old City, thronged with pilgrims come with hopes and tears, thanks and pleas, Hannah inserted *kvitlach* in a niche between blocks of the Wall. One petition of hers asked God to forgive Rupert—look what a lovely time he was showing her posthumously. Another asked Rupert's forgiveness for her having missed the funeral.

Sheldon deposited just one note in the Wall. Asked his request, he told of the wise man whose king commanded him to guess whether a bird in the monarch's hand was alive or dead. If I say yes, replied the wise man, the royal hand would crush the bird to death; if no, the king would let the bird live. The decision, then, was entirely in the king's hands. "So it is with me," Sheldon concluded. "My note is in the Wall, my life is in your hands. Say yes, Mrs. Trilling."

"Yes to what?"

"Marry me."

"Me? *Marry* you? *Good heavens!*" Hannah hadn't been so taken by surprise since her wedding night.

"You do want to marry me off. So why not let *me* pick the bride?"

It took a week to persuade her. Even then, she would go no further than engagement. Love's halfway house. There were Rupert's good name and her own to consider, as well as her children. Throughout,

Mr. Wilson didn't know what to do for her next; Hannah hadn't been pampered so much since the days before she'd been weaned. So after a while she came around to thinking, Well, why not? Rupert had taken plenty of flyers in the market. Wasn't she entitled to just one?

"Mom? . . . *Mom!*"

Josh's cry roused Hannah from her reverie.

"Know what all the experts say, Mom? A new widow should do nothing drastic for at least one full year. She's much too vulnerable."

"Josh, do *you* know what President Kennedy said after the Bay of Pigs about so-called experts?" Hannah sought to prepare her family, first impressions being so important. "Now, please don't jump to the wrong conclusions. You really cannot tell a book by its cover. Don't be put off by appearance."

"Sure, Mom, of course. Sheldon is stacked with personality, right?" Josh smiled.

"You never did tell us why you like Sheldon. Are you that miserable?"

"Miserable? Not any more." Getting out of the car, Hannah ran her fingers through her hair, bit her lips and pinched her cheeks.

"Don't bother," Debbie whispered. "You look gurrreat."

How dilapidated the old neighborhood and run-down Hannah's building. Seen with a fresh eye after five weeks away, the squalor and shabbiness made her flinch. Thank heaven she'd be moving away.

So bizarre the children's reaction to Sheldon. When he opened the apartment door, Sandra, looking right past him, asked about the old drapes Hannah had told Sheldon to throw out. Even after Debbie fetched the drapes from the incinerator room, she didn't calm down, claiming those were the *wrong* drapes and asking what happened to the ones from Bloomingdale's. And from Josh, "How old are you?"

Sheldon smiled. "I'll show you my driver's license if you show me yours."

Hannah pointed out the age difference between her and Sheldon was half of that between Fredric March and Norma Shearer when they ran off to get married in *The Barretts of Wimpole Street*.

"So," Josh began. "About your intentions."

Sheldon chuckled. "You sound like me grilling my daughter's boy friends."

"Do any good, the grilling?"

"Nah. When a woman makes up her mind—well, you know how women are. Then again, maybe you don't know. Never been married, Josh, have you?"

Hannah sprang to his defense. "Any day now."

Smarting, Josh fished the pack of Israeli cigarettes out of Hannah's pocketbook. "And you, I'm sure, know Bette Davis intimately."

"Romantic as hell, that shtick. *You* should try it, Josh. Now, your *mother* would do something that drove *me* absolutely wild."

"I don't want to hear it!"

"*I* do," said Hannah, curious. "What was it?"

"Tipping people with shares of stock. Fun-ny."

"Mom, you didn't!"

"You found that *romantic*, Mr. Wilson?"

"Sheldon, call me Sheldon. Sandra, you think I'm the only one in the world turned on by money?"

"Your own or *other* people's?"

"*Money* doesn't distinguish, why should I? And like most things in life, money is enjoyed much more in tandem. Spending it by yourself, I've found, is like making love by yourself."

"You do have a way with sophistry."

Hannah apologized. "They're just overprotective, my children. I'm sure your daughter is, too. Overprotective."

"Marilyn? Nah. The sink-or-swim type. You know, If you can't take the heat, get the hell out of my sight."

"She *must* be, Sheldon. Concerned, I mean. Didn't you tell me she sees you every single day?"

"Can't help it, sweetheart. We live right next door to each other. Hey, look. I love your mother"—he turned to the children—"and I want to marry her, that's the story."

Hannah felt her cheeks grow warm. "A fairy tale, really, isn't it?"

"Exactly," the children said in unison.

"Guys, I know how hard it is for children to think of a parent as a sex object *also*."

Hannah *wished* Sheldon hadn't said that. What would the children think?

"I suppose," Sandra said, "you fell in love with Mom at first sight."

"Nah. No such thing. "I *decided* to love your mother. Doesn't just

{156}

happen, love. It has to be a *leap*. Planned. Almost like the invasion of Normandy."

"The leap of love," Josh repeated, impressed despite himself.

Hannah intervened. "When did you do it, Sheldon? Decide to leap." Yet when he turned to look into her eyes and started to speak, she cut him off, too embarrassed. "No, not me. Tell *them*. I have to unpack."

Having learned to take everything in stride but praise, she hurried from the living room into the bedroom and shut the door. Her thoughts needed regrouping after the sea change. What had seemed not unnatural in the ethereal golden glow of Jerusalem was not receiving universal raves at home in New York's grit, real life. Ah, but she who hesitates is lost. On the other hand, marry in haste, repent at leisure.

Hoping to be convinced all over again of the correctness of her impetuous decision, she opened the door, to hear.

". . . the Captain's Welcome Aboard. I *have* to tell you about that night. I was in the QE2's Grand Lounge when people started pointing toward the stairway, murmuring. I looked up and there was this regal, shapely stranger in a clinging black gown with a white ruffle, a rose peeping out from between—"

"My *nightgown?*" exclaimed Sandra. "Well, it is a long dress, but I bought it to *sleep* in. Cost exactly twelve dollars. Reduced, of course, from—"

"Never saw an entrance like that. Well, maybe Cinderella at another ball, which I wasn't invited to. Everyone was talking about her. People at our table, adjacent ones too, fell over themselves telling her how pretty she was."

Hannah shut the door. Still, it was important to hear whether the children were won over. Again she opened the door.

". . . The warm relationship with this Irish stewardess who never knew from Jews before. At my bank I've learned to judge people not by how they act to the president and other officers, but to the guards, who are treated like wallpaper.

"Then I discovered the enormous emotional strain your mother was under. Most people take out their troubles on everyone around them. Not her. And she had cause. *Boy*, did she ever! Tell me, which one of you takes after your father? Both? No matter. Anyway, soon I found myself inclined to reach out to your mother. That's what love is, you know. A reaching out."

Sandra broke in, accusingly. "So you spirited her off to Israel."

"No, just encouraged her. She was the leader, I followed. But once we reached Jerusalem—Your mother seemed intent on *avoiding* the sights. Our first morning there, instead of touring, she insisted on going to an army hospital. The second day, it was an orphanage. And the third, to tend the sick family of her chambermaid. Her *chambermaid!*

" 'Donate some stock to those wounded in the Yom Kippur War, to the orphanages,' I told her. 'To your chambermaid too, if you want. And let's tour Israel, which is what tourists come to Israel to *do.*' But your mother said, 'It's not enough.' So I told her to donate some bonds as well. Still too little for Hannah. 'No *amount* is enough,' she said. 'I have to spend *time* with these people.'

"Shall I be honest? I felt like shoving your mother into the King David's pool and drowning her. Well, don't look so shocked. Didn't do it, did I? Instead, at that very moment, when she exasperated me most, I chose instead to love the woman. Nor was I the only one impressed. At the hotel Hannah made friends with the widow of the mayor of Tel Aviv who followed her around like a puppy, and also with . . ."

Lovely speech. So why did it give Hannah pause? That word, drowning. Rupert was the partner she had chosen for making babies, but Sheldon would be a choice even more intimate. In his bed she would die. If a marriage didn't pan out, one could walk away. But from a deathbed?

Back Hannah hurried to the living room.

". . . any further questions, guys? Or does the prosecution rest?"

"Just one.

"Be my guest, Sandra."

"What does your daughter think of this?"

Quickly, Hannah said, "She'll be mad as hell, I'm sure."

"Sweetheart, what a thing to say!"

"Well, does your daughter approve?"

"How could she? Doesn't know about it yet."

"Suppose you tell her, then."

Josh pointed to the phone. "Call her."

"On the *phone?*" Hannah asked apprehensively.

Sandra walked to the phone, picked it up and held it out.

Hannah cried, "No, Sheldon! Don't do it."

"Sweetheart, *my* daughter is a honey." Confidently, he took the phone and dialed. "Hi, Marilyn . . . Yes, it's your wandering Dad. No, back *to* the wars . . . Good, wonderful . . . Yes, sure do have something to tell you. Something terrific . . . Uh-huh, about that woman I wrote you about . . . Bingo! You guessed right the first time. Hannah and I are—" A shriek erupted from the phone, so loud Sheldon jerked the earpiece away.

"See?" said Hannah. "She's hysterical."

With a big smile Sheldon held out the phone, which resounded with a series of whoops. Followed by "You did it, Daddy, you really pulled it off!"

"Have to cut this short now, Marilyn. I'm with my sweet Hannah and her kids . . . Well, nothing like their mother, but I'm not marrying *them.*" Hanging up, he addressed Hannah with a jubilant smile.

Things didn't seem to be working out. If the only one to rhapsodize over their engagement had never met her, perhaps something was unkosher here. Out of the frying pan, into the fire?

"Didn't anyone hear me?" Sheldon said, puzzled. "Why the long faces? Marilyn is making us this big party—"

"We heard, we heard," Sandra said. "So did Mom."

All of a sudden, Hannah felt completely exhausted. "I'd like to lie down," she announced.

Smart enough not to press matters now that their point had been made, if not confirmed, the children left in short order. Why put all her trust in a man she'd known a mere five weeks?

Sheldon drew her down beside him on the couch. "Debbie is lovely. Takes after you. But those kids of yours, sweetheart. They'd make one terrific hanging judge."

She pulled back. "Marilyn didn't even ask to meet me before giving her consent."

"Who needs her consent? I used to *diaper* Marilyn."

{159}

"Oh, why couldn't she have put up a fight! For all she knows, I could be a-a-a female Bluebeard."

"Sweetheart, Marilyn trusts my judgement. So do I. The question is, do you trust yours?"

"Me? Sheldon, I don't even know if I *have* any judgment."

"What's happened, sweetheart? Just yesterday—"

Yesterday had been wonderful. All the days with Sheldon, wonderful. "The trip to Israel. You encouraged me to go. Yes, you did."

"I wanted you all to myself, sweetheart. Is that a crime? Any regrets?"

"Oh, no! As long as I live I'll never forget Jerusalem."

"Then let's set the date."

"The date? You mean, for a *wedding?*"

"No, sweetheart. For the next moon shot." He wrapped her in his arms. "You've kept me on such a long leash, and I love short ones."

"Oh!" Hannah put up a struggle, a weak one. "Sheldon dear, speaking of . . . premarital . . . premarital . . . premarital . . ." She could not get the next word to roll off her tongue into Sheldon's ear which was touching her lips, while he kissed her neck.

"Well, I'm all in favor so long as it doesn't hold up the wedding ceremony . . . Hey, sweetheart! Why so solemn? That was a *joke.*"

"Agreement, Sheldon. I was thinking more in terms of that. An agreement."

"You mean, no more than twice a night, sweetheart? I don't know if I can agree to *that*. You know how men are. Animals."

"I mean," she whispered hoarsely, "did you know Jackie Kennedy and Aristotle Onassis did it?"

"I always suspected. People don't get married in order *not* to do it."

"No, no, no—"

"Well, it isn't the *only* reason. So they tell me." He drew back and took her face between his hands. "Sweetheart, what are we talking about here, anyway? Do you have any inkling?"

Hannah blurted it out like one long word. "Don'tyouthink-allyourassetsshouldgoeventuallytoyourdaughterMarilyn?"

"What's that?"

Slower, this time: "I'm more than willing to sign away any claim of mine to anything of yours, Sheldon."

He stiffened. "That's generous of you, sweetheart. But who on earth asked you? Couldn't have been your children."

"My children?"

"Naturally, the dears want me to sign away all claims of *mine* beforehand. Right?"

"Well, it's . . . in tandem."

Sheldon jumped to his feet. "So they've convinced you I'm a hustler!"

"No, Sheldon, no!"

"Here, I'm committing my life to you, coupling my future to yours, and you think it all just a *scam.*"

"Sheldon, I never—I *swear*—"

"Well, what do you think those kids of yours are after? Your blessings?"

"Sheldon, I know them *longer*. And they signed my menu—"

"Rupert, who never took you as far as Lincoln Center, you knew longer *yet*."

"Yes, but *he* can't do me any harm now."

"And I can—right? Oh, boy! I never, never dreamed the Widow Flower could *sting* so. A sting like a red-hot poker."

"The Little Flower?" (Mayor La Guardia?)

"The *Widow* Flower. What I call all those women who blossom after planting a husband six feet under." He started for the door. "Goodbye, Hannah."

She hurried after him. "Wait, Sheldon! Don't go. Please stay. There's good reason for what you call my blossoming—"

He paused long enough to say, "Sure there is. Nothing makes better fertilizer than a dead husband." And out the front door.

Hannah stood rooted to the spot. Never having fought before with husband or sweetheart, she had no idea how to go about it. And by the time she decided to make up with Sheldon, the elevator had taken him down. Down three flights of stairs she ran to say that a quarrel was nothing but the smoke of love.

The elevator was empty, however, and the night outside concealing. *Gone!*

*   *   *

{ 161 }

Hannah hadn't had much luck with men. Not that she'd had so many, and the two that should have been retained she'd given the boot. In the few weeks since Sheldon's exodus, life began to be too much for her. Death and revelation, engagement and disengagement. Butterfly for a month, she felt herself slowly changing back into a caterpillar. Any more bedtime, the wilting Widow Flower would decompose.

Several times she called information for Sheldon's phone number. But he wasn't even listed as being *un*listed. The man had no phone or—the last operator said—was living with somebody who did have one. Did Hannah know her name? "*Her* name." Stood to reason. A handsome charmer like Sheldon never did need Hannah's help to get himself a her.

But how long would a person lie around the house brooding? "Today is the day I do something, really do something," she vowed on arising that Sunday just before noon.

After breakfasting on the remains of a half-gallon container of ice cream, Hannah borrowed a neighbor's infant. He just lay in his carriage, still fresh from the womb, cooing. How foolish to rejoice at a birth and to cry at a funeral. What worse thing can befall the dead? But who knows what the future will be unloading on a newborn?

Hannah ignored the doorbell. But it rang again and again.

"I know you're in there. Mrs. Sierra just told me. It's Leo."

As if she wasn't depressed enough, but she had to admit the answer to nobody's prayer. Didn't want the neighbors disturbed. It wasn't their fault, the shambles her life had become.

Inseparable brown paper bag in hand, Leo began, "You're looking good and *zoftig*. Like the Hannah of old. Couple of weeks ago, when they let you out, you were so thin. Cheeks flushed, eyes shiny. A *shreck*."

Leo just wasn't used to seeing her ecstatic.

"Glad to see you getting back to normal, Hannah. I'm really surprised at the hospital."

How many times did she have to tell the man! "I was *not* in some hospital, Leo. You've heard of the Queen Elizabeth?"

He nodded. "Sure, sure. Of course. You never had a nervous breakdown when Rupert . . . you-know."

"Leo, I did *not* have a nervous breakdown."

" 'Cause I can't tell you how much I *admire* you, Hannah. There are too few widows in this world who . . . go straight into the Queen Elizabeth . . . the day of a husband's funeral."

Certainly, Hannah had been the newest widow aboard. The QE2 had teemed with widows, but none fresher.

"Such a devoted wife you were, Hannah. Every man should be blessed with at least one."

"Yes, and every husband should have at least one widow."

"Right. About your, uh, trip. They treated you nice? Good staff? Well-trained?"

"Oh, yes! It was everything I never dreamed of. Before, who had time to dream?"

He handed her the brown paper bag, "Ever make a standing crown roast? I threw in some chopped meat to stuff it with. Just in case you want to go whole hog."

"Again lamb chops? No caviar and champagne for a change? Oh, well. Maybe I'll make a lamb chop salad."

"Are you crazy? Sorry! I mean, it's good having you back, Hannah. That's the main thing. Look, I understand how it is. Don't think I don't. Hard for a woman alone. Helpless, unnecessary. I'll tell you a secret, Hannah. It's hard even for a *man* to live all by himself. And me a physician yet. But forty years together with Eleanor, approximately, is a whole lot. Can't remember a time I wasn't married. At night sometimes, I find myself still calling out for her. 'Eleanor, where's the TV Guide?' Or, 'Eleanor, get me a beer.' And there's no reply. It's a lonely life without Eleanor, let me tell you."

"Leo, who's Eleanor?"

"I don't believe it! How could you forget my Eleanor!"

"Leo, your wife's name was Laraine."

"That's right. Of course." Not the least bit flustered, Leo continued, "So much alike, women. Men, nobody mixes up. Me with Rupert, for example. Men are much more you-know. Take Eleanor. Nice in the same way my wife Laraine was nice. Sweet. She was the first girl I proposed to, Eleanor. Are you following me? But she married some lawyer, who went to jail later on for mail fraud. Served her right. Hannah? Was there anyone who put in a bid before Rupert?"

"I had four other proposals. Well, this Mike proposed all four times. Then Sheldon, a couple of weeks ago. But I turned him down."

"A couple of weeks ago? No! Hannah, you surprise me. I'm shocked. I really am."

"You think it's so awful?"

"I certainly do. Worse than awful. Your not telling me before. Here, I've been waiting around for a decent interval before speaking up."

"How's that?"

"You don't think I go around passing out lamb chops right and left to just anybody, do you? As soon as I heard Rupert was checking out, I thought—God rest his soul—we'd make a good team, you and me. You need a man to look after you, I'm very comfortable. It's a natural. So what do you say, Hannah?"

What was going on here! Was she perhaps sending out subliminal hot flashes? *Available! Come and Get It!* Love, of course, this certainly wasn't. More like Leo's aversion to his own company, and who could blame him? In the darkness of the night she too had this urge to reach out and touch. A human being is lonely for another human being nearby. Rupert was not a talkative person, but he was always there. A presence. Someone to share with. Now, there was this emptiness all around that never filled up. But with *Leo?* A sane person didn't plug a cavity with junk food. Not unless she was asking for a toothache.

". . . and that's what my lawyer told me, Hannah."

"Lawyer?"

"He'll draw it up. Premarital contract. Standard nowadays."

So Leo had already spoken to Sandra and Josh. *Him* they had approved! "You don't find it insulting, signing such a thing?"

"Why insulting? I don't want any of your money, Hannah. Not a penny. It should all go, when you . . . you-know, to your own flesh and blood. Two of my sons agree wholeheartedly."

"And the other two?"

"*Them* I'm not on speaking terms with."

Maybe the man *was* capable of feeling. "That's so magnanimous, giving up all claim to my money." Unlike Sheldon, for all his talk of love. Go, figure. Impulsively, she kissed Leo on the cheek.

His calves' eyes lit up. "Let's celebrate, Hannah! Caviar it is! Be right back." Starting for the door, he automatically scooped up his brown paper bag on the way. "Oh, forgot!" He put the paper bag down. "We're engaged now." And out the door.

Engaged? Who said? For the life of her, Hannah couldn't piece together what had just happened. He had said . . . and she had . . . and he . . . then, her kiss. To show appreciation, that was *all*. Desperate for marriage she wasn't. Only for some cuddling now and then. There was more tenderness in that than in the other thing.

Still, she was growing older. No. Old. Not that she ever *felt* old. But who'd believe that? Old is what people saw in the white hair, liver spots. And what good was it to stay young inside all by yourself?

"Googoogoogoogoo." Baby Joey had woken up.

Hannah went over, took his hands and played with them. "Tell me, Joey, what do *you* think I should do?" More cooing—"Uh-huh, uh-huh, uh-huh"—followed by a belch. "Well, *that* makes sense. More sense than I can come up with myself right now. You stay right there. Be back soon. The bath is calling."

There was nothing like a tub of warmth. A *mechayah*. No wonder newborns howled on being dispossessed. Hold on! Was that someone moving around the apartment?

Sandra and Josh had made a dozen sets of keys, which they distributed to everyone in the neighborhood except perhaps for a burglar or two. That was in addition to adding an extra lock on her front door and installing two memory phones with their numbers and the doctor's and police's punched in, plus an electronic beeper to wear on her person, just in case she forgot the location of the phones. All this despite her moving out in a few weeks. Still, the children meant well. In *this* respect. Electronically and phone-wise, Hannah was well-provided for.

"Grandma? You in there?" Debbie, bless her, was knocking at the bathroom door.

"Be right with you, my darling." Hannah got out of the tub, dried herself quickly, and put on a robe.

"What's taking so long?" Debbie, opening the the bathroom door and seeing Hannah on her knees, ran inside and grabbed the sponge away, which resulted in a yelling battle.

Clean up after her? Never! But Debbie wouldn't relinquish the sponge until Hannah swore on her life.

A question. Why wouldn't Grandma ever accept assistance?

"There's an old Yiddish saying: 'When a parent helps a child, they both smile; when a child must help a parent, both cry.' But what happened to the senior class play you were trying out for?"

"I got the lead, Grandma! And the director is inviting agents and producers to the opening. If just *one* of them takes a liking to me—"

"What about college, Debbie?"

"Grandma, the sooner an actor starts acting—"

"So where's Shirley Temple today? Debbie, if I had your opportunity—"

"But you do, Grandma. What's stopping you now?"

"College? At my age?"

"Either go to college, Grandma, or marry Sheldon."

"Sheldon? He could steal me blind, my darling."

Debbie tossed her long, auburn hair. "What do *you* care? Have you heard from him?"

"You know these shipboard romances."

"*Call* him, Grandma."

"Oh . . . I couldn't do a thing like that."

"What do you have to lose? If you won't . . ." Debbie picked up the phone. "I'd like the number—"

Hannah took the phone away and hung up. "Sheldon is living with somebody."

"Can't be. It's been just two weeks."

"Some men are speedy."

"Oh! I'm so sorry, Grandma!"

"Don't be, Debbie. There's plenty of other fish in the barrel. Cousin Leo just proposed."

"*Cousin Leo?* Grandma, you can't be *that* hard-up."

"Loneliness makes strange bedfellows, Debbie. And he's a doctor, remember. Should come in handy for repairs."

Hannah was pouring a glass of orange juice in the kitchen when the doorbell rang. Had to be Leo, back with the caviar, a nice change of pace from Sunday morning lox. With Debbie inclined to bar what she called the man with the personality of a blunt instrument, Hannah went to admit him.

But the door opened on Sheldon, red bandanna tied carelessly around his still tanned throat. "*Oh . . . !*" The glass of juice slipped from her hand and spilled all over the linoleum in the foyer.

Whipping out a handkerchief, Sheldon bent over and wiped up the spill. He looked so handsome, lithe body in a powder blue T-shirt, blue jeans and blue suede shoes with tassels.

Debbie wheeled the baby carriage right past Sheldon. "So nice to see you again, Mr. Wilson." Out they scooted.

Sheldon dropped the sopping handkerchief into the candy dish full of stale cigarette butts, then turned to size up Hannah. "Oh, boy! You look like hell."

"As good as all that?"

"What's happened? When I left—"

She turned away. "There's your answer. You left. After having transformed me."

"Baloney! Nobody can change anybody else. It's impossible enough changing oneself. All I did, Hannah, was help you become what you are."

"And what's that?"

"Ever been to the Metropolitan? Well, I was there once when this man was restoring a work of art. Didn't add a thing to the painting. Not a brush stroke. What he did was remove the grime that had collected over the years. Until the work's original beauty stood revealed once more."

(A work of art, he'd said.) She turned toward him.

"Oh, Hannah, when I see you now! And *I've* done this. Deserting you in a huff because my feelings were hurt."

"I drove you away, Sheldon."

"No, you didn't."

"My children, then."

"Not them, either. It was the truth that scared me off, Hannah. Might as well confess."

Her heart sank. "You don't want me."

"That's a dirty lie!"

"Then, what?"

Sheldon turned away. "Let me begin at the end, Hannah. I said I'm in banking."

"I remember."

"Well, I do work in a bank. As an officer."

"You told me that."

"A *security* officer. The one who guards other people's money. Because I have none of my own."

"What? But that expensive cruise. And the trip to Israel."

"Someone staked me. Oh, this is too embarrassing."

"The someone you're living with?"

"You *know?* Well, no more. I'm living now, temporarily, at a Y in Manhattan. It was either that or punch him out."

"Him? You were living with a *him?*"

"My son-in-law. You see, my daughter took me in after my wife died. When I said my daughter and I lived next door to each other, I meant *next door.*"

"So *she* staked you."

"Yes. To marry me off to a rich widow."

"*Oh!*"

"Hannah, when you asked me to sign that prenuptial thing—"

"You saw yourself losing a small fortune."

"I was *afraid* you'd think that. But I could never marry a woman for her money. Not me. Marilyn just persuaded me to marry a woman *with* money. I simply can't afford one without the other. They have to be, well, in tandem. Still paying off my wife's medical bills. But I could never marry just *any* monied woman. I chose you, Hannah, because you have so much *more* than money."

"Sure. Of course. I have gullibility."

"Hannah, I should have been honest with you up front, and afterwards it was too late. The private detective would have found out all about my finances."

"*What* private detective?"

"The one your kids would have hired. They're playing for big stakes."

"And you, Sheldon?"

His cheeks turned red. "My only mistake was not making a clean breast at the start. But I'm new at this. It isn't as if I've made a practice of cruising rich widows."

{168}

"What about the night you proposed? You could have told me then. At the Wall, before God."

"Would the princess have said yes to the pauper?"

"You think any self-respecting woman would marry a man who's passionately attracted to her money?"

"Is intelligence, say, a superior inspiration for loving? My son-in-law writes brilliant newspaper editorials, and *still* he's a creep. Is beauty, perhaps, a better reason? Beauty fades. What, then?"

"Well, at least the face remains. The principal resource stays intact."

"In *any* case, money is *all* you'd lose," he retorted. "Never in a million years would I exploit your goodness, Hannah, which is the very heart of you."

Gravely, she said, "Is it really so peculiar, Sheldon? My wanting to live for a change on my *husband's* money?"

He dazzled her with the wide smile she'd been dreaming of for weeks. "Then who would live on *yours?*"

The man had an answer for everything! But was that so bad? What she craved now was answers, whether or not they made sense. "Tell me, Sheldon. Why did you come here?"

"I owed you for our happy five weeks together, Hannah. Couldn't let you blame yourself for my vanishing act. Had to explain. And ask again for your hand."

She could hardly get the words out. "*Well*, then! Once you sign that silly thing—"

A shrug of his broad shoulders. "Can't do that, Hannah. As good as a signed confession. Like proclaiming to one and all, 'I am not a crook.' Remember the last man to make that declaration? He *was* a crook."

"Exactly what are you proposing, then?"

"I'm not here to bargain, if that's what you mean. Let me tell you something about myself. No, everything." Sheldon spoke of the dress house he'd owned for twenty-seven years. It had gone bankrupt two years before his wife was incapacitated by a stroke. Medical expenses wiped out the balance of his assets. His home could have been saved if he'd divorced his wife, making her eligible for Medicaid. Marilyn, who loved her mother, begged Sheldon to divorce. But the best doctors and finest nursing homes didn't accept Medicaid patients. Sheldon could never do that to his wife of thirty-four years. No, not out of false pride. "Self-esteem. Without it I'm a big nothing. And that's what I offer you, Hannah. Self-esteem. Mine feeding yours, yours nurturing mine. We would have a shared self. That's what marriage is, you know. Two people with one scenario. Think now, Hannah, think what the two of us can do with life *together*."

Enticing word, together, to someone who had never lived apart. Sheldon was back, rejuvenating her, the judgment hers alone to make. Yet, with what new evidence? Only that he had lied. About *that* he was honest. If his word were a bridge, would she dare to cross? "Sheldon—"

The doorbell interrupted.

Hannah didn't want to answer, but pesky Leo would never leave her alone. When she opened the door, there he was, smelling of cologne and clutching a suitcase.

"Since when does caviar come in luggage, Leo?"

He bridled at the sight of Sheldon. "What's *Tarzan* doing here?"

"This is Sheldon, Leo. Leo, Sheldon. Well, I'm still waiting. Why the suitcase?"

He pulled her off to the side. "The gourmet shop being around the corner from my place, I just stopped to pick up a few things."

"*What* things?"

He wouldn't say, until Sheldon seized the case. "Nothing. A change or two of clothing and a spritz cologne . . . Well, we *are* engaged, Hannah."

"*Engaged?*" Sheldon exclaimed.

"But if you don't want to you-know, Hannah, we just wouldn't. You-know is the furthest thing from my mind, believe me."

"You better believe it, buster."

Two men squabbling over her. Was it possible? What did they want from her? Or she from them? Who needed all this hoo-hah at her age?

Just then, in came the children. Hannah asked everyone to sit down in the living room, while she brought out a nice bowl of fruit and collected her thoughts. To get this much attention, Hannah usually had to give birth or inherit.

"Cousin Leo's proposed," Debbie volunteered. "And I just bet Sheldon's renewed his proposal. *Grandmère fatale.*"

"*No!*"

The children demanded to know what Hannah had told each man.

"One thing's certain," Sandra said. "You can't marry a fortune hunter."

"Mom," said Josh, "I won't let you marry Leo."

"But he's agreed to that premarital thing. Leo wants me for myself alone."

"Sandra! If you don't tell Mom, I will."

"Tell me what, Josh?"

"Mom, Leo doesn't want a cent of yours—"

"Absolutely correct," Leo said. "One hundred percent."

"—because he thinks a cent is all you've got. Nobody knows Dad left you two hundred and fifty thousand dollars. We all swore each other to secrecy."

Leo's mouth flew open, as his eyes formed perfect zeroes. "What's this? What's this?"

"Not even Charlie knows, Mom. I think Sandra was afraid he'd put out a contract on you with one of his clients."

"*Two hundred and fifty thousand dollars!*" Leo fell onto the couch. "I'm dying!"

"That prenuptial business," Josh said. "Leo's loving way to make sure you wouldn't get a cent of *his*."

Leo exploded. "My *sons* made me do it, Hannah. It's all *their* doing, damn them."

So he had wanted *her* to sign. "How dare you, Leo! How dare you! Taking me for a—a—a—"

Sweetly, Sheldon suggested, "Fortune hunter? Gigolo?"

How Hannah had humiliated him for no good reason. "Forgive me, Sheldon, please forgive me."

"Only if you marry me, sweetheart."

"Way to go, Grandma! Go for it!" Debbie jumped in

Josh held up a hand. "Hold it, everyone, just hold it!"

The plastic covers crackled as Sandra suddenly dropped into a club chair and burst into tears. "Oh, I'm so *ashamed*." She covered her face with her hands. "To think of sacrificing you to Leo. Not that I'd ever have gone through with it. *Still* . . . So afraid money wouldn't be available soon enough to get me—" She checked herself.

{171}

Hannah, devoted mother once more, asked, "What is it? What do you need that bad, Sandra?"

"Can't imagine what came over me! I apologize." Sandra wiped her eyes and stood up.

"What is it my money can buy you? Tell me, dear."

"Not your problem, Mom. Something I have to work out on my own. What I need right now is a drink of water."

As soon as her mother went into the kitchen, Debbie reported matter-of-factly, "Mother wants a divorce." Hannah was shocked. Josh, too. Even Debbie herself, for putting it into words. "Actually, Mother's never said that. Don't know why I did."

The news didn't entirely displease Hannah. She pressed Sandra, on her return, until she finally spoke out.

"Whenever I try to negotiate our differences, Charlie reels off a list of younger women ready to eat him up exactly as is, that prize. I got no leverage!"

Josh snorted. "And everyone's urging marriage on *me!*"

Sheldon seized Hannah's hand. "What else does life offer *but* chance? So grab it now with both hands. What do you say, sweetheart?"

Leo intervened. "Remember, Hannah, I'm a cousin. By rights, you should keep yourself in the family."

Everyone started talking at once. All these demands flying at her. *Marry* me. No, marry *me*. No, marry *him*. No, marry *nobody*. Finally, she stated, "I've come to a decision."

Their expectant looks unnerved her. She'd have to disappoint someone there, perhaps several. That weighed on her mind. And what if she ruled wrongly?

"First, we eat. Then my ruling." And after brunch, hesitantly, "This is my final word." Deep breath, long pause. "I'll announce it the day I move out of this apartment." (By then, Hannah should have *definitely* made up her mind. She hoped.)

"*Four weeks?!*"

"Well, look how long it took Scarlett O'Hara to choose between Clark Gable and Leslie Howard."

"Well, all *right!*" Debbie, certain now of the outcome, gave her grandmother a thumb's up and a big wink.

12

EVERY unescorted older woman on the street now gave Sandra a twinge. Such a solitary figure: *One*. Was her mother being cheated out of what was rightfully hers? A full life of her own. Had Sheldon been misjudged? An older woman loved is winter with flowers—and Mom so loved flowers.

"Stop mooning around and hire a private eye," said Debbie. "Check out Grandma's dreamboat."

"Ridiculous!" (Private detectives were movie and TV fantasy figures hip deep in mayhem, murder and nymphomania, circles Sandra didn't ordinarily travel in.)

"Why? Before buying a house, people get someone to do a title search, right?"

The P.I. found through the Yellow Pages assured Sandra lots of people in these sophisticated times were investigating prospective mates—ever-increasingly, a parent's, sometimes a grandparent's. "Entirely logical. Too much is at stake to marry blindly."

"Yes," said Sandra, "people's entire future happiness."

"Money," said the P.I.

Charlie ruled the enterprise irrelevant. "What could an investigation have unearthed to stop your marrying *me?*"

True. Who could predict the future of any marriage? Or why mates mutate. Or how over the years lovers develop an overriding passion to put the other down. Or do him or her in. Marriage, Sandra sometimes thought, is the only misfortune people pray for.

Sheldon was a decorated veteran of the Normandy invasion, the P.I. reported in due time, a highly regarded dress manufacturer until he filed for bankruptcy, and so far as could be ascertained, not a blatantly unfaithful husband.

Sandra broke in. "Was his marriage a happy one?"

"Hey, you're asking the impossible, lady. Happy? Often, husbands and wives lie about that even to themselves. Who wants to think himself a loser in the love department?"

Friends spoke well of Sheldon, naturally. Detractors thought him flashy, a bit too smooth, and mentioned his three-year membership in Gamblers Anonymous. Because nobody would back a new dress venture of a sixty-six-year-old bankrupt ex-gambler, and pride kept him from working as an employee in an industry where he'd been a boss, Sheldon had taken a temporary job as security officer in a distant county to get out of his daughter's house and give structure to his day. He was now seeking more suitable employment elsewhere.

"As a husband?"

"For thousands of years women otherwise unemployed regarded wifehood a legit occupation. Do you believe in a double standard?"

"Damn right I do! Does Sheldon want my mother for the right reasons? Will he be a good husband?"

"The only thing I don't draw, lady, is conclusions."

On the one hand, Sheldon, the hunk in a hurry, had neither means nor prospects. On the other . . . *was* there another hand?

"Actually, I was inclined to think Sheldon something of a hustler. Most people are. Nature of the beast. Look at public officials. Would you want your mother to marry one of *them?* But then I observed her for a few hours. Let me tell you something. A man doesn't have to be a hustler to want Hannah Trilling."

Wanting was one thing, making her happy another.

"If you push me, I'd say they have as good a chance as any other second marriage today. Sixty-forty."

"Which way?"

"Hard to call."

Briefed, Josh surprised Sandra by saying he was waiting to hear from *his* P.I. Yes, remorse set in every time he saw an older woman walking along hand in hand with some man, going out together or heading home. "There but for her children, I think, goes Mom. And not just accompanied. Cherished."

Aside from the gambling problem, now presumably licked, no skeletons were discovered in Sheldon's closet. Josh's investigator confessed to finding Mom's suitor terribly charming, extremely attractive, decidedly sexy.

"Josh! You hired a gay P.I.?"

"A *female* P.I. Anyway, she says she'd take on Sheldon herself if she wasn't living with someone now. Sandra, Queen Elizabeth's done pretty well with Prince Philip, who *also* has no steady job."

The Sunday morning they came to Brooklyn to pack up Mom's belongings, only to find she had packed everything herself, Sandra and Josh handed over the reports. Read, they said.

Mom smiled. "Sheldon *said* you'd be hiring private detectives."

"Not to blackball him, honest. To prove he's right for you."

"Well, how kosher *is* Sheldon?"

"See for yourself. Whatever you decide . . ."

". . . we're with you one hundred percent," Josh concluded.

"Well! Isn't that—" Mom choked up. "As it happens, I already decided. And so informed Sheldon."

Sandra caught her breath, unsure what she wanted, which was better for Mom. A great marriage was what she deserved, but how many satisfying marriages were there in existence? Still, a life alone also had its problems, not the least of which was loneliness. Next door to Sandra lived a widow who conversed with her two dogs as if they were human. Didn't consider them to be pets at all—too patronizing a term, she said—but called them "companion animals."

"Mom, what did you tell Sheldon? Yes? No? To be continued?"

"Wait." Mom began, "In Galicia marriage usually took place between teenagers. Rightly so. The older you get, the more aware you become of its pitfalls. Just like surgery. Every day patients go cheerfully under the knife. They don't know any better. Have no idea of all the things that can go wrong. But when Cousin Leo had a hernia, him being a doctor, he had to be dragged into the operating room, drugged."

"Does that mean—?"

"Yes—"

"That's what you told Sheldon? Yes?"

Mom held up a hand. "Let me tell you of this perfectly lovely dream I had a few nights ago. I was walking down the aisle on the arm of my parents, Mother as well as Papa. Ahead was the *chuppah*, which filled me with such joy. My wedding day was the happiest day of my life. Till I had the two of you, the *other* happiest days of my life."

"Well? Who was standing under the *chuppah?* Dad?"

Mom shook her head.

"Sheldon?"

Another shake of the head.

"Not Leo! I'll *die* if it was Leo."

"*Nobody,*" said Mom. "Nobody at all."

"*Nobody?*"

"Yet I felt so very happy. That's what made me write Sheldon the next day. Though I'd always be grateful for his help, it was off between us. Hurt me to hurt him like that. But I just can't put myself through it now. I've done that already, marriage."

"No marriage?"

"Well, it isn't as if I can have more children."

"People marry for other reasons too, Mom."

"All my life I've lived in a crowd, supporting one and all. Parents, nine brothers and sisters, husband, children, relatives, friends, neighbors. For a change I'd like to support *me*. Try being my *own* Prince Charming."

"What about love, Mom?"

"What about it?"

"Everyone needs love," said Josh.

"True, very true. Love *is* what the world needs. Though not in the way they say. There was this movie in the forties advertised with the line: 'A woman is beautiful only when she is loved.' Never thought so then, don't think so now. Me, I believe a person is beautiful only when she herself does the loving. Well, the commandments say, 'Love thy neighbor,' and 'Love thy God.' Nowhere does the Bible command, '*Be* loved.'

"No second marriage *ever?*"

"I wouldn't say *never*. Perhaps when husbands come with warranties. Love without trust is like religion without faith. My entire life has been spent trusting others. Loved, I don't have to be. But trusted, you bet. And Sheldon refuses to agree premaritally. So, children, the rest of my life I'd prefer to live at my *own* mercy. Not anyone else's."

"No husband?" Sandra felt very sad.

"Only last Wednesday I got together for lunch with this nice stewardess from the QE2. And during the week there have been other lovely experiences. So why bet my entire future now on just one individual?"

"Don't you want a relationship more sustained, more intimate than lunch?"

"My dears, lunch or dinner out is more than I got from your father during the last eleven years. Why expect better treatment from a Sheldon, who I never did a thing for?"

"Because he *loves* you," Josh said. "The way he spoke about you. Such eloquence."

"Eloquence is instantly recognizable. But love? That's something you can determine only after the fact. Way after."

"So that's your decision?" Tears sprang to Sandra's eyes. "Just you by yourself?"

Mom drew herself up to her full height. "No 'just.' *Me*. And not by myself. So long as I have *Tattenyu*."

"But Mom. Is God *enough?*"

"Yes, God willing. Well, we'll see soon enough, won't we?"

Later, Josh asked how Sandra felt about Mom's decision. "All that religious talk. Our mother the nun. Bride of God."

Sandra heaved a sigh. "Heaven knows there are *worse* husbands."

If Mom at sixty-nine could brave being single, Sandra in her mid-forties could have it out with Charlie, who seemed to think he got her to love him once, why did he have to keep trying after that? Mothers and sweethearts were crazy enough to love eternally, but not wives. If the Heller marriage was to continue, there had to be changes; otherwise, the hell with it. What initially soured the relationship was Charlie's switch to defending the same creeps he used to prosecute as an assistant D.A. For big fat fees.

No wives of his acquaintance, Charlie charged, took such violent exception to their husbands' chosen professions.

"Of course not. All those wives are married to mafiosi. They wouldn't dare."

But America's system of justice entitled everyone to the best defense.

"Also true. But what other professionals specialize in treating mobsters? Doctors specialize, but in curing diseases. Not in inflicting them on society."

As a lawyer, Charlie was *obliged* to defend clients.

"Granted, but no lawyer is obliged to hire himself out to bastards. Lawyers are corrupting the nation's sense of right and wrong. No longer are courts finding in favor of innocent defendants, but of the smarter lawyers."

At which point Charlie would fly into a rage. "I married a woman, I got me a critic! No, a *prosecutor*."

The decision to confront him was simple compared to going about it. As a miser can never be satisfied with additional riches, no amount of proofs of love ever appeased Charlie. In what supplementary ways was she loving him *lately?* Not by quitting her job to concentrate on him and home. (Though before she started working as a vocational guidance counselor, he called her a parasite.) Nor by severing all distracting ties to her family the way he'd done with his own (whom he detested). Certainly not by meeting all of Charlie's needs (which he could never articulate).

Happily, Sandra knew a place that prepared meals cunningly designed to convince husbands and guests they had been slavishly cooked at home. It was a great success, the six-course meal, Charlie duly appreciative.

"Thought after all our eating out and TV dinners, you'd forgotten how to cook. Lost all desire."

(Why should a wife who worked full-time be bothered to cook

what others did better anyway? Whenever the toilet got stopped up, did she ask Charlie to fix it, or call a plumber?) Sandra smiled sweetly.

"Isn't my birthday or anything."

"Charlie, let's talk."

"I *knew* there was a catch!"

"I said, Let's *talk*. Not, Let's tear each other apart. Charlie, I can't go on living like this. With silences broken only by temper tantrums. Why do you save all your not inconsiderable charm for the office and for strangers?"

Jumping to his feet in a mad dash from the den, he knocked over a plant, pausing only to kick some earth in Sandra's direction.

She pursued him into the bathroom before he could lock the door. "Charlie, if you don't talk to me now, you'll have to talk to my lawyer."

He exploded. "You are *threatening* me? A man who threatens witnesses every day of the week?"

"No threat, Charlie. Simple statement of fact. In a word, divorce. There, I've actually *said* it."

"You must be insane! Know how many women I can get with a snap of my fingers? Just one snap and—"

With some surprise she heard herself say, "Go ahead, snap away. Charlie, when your gray hair turned green after you colored it with that rinse and you panicked, who took you to a beauty parlor to get it dyed so you'd look normal again?" (Of all things, why *that?*)

In a moment charges and counter charges flew thick and fast. "Faultfinding," "griping," "nagging," "contentious," "demanding" vied with "brooding," "sulky," "testy," "hostile," "disparaging." Then, "What *happened?*" In unison: "Why did you *change?*"

At which point Sandra burst out crying.

Charlie sneered, "Tears, the first refuge of a woman. I don't know about you"—swiftly he stripped off his clothes—"but I'm taking a shower." And ducked into the shower stall.

There could be no retreat. Sandra stepped out of the lounging pajamas and into the shower stall. Wiping water from her eyes, she listed the options. "Continue as we are, which I refuse. Divorce, which will cost you plenty. Or marriage counseling."

Charlie twisted a knob as if it were a throat.

Too late to save the thirty-five dollar hairdo going down the drain. Sandra reached out and shut off the water. "When you had that bladder infection, Charlie. If you hadn't gone for help, the bed would still be wet. It's not a sign of weakness, going for counseling. It's a sign of strength."

"You're telling *me* about strength? Litigation is jungle warfare, one on one, with a loser guaranteed each and every time. Any idea what it takes to get up each morning, knowing that day you may be defeated in open court with all the world looking on?"

"Why do it then? You don't have to prove anything."

"Maybe not to *you*, Sandra. But any lawyer who has nothing to prove will never prove a thing, ever." Long gone was the anticipated thrill of winning of years ago. Replaced now by fatigue, apathy, ulcers and lack of wifely appreciation.

Symptoms, all. "Charlie, burnout is nature's way of telling you to cease and desist. To balance a career with a personal life."

"The law is my life, Sandra. A man is what he *does*. Unlike a woman, who is merely what she feels."

"Then do something *else*, Charlie. Something worthwhile. Pro bono work. Or university president. More and more of them are coming from the ranks of lawyers."

"University president—me?" He looked pleased.

(Rarely failed, flattery. Mother's milk to men. And women were supposed to be the vain ones.) "Why not? You have the necessary management skills and a broad range of experience. That's one of the things we can discuss with the marriage counselor." Plus the obsessive-compulsiveness of trial lawyers who can't see family relationships for the microscopic details of their cases.

"And what was that about considerable charm?"

Did she say *that*? Well, as long as it turned him on. She couldn't remember the last time she'd seen Charlie trembling so from top to bottom. All of a sudden, so was she.

Neither with desire, however. Shivering, he exclaimed, "Why'd you cut off the hot water? It's freezing! When I tell your marriage counselor what an *idiot* you are—"

13

*T*HERE was no need for cagelike steel gates on the windows of Hannah's new abode at Lincoln Plaza. A marble lobby big as a cornfield, high as the sky. Doormen, not one but two, to wish you a nice day, call taxis, help with packages. Behind a marble desk with fresh flowers, a concierge to announce guests and bar burglars. Elevators by the half-dozen, which never broke down. Central Park a few blocks away—nature practically on call.

Hannah bought all the previous tenant's attractive furnishings. Life had never been so effortless. Shops that delivered. A cleaning lady each and every week. Yes, an honest-to-God cleaning lady.

And yet . . . and yet . . .

——*And yet, Hannah?*

——I feel . . . I don't know . . . a void.

——*Second thoughts?*

——*No* thoughts. That's the trouble.

——*None about Sheldon?*

——Well, from time to time. It's wonderful being swept off one's feet every forty-five years or so.

——*You can still make it permanent, Hannah. Just pick up the phone and call him.*

——Ah, who in the world *stays* swept off her feet? Sooner or later, a person is bound to come down to earth. And she doesn't always land on her toes.

——*No thoughts of marriage, then?*

——Well, once a person has been burned by the hot, she blows on the cold. Me, I was never a terrific success matching up others. Foolish to think I'd do any better matching up myself.

——*But the rewards of marriage are enormous.*

——They *should* be, the risks being so great. Like the lottery. One dollar gets you ten million, because the odds are stacked against you.

——*There's nothing like a happy marriage, though.*

——Oh, yes! I agree. A happy marriage is a work of art: an act of the imagination. It's divine.

——*So?*

——But a *bad* marriage! Nothing's worse. And from all my listening all these years, I've learned even *good* marriages can go bad. Didn't it happen to me? People tend to grow unhappy as they grow older, and their only enjoyment is blaming those closest. Who wants to be a lightning rod at my age?

——*You're afraid to take another chance?*

——Youngsters can defy arithmetic. They marry in the belief that one plus one equals one. Not us oldsters. We can add.

——*What about a partnership?*

——That's the ideal. But it's an ideal because it's never realized. Who has a *third* chance in life?. . . Still, it does hurt me.

——*What?*

——Hurting Sheldon. I don't want anyone's feelings hurt. It's a sin.

——*Better* you *should be hurt?*

——I didn't say that. Did I say that?

——*Somebody's not going to get what he or she wants. You think that somebody should be you?*

——I'm *also* a somebody. Isn't that so?

——*Right. So why aren't you behaving like a somebody?*

——What does that mean?

——*You know very well what I mean, Hannah.*

——Well . . . it's hard, so hard.

——*Moping around the apartment. Eating out of cans. Defrosting frozen vegetables in your mouth. Freezing garbage to avoid taking it out to the incinerator. Why, Hannah?*

——I don't know. Just don't have the strength anymore. I'm so ashamed.

——*Ashamed?*

——Of not being able to pull myself together. Me, always such a capable person. Now, look. Watching television in the *daytime*. Me, who always regarded daytime TV as a glass teat for tots. Always used to be so busy busy busy. Now, nobody's home. Everything is too much. Me, who breezed through menopause without realizing till it was all over.

——*Maybe you should talk to somebody. Some nice Jewish psychiatrist.*

——Expose myself to a complete stranger? Too embarrassing. I'd rather talk things over with you who knows me since I was born. *Feels for me.*

——*So tell me what's troubling you.*

——If I only knew! If I only knew! Here I'm free as a bird, and yet . . .

——*You know, there is such a thing as too* much *freedom. Too many choices. Too good a thing.*

——Too much, too late?

——*Perhaps.*

——Then I have to chance that, don't I?

——*Chance eating tuna fish out of a can forever while standing up?*

——Not on Shabbas, of course. Never do that on Shabbas. Or when the cleaning lady is coming.

——*That still leaves five whole empty days a week, Hannah.*

——Very lucky, my cleaning lady. What she does, she's doing for somebody.

——*Well, so are you when you prepare meals during the week, go out.*

——What are you talking about? Who am I doing it for?

——*For yourself, Hannah.*

——Oh. Well, that's not the same thing.

——*When it comes to doing things for yourself . . .*

——It's simply not worth the effort.

{ 183 }

——*Who's not worth the effort? You?*

——Did I say that?

——*Didn't you? Let's say a dozen people were dropping by tonight. How hard would it be for you to whip up dinner?*

——Well, it wouldn't be easy. But I'd do it. Love to.

——*Because it was for others. But you yourself don't rate?*

——I've never done *anything* for myself alone. Don't know where to begin. Don't misunderstand. I'm no saint. Just a woman.

——*Others deserve better than you?*

——I didn't say that. But a person can't change her nature.

——*If you say so, Hannah. So go on eating out of cans—*

——But I *hate* all that!

——*Then what are you going to do about it?*

——What *should* I do? Oh, I know what you want me to say.

——*Don't say it, Hannah, unless you mean to do it.*

——The first thing now is get out of bed. Well, it's eleven o'clock. Then, shower and dress. How's that?

——*And then?*

——Throw out every single can of tuna fish. Maybe my TV too. Turning my brain to tapicoa pudding.

——*That's a start, Hannah. This is all very hard for you, I know. But you can do it. Yes.*

——Think so? Can turn my life around?

——*I know so. If you will it.*

——Dear God! Thank You. I'll try. Yes, I will. Just watch. *Tattenyu?* I so want you to be proud of me.

——*Sure, Hannah. Be strong now and of good courage. And hang in there.*

14

NOW came the marketing of Josh's novel, the crucible of commerce, under direct threat of his publisher: Promote or perish, move your ass or be remaindered.

The marketplace had only a dozen or two competing soaps, toothpastes, toilet papers. But *Captain O Captain* was vying with over 40,000 other products published that same year, some bearing big brand names. Too late now, alas, to retitle his novel *Naked Came I*. (From the Book of Job, should anyone accuse Josh of pandering to trade or people's basest instincts, assuming those weren't identical.)

A big disappointment was the mere 15,000 copies that constituted *Captain O Captain's* first and second printings combined. "Don't the early great reviews *count?*" Josh asked his publisher.

"*Certainly*. To your entire family."

Enter promotion, a way of advertising free of charge, the paid kind being inordinately expensive. The publicist's first idea was to find some scandal connected either with the book or the author, or concoct one. When none came to mind, Josh took leave from his job to flog *Captain O Captain* cross-country on local radio and TV.

Provided invitations to appear could be wangled. Interviewers who never read the book could discuss at length a nonfiction subject or thesis, however inane. With a novel, however, the host would have to talk of stuff guaranteed to glaze eyes, deafen ears, deaden brains, all desperately needed to absorb upcoming commercials. It helped that half the critics thought *Captain O Captain* funny with a serious theme while the other half called it a serious work that was funny. Raised by parents deft at banter, Josh enjoyed kidding. And when the interviewer wasn't listening (some read questions off cue cards without attending to replies), he slipped in something of substance. Once, when a host was too stoned to sit upright, Josh taped answers to queries he put to himself, queries the sobered-up host taped the following day, then spliced into the show.

Less productive were other appearances. In Cleveland the host of what Josh thought was a half-hour show spent ten minutes asking about brassieres (the business of the father of Josh's protagonist), then ended the program. In St. Louis Josh shared a show (sponsored by a dairy company) with a live cow. In Los Angeles he was asked repeatedly about his stable of white " 'ho's" until during a commercial break the host was informed he'd been using the list of questions prepared for his next guest, a slick pimp promoting his autobiography. In San Francisco Josh's mention of Reinhold Niebuhr triggered fifty minutes of vicious on-air call-ins accusing the great Protestant theologian of being a communist pervert. Yet when Josh apologized afterwards for having attracted all those crackpots, the host exclaimed, "Are you kidding? That was the best damn show I've had all year!"

Why expect audiences of interviewers, who cracked more bottles of liquor than books, to read? Yet *Captain O Captain* was going into a fourth printing, and someone who caught Josh on TV in Los Angeles booked him for a morning network show hosted by TV's leading woman interviewer, Bonita Weller.

That brought Josh back to New York, down with a severe case of nerves. A *national* TV program viewed by *millions*—

Sandra comforted him with: "So what if you flop? You're a U.S. citizen. They can't deport you."

Friends called to congratulate and warn. Bonita Weller was one tough hombre. Several interviewees had departed her show as walking wounded. Blood was what she'd be after to juice up the interview. And nobody could rush in to staunch the flow, with the show live.

To ensure a good night's sleep before the 7:00 A.M. inquisition, Josh retired the night before at ten-fifteen, then spent two hours watching the clock before raiding a bottle of sleeping pills. Exactly an hour later, took a second pill, perhaps some time later a third. So hard to recall anything with a brain encased in what felt like baby bunting . . .

. . . Mom was standing there, shaking Josh, while off to the side the building superintendent was pointing upward. "Mr. Trilling, is that a *mirror?*"

"What?"

"On the ceiling. A *magnifying* mirror?"

"That's no *mirror*. Well, a ladies' *make-up* mirror. Jut six by six *inches*. Put there as a *gag*."

"A gag? Well, if you say so, Mr. Trilling."

After sending the super away, Josh stumbled into the shower and turned on the cold water till he vibrated himself awake. Over a pint of hot black coffee, Mom explained she'd been phoning since 5:30 A.M. to assure Josh he'd be so wonderful on the show he'd doubtlessly be asked to stay on as a regular. Receiving no response, she had taxied over to find Josh had slept through his alarm and all phone calls. Mom waited around to check out Josh's attire—ties were usually worn *inside* collars—then ushered him downstairs.

He turned nervously toward her. "Mom—"

"Don't worry. Mommy's not going with sonny boy. He's a big boy now, aren't you?" Twice she gave his destination to the cab driver, then had each of them repeat it. As the taxi pulled away, cried, "Bonita Weller is Jewish and single."

At the studio Josh was rushed into make-up, whose artist pencilled in a widow's peak when Josh nodded amiably to a question he couldn't quite make out. When removed at Josh's insistence, what remained made his forehead look as if it had five o'clock shadow. Led to a chair, he found a cocker spaniel in an adjoining one. What was the *dog* doing there? This cocker *also* wrote a book. Small joke. He was actually an actor in a dog food commercial, which paid thousands of dollars more than the nothing that Josh was getting. As soon as the thought entered his mind to stage a violent on-air protest over discrimination against humans, Josh realized he wasn't quite back to normal yet.

Someone guided him to a seat behind a table under hot, blinding lights and hung a small lavaliere microphone around his neck. Soon a redolent woman sat down. Bonita Weller, a striking, slender, beautifully dressed brunette, mid-thirties, with a brisk manner and supreme self-assurance.

"My mother wants me to marry you. What do you think? Interested?" Josh said. *Thought* he said, for there was no response from Bonita Weller, busily shuffling papers.

She whirled toward him. (In his befogged state any sudden movement was a whirl.) And speared him with her dark eyes. "Nervous?"

"No," he replied. "Panic-stricken."

"Good," she said. "Gets the adrenalin flowing."

(Could adrenalin flow through blood that had jelled?) "Miss Weller, I mean, *Ms.* Weller? Be kind. I'm just a novelist." (He was so embarrassed to hear a grown male plead for his honor.)

And then Bonita was speaking. To the entire United States of America. Looking straight into the camera, she introduced him.

Some of the words sounded familiar—his name and the title of his novel, but that was about all. Josh had gone stark staring deaf! All he could hear was a voice within, yelling, *Wake up! Wake up! Wake up!*

Bonita turned to him. "Suppose you start off by telling me which is your favorite part of *Captain O Captain.*"

God bless Bonita! The only thing that stopped Josh from leaning over and licking her face in gratitude was that just then not only couldn't he pick out a favorite part of his novel. He couldn't recall one thing in it.

"Suppose, *sir*," Bonita repeated, sternly, "you cite your favorite part of the novel."

"Oh, that's easy," said Josh. "My favorite part of *Captain O Captain* is pages one through 277."

That got a chuckle, and the interview proceeded as Josh dredged up answers given to similar questions during his eighteen days on the road. To ward off the rigor mortis that threatened his rubbery tongue, he reached under the table and pinched an inner left thigh, praying it was not Bonita Weller's.

Afterwards, she said with a smile, "Now that wasn't so bad, was it?"

Josh, however, could remember nothing of the ordeal. Rushing out of the studio, face burning when a member of the staff drew attention to an open fly, he hurried home, buried the phone and fell into bed, dead to the world.

And awoke that afternoon a personality. On the way to work strangers stopped Josh on the street to ask about Bonita. The elevator operator in his office building congratulated him; in a restaurant, whose waitress commented on the show, a couple insisted on buying him dinner. All this had little to do with his performance, to be sure, and everything to do with fame, secularized canonization. Josh had been granted twenty-four hours in the limelight until the next celebrity was anointed the following day to eclipse him.

One viewer, tracking Josh down to his office days later, phoned to say he'd bought a dozen copies of *Captain O Captain* and invited Josh to lunch at any restaurant of his choice. He named the Four Seasons, so expensive only authors and editors of blockbusters dined there along with the richer and the richest. Called Wednesday from the Four Seasons, Josh, embarrassed to have treated the lunch date as a joke, went to meet Aaron Kogan. Well, the man had bought more copies than Sandra.

"Everyone calls me Aaron" was in his late sixties, tall, good-looking, silver-haired, blue-eyed, richly tanned, very well dressed. A native Bostonian, he had flown to New York just to meet Josh. That would sound perfectly reasonable to Norman Mailer, but not to Josh who wouldn't fly anywhere to meet himself. Once Aaron began praising *Captain O Captain*, however, all doubts about the man vanished, and Josh felt cheated when Aaron scanted the opening and concluding paragraphs, perfect gems.

All of a sudden, without any transition whatsoever, Aaron was talking of Boston's chronic diseases hospital, which, it turned out, had yet to be built. This despite the city's desperate need for one. And Aaron was the one who would do it. Was he a physician?

contractor? No, simply an ordinary citizen with an extraordinary amount of money. "On my sixty-ninth birthday I said to myself, 'Aaron, you've made lots of dough. Now, what are you going to do with it? Were you put on earth just to pile up money? Of course, no one person can erase all of the world's troubles. But why not a little bit?" From his wallet Aaron took out a photograph of his mother, who had worked for decades for Boston's Jewish home for the aged, now being phased out. She was his inspiration.

How many others were involved in this project?

"Well, so far, up till this minute, just me and my wife Elaine. But that's enough for now. You know, 'One with God is a majority.' "

A kook, pure and simple. Which individual alone had ever founded an institution from scratch? Moses at Mount Sinai. But he had the Lord God for backer. Still, the lunch had been delicious.

Leaning forward, tie falling into his just emptied coffee cup, Aaron à la a Kennedy running for office, "I need your help."

"*My* help?" A bachelor with a Haagen-Daz-induced cholesterol count of 295 living in one room? An editor whose magazine had just been swallowed up by a conglomerate out to cut costs and eliminate fatty personnel? A writer with no idea for that all-important second novel? If anyone needed assistance, it was Josh.

"I'm organizing a fundraising dinner and inviting the cream of Boston society. Well, the Jewish cream."

"How . . . nice." (So Aaron was putting the arm on Josh for a donation that would exceed the cost of this lunch.)

"And I want you, Josh, to be the main speaker."

A bit of chocolate mousse sprayed out of Josh's mouth on to the table cloth. "*Me?* The last time I spoke in public was at my bar mitzvah. So nervous I declared: 'Hear O Israel, the Lord our God, the Lord is Two.' "

"I'm not looking for a mouthpiece, Josh. I want a heart. That chapter in your novel about the chronic diseases hospital. It moved us so. Josh, all you have to do at the dinner is get up and talk about that."

"Aaron, everyone knows novelists can't speak. If they could, they'd never write. As for me, I *phumpha*."

"You what?"

"Talk through my nose." So much of Josh's verbal output made regular detours through his sinuses, Mom was always suggesting he get himself a word job.

Aaron, however, would not take *No, not me—you've got the wrongest guy possible* for a refusal.

"Of *course*, we'll lunch again. *Soon*," Josh said on parting. *"Real soon. Certainly."* Which to any New Yorker meant, Don't hold your breath.

Not to Aaron, though. For weeks he phoned every other day to invite Josh for another lunch, then followed up with long letters detailing his plans for his hospital. Clearly a nut case.

Only Mom didn't chuckle or tap her forehead. "Mmmm," she said, "mmmm." Then, after awhile, "Who knows? Maybe. Maybe . . ."

"Maybe *what?*"

"Maybe that's exactly what Boston needs. A *mashugana.*"

Aaron could be a con artist. Who else would be so intent on raising millions for a hospital-in-formation that had no land to build on nor plans?

None of this fazed Mom. "Maybe that's why your book was written, Josh. And maybe it wasn't Aaron Kogan who chose you."

"Who else?"

"God."

"Oh, Mom. You think God reads novels?"

"Moses also *phumphaed*. And remember how Jerusalem's Hadassah Hospital got started, Josh?"

"Terrific! Dad wanted an accountant in the family, you want me to be Henrietta Szold."

"Josh, how many favors have I ever asked of you?"

None, aside from her nagging him to get married. ("If *Frankenstein* could find somebody to marry him," she'd say.) So Josh consulted several friends in Boston who reported—wonder of wonders— Aaron was indeed legit, a philanthropist who liked to do with money what Johnny Appleseed did with pits. And a dozen more long distance phone calls convinced Josh it would take less time to write the damn appeal, travel to Boston and deliver it than to fend off a monomaniac for the rest of his life.

It took two weekends to draft the speech and another to polish it. To serve as editor, that person who sees the manuscript as the writer himself would in six months' time, when he could read it with a fresh eye, Josh chose a contributor to his magazine, Laurel Rabin, a pretty, dark-haired, thirtyish associate professor of psychology with hazel eyes and a smoky voice. She had written that women were much better than men at sharing themselves, and Josh wanted to prove himself different enough for her to invite over for a sharing weekend.

Like a shrink, Laurel offered no comments on the speech, but asked questions. "Why has your mother been visiting the hospital all these years week in, week out?"

"It's her nature."

"Never asked why?"

"Why do you counsel runaways at that teen shelter in Times Square?"

"We're talking about your mother, not me."

"Well, she's a genuinely good person. A *practitioner* of good."

"Interesting. There's this project of mine, to determine the *source* of goodness. You see, by now everyone knows, more or less, what makes evildoers tick. But nobody knows what generates altruism. One of the great unsolved mysteries of science."

"*Nobody* knows?"

"Oh, there are theories aplenty to account for altruism. A sublimated form of egoism. Repression rechanneled. Cultural hypocrisy. Original sin in reverse. The latest theory sees altruism as acts performed *unwittingly* for the survival of the species. Plenty of witless theories like that. So the more I've studied neurotics, psychopaths, sociopaths, the more convinced I've become that what's needed is a study of benevolence."

Laurel wanted to write a book about the *other* side of the Holocaust. The Righteous Gentiles, albeit few in number, who risked their lives to save Jews from the Nazis and their collaborators. "Such a study is needed to restore people's faith in the possibility of the good. Without that faith, without good human beings to emulate, evil will surely eclipse goodness one day. Only by fathoming good people can we create a new moral ambience in which to raise children, transmit goodness to future generations."

But . . . "What about my *speech*, Laurel?"

"Oh, that. Well-written. But as a speech, not so hot. Yours is an *essay*, and an essay is directed at. . . ." She tapped her forehead. "Not . . ." She touched her softly contoured left breast, nestled inside a rosy pink angora sweater.

"Any suggestions how to round it out, make it more felt?"

"Scrap it."

"Scrap it?"

A nod of the head dislodged an auburn wave which tumbled over her high forehead. "Do as the man said. Let your mother's actions and motivations speak for you. After all, a speaker you're not. So just be yourself."

Josh wanted to call the whole thing off. But the dinner was already heavily advertised, and in a fit of optimism Aaron had brought 300 copies of *Captain O Captain* to distribute gratis to imagined guests. (As for being himself, Debbie said that was impossible on short notice. "Know how long it takes an actor to learn how to act natural? Forever.") He appended the P.R. man's concluding pitch to index cards of new material and finally stopped fussing. No career was to be made out of one speech that no New Yorker would hear nor Bostonian remember.

Then, wonder of wonders, *Captain O Captain* made the best seller lists! (Which instantly changed Josh's disdain for the kinds of books that became bestsellers and of the lowbrows who bought them.) Word of mouth, apparently, did it. Josh himself did not discount the power of prayer for revenge on the forty-nine publishers and agents who had rejected his novel, several of whom soon asked for his next novel, ". . . if it's half as wonderful as your first." Now, women previously scheduled for hairwashing whenever Josh wanted a date were offering to wash *his* hair.

Not Laurel Rabin, however, who quoted Alfred Lord Tennyson. "Man dreams of fame while woman wakes to love."

" 'Whoso loves believes the impossible.' Elizabeth Barrett Browning." Case closed. (Or was it?)

Mom was invited to the fundraiser, possibly because Aaron needed a third for dinner; how many Bostonians would pay good money to have their pockets picked? In any event, the 300 copies of

Captain O Captain couldn't be returned, Josh having deliberately autographed them. Aaron also arranged a chauffeured ride from Manhattan. According to Sandra, the big question was, What would Mom wear?

Not the black nightgown with the white ruffle, not in Boston. Nor a beaded dress Sandra bought at Saks. At Loehmann's Mom picked up a lovely form-fitting gown of white wool with long sleeves and gold embroidery around the neckline. but Josh's heart sank when he cut off the designer label and price tag. Reduced, the gown cost exactly $13.95. And no jewelry?

"My most valuable pieces of silver are Sabbath candlesticks," Mom said. "Want me to wear those?"

The chauffeur had taken ill. There was the shuttle flight to Boston, but Mrs. Pomerance insisted on driving back to Boston by herself. That, Josh couldn't allow, for the woman had just been discharged from Memorial Sloan-Kettering Cancer Center.

Slight, bejeweled and bewigged, with a sallow complexion, Mrs. Pomerance was very gracious. "You're so pretty," she told Mom. "And such a beautiful gown."

"So are you," Mom replied. "And what a car. You could entertain in it."

Josh stuck the two women in the back of the stretch limo to keep each other company while he concentrated on withstanding anxiety attacks. The nerve of him to appeal for millions of dollars for a nonexistent hospital, when it had taken him four years to land a thousand dollar advance for a book already written. Even longer as a teenager to get his allowance raised by his own flesh and blood.

Unfortunately, no mishap prevented the car from reaching the Boston hotel, where there were over 400 people in attendance. So Josh's flop would be on a *gigantic* scale. The word of mouth *epidemic*. How did candidates for public office speak continuously in public? Only by possessing King Kong-size egos and lacking all imagination.

After a photo session, he heard people talking of a mysterious elegant beauty in white who wore no jewelry. "She doesn't need any," someone remarked. "That woman has radiance."

Josh, better after overdosing on antacids, found Mrs. Pomerance holding Mom's hand. Soon they were joined by Mrs. Kogan, a pretty, friendly, vivacious woman with blue eyes and a chirping voice, who handed them drinks. "Sorry they didn't have any beer, Mrs. Trilling. Will ginger ale do?"

(*Beer?* The bartender must still be laughing. And telling the world.)

When Mom excused herself to go to the ladies room and Mrs. Kogan went along to show the way, Mrs. Pomerance mentioned switching from a table up front to Mom's in the back. Thanking her, Josh said it was unnecessary. Mrs. Kogan would be looking after his mother.

Mrs. Pomerance shook her head. "You don't understand. It's for *my* benefit. Almost a year now I've been undergoing chemotherapy and radiation. But after four hours in the car with your mother, tonight I feel really good for the first time in ages. Speaking with her, I felt as if I were—what can I tell you?—being healed."

Moments later, dinner was announced, and Josh was surprised to see Mom in the midst of the committeemen with him. Even more surprised she'd been invited to sit on the dais.

Some people had complained of Aaron's pressuring them to attend the dinner, one committee member told Josh. "Me, I think everyone here should kiss his feet. My father has Alzheimer's."

A string quartet accompanied the group's entry into the ballroom, and an M.C. introduced everyone at the head table but Mom, whose name wasn't on his list. That added to the mystery. Too famous to need an introduction?

There was the meal to get through. Why weren't afterdinner speeches delivered beforehand, so the condemned could eat a hearty meal later on (assuming there was an afterlife)? Clearly, *The Book of Lists* had it right: people's second greatest fear was fear of death; their greatest fear, public speaking.

After countless words of welcome by Aaron and several others, during which Josh drank three glasses of water, his lips having turned to parchment, tongue to sand paper, throat to the Sahara, he was introduced. So Josh assumed after the last speaker turned expectantly toward him, saying, "Nu, *boychik?*" Marching to the podium like a man seemed the appropriate response.

God! Trained on him like rifles of a firing squad were a thousand eyes. It had never occurred to Josh, preparing his talk, the audience would be *watching* him talk. Somehow, he'd thought of them as all *ears*. Would it sound silly to ask everyone there to lower his or her gaze?

"Before I start to speak, I'd like to *say* something," Josh ad libbed, and the audience tittered. "I am not a public speaker. My friends said I should tell you that right away, before you discovered it for yourselves."

Chuckles from the crowd, which relaxed him. Eyes fixed on Mrs. Pomerance, at her front table, Josh directed his words at her and, as she smiled in encouragement, related to this woman how he first became aware there was such a thing as a chronic diseases hospital. Of its pitiable patients, forlorn, incapacitated, desolate. Of Mom on her weekly rounds, running errands, singing to the patients, touching, always touching them. Of the word most often heard, said by visitors to their mothers, whispered by mothers themselves after the visitors' departure. *Mama.* Of the second word most often uttered, usually in supplication, sometimes cursed. *God.*

By then, Josh, who hadn't referred to his index cards on the lectern, was able to shift his gaze to others, which he hazarded only at the end of a sentence. Practically no coughing, a good sign, and nobody signaled for more coffee as, choking up, he recounted his own hospital experiences. People were actually *listening!*

Wise to quit before they tuned out. Citing the grievous absence of a chronic diseases hospital in Boston, one of America's great medical centers, Josh pushed aside his index cards to look at the ghostwritten appeal. And saw nothing from the height of 6′2″ but a *blur*. The lectern, adjusted for speakers all much shorter than Josh, was too far away to decipher there what had been perfectly clear when held in hand while practicing at home. Unless hoisted now with shaking fingers. Slowly bending his knees, Josh scrunched down, but too rattled to read the manuscript with ease, had to improvise a conclusion.

In one minute he would lose his audience. He *knew* it. His halting delivery was that of someone who didn't know where his next phrase was coming from. Like an anchorman with a Teleprompter on the blink.

The audience was no longer scrutinizing him. First one, then another, then more and more were looking off to the side. Far more distressing than those stares at the start was seeing them now directed *away* from him. Individuals, nudging companions, were pointing somewhere to Josh's right. What the hell was going on! Still talking, he followed the audience's gaze down the length of the dais all the way to Mom.

Erect as ever, she was sitting with her everpresent smile, now frozen to that warm face, as down her cheeks rolled tear after tear, the effect that of a rain shower on a sunny day. Evidently experiencing flashbacks to the incurables, she was digging a knife blade into the palm of her left hand to stem the flow of tears. People were still listening to him, or maybe they weren't—hard to tell—but all of them were watching her.

Quickly, Josh concluded: "Just remember this: money can be the root of all good. Contributions of yours will build *your* hospital. Come, share the dream. In a world of destruction and disease, this is your golden opportunity to be healers."

On the shuttle flight back to New York, Josh told his mother, "Know something? I think you saved my *tuches*."

Mom beamed. "And what shall I say about *you?*" she said, eyes aglow. "I don't have enough words for someone who worked a miracle."

First on his feet following the talk was Aaron, who tendered $100,000. Pledges totaled $892,000. (Including the $750 honorarium that Josh was returning.) A magnificent tribute to the assembled's faith in the New England Sholom Hospital. Its acronym, NES, noted the rabbi in the closing benediction, was the Hebrew word for *miracle*.

15

MANY of Sandra's friends were seeing psychiatrists aggressively indifferent to salvaging marriages, concentrating on "self-actualization," what was best for themselves as *individuals*. In Sandra's book, jargon for selfishness. The closest she herself had come to marital counseling was via a couple of neighbors, a dashing airline pilot and his sultry, voluptuous wife, a former stewardess who favored a heavy, almost fetid perfume. Because, Kate explained, of the way it combined with her body's chemistry, as unique as a fingerprint. (But no fingerprint ever gave Sandra a headache.)

Much to everyone's embarrassment, Kate often made cracks in front of company about her husband's sex drive. The day after another such put down—"no lift-off to his libido, flaps always down"—Victor stopped by to ask Sandra to get his wife to do him an intimate favor.

"Pave?" (That made more sense than what Sandra thought she'd heard.)"

"*Bathe.*" Eyes averted. "Kate takes a bath once a month, then bitches to one and all I won't come near. You've heard her, Sandra. And smelled her too. It's like driving into a cesspool, making love to that woman."

Involve herself? No way. But the next time Kate spoke at unbearable length of her sexless union, in the beauty parlor under an adjoining hair dryer, Sandra said what turned Charlie on was bath oil, reason for her to bathe every single day of the week. As did he.

Kate reacted with shock. "Are you two *mad?* Ravaging a woman's most alluring organ and man's biggest."

"*What* is woman's most alluring organ? Did you say man's *biggest?*" Sandra asked, mystified, just as the hair dryers went off.

Everyone in the shop leaned forward to catch the reply.

"Skin, silly. Too much bathing shrivels it all up like a prune. Well, look at yourself, Sandra. How do you think I keep myself so soft and supple and seductive? So now you know my beauty secret. Lots of no soap and less water."

Kate's skin did indeed look good, with the sheen that an overripe fruit develops just before turning rotten. But what, Sandra asked, was Kate saving her skin *for?* A brief, soft-spoken lecture on personal hygiene fell, like all unsolicited advice, on deaf ears—in this case, unwashed too. Soon, the neighbors turned to a marriage counselor. He, failing to modify Kate's obsession, urged a variation of the French option—Victor's stuffing wads of cotton saturated with perfume up his nose.

"Up *yours,*" retorted Victor. Not long afterwards, the couple divorced.

For six months nobody dated Kate a second time. But after borrowing a bottle of bath oil from Sandra, who urged its use even when the moon was not full, within the year Kate married. Only to resume nonbathing, and divorcing. At which time Sandra washed her hands of Kate.

Now, Sandra had gotten Charlie to go along for counseling, though she herself could never understand why any twosome would turn itself into a *ménage à trois.* Why couldn't a couple, intimate for decades, simply talk to each other without a kibitzer at hand? Was opening up one's mouth or a beloved's so difficult it needed a third party to pry it open?

Mom, after Dad's death, had profited enormously from three months of therapy, emerging energized and vibrant and young in attitude, demeanor, appearance. Her intensive therapy—some eight hours per week—had been conducted by those who knew her and the entire familial context very well, Sandra and Josh. Impossible for children, friends and professionals argued, devoid of the necessary objectivity, to serve as a parent's therapist. Nevertheless, it worked. Because of Mom's openness and receptivity. After all those years of holding everything in, she divulged all, and rejected no hypothesis. Mom would say, "I don't know. Seems unlikely. But let me mull that over." Now, who knew how many weekly fifty-minute sessions it would take for a foreign marriage counselor to sort out Sandra's claims and Charlie's counterclaims from the truth? (At a surprise Golden Wedding Anniversary party Sandra's friends threw their parents, the mother exclaimed, "Why a *party?* I didn't have *one* good day with your father!" And was told, "Ssh, Mama, sssh. Just enjoy, celebrate.")

They were not dealing here in *truth* so much as in *perceptions*, said the M.C., whose watchword was "evenhandedness." He'd be focusing neither on Sandra nor on Charlie but on their *relationship*, to which each partner had contributed *equally*.

(Yeah, sure, nobody was all black and white, but penguinlike, and Victor had contributed equally to his divorce by not drowning Kate or himself in Chanel No. 5.)

When Sandra traced her distancing herself emotionally from Charlie to his taking on loathsome defendants, the M.C. commented, "That's only a *symptom*. You wouldn't weed your garden from the ground *up*, would you? Let's unearth the root *cause*, shall we?"

But Charlie's symptom *was* the disease afflicting her marriage. Who needed *insight?* Charlie just should alter his disgustingly immoral behavior. Why didn't the M.C. take Sandra's word?

"*No* marriage breaks up on account of overhanging high-minded moral *principles*. They founder on underlying *emotions*."

Charlie, for his part, said nothing. During the first few sessions he who never shut up in a courtroom or office sat mute. Which left all the talking up to Sandra who, paying $75 per, wanted her money's worth. Costing at least $12.50 per was the time it took the

M.C. to fumble for cigarettes and light up and puff away between pronouncements, *all on her time*. But mention of that cost an additional $30, while he analyzed her hostile reaction. To add insult to robbery, the M.C. handed over a monograph entitled, "The Compulsive Talker Wife and the Silent Husband: Cause and Effect?" So during the following meetings, Sandra held her tongue while hundreds of dollars were flushed from the Heller bank account into the M.C.'s during silences so deep they could hear each other's stomach rumble.

Finally, Charlie spoke up. "My wife," he said. "She doesn't understand me, she under*mines* me."

(No wonder he'd been so still. Adam too had taken his troubles like a man, blaming them all on his wife.) "Charlie dear," Sandra responded. "I don't *want* to understand you. I just want you to *change*."

"If you loved me, Sandra, you'd prove it by accepting me in toto—"

She cut in. "Charlie, your own parents never loved you in toto. Why should I? *Unless—*"

"That's right, hold it over me that you have a loving mother—"

"It would make you happier if I had a hating mother?"

"A mother you love more than you love me."

"Well, Mom *behaves* lovably."

"The hell with your mother! All that greenhorn's fault you're loaded to the gills with scruples!"

"Ah, that's *good. Very* good!" exclaimed the M.C. "Now, at long last we are starting to make *progress*." The fifty minutes being up, he immediately ended the session.

Nor was Charlie the only one not to appreciate Mom. There was the social worker at the local senior citizen center. Mom signed up for an art class, but the free lunch program made her feel like a charity case. After donating some money, she ate there several weeks, then stopped. The social worker in charge was "not a nice person"—the worst thing Mom ever said about anyone. So to smooth things over, Sandra went to the center.

"You're the daughter of *that* woman?" exclaimed Mrs. Bloomengarten, who, in her size twenty, ketchup-stained, black and blue muumuu, looked like a large bruise. Her unevenly cut, home-colored apricot hair would on a teenager have passed for a punk hairdo. "Difficult woman. So troublesome."

Difficult? Troublesome?

"She tried to boss me around! Walks in here, a perfect nobody, tries to take over. Telling me, a trained social worker with a master's degree and two and a half decades of experience, I should provide mental stimulation—for people who can't even remember their own addresses. Call my boys and girls not by their first names—but mister and missus, if you please. Get them involved, she says. How, *romantically?* Have them help others. People who can't even help themselves! Visit shut-ins, bring them meals. Call them up for chats."

"She does that herself."

"Too much mayonnaise in the egg salad, cholesterol everywhere. Just because her highness watches her weight. Some of us have an entirely different bone structure, she doesn't want to recognize."

"Mom only meant—"

"Coming in here every day dressed to the nines, showing off her figure in fancy expensive clothes. How do you think that makes people here feel?"

A woman who wore a twelve-dollar nightgown to the Captain's Ball and an evening gown that cost $13.95? "Nothing of hers costs more than twenty-five dollars. At discount stores."

Mrs. Bloomengarten snapped, "Don't tell *me* what they cost. Don't *I* buy clothes? Every day your mother comes in here looking ready to party. What right does she have to make everyone here feel shabby and unkempt?"

The funny thing was that Mom wouldn't wear her new clothes to the chronic diseases hospital, for fear the patients might resent them. Sandra had to convince her that nobody there would begrudge her. Sure enough, pleased by the new finery and trips abroad, they urged her again and again to talk about them. "You are our eyes and ears and legs," said the paraplegic. "Our vicarious life. Go, live."

Mrs. Bloomengarten was saying, ". . . looking down her nose at my choice of reading matter, because she's an intellectual. Such arrogance! Flaunting your brother's book."

Intellectual?

"What's more, I don't give a damn if you and Henry Kissinger *are* cousins."

Henry Kissinger?

"You seem surprised. Was your mother lying?"

"Don't be silly. Well, Cousin Henry told us never to mention our relationship. Security reasons . . ."

An elderly couple interrupted with a request. "The cheesecake was so creamy, Mrs. Bloomengarten. Can we maybe have seconds? We'd be ever so grateful."

The social worker smiled expansively. "Of course, Abie. Because all week long you and Sadie have been such a good boy and good girl. Here, I'll give you a note for Cookie." After they left, "See how well-behaved those two are? My pet people. And they look up to me like God. Not like highfalutin' Hannah."

In truth, Mrs. Bloomengarten was *not* a nice slattern. Still, did Mom put down her taste in literature?

"I should pick up the *National Enquirer?*"

What was this about Henry Kissinger?

"I met his aunt and uncle in Israel. Wonderful traditional Jews. Very upset a nephew of theirs had married a gentile."

Where did Mrs. Bloomengarten get the idea . . .?

"She was reading the *National Enquirer*. Seeing Kissinger's picture, I said his family was very lovely, my kind of observant people. With backgrounds so similar, we could be *mishpocha*. But that Mrs. Bloomengarten doesn't listen. Never holds conversations, only audiences."

Lunch at the center was clearly out. But art class stayed in, though considering them amateurish, Mom wouldn't show her sketches. And after joining a nearby synagogue, she signed up for sisterhood and adult education classes. Got season tickets to the Met, City Opera, American Ballet Theater, the Philharmonic. Frequented museums, bought art books. Every evening when Sandra phoned to ask about that day's meeting, matinee, class, museum, whatever, Mom's reply was invariably the same.

"You know me, dear. I *always* have a good time. *Wherever* I go."

Not bad for a seventy-year-old. Theories propounded by psychoanalysts led one to expect an exchange of roles as Mom aged, with

Sandra playing the parent. Never happened. While she was no longer dependent on Mom, even heading for fifty Sandra still could use nurturing.

What did change was their conversations. Just as Sandra had relived childhood's wonder through Zack and Debbie, she was now experiencing through Mom's eyes art and ballet and opera, and the joys of extremely late middle age. That made Sandra recast her image of Mom, who was evidently something in *addition* to a mother.

In a few months Mom was graduated to oils. Were her sketches that good? She didn't think so. "My teacher's standards are lower than mine." Her first oils, copies of picture post cards, were so good, Sandra wondered how much the art teacher had participated. The more accomplished the new paintings, the more Sandra's doubts grew. So one Sunday she brought over a photograph of a Gaughin to copy. But Mom refused because the no-goodnik had deserted his wife and children to go off to the South Seas to make whoopee.

"Monet, on the other hand, was a mensch. Did you know he came to the support of Captain Dreyfus?"

Taking out a book on French Impressionists, Mom opened to Monet's *Tulip Field* and copied it. The result was astonishing, after just a few hours. All these years, where had this talent been hiding? Why hadn't anyone known of it? Well, she used to draw, when young, but the only art that interested the family was singing, her cousin Simon's.

The art teacher confirmed Mom was indeed talented, with nothing more to learn at the center. Should enroll in a professional art school. Sandra signed her up.

Painting, Mom forgot everything—bad news on TV, arthritis, worries, lunch, sometimes dinner. There was so much to learn—perspective, mixing colors, different strokes and brushes, contrast, a new vocabulary. Three afternoons a week nothing deterred her from transporting easel, paint box and canvases to West 57th Street in a wagon, covered in rainy weather with a shower curtain, herself in zero weather with extra sweaters and leg warmers and lined boots. Neighbors called her as reliable as the U.S. mail.

About her new love everything delighted Mom except washing her brushes for hours in turpentine—and the artist's model, a tall, engaging black man in his early fifties with a leonine head, graying hair and gracefully proportioned body. His posing in the nude troubled her. Not because of prudishness, which only took her several months to subdue. She felt that Rodney, supplementing his income with this second job, was being taken advantage of and demeaning himself. Clothed people observing naked ones reminded her of Nazi concentration camps, whose first step in dehumanizing prisoners was stripping them of all attire and dignity. Mom's fellow artists scoffed at that thought, but would any of *them* pose in the nude? Not one said yes.

She contacted several prospective employers, and disregarding Sandra's warning not to get involved, invited Rodney out to supper one evening. But before submitting the list of contacts, she inquired about his family.

Happily married for twenty-seven years, Rodney had four fine children, two college graduates. No one knew about his posing in the nude; it would have given his very proper wife apoplexy. No telling his friends either, for fear his secret would get out. Then, just as Mom opened her purse for the list of jobs Rodney could tell the whole world about, he continued,

"I like what I do. Not to show off my well-built body, which would make me just a flasher. I'm *good* at my job. Hard to keep perfectly still for twenty-five minutes at a time. I'm a big help to artists just starting out. When I think of so much money—tuition, canvas, paints—all invested in Rodney! All over this city you can see sketches and paintings of yours truly. Why, I must be the most famous unknown in all of New York. Yes, I do take pride in my work."

Parting, he thanked Mom profusely. "I've been posing for some twenty years now. Been studied so closely, people here know my body parts better than my wife does, or I myself. But this is the first time someone's taken me out for a swell dinner."

Sandra asked about the list of contacts. Was Rodney equally appreciative of that?

"Changed my mind about giving it to him. I'll stick to forging Van Goghs."

Mom loved his early Paris paintings. Renoir also became a favorite, for his persevering to paint despite being wheelchair-bound in his later years and fingers crippled by rheumatoid arthritis. *The pain passes*, he declared, strapping brushes to his hands, *the beauty remains.*

"Renoir's message was very simple," she noted. "It was joy."

Soon Mom was creating originals, which awed her as much as Sandra. "Did I really paint that?" she'd say. "No, couldn't have been *me*. Maybe *through* me." Her favorite subjects were landscapes like those of Galicia's countryside, her Vitebsk. Several portraits too, one of Rouault's *Jesus.* ("Just about everything he taught was Jewish. You can't hold Jesus responsible for that fellow who commercialized him, what's his name, Paul.") Another, an original called *Past Present Future*, showed three men standing before the Ark reading from a Torah scroll—one elderly, the second middle-aged, the third young. "I wanted to name it *Transmission*," she said with a smile. "But I was afraid people would ask if it was automatic or manual."

Yes, Mom was having a ball. "Know something?" Sandra said. "Everyone envies me for having you for a mother."

"To tell the truth, *I* envy me. Yes, this baby's come a long way."

At her synagogue Mom made a suggestion nobody thought troublesome. After Mom volunteered to set it up, it was even acted upon. Every Thursday congregants brought in food, which was donated the following day to indigent neighbors of all faiths. A corps of volunteers signed up to help, among whom Mom made some nice friends. Sandra had hoped for a male friend or two. Actually, a suitor, now that she'd come around to acknowledging Mom's sexuality. Whenever the matter was broached, however, Mom would say she'd had her shot at matrimony; now it was Josh's turn to play Russian roulette.

As for Sandra's marriage, to fake more of an interest in Charlie, every other night of the week Sandra now served gourmet meals, courtesy of Best's Kept Secrets. That made Charlie feel loved, all the while he was chewing and swallowing and digesting. But what about quid pro quo? Was it asking too much of that mouthpiece for undesirables to represent people Sandra wouldn't be embarrassed to death being seen with in public?

"Your brother's all over radio and TV these days," Charlie snapped. "Have you asked *him* to drop out of sight?"

"In your case, Charlie, out of sight would be a giant step forward."

"You want a nonentity for a husband? Someone nobody in the world knows is alive and kicking?"

"*I'd* know, Charlie. You don't have to scale the heights for me. Just climb out of the gutter."

When Town Hall invited him to participate in a symposium on proposed legislation to freeze a defendant's assets that may have been amassed illegally, then confiscate them after conviction, Sandra accompanied Charlie there. Though dressed in a dapper suit she had bought him for the occasion, he didn't let her read his speech beforehand. So Sandra could only pray nothing would be said to shame her and their children and future generations. Like, "Give me money or my client death."

Speaking in favor of the proposal, a congressman argued, "At issue is whether lawyers should benefit from the ill-gotten monies of criminals and murderers. In essence, become their legal partners in crime." The proposed law would provide defendants with able, court-appointed counsel paid for by the Government.

Charlie, the second speaker, strode to center stage and pounded hard enough to resuscitate any podium that was suffering cardiac arrest. "Such a law would shake the very foundations of our criminal justice system! No experienced lawyer will take on a defendant if, in the event of a conviction, the Government can appropriate all legal fees paid. Any such law that deprives defendants of the right to counsel *of their choice* is ipso facto unconstitutional. What happens to the American presumption of innocence?"

During the question and answer period, Sandra felt compelled to disassociate herself from Charlie's views by getting up to say, "Yes, I have a question. Is there such a thing as legal *ethics?* Is that ever taught in law schools? You think an accused murderer, say, who is the beneficiary of the victim's life insurance, should be able to use the proceeds of the insurance policy to pay legal fees? Or a narcotics trafficker use drug money? Or a bank robber stolen money? Why should financially successful criminals merit special constitutional protection? *That,*" she concluded, to a big round of applause and some laughter, "is my question."

Charlie replied, to far more laughter than applause, "Does each question of yours, *Ms.,* always come in a dozen parts?"

The ride home was long and silent. Sandra wasn't sure what was troubling Charlie the most. But if things didn't change between them very soon, who'd care any longer what disturbed that nudnik?

At the door to their house, Charlie suddenly turned on her and shouted loud enough for all the neighbors to hear, "What do you want, Sandra? What is it you want? Well, you can't have them! They're mine, *both* of them."

"You think I want to take the *children* away from you?"

"Who's talking about children?"

"Oh, *them*. Charlie, you can pickle them. It's tough enough being a woman."

Forty dollars of their next counseling session was expended on his blow-by-blow account of the symposium, after which the M.C. repeated Charlie's question, "What is it you *want*, Sandra? We're searching here for *cause*."

By way of answer she drew from her pocketbook a diary of the year Charlie had started taking on clients guilty as hell. The M.C. looked it over—another thirty dollars' worth—then exclaimed, "*Well, well!* Documentation of your wife's gradual disaffection, the shadier the clients you accepted. All right for me to show this to Charlie?"

Sandra nodded.

"Yessir, looks to me like the *smoking gun*. Yes, the *breakthrough* we're all looking for!"

Another long and silent ride home—this time without any screaming at the door. Charlie took the diary into his study and when he emerged, his eyes were puffy. "This is the way you've felt about me, Sandra? All this love and regard while I was an assistant D.A.?"

"Yes, Charlie."

"But I was making *peanuts!*"

"No accounting for tastes. There are those who are partial to peanuts. Monkeys, for example."

"Why didn't you ever *say* so before? You think they can be revived? The feelings expressed here."

"Maybe. Love never dies. Though it can be asphyxiated."

"This very appealing man in your diary. Think *he* can be resurrected?"

"Well, it's happened before. Look at Jesus—"

{208}

Charlie did something then that came harder to him than crying. He laughed out loud.

A *start!* If Sandra lived to be a hundred and twenty, she would never understand why neither Charlie nor the M.C. believed her all those months she spoke those very same words again and again. Yet, both now swallowed whole the diary she had forged.

16

*I*N the fall of 1976 Miriam died, the two of her: the beautiful tomboy and the pitiable stroke victim. For the one Hannah grieved. For the other she was relieved—no more torment. Such a pity that death had taken her piecemeal, not in one gulp.

God was not to blame, however. One thing Hannah reaffirmed from her long association with the chronic diseases hospital: in no way was He all-powerful as advertised. No deity, certainly not the one Hannah worshiped, would allow suffering like Miriam's and her ward companions'. Like them, God Himself probably needed help in alleviating pain and tragedy, perhaps even to ward off despair of His own.

Thoughts of the New England Sholom Hospital afforded some consolation. Aaron Kogan had written Josh: "You have provided the inspiration to make my vision of a chronic disease and rehabilitation hospital a reality . . ." Josh, in turn, had been inspired by Miriam.

Funeral arrangements were made by Hannah's big brother Ben, who regarded himself as the family patriarch by virtue of his age, sage by virtue of his million dollars, and pious by virtue of hobnobbing with ultra-Orthodox rabbis. Forty years before, he hosted the wedding for a younger sister at his fancy kosher restaurant (a restaurant financed in part by a loan from Rupert and whose first waitress, unpaid, was Hannah). The officiating rabbi, a friend of Ben's, spoke at stupefying length not about the bride and groom or their marriage, but about Ben and his generosity in hosting the affair for his poor relation, Little Orphan Annie to Ben's hairy Daddy Warbucks. Years later, at Papa's funeral, the same rabbi delivered a eulogy that mentioned the deceased only in the last paragraph. The rest was a tribute to Ben, a substantial contributor to his ultra-Orthodox yeshiva. (Afterwards, Josh remarked, "It's as if that rabbi were extolling Grandpa's germ plasm, and not even all of it. Just one ejaculate.")

Because Rabbi Belzer had known Miriam before misfortune struck, Hannah wanted him to officiate. But he was out of town. Her own rabbi from Brooklyn, president of the New York Board of Rabbis, was vetoed by Ben for being a Conservative Jew. (As if Jews didn't have enough enemies. Some had to manufacture additional ones out of their very own. Like Israel's perennial controversy over "who's a Jew?" Hannah would have settled it once and for all by legislating, à la Abbott & Costello, that Who is indeed a Jew. Period.) To avoid a quarrel, Hannah told her brother to bring a rabbi other than his pal. "Someone *nice*."

Apparently, someone nice was unavailable. Ben showed up at the funeral chapel with no rabbi at all. "*I* will officiate," he announced.

"*You* officiate? You think yourself ordained by money?"

"You don't know Jewish law, my dear sister. Doesn't require a rabbi at a funeral. And I know all the prayers."

"Prayers, yes. What you never knew, Ben, was to visit Miriam."

"It would upset me terribly, seeing Miriam crippled like that. Everyone knows about my sensitive nature. But I'll make her one swell eulogy now, you'll see."

"Over my dead body, Ben." (Two eulogies were more than enough for a man still living.)

"What's that?"

"You can officiate at your own funeral, not Miriam's."

"Such talk! I'm shocked, Hannah, really surprised. But maybe I shouldn't be. Funeral drive you crazy, don't they? At Papa's you got hysterical, and at Rupert's you took a hike."

"*Funerals* don't drive me crazy. *People* do." (Ben had pressured Miriam into marrying a man she disliked, after which he ignored her for the rest of her life. First for being poor, then for being hapless.) "Find someplace *else* to shine, Ben."

"The funeral starts in twenty minutes, Hannah. If I don't officiate, who will? You?"

She recalled being excluded from her mother's burial because of her chromosomes. "Thank you so much for the idea."

Ben's eyes narrowed in disdain. "You're a *woman*."

"I will officiate, and that's that."

Sandra and Josh changed her mind. The strain might be too much, the proceedings spoiled. To everyone's surprise, including his own, Josh volunteered. He'd use the section in his New England Sholom talk about Miriam.

"Fine. Just right, Josh. Only, use your description of Miriam *before* her stroke. The good soul she was. And not a word about me, you hear? Only that I loved her very much, as did everyone else"—Hannah's voice cracked—"and always will."

Everyone was astonished to see Josh step up to the pulpit. (No rabbi? Was there a rabbi strike? Ben hadn't called one? Unbelievable!) Unlike too many eulogies, which seemed written and delivered by an announcer unfamiliar with the product, Josh's words came from the heart in a voice filled with emotion. So afterwards, lots of relatives placed orders with Josh to host their farewells too, Hannah among them.

He made a face.

"You think it goes on forever, life?" she said. "Every song has its end."

"Some songs last and last. Classics."

"Songs, yes. But composers? Still, if their melodies linger on, that's more than enough."

Now Hannah couldn't help thinking of it. No problem, death; it was the ticket of admission to the World-to-Come. But dying. How to get there from here with dignity unimpaired and no drawn-out leavetaking such as Miriam's that would burden the family? If only one could simply disappear one day in a cloud of dust, like the Lone Ranger.

Sitting *shiva* at Sandra's, she was asked several times if Sheldon should be summoned. No, she said. Sandra and Josh were very solicitous, asking day and night what they could do. Darling Debbie, a Barnard junior, still was intent on a career in the theater. Dynamic Zack, law student, talked deals. Even Charlie was less overbearing. Having sworn off high-profile criminal defendants, he was now directing his zeal at the local temple, sights set on becoming president. ("Well," said Sandra, "if they could send a man to the moon.") Hannah envisioned Charlie's leading a takeover of all neighboring synagogues and going on TV to proclaim himself Pharaoh.

Leo came with a date, a plump ash blonde. (When very young and very broke, Josh sometimes took a girl to the predinner smorgasbord at a stranger's wedding or bar mitzvah reception. But never to a *shiva*, which should go down in *The Guinness Book of World Records* as the cheapest date in history.)

It astonished Leo that Hannah had no inkling who his companion was. "My first lady love. I've told you about Laraine."

"Leo dearest," said the woman sweetly. "I'm *Eleanor*."

"Of course," he said. "We've decided on a big wedding. Well, why not? Honeymoon hotel with heart-shaped hot tubs. See what you're missing, Hannah?"

Much to Hannah's surprise, Rabbi Belzer came. Forgetting the impropriety of welcoming callers to *shiva*, she scrambled up from the low wooden stool to greet him. The rabbi looked remarkably unchanged, though almost a quarter of a century had passed since he'd left Brooklyn to lead one of Manhattan's largest Orthodox congregations. A dozen pounds heavier, hair and moustache only partially gray, face unlined, voice young, clever brown eyes shining. The biggest difference was his woolen suit, that of a British prime minister, which weighed more than the entire wardrobe he'd brought with him from Galicia.

"*Shiva* is no time to talk philosophy," the D.D. and Ph.D. in comparative literature began. "Look what I found, Hannah." He handed over a faded snapshot from the twenties.

She gasped to see the Brody family, Miriam among them. So beautiful, slim, carefree, vibrant.

"I can visualize your wedding now, Hannah. Our youth."

"The past," she said, "is a faraway country. Youth its capital."

"Not that far removed. Even under these sad circumstances, you're looking good, Hannah. Marriage must have agreed with you. Shows in your face."

A fraction of a moment's hesitation. "Yes."

After a like pause, "I'm pleased."

Quickly, "I was happily married for a good thirty-three years."

"Lucky. I imagine your father told you about my own marriage."

She shook her head.

"No? Really? Good."

As newcomers arrived, Hannah asked to see the rabbi in private outside. In the backyard, whose crisp autumn air Miriam would never again feel nipping at her skin, there were trees like those she loved to climb in Galicia, jumping like a boy from branch to branch. After Mother's death, she never climbed another tree. Childhood, Miriam said, had ended.

Hannah turned to the rabbi. "Why haven't you remarried?" Then, after unintentionally startling Rabbi Belzer, came the belated explanation. Her brief engagement to Sheldon, the children's objections, her second thoughts, their guilt feelings, entirely baseless. "Your reason, Rabbi, when I tell my children, will relieve them."

"My reason? Let me see now." He walked over to a tree and tore off a leaf turned to flame. "I'm a believer, of course. In God," he said, studying it. "About romantic love, however, I'm an agnostic. It demands a tremendous imagination, this bestowal of the highest value on another frail human being. When that love frequently turns into naked politics, an exercise in power plays. Nietzsche characterized romantic love as 'the most ingenuous expression of egoism parading as its opposite.' "

Hannah could hardly transmit comments she didn't quite fathom. "Isn't it a great mitzvah to marry?"

"Yes. Of course. Certainly. To marry—once. To have children—twice. Both obligations I fulfilled. Of course, men, having more fragile egos than women, need a spouse more. But as a rabbi, I do have a congregation to shower affection on, lives to participate in. As for being the center of attention, which every man covets, I hold center stage whenever I preach. Just enough. Too much recognition, like too much money, makes one greedy. Insatiable."

"Then an unmarried life can be complete?"

"Well, mine is good, thank God. I have my health. Purpose. When you pray, you talk to God; when you study Torah, God talks to you. Answers you."

"I'm so glad for you."

After a pause, "But you asked whether my life is *complete*. Well, the truth is, nobody has lived the life he or she contemplated. Or planned. Who is so quick as to enjoy life? Still and all, when I look back from the vantage point of over three score years and ten, there seems to have been a coherence I wasn't entirely aware of. A distinct trajectory. My life does seem to have been plotted, like some novel." Wistfully, he added, "Although not by me." Then, probably grown too personal, he spoke of Josh's book. "A Jew who is not highly neurotic, an obsessive or a self-hater, is a rarity in contemporary literature. My thanks to your son for having created a happy Jew. Your influence, I suspect."

Looking back, what did Hannah see? Sometimes her life seemed to be a dream being dreamed by someone other than herself. Who? God? Well, who else was there?

Rabbi Belzer checked his wristwatch. "Have to leave now. *Ha-makom yenacheim eschem betoch she-ar aveilei Tziyon.*" He led her back to the house, pausing at the threshold. "If this encounter of ours took place in a novel, Hannah, you know how it would end, don't you?"

She shook her head.

He just smiled.

"Oh," she said. "Well, it wouldn't have worked."

"Why?"

She smiled. "Sitting apart in a segregated women's gallery. I wouldn't stand for that any more."

The rabbi chuckled.

"But what should I tell my children? About my not remarrying. Nietzsche I can't even spell."

"Let *me* tell them, Hannah. Not to fool with success. As the

{215}

Talmud says, If it ain't broke, don't fix it. Just keep up the good fight. Life. It is *very* good. But it *is* a fight."

"And the older you grow, the tougher?"

"Don't say older. Don't even *think* older. Think *wiser*. With each passing year a person gets deeper into life."

(Deeper and deeper? Until one is planted?)

"So keep on swinging, Hannah. Till that final bell."

Every night that week Sandra tucked her mother in. Excessive, such attention, but she allowed it: receiving can be a form of giving. Once, after a goodnight kiss, Sandra picked a couple of eyelashes off her mother's cheek, placed them in the palm of her left hand and held them up to Hannah's mouth.

"Make a wish, Mom. No, *two*."

Recalling all the times she had asked her children to wish on eyelashes, Hannah pursed her lips, then blew.

"No more, both gone! Tell me, Mom. What did you wish?"

She hesitated.

"Well?"

"If I tell you . . ."

"It won't come true? An old wives' tale."

"What do you think I am, a *young* wife? Well, all right. I wished for Josh to get married. I worry about his being alone, nobody to look after him. You think it's *my* fault, his being a bachelor? Maybe I was too close to him, or maybe I was too distant. Or maybe I just wasn't equidistant enough."

"Don't be silly, Mom. Josh's just slow. All that thinking. Clogs desire, retards romance. Remember, it wasn't their brainpower that made Romeo and Juliet famous. Not to worry. Josh will get married—"

"Before I—" She checked herself.

"You'll see. Now, go on. Your second wish."

She hesitated. "If I tell you . . ."

"Yes, Mom?"

"It may . . . bother you."

"Nonsense."

"Well, I wished that I would . . ."

"Go on, go on."

". . . die well."

Sandra winced. Then joked, "But nobody well dies. You know that."

"Dying, dear, is like parenting. There are no second chances. You have to carry it off the very first time."

"Oh, Mom, everyone wishes that. To carry it off well. Me, too."

"Everyone isn't as old as me, dear." Too grim for Sandra, this conversation. "No, I'm wrong. Methuselah was."

Driving her back home after *shiva*, Sandra tried to cheer Hannah: Miriam was at peace at long last. "And you don't have to visit that horrible hospital anymore, thank God. That place is enough to make anyone sick."

"What are you talking about? Abandon all my friends?"

"You're not going to continue going! I won't let you."

"Whoever fails to help the sick, it's as if he or she shed their blood. The Talmud says. Besides, what else would I do with my Tuesdays?"

Five weeks later, Hannah just had to get away for a while. It disturbed her, seeing someone else in Miriam's hospital bed. Who was that intruder? Such irrationality indicated a vacation was in order. So taking temporary leave of the patients, she went to Miami Beach.

To an oceanside hotel that called for evening gowns on Sabbath Eve and Saturday night and served three meals daily. Where a weeknight's entertainment consisted of guests, all very pleasant people, boasting to each other of *yichus*, illustrious relatives. A son who was a this, a daughter a that, a brother a big deal and, when hard put, an in-law such a big shot he was under indictment for something or other.

There Hannah also met a big philanthropist who made his wife hand-wash and iron his shirts. Another millionaire had his wife return a fifteen-dollar skirt because, he said, she wouldn't live to wear all those she already had. The women, when counseled to stand up to their husbands, were forbidden to associate anymore with "that radical Mrs. Trilling."

Just the right place for rehabilitation, kitschy Miami Beach. Though the architecture glitzy, the weather was balmy, the foliage lush, the living too easy. Lots of cultural activities. At a local Y Hannah resumed painting, the best medicine of all.

To lift her spirits also there were Josh's good friends, the Kogans, who maintained a second home in Palm Beach and invited Hannah to spend the day at their club, founded by Jews when the Protestant clubs barred them. A bellhop drove her the ninety miles north to the island with streets immaculate enough to eat off and sumptuous estates of Old World architecture and, for the poorer multimillion-aires, contemporary ranch homes and lavish condominum complexes. Lining the city's axis, Worth Avenue, were boutiques where prices resembled telephone numbers. On sale were cashmere sweaters in sixty-six colors. Quail eggs. Silken *faux* fruit. Art that responded to noise and light, some emitting sounds. Jewelry costing hundreds of thousands of dollars. Just the place for those in need of keeping up with the Rockefellers. No wonder Aaron Kogan was planning to hold that year's hospital fundraising dinner in Palm Beach.

On one side of the stately Palm Beach Country Club was the Atlantic, an antique porcelain blue, on the other an emerald green golf course, in its driveway exotic automobiles that probably ran on stocks and bonds. Apparently, Hannah knew others in Palm Beach besides the unpretentious, down-to-earth Kogans. A woman several years her senior waved, crossed the grand foyer of the club and came forward with a toothy smile.

Though unable to identify the familiar slim, handsome square-jawed brunette, Hannah returned the greeting. Why on earth couldn't she place the woman? How embarrassing! Whenever this sort of thing happened, she pretended to know the acquaintance's identity while fishing for clues. But this woman's brisk, no-nonsense air would brook no subterfuge.

Sheepishly, Hannah said, "Queen Elizabeth?"

The woman stopped short. "Been mistaken for lots of people in my time. But never for *her*."

"The *ship*. The QE2."

"Oh. No."

"Jerusalem? Is that where we've met? The King David Hotel?"

"No."

"Not Brooklyn."

"You're absolutely right. Not Brooklyn." A wave to someone behind Hannah. "Sorry. My game's waiting." Brushing by, she hurried to the entrance to embrace another sportily attired woman, loaded down with a bag of clubs. The person she'd probably been waving at all along. They left together.

Someone tapped Hannah on the shoulder. "Don't you *know* who that is?" (A corpulent seventyish brunette weighed down with heavy make-up, jewelry, muddy hair dye.)

"*Thought* I did, but . . ."

The woman snickered condescendingly. "That's Rose Kennedy. Kennedy. She's a member of our club. When the Kennedy's first bought their mansion in Palm Beach, no club but ours accepted Catholics. Once Jack became President, all the WASP clubs were after Mrs. Kennedy, of course. But she'd have none of them. Boy, some life that lucky lady has led!"

"Lucky?" With a no-goodnik husband, two children assassinated, two others killed in plane crashes, a retarded daughter. "Did you say lucky?"

The woman nodded vigorously, setting earrings, pearls and brace-lets a quiver. "Daughter of the mayor of Boston. Mother of one president of the United States. Probably of another, Teddy. Wife of the ambassador to England, who was Gloria Swanson's lover. *Fabulous* life!"

"I do hope your own life is *less* fabulous."

"Oh, I've done all right for myself. Belong to the Palm Beach Country Club, don't I? Say, you're new here, aren't you?"

"A visitor. Here to see the Kogans."

"That Elaine. Too happy with her husband. So irritating. And better watch out for that Aaron, always fundraising for Boston. Know what *I* say? Charity begins at home. Mine is New York. Park Avenue. You?"

"Also New York. The West Side."

"I'm really surprised. You look like Park Avenue."

Hannah smiled. "Well, looks can be deceiving. I lived nearly all my entire adult life in Brooklyn."

"Oh, I've heard of that."

Probably Hannah's imagination, but all of a sudden something about this woman struck her also as familiar. "Excuse me. Are you a celebrity too?"

Just then Mrs. Kogan appeared. (Such a contrast between the two women. One warm, buoyant, smiling, modest; the other cold, sullen, forbidding, pompous.) "You know Fannette Ellenbogen from New York?"

"Fanny?!"

"No, not Fanny. *Fannette.* It's *French.*"

Why was there no vestige of Fanny's one-time attractiveness? True, almost forty years had passed since that night at the Plaza. Her face and figure bloated now. But what transformed her so drastically was her expression: just plain mean. "Fannette, I'm Hannette—I mean, Hannah. Hannah Trilling."

She changed colors. *"No!* Your hair. Snow white. And you've *lost* weight."

Mrs. Kogan said, "You two *do* know each other." She graciously withdrew to let them catch up on old times. "Aaron and I will be waiting in the dining room."

The two women scrutinized each other. Seeing Rabbi Belzer, Hannah had felt alert, cheerful, rejuvenated; now she felt uneasy, depressed, old. And what did Fanny see? Feel?"

"Yes, Hannah, both of us have made it. Palm Beach!"

What had separated them? Fanny had been her one friend. "Not that it matters anymore. Happened to two other people. But we were so close, you and I. Why exclude me from your wedding?"

"Well, if you *must* know." She shrugged. "Look. My dates who you always invited over. All they talked about later on was you. Not Fanny. *Hannah.* Why I never brought Maurice around. As for my wedding. Is it so terrible for a bride to want to be the star of her own affair. Understandable, isn't it? Well? *Say* something, Hannah."

"I can't believe it!"

"You've never been jealous, Hannah?"

"I *value* people. For all sorts of qualities. Philanthropists like the Kogans I admire tremendously. But jealous?" She shook her head.

"I don't believe you. Everyone's jealous. Everyone. Look at Rupert. *He* was jealous. Of you."

"Ridiculous!"

"Oh, yeah? He was always saying everyone thought you a *malach*. Over and over again he said that."

"*Malach* means *angel*. That's a compliment."

"Not the way *he* said it. Rupert was jealous of your nature, contented disposition. He never felt fulfilled like you. Tough living with someone appreciative of every little thing and every person she meets, while you yourself are dissatisfied. And he needed you. Men resent that, needing women. Well, if you don't believe me, go, ask Rupert."

Hannah hesitated before replying. "I can't do that, Fanny."

"Oh . . . Well. Sorry. Maurice is also a goner. Of course, he was a good deal older than me. And twenty-two years of marriage was more than I bargained for. Got me my three sons, though. Millionaires, all of them. They run the business now. *My* business. You have any more children after your daughter? I remember how you wanted more."

"A wonderful boy. I'm very thankful."

"Just one boy? . . . So tell me, Hannah, what do *your* children do?"

"Do?" Sandra and her vocational guidance, Josh and the New England Sholom Hospital, each a mensch. "They feel for people, help them," Hannah said. "Give people something to smile about."

Three

17

JOSH never experienced the wonder of flesh and blood of his very own being born, growing, developing. *Captain O Captain* was the closest he had come, but to consider himself a creator would have been, to him, pretentious. When the publisher conveyed his salesmen's pleasure at escorting a writer around, becoming acquainted, Josh asked who it was they'd been shepherding. Then repeated the question until the publisher finally responded, "Didn't *you* just return from a promotion tour, you twit?"

To Josh, however, a writer was Tolstoy, Cervantes, Mann, Wilde, Homer, Sholom Aleichem, Job. None of whom, all happily dead, had to contend with the question that was never posed by interviewers, family, friends to someone still breastfeeding a newborn, "When's the *next* one due?" With *Captain O Captain* optioned to a movie producer, Josh could postpone new work while he reshaped his book into a screenplay. Alas, there were civilizations that worshipped fools, and Hollywood was one of them: the movie producer wanted the novel's plot as well as protagonist's religion altered. But, unless pressured by financial backers in New York, not his sex. So the movie was never made and Josh publicly embarrassed. But when the option lapsed, neither was his bank account augmented.

The publisher wanted Josh's two-book contract fulfilled with a novel about the Peace Corps. Informed it would entail enlisting in the Third World, where he'd be prey to diseases with no cures and facilities with no toilets, the publisher said, "Well, of course. You do want your novel to be *authentic.*" The opening section of the novel Josh subsequently wrote without benefit of publisher's fertilization was rejected, whereupon he received permission to submit it elsewhere. (Meanwhile, everyone was asking why a bestselling author didn't quit his job as magazine editor and run through his fortune. Go, tell people the overwhelming portion of monies earned by *Captain O Captain* went to the paperback publisher. Because no other house bid on what they did not consider a mass market book, he bought for $10,000, plus a royalty of four cents per copy—split fifty-fifty with the hard-cover publisher—what became the number four national bestseller for six months. That, dumb writer Josh was told, was smart business.)

Just as soon as another publisher accepted Josh's new work, his first one decided to publish what he had termed unprintable—after radical revisions. Yet he'd already granted Josh a release. "Ah," said the publisher, "do you have that in *writing?*" It took over a year for the second publisher to get the matter straightened out, after which there was the book itself to complete despite the erosion of Josh's initial enthusiasm, which fueled his imagination far more than did the advance. Why O why hadn't anyone warned him there was a hell of a lot more to the profession of writing than merely writing?

Balancing all that aggravation was the New England Sholom Hospital. The $900,000 raised at the 1974 dinner was used to buy a large tract of land on the outskirts of Boston and hire an architect. It took three years to get the approval of Massachusetts' Public Health Council, which granted permission for 120 beds. Every year Aaron Kogan asked Josh to speak at the fundraising dinner. But what could be added? So Josh always declined, several times, only to have his objections overridden. It wasn't possible to withstand someone who said, time and again, "Without you, Josh, the New England Sholom Hospital would never have been built." Each time he responded, "Tell me that once more, Aaron, and I'll believe it."

Josh delighted in viewing the obsession of the genuinely good Kogans translated into a medical center presently expanded to 210 beds, with an out-patient department and facilities for a day-care program. Those it could not restore to independent functioning, the NES staff taught skills necessary to live with disabilities, while those too sick for nursing homes were treated as guests in a first-class hotel. The hospital contained no wards, only semiprivate rooms with bathrooms, each overlooking landscaped gardens.

One year Aaron invited Dr. Christiaan Barnard to pinchhit. The following year Josh was prevailed upon once more. "The music just wasn't there. Nor the donations." Throughout the year Aaron played for potential donors tapes of Josh's previous appeals, which yielded more immediate results than did his new novel, still in progress and threatening to become the work of a lifetime.

So, the way parents count the years by watching their children put on weight and inches, walk, talk, run, start school, Josh observed the hospital, *his* hospital, break ground, build, establish a nationwide reputation. Over fifty hospitals in Massachusetts and Rhode Island now regularly referred their post-acute patients to NES. In his wallet, where others carried pictures of their children, Josh carried its photographs.

Always hard up for new material, Josh would pick everyone's brains as soon as he made shuttle reservations for the annual pilgrimage to Boston. How many different ways were there, after all, to ask for funds for the same institution? Only the I.R.S. didn't have to worry about inspiring people to continue to give.

One year Mom responded with impressions of Israel's two very different seas, both fed by the Jordan's sweet water. Lots of fish swim in the Sea of Galilee, its banks lined with trees and youngsters at play. A happy sight. To the south the Jordan flows into another area, where no fish swim, no tree grows, no birds sing. From these waters nobody drinks, and anyone swimming in it has to be scrubbed clean with soap and water. What makes the difference between these two Israeli seas?

"That's easy," Josh said. "One is fresh water, the other full of salt and phosphates and other chemicals."

She shook her head. "*This* is the difference. The Sea of Galilee gets sweet water from the Jordan, but it doesn't keep any. Whenever

{227}

water flows in, the sea releases water of its own. But the other sea hoards all its water. Every drop it gets, it keeps to itself. Because the Sea of Galilee gives, it lives. The other sea gives up nothing ever. That's why people call it the Dead Sea."

That parable made such a hit at the brunch, that Josh worked it into the new novel, where it did not belong. The next year Laurel Rabin again helped out. So successful was that speech—$536,000 was raised—he proposed on returning from Boston. After first making a pitch for living together.

"No way, José. Want to buy in now, when the merchandise is fresh and sweet, fine. But no more free samples. It just expired, your learner's permit."

Finally, out it came: ". . . marry me?"

"Sure you're ready, Josh? You haven't hit forty yet."

"Is that an affirmative? Or a tentative?"

"What do you think?"

"I stopped thinking when I decided to marry you."

"I think you might be better off with a wife who's imaginary. No restraints. Follow the wallow."

"Make imaginary love? Imaginary children? Imaginary problems? Does sound good, the imaginary problems."

"Want to edit your proposal, Josh?"

"Look here, Laurel. If this sparring is a foretaste of married life—"

"You think sparring ends with marriage? Can you take it?"

"Sparring? Or marriage?"

"There's a difference?"

"Oh, I can take it, I suppose. If you can."

"Take the joyous conflict of minds and wills?"

"Well, not if it doesn't include bodies, Laurel."

"So let's throw in bodies. By all means, bodies."

"What about vows to observe and to celebrate each other's individualities?"

"Such a mouthful. But why not?"

"Laurel? Think I got lost somewhere at the last turn of phrase. Did you just—?" There had been this lurking dread that Laurel would decline out of revenge for all his years of nonproposing. "You have just made me the *happiest* . . ."

In the middle of the night, panic struck. As much as Josh had feared rejection, acceptance shortcircuited his nervous system. Now all his limitless choices were to be condensed into one 5′6″, 129 lb., admittedly great looker with auburn hair, smoky voice, and large, wide-set hazel eyes. Gone the thrilling anticipation of meeting someone new. No more holding out for Ms. perfection, who might well appear on the scene at his wedding reception. Worse yet, Laurel could read Josh like one of the pop psych articles she wrote. To be completely understood put one at constant risk of disenchanting. Easier for a relationship to survive infidelity than boring a spouse to death.

And what did it profit a man if he gained a wife, but lost control? Matrimony could never afford a man the sense of power, of mastery, derived from a career. At his magazine Josh had put in the hours, developed the expertise, delivered the goods, all of which earned him the title of managing editor. But who ever worked his way up in marriage to husband-in-chief?

Wedlock, as the word itself implied, locked people in, rendered them all to vulnerable. Friends of Josh noted a loss of self in merging, a dwindling of dominion, as one was obliged to pleasure another in what was not just another one-night stand, but a repeat business. Time after time a husband had to keep going back to the same old well. Often that required taking extraordinary if not heroic measures to keep it from running dry. What suited a woman's nature, marriage, could well undermine a man's.

But O the bleak alternative!

In love there was no safety net. A high-risk endeavor. Yet it was only in spending the self that one can enrich the self. Worked that way with Josh's novels. And wasn't the marriage the grandest of fictions shared? Woman believing in man, he in her, together in a world of their own devising.

At dawn Josh woke up Laurel to say: "I am *convinced* we're doing the right thing."

"Isn't that what nations declare every time they start hostilities?" She rolled away.

He took her by the shoulders and shook her hard. "But nations don't *love* each other."

"I didn't hear any talk of love."

"Didn't I say I love you, Laurel?"

"All those *other* difficult syllables to pronounce. 'Will . . . you . . . mar . . . rrrr . . . ry . . . m-m-m-me?' "

"Well, I do, of course."

"Do what?"

"You know."

"Say it. Or do writers function only on paper with pencil? No? Perhaps saying it in unison would make it easier."

Together: "I love you." And fell into each other's arms, laughing till the tears came.

When Mom heard of the engagement, her face lit up like a Hanukkah menorah. "Now I can rest in peace! Couldn't be more thrilled! Until, of course, your children come. Lovely Laurel. So appealing, funny, good. And she loves you so much. But then, who wouldn't?"

What about Mom? Had she never reconsidered marriage?

"By now, Josh, the average age of men my age is deceased. Why spend my remaining years nursing someone? Or burying him?"

But a life without love?

Intimacy alone didn't spawn true happiness. A relationship could be a cornerstone of one's life, but cornerstones came in fours. Life's meaning didn't stem entirely from love. It couldn't bear all that weight. "People need other things as well."

Man is a social animal, Aristotle said. In need of emotional attachments, said Freud.

"Sure, of course. I don't know from Aristotle. He lived before my time. But look at Freud. His writings deal exclusively with the development of his *ideas*. Hardly a word about his *own* emotional attachments. Doesn't that tell you *something?*"

Nevertheless, it still bothered Josh, who quoted Laurel: "The ability to form a lasting relationship is a sign of emotional maturity."

"Very true. But so is the ability to be alone, solace yourself. Make yourself feel better on your own."

Josh threw up his hands. "So tell me this, Mom. Why am *I* getting married?"

"Very simple. If you let Laurel get away, I'll murder you."

That question haunted Josh. Wasn't marriage an extreme remedy for loneliness? Perhaps overkill. Being open, sharing feelings, emotional disclosure were women's stock in trade; Josh, however, would sooner play tennis with them or produce a novel. What if he got fed up with Laurel one night and told her to go home? She could claim, rightly, she *was* home.

There was always divorce, of course, the fuse for overloaded marriages. But, Josh asked himself on the way to the synagogue, should someone fitfully thinking divorce be getting married? Walking down the aisle he answered himself, Think you're the only one in history to be put through this ordeal? Throughout the ages billions of people the world over have endured it, some happily. If they could do it—jocks, illiterates, blue-collar workers, Republicans—so can Josh Trilling.

After the ceremony, Laurel confessed an impulse to run like hell. "Who *was* this sweaty, glassy-eyed stranger standing beside me under the *chuppah*, squeezing my hand and hurting my knuckles, fumbling with my right forefinger, stamping on my foot instead of on the wine glass, the klutz!"

All mutual doubts were jettisoned during the reception, as friends hoisted bride and groom on chairs and whirled them up toward the ceiling, knocking their heads against the glass chandeliers. Compared to eyes being poked out or a possible brain concussion from a fall, marriage held no terrors. Later on, since Josh was the *muzhinki*, last child in the family to be wed, the band played the *kreindel-tanz* while everyone danced around Mom, crowned with a garland of flowers and seated on a chair in the center of the ballroom, and offered mazel tovs.

Mom, in seventh heaven, beamed. "Who knows? Maybe Josh and Laurel will be the ones to produce the Messiah. God knows this world needs him now."

"Does that mean," Laurel asked, "you've given up on *Josh?*"

Funny, the marriage itself proved no sweat at all. Apparently, nothing was as fearsome as its prospect, probably not even excluding death. Wedded life was harmony and contentment beyond Josh's imaginings—for the time being. After all those jokes about clashes between in-laws, some observed first hand, Josh had expected friction, sparks. Never happened. Laurel's explanation: Usually those hostile to their *own* mothers battle mothers-in-law. She felt no jealousy. "Every woman with brains knows that in the long run how a man treats his mother is the way he'll treat his wife."

Mom admired Laurel's intellect and loved her warm heart and dry humor, qualities that turned Josh on (though to his friends he spoke of her sensuality). Laurel, in turn, appreciated Mom's sweetness and grace—which her own mother never possessed—as well as independence. But why on earth conceal illness? The family learned of it only afterwards, when Mom would say how much better she was feeling *now*.

Above all, Laurel loved Mom for never asking when she'd be having a baby, Messiah or no. Everyone else did, tactlessly, as without issue the years passed. Tests had confirmed the unlikelihood of Laurel's conceiving, something she couldn't bring herself to talk about. Repeatedly, Josh assured her, "My love for the unique personage who is Laurel is in no way conditional."

"Of course unique. Nearly all other female personages can conceive."

"Didn't you hear me use the word *love?* Why must you focus on the unborn?"

"You mean the *never*-to-be-born, don't you?"

Neither wanted to discuss having children by other means. Each had reservations, some sensible, others not, still others unconscious. By the time they had decided to adopt, it was too late. Waiting lists were too long—and Laurel in her late thirties and Josh, past forty, were deemed too old. Dead end?

As the latest fad, one involving babies along with a soupçon of unorthodox sex, surrogate parenthood was being chewed over piously by the media. Having an aversion to the idea, Laurel sought a pre-emptive veto, raising the matter with Mom, who would surely disapprove of something so radical.

But she said, "Nothing new, surrogate motherhood. It's in the Bible." The patriarchs had children by women other than their wives. Often the wives themselves made the match." She added, "Afterwards, Sarah and Rachel did conceive. Wonderful babies."

"Be honest now," Laurel said. "You want Josh to have a baby even if I can't. By hook or by surrogate. Isn't that so?"

Mom shook her head emphatically. "The baby would be just as much *yours*, Laurel. According to Judaism, whoever raises a child is the *real* parent."

"Today's surrogate mothers being all married, that makes it adultery. In our case, doubled."

"Adultery? When there isn't so much as a handshake between the man and woman? Not even a how-do-you-do. Why not think of it as a form of lend-lease?"

Mom soon took to painting pictures of children and birds and animals suitable for a nursery. Better nagging through art, Laurel called it. By now, all of Mom's walls, her children's and grandchildren's as well, were covered with paintings. On Parkside Avenue, Mom *shepped nachas* from her apartment's neatness and cleanliness, the shine on the kitchen floor and the foyer linoleum, the freshly ironed curtains on the windows—at that time her only creative outlet. Now she had her artistry. Often Josh asked who painted all those extraordinary works. Was it Renoir? Monet? Rembrandt?

She would reply, "Me, myself and I." In wonder, "Can you beat that!"

Her enthusiasms proved contagious. Josh studied enough art books to answer most relevant queries in crossword puzzles. And Sandra fast became a ballet fan, who rhapsodized about line and extension, with lots of French words and Russian names thrown in.

It was Josh's idea to give Mom a showing in her apartment. So many people came, they ran out of champagne and noodle pudding.

As usual, Cousin Leo could always be counted on for amusement. Spying an evocative Galician landscape on the easel in the bedroom, he kissed the painting, whose still-wet paint had to be removed from his lips with turpentine. Then insisted only kisses could erase the taste and sex kill the smell. But when he invited a pretty woman into the bathroom for a physical examination, Josh realized something was amiss and suggested Leo be seen by a gerontologist. His wife shrugged it off. "Nothing's the matter with that fool. Leo's just *old*. I'm two and a half years younger than him, you know."

Josh hoped Mom hadn't noticed Leo's inappropriate behavior. She had a full enough case load without adding him to her list, and Leo had four sons to look after him.

One guest said how lucky Mom was to have such devoted children. Mom wasn't lucky, Sandra remarked, she was *deserving*. The woman scowled. "What world do *you* live in? Who on earth gets what they deserve?"

The dozens of paintings, which covered the walls of the living room, dining room and foyer, amazed nearly everyone. "If I could paint like this," said her beloved Rebbitzen Silverstein from Brooklyn, "I'd go up on the roof of this building and shout it to the world." The wife of the owner of an art gallery commended Mom's intensity of feeling, use of color, feathery strokes, reverielike style, as if scattering flower petals. Which Impressionist had influenced her the most?

"Berthe Morisot," she replied.

"Who?" said everyone.

A painter's painter, reported the gallery owner's wife, who created form through color. Morisot was noted for her subtlety, shimmers of iridescent light. Yet despite being the only woman invited to participate in the first Impressionist show in Paris in 1874, she had been relatively neglected by scholars and collectors.

Mom added, "Pity she never got the credit due her for having influenced Manet, Monet, Renoir, Degas. Think that has something to do with her being a woman?"

There were several late arrivals, among them the QE2 stewardess with whom Mom had been corresponding for years. (Mention of a recently diagnosed pregnancy had Josh steering her far away from Laurel.) And a tall, striking, black middle-aged man with a shaggy head, broad shoulders, trim build, smilingly introduced himself as Mom's professor of anatomy.

"Don't you recognize me?" said Rodney.

"From where?" (Did he say *anatomy?*)

"Let me show you." He disappeared into the crowd, returning some fifteen minutes later to ask, "Where *am* I?"

"You don't know?"

"Is there another room here?"

"You mean a *secret* room?" Just as Josh was about to usher the eccentric out, Mom appeared and greeted him like an old friend.

Rodney said, "Can't find my portrait anywhere."

"It's here. Well, in the closet." She hastened to explain, "This crowd might not . . . understand."

"Understand what? My posing?" The man seemed hurt.

"No, no, not *you*, Rodney. *Me. My* painting *it*."

When Sandra came over to welcome Rodney, whom she recognized from his portrait, Josh, annoyed at being left out, insisted on seeing it, too. Reluctantly, Mom led him and Sandra and Rodney into the bedroom; Charlie, Zack and Debbie tagged along. Inside, she locked the door behind them before taking two unframed canvases from the closet.

Debbie clapped her hands and exclaimed, "Oh, *wow*, Grandma!"

"I'll take the blonde," said Charlie.

Mom turned to Rodney, her expression saying, See what I mean?

One was a nude study of Rodney, the other of a voluptuous blonde, each powerfully yet lyrically done. Both looked peculiarly chaste even when placed side by side, which made it seem they were ogling each other.

Mom said, "One thing to see nudes in the museum. But on a grandmother's wall? With a rabbi present?"

"Your religion holds the human body in contempt?" asked Rodney.

"On the contrary. Being God's creation, it's holy. But Jews show respect for the body's dignity with clothing. Just as we cover our heads in temple to show reverence."

Charlie picked up a sheaf of nude sketches off a closet shelf. "Then why—?"

"Improved my portraits, sketching what's underneath clothes. But just because something *can* be done doesn't mean it *should* be. I mean by *me*. No objections to *others'* doing nudes. I admire them. Well, except Francis Bacon, whose nudes are freaky slabs of beef."

"The *zoftig* blonde, Grandma." Zack reached out for a canvas. "I'll see her home."

{235}

Everyone else at the showing also wanted paintings, many even offering to pay. Sold, the paintings would disappear from view, vanish as if they had never been. Josh wouldn't allow that. Sell what could never be duplicated? Sacrilege.

Okay, said several people, we'd love *gifts*. Mom found it impossible to refuse until Sandra intervened.

"Sorry. Money, Mom can give away freely. All hers to dispose of. But not paintings. They are my inheritance and Josh's."

One neighbor made Mom an offer she herself refused with ease. "I'd love a copy of that painting of the three men reading the Torah. Not for nothing, understand. Let me commission you. Tell me how much the canvas and paints cost."

A triumphant afternoon all in all. Add to that the senior citizen's production of *Fiddler on the Roof* in which Mom stopped the show singing "Sunrise, Sunset."

It was another good year for Mom and her children. This at a time when Alzheimer's disease was stalking the land.

18

NEXT to being born, it was the smartest move of Zack's life, leaving the practice of law for Wall Street. Naturally, Dad hadn't seen it that way. All he knew was what he could count, and investment banking had initially meant a five-figure cut in salary. Anyone spurning cash in the here and now for a mother lode by-and-by, Dad thought a fiscal defective. But his had always been a nickel-and-dime mentality; thinking big gave Dad a migraine. Luckily, he rarely did.

Now that money was rolling in, invested in a new home in Westport, Connecticut, a Mercedes and a few other necessities, Dad had changed his tune. From "your idiot son" to Mother to "my boy Zack" to the whole world. Trust her, however, to be perverse. On Mother's visit, she zeroed in on his car.

"You had to buy from Daimler-Benz, a company that used slave labor during the war? And still refuses to pay compensation? A stand backed up by West German courts." Next, a lecture on the overriding importance of *Menschlichkeit*. "Without that, a person has trouble distinguishing net worth from self–."

Before she could reveal that money couldn't buy happiness or cure baldness, Zack cut in. "You must be the only adult around who doesn't appreciate what net worth *means*. Freedom now. Look at Grandma. Where was she before she came into money?" He raised his voice to drown hers out. "Do you know a full third of Yale's senior class this year applied to First Boston Corporation? Not to mention all the resumés from professors and journalists my company receives every day. Even from clergymen and medical students, yes. The dirty little open secret is that *everybody's* horny for wealth."

"You're telling me something *new*? But how much money is *enough*? And to what *lengths* will a person go? Forsaking *which* values?"

"Hey, give me a break!"

Parents were meant to be moral guides. The Hebrew words for parents, teachers and Torah are all derived from the same Hebrew root, to instruct. The woman never lightened up. Yakety yakety-yak. No mother ever volunteered for retirement—that's why South Florida was invented. To get parents out of children's hair.

Look where Mother had guided Debbie, who had gone dutifully to college instead of drama school, then found it impossible to gain a toehold in acting. So she had settled for the goal of all good little Jewish boys of the previous generation, medicine. A genuine contribution to society, Debbie rationalized, because women, being the compassionate sex, make better physicians. If that were so, Zack must have been dating a third sex. For it wasn't from chastity alone that the sexual revolution had liberated females.

". . . The trouble with you, Zack, you think you are what you spend."

Spending—evil? It only fueled the American economy, that's all, kept it afloat. Consumerism was the proud equal of any other ism. A spendthrift always makes sure to look his best, never becomes addicted to alcohol or drugs or sex. Such transgressions would disrupt his career, interfere with cash flow, drain the bacon brought home.

With that year's near six-figure bonus, Mother's was the only negative note in a chorus of praise. And there was plenty more where that came from, all for Zack's earning. Advising corporations on raising capital via new stock issues and acquiring other companies had become the gold rush of the eighties. Growing along with his investment house, now larger than some of its clients, Zack had struck it rich by regularly instructing corporate heads two decades and more his senior. And they *heeded* him! Such deference might yet cost Zack his humility. But hell, a guy had to lose it *some* day.

Anyone impatient with the slow but steady, hard but honest way, could mine even more gold by simply disregarding all the nitpicking regulations and niceties. Several of his colleagues hailed as financial geniuses by the media, which displayed their lavish estates, were trading inside knowledge. Tempting as were these victimless—well, they weren't crimes, exactly—Zack could wait several years to become a millionaire. A murderous schedule kept him from furnishing his house, as it was, or spending more than his income. Some nights he never even made it home to Westport, but crashed at a friend's in the city, or slept at a hotel. Yet who gave a thought to Zack's grueling schedule?

Jealous, everyone not making the big bucks was. It showed in the gleefully spiteful jokes about "paper entrepreneurs," about yuppies having made selfishness respectable, in the polls characterizing them as greedy egomaniacs consumed by consumption. As if all there was to investment banking was cooking up gimmicks to transfer money from one pocket to another. His burgeoning wealth was a pittance compared to what he had earned for his boss, R. J. Whittier, who certainly wasn't rewarding Zack for good looks and charisma, hefty though his were.

"What's needed to set the record right," R.J. often said, "is an antidefamation league for investment bankers."

The truth was young people begrudged those their own age making pots of money, perhaps flaunting it, while older ones couldn't stand their juniors' enjoying what they considered the prerogatives of middle age: the good life and beautiful, young, firm-bodied women. As if the only way of paying one's dues was with bald heads, pot bellies, impotence.

Pity there wasn't nearly time enough for all the women Zack wanted or, money being the greatest of turn-ons, the even larger number after him. There were those who yearned to make a career out of Zack, which pleased him. How terrific to be the center of attention, a woman's entire life, her reason for being. Yet, wouldn't that be a mite enveloping, smothering? And shouldn't a woman contribute something more than just herself to a relationship? A fortune of her own would be nice.

Not that Zack had the time to figure it all out. Work barely left him enough leisure to love them before leaving. Dismissing his ever kindly parting words "I love you more than life itself, but in the vast scheme of things . . ." —they'd attack his so-called insensitivity. Just like you-know-who. Scratch a female, and there was Mother!

Despite the crushing workload, Zack felt happiest on the job. No need there to justify himself to those who indicted his lifestyle or his firm's engineering of corporate takeovers for giant fees. To those attributing the mammoth U.S. budget and trade deficits to America's producing corporate raiders, mergers, arbitragers, greenmailers, while Japan was producing goods, Zack's boss offered a gentleman's version of "Nuts."

"Restructuring is what the doctor ordered for the eighties," R. J. Whittier argued cogently, "to restore America's competitiveness, lost during the complacent sixties and seventies by failing to innovate, improve product quality, find new markets. Our economy *needs* lots of creative destruction." Mergers had eliminated inept management, reduced corporate overhead, increased the value of assets, steadily decreased unemployment, driven up productivity.

Mergers had also made people like R.J. grossly affluent. Not that coming from an old-monied New England family, he'd started out a pauper. Half a million R.J. sank into a sailboat he raced off Miami, source of his perpetual tan. When he was invited aboard the sleek 45-foot, light-hulled, aluminum beauty, which was outfitted with $100,000 worth of computerized equipment, Zack knew he had really arrived. While the deck pitched, the wind flayed, spray battered, the sun baked, the body rebelled, effectively keeping nausea at bay were the thoughts of a junior partnership that crisscrossed his mind.

Thoughts furthered after a partner passed a comment about Zack's attire, whereupon back in New York R.J. himself introduced Zack to Paul Stuart, "known, more so than Brooks Brothers, for catering to people of substance and style," and to Hermes neckwear at $75 a tie. "Only the gauche show off the horse-and-carriage trademark on the front of the narrow tail," he counseled. "Those familiar with Hermès recognize it at once; anyone else there's no reason to impress."

R.J. had become Zack's role model. Same haircut, some of the same mannerisms and gestures; sometimes, like R.J., Zack ordered cole slaw at lunch, forgetting cabbage repeated on him till suppertime. Colleagues who had no appreciation for any show of allegiance—homage, really—called this "sucking up to the boss." Laughable, from fellows who stabbed the air with their right forefingers à la the Kennedys and R.J.

Only in his late forties, the genius behind many a corporate takeover, a born leader with panache, enviable WASP reserve, R. J. Whittier was surely worth emulating. Capped by an exquisite society wife and two children out of a Ralph Lauren ad, R.J. himself looked like a Marlboro man with the brains to have kicked the smoking habit.

So arriving one day for an appointment, Zack was taken aback to see his boss on the phone just listening for a good seven minutes straight, with only a nod every once in a while and an occasional "Uh-huh" or "Yes, but—" As soon as he hung up with a *"Damn!"*, R.J. hurried from behind his desk to stretch out on the thick Chinese carpet. "Back spasm." He put himself through a series of exercises that relaxed his head and neck muscles, then his shoulders and arms, invoking all the while murmured images of balmy Hawaiian waves washing over him.

Zack finally asked, at a loss, "Anything I can do, R.J.?"

"I *wish!* But no."

"These spasms happen often?"

"Depends on my mother. How often she calls."

"Your *mother?* Never thought a man like you had a mother. I mean—"

"Do *I* have a mother!" WASP reserve in meltdown, he spoke of her, ranted. After the sudden death of R.J.'s father earlier that year and a subsequent heart attack, she had impulsively sold her mansion in Boston and moved to New York to get on R.J.'s nerves. His wife didn't get along with her mother-in-law—they mixed like oil and fire.

And despite doctor's orders to be up and about, Mrs. Whittier was playing the invalid, putting R.J. through the wringer. He was at his wits' end, trying to cope with her mounting demands on his time, sanity.

Feeling a sudden bonding—us men against them mothers—Zack said, "I may have just the medicine for your mother." (And perhaps a partnership for himself.) "My grandmother, who lives in the same neighborhood, is a healer."

"Faith? Gypsy? What?"

Zack related Uncle Josh's favorite story about Boston's Mrs. Pomerance. "My grandmother has this talent for making people feel good. Once she befriends a person—"

"Call your grandmother," exclaimed R.J. "*Hire* her. Now."

"Right. Oh, yes. Just one thing you should know. She's Jewish, my grandmother."

R.J. looked amused. "Zachary, I didn't think you had *converted* to Judaism."

Instead of simply handing Grandma her assignment, Zack took her to call on Mrs. Whittier, on Riverside Drive in a penthouse duplex overlooking the Hudson. Answering the door was a soft-spoken, middle-aged man to whom Grandma introduced herself.

"I am Bailey the butler. Let me show you to the drawing room."

Grandma asked what a butler did. Zack had no idea.

"Lovely view!" Grandma pointed out the window. "On a clear day you can see New Jersey."

"Who on earth would *want* to see New Jersey?" said a voice behind them. "On *any* day."

Introduction to the handsome seventy-year-old silver-haired patrician, with steel gray eyes that matched her silk dressing gown, spitting image of her son. "Won't you be seated? Some sherry, perhaps?" (Grandma accepted, probably thinking she'd been offered cherry, as in soda.) Almost concurrently: "I've been living here four months, and not one soul has come to call. Except my son. When the moon is blue."

Grandma tried to placate the woman. "It's a real shame, the way big cities are. So impersonal. Have you been to church here? A good place to meet people."

"A lot better than a singles' bar," Zack joked.

Mrs. W. never cracked a smile. "I do not solicit attention. It's the church's place to seek out strangers, make them feel welcome. That's how it's done in Boston, where the mayor, I might add, calls on me. Well, I did attend church here. Nobody paid me any mind. Never went back. Never will."

"There are other organizations—" Grandma began.

"Not up to that. Had a heart attack."

"What a coincidence. So did I. Frightened me so. At first. But after talking to myself day and night, I finally talked myself out of —"

"My heart attack was *massive*."

"*Another* coincidence . . ."

Grandma got exactly nowhere. Yet Mrs. W. did invite her back.

Zack didn't have to talk Grandma into returning, for she took pity on the aristocratic fishwife. Even asked several occupants of Mrs. W.'s building to pay her a visit. A few went—once.

Next, Grandma went to the nearest church, possibly her first time in any Christian house of God, to ask its minister to welcome Mrs. W. personally to the community. Complying, he was sent packing for being from a denomination on the wrong side of the tracks. So Grandma approached the highest church in the neighborhood, whose Episcopalian priest went calling on Mrs. W., fortified with several church ladies. Same diatribe, no soap. None returned.

Having noticed Mrs. W.'s skill at calligraphy, Grandma had her own rabbi ask Mrs. W. to teach a class at the temple. "Be an *employee?*" Mrs. W. replied in high dudgeon. The rabbi's reply— "Who said anything about *paying* you?"—sparked a tirade. At which point Grandma gave up on the injustice collector, for which Zack made excuses.

There was a decided change in R.J.'s attitude. One day when they came to work wearing the identical Paul Stuart, R.J.'s secretary told Zack to come back from lunch in a different suit. And another invitation to sail never materialized.

Weeks later, however, Mrs. W. was hospitalized with a suspected heart attack, and R.J. turned to Zack. "All tests are negative, but she's terribly depressed. Perhaps your grandmother might—"

Grateful for the second chance, Zack escorted Grandma to the hospital.

Congratulated on her clean bill of health, Mrs. W. snapped, "You've been talking to my son. Well, there's nothing clean about heart disease."

"Think of all the things you *can* do," Grandma urged. "The trick is to *try*. I speak from experience."

"I can't—"

Grandma spoke of the New England Sholom Hospital. The great strides made there in restoring cardiacs and others to nearly full functioning.

"That's a *Jewish* hospital, isn't it?"

"Only the money that built it and the founders are Jewish. The patients and the diseases are nonsectarian."

"What about the visitors?" Mrs. W. was off and running with her familiar I-hate-New Yorkers theme song.

"*Enough*, already!" Grandma burst out. "Kvetch, kvetch, kvetch. Is there anyone or anything in this world that doesn't displease you? What's making your highness sick is self-pity. High time you took yourself in hand and did something besides kvetch. Tried hard. Pushed yourself. There's a Yiddish saying, A person's worst enemies can't wish her what she thinks up for herself." Out of the room she strode.

Partnership? Hell, now Zack would be lucky to qualify for unemployment insurance. After apologizing profusely to Mrs. W., rendered speechless for once, he raced after Grandma. He would make her do penance; neither Zack's house nor Mercedes was fully paid for. Near the nurses' station, bending over the water fountain, was Grandma.

"Have you gone mad! Losing your temper with a poor sick old lady—"

Straightening up, Grandma opened her pocketbook, withdrew a lace handkerchief and dried her lips. "Who lost a temper?"

"The way you attacked. Grandma, march yourself back to Mrs. W. this minute and—"

"You're shouting, Zack." She put a finger to her lips. "Calm down."

"*I* should calm down? When *you* just—" He stopped short, suddenly aware that Grandma, now restoring the hankie to her pocketbook, didn't look the least bit perturbed.

"Mrs. Whittier is none of the things you said, Zack. Not old—I'm ten years her senior. Poor? Sick, maybe. But a far cry from dying. I checked with her doctor. As for blowing up, I just pretended."

"*Pretended?*"

"An act. I was getting nowhere with that woman. *Nobody* was. After so many months of self-pity, which is what's incapacitating her, I had to do *something*. Too much sympathy has only made Mrs. Whittier worse. Convinced her everything she says is true. Everyone's who's tried to help she's driven away. So I thought a little shock therapy—"

"Shock therapy?"

"Instead of excessive compassion. There's a story in the Talmud—"

"What's the *Talmud* got to do with a Daughter of the American Revolution, for crying out loud!"

"Wait, Zack. Listen." According to legend, God in the beginning couldn't make up His mind whether to create the world according to the principles of justice or those of mercy. Total justice was like icy water that cracks any glass it's poured into. Just as total mercy, like burning hot water, bursts a glass. So in the end God created the world with a mixture of *both*. Justice *and* mercy. "Anyway, Zack, I didn't have anything to lose."

She didn't. But once R.J. learned of Grandma's insulting behavior . . .

Thursday and Friday Zack called in sick, then took the phone off the hook and tried to addict himself to alcohol. Perhaps by the time he returned to the office the following week, either Russia or the United States would have invaded some country or other and taken the heat off him.

Monday morning Zack was the first one at work, where he hid out in his office, hoping his return would go unnoticed. He prepared excuses for Grandma's onslaught. Old age. Hallucination. Insanity inherited from a grandson who thought a grandmother could shoot him to the top.

At ten-forty-five the mail was delivered. One letter was addressed by hand in beautiful flowing calligraphy, the sender Mrs. W. Zack wouldn't read the letter on an empty stomach, and why kill his appetite for lunch? Finally opened, after Zack had downed two drinks and some Tums, the letter read:

I am the one who should apologize. My behavior of late has not been the sort one takes pride in. Nor the kind that would have helped my ancestors survive their first winter in the New World.

What your grandmother said is, of course, true. I have been indulging far too long in self-pity, which takes all our weaknesses and makes them even weaker. And troubles hurt the most when they are self-inflicted.

I shall try to change. I *must*. It is no pleasure, believe me, living with the common scold I have become. And when I see myself succeeding, my former self restored, I should like to have you and your sweet grandmother come to tea. With no more sympathy.

Zack let out a whoop, dashed by his secretary, ran outside and took a cab over to Grandma. She too had received a letter from Mrs. W., which came as a big surprise.

"What opening up a big mouth can accomplish!" she exclaimed. "So many *other* people I could be insulting. I'm going to make a list."

Zack swept her up into her arms and kissed her on the mouth, then on each cheek. "Grandma, you are *terrific!*"

"You think so, Zack?"

"*Absotively, postitutely!*"

She heaved a sigh. "Then why didn't I help my aunt when she was being beaten by her stepmother? And the surgeon who saved your grandfather's life—"

19

*H*ANNAH had never seen anyone make a U-turn in life like Mrs. Whittier's. Now a woman transformed, pleasant and uncomplaining and on the go. The two went places together and spoke regularly on the phone. Though rarely about their respective families. Since Mrs. Whittier, a very private person, never extolled her son and picture-perfect family, displayed in the society pages, naturally Hannah refrained from boasting of Josh and Laurel, Sandra, Zack and Debbie.

There was no more unsolicited advice; instead, Hannah made a point of seeking Mrs. Whittier's. About calligraphy. How to research one's family tree, start a New York chapter of NES. And asked about her forebears, the Kennedys politics in general, about which she was very knowledgeable. Always responsive, Mrs. Whittier proved cordial, after the fashion of one struggling to overcome the training that to reveal one's emotions was bad form. Once, when Hannah was ill, Mrs. Whittier sent over enough food to feed a kosher army.

Clearly, the previous Mrs. Whittier had been possessed by a

dybbuk, now exorcised. So Hannah was sorry to learn of her decision to return to Boston for good. Yet a wise move, for there was a supportive network of old friends and associations that, at her age, a woman of her temperament could never develop in a strange city. But what of son and family?

"By air Boston is only an hour away from New York," she remarked. "A lot closer than a yacht in Miami."

As a surprise gift, Hannah painted Mrs. Whittier's portrait, copied from a glamorous thirty-five-year-old black and white photograph, provided on the sly by her butler. Hannah invited her friend over for lunch, but intent on finishing the portrait, had neglected to buy the necessary provisions.

At the back of the refrigerator she had found a forgotten container of cottage cheese, moldy from neglect—perfect for a Galician cheese omelet. But cholesterol was bad for Mrs. Whittier. Instead, Hannah dumped whatever was in the vegetable and fruit bins into a huge salad, which made a big hit.

"So original, combining vegetables with fruit. Looks like a sunrise."

An artistic success, the meal. "Now for dessert."

"I just love pistachio ice cream." One taste, however, had Mrs. Whittier gagging.

Hannah too. The container she had snatched from the freezer held pea soup! So *embarrassing*. She apologized half a dozen times.

Mrs. Whittier just chuckled.

"*Next* time," Hannah vowed "I take you *out* to lunch."

A deep sigh. "I shall miss you, Mrs. Trilling."

"Likewise." Neither of them had any idea when they'd be seeing each other again. If ever. "Nobody ever had too many friends."

"Now, then." From her purse Mrs. Whittier took out a box which she handed over. Inside was an exquisite pin fashioned in the shape of a rose, with leaves of emeralds, petals of rubies and a small diamond in the center. "The petals can be opened and closed. See? My mother's."

"Oh . . . ! But I can't—"

"You must, Mrs. Trilling."

"Your daughter-in-law—"

"That *witch?* Forgive me! Just slipped out. Tell me, how is *your* daughter-in-law? You never mention her."

Hannah wouldn't speak of Laurel, for she loved her. But Charlie was fair game. "Well my son-in-law is improving. At dinner last Sunday, he did push the platter of asparagus in my direction. At least six inches."

Mrs. Whittier sighed. "The only thing my daughter-in-law would offer me would be hemlock." In a moment, feelings pent-up for ten years spilled out. About a daughter-in-law who restricted her wedding ceremony to family, of which she had eighty-six and the Whittiers seven. Who, because her dress was the wrong shade of pink, stopped talking to her the next day. Who never invited the Whittiers to her home or visited them. Who, after Mr. and Mrs. Whittier had spent hours placing a long-distance call from Scotland to their son in New York on his birthday, answered the phone with: "Sorry, R.J.'s eating now. Call back in an hour." And hung up.

But instead of outrage, as justified as it would have been counterproductive, Hannah reacted with giggles. "Your daughter-in-law must hold the record for the world's *awfulest* excuse for a human being!" More giggles, like internal jogging.

"I'm glad *you* think it's funny," Mrs. Whittier began, but the giggling proved infectious, and unable to keep a straight face, she joined in. "Well, I suppose if you can't burn witches any more, laugh at them."

Hannah presented her friend with a personally inscribed copy of Josh's new, well-received bestseller, whose title was too long and too difficult to remember. (Why couldn't he have named it *Captain O Captain II?*) Then led her to the portrait.

Mrs. Whittier was flabbergasted. "Why, that's *me!* A hundred years ago. You painted my cloak red? Like Little Red Riding Hood. Stunning!"

Hannah was pleased.

She sat down on the bed. "Might as well finish what I started, Grandma. I owe you an explanation—"

"You don't owe me anything, Mrs. Whittier."

"About my insufferable behavior—"

"Ancient history."

"Please, Mrs. Trilling. It's important for me to, well, lance the boil. My ranting and raving about nobody visiting? Well, *strangers* weren't upsetting me. It was, to be candid, R.J." Her good relationship with him had deteriorated right after his marriage, when his wife went on the warpath about anything and everything. Mr. Whittier had kept her from taking these shenanigans too much to heart. Then, he was dead. R.J. and his family came for the funeral, never to return until Mrs. Whittier's heart attack four months later. Only he came for one afternoon and left. A few months later, on impulse, Mrs. Whittier sold her house and moved to New York. Her family, she told friends, wanted her near. The truth was she felt publicly humiliated. "Please understand, Mrs. Trilling. I was never possessive. But when one wakes up to find a husband dead beside her in bed, then suffers a severe heart attack . . . Well, defenses painstakingly built up over a lifetime crumble. Hence, the panicky flight to New York, where I encountered a son more concerned about his tan than about me. So . . . I took to phoning him. Haranguing everyone. Because I could never come out with the truth. Hurt too much. But that day in the hospital when you lost patience with me—"

"I didn't, Mrs. Whittier. Really, I didn't. It was just a big act. *Honest.*"

"You're an awfully good actress.

How to ease the pain of a neglected mother? Perhaps by joining in. "Every parent wonders now and again, Mrs. Whittier, whether children are worth all the effort. And sometimes they're not. Did I ever tell you about *my* children?" (God forgive Hannah.) "They *also* could be a whole lot better, because . . ."

All week long Hannah looked forward to Sunday morning's Galician blue-greenish cheese omelet, which turned out so delicious, she planned on placing a standing order with the grocer for any cheese of his that had turned. Later on, after a leisurely bath, she got dressed and went downstairs.

The concierge exclaimed, "Mrs. Trilling! Am I glad to see *you!*" He'd been calling her apartment while she was in the bath, and grown concerned there was no reply. To a policeman approaching the desk, he said, "This is 11-F. *She's* okay."

"Must be *12-F*. You have the key?"

"Uh-uh. That second lock on the door 12-F added on his own."

On her return home from the park, the concierge looked much happier. "No body inside 12-F. Everyone in the F line fine and dandy."

"Why shouldn't they be?"

"That foul odor, which you're too much of a lady to mention, Mrs. Trilling. People thought someone had expired several days before. But the police found nothing."

"My O my O my!" The smell of Hannah's Galician delicacy must have wafted up and down her line through her kitchen vents. "How did the police get inside 12-F?"

"Broke down the door. Why, what's the matter, Mrs. Trilling? You okay?"

"If you hadn't spotted me earlier . . . I was just thinking . . . it would have been *my* apartment the police would have broken into."

Hannah was still scrubbing the kitchen, after having sprayed the kitchen vents with her best cologne, when Sandra stopped by.

"Mom, nobody soaks a frying pan in *ammonia*. And what's that god-awful smell?"

"A blend of Mr. Clean and Chanel No. 5 and rotten cheese." After swearing Sandra to secrecy, Hannah revealed what neighbors thought was a body moldering had been her Sunday breakfast treat.

Sandra collapsed onto the couch. "They actually *broke down* the door?" Tears ran from her eyes. "But, Mom. You swore never to cook that mess again after what happened the *last* time."

"*What* last time?"

"When we took that basement apartment in the mountains for two weeks one summer? After you made that really rotten cheese omelet, the owner of the rooming house tore up all the linoleum and some of the floorboards and emptied out all his closets, looking for the herd of mice he thought had died. You remember, Mom."

"Ridiculous! You just made that up."

"What?"

"Would I feed us dead mice? Never happened. Would I *repeat* such a mistake?"

"Ask Josh."

"Josh? He wasn't even born then."

"Of course he was, Mom. He was seven years old."

"You expect a toot to remember? Better than me? I like that!"

Sandra changed the subject. But the look in her eye remained. The look that said, Something's wrong.

So. It was happening to Hannah too, what she had seen befalling contemporaries. Forgetting. Memory loss. Trouble switching off the TV's remote control. Only a few years before, they had all made jokes about senility. No more, now they were truly at risk. And too busy supplying each other with words for speech grown hesitant. Though everyone resented being helped.

Hannah wasn't sure when they had begun, the changes. She wasn't sure exactly what had happened, or even if it did. Her health was good. She still was complimented on her appearance, her voice that of someone young. (But her handwriting had gotten wobbly.) She enjoyed her life, people, surroundings, activities. And yet . . .

There was *something* different. She knew it. Hard to pinpoint. Was this what was meant by old age? Feeling differences one couldn't decipher? To prepare her for what someone with a tinny sense of humor called "The Golden Years," the children had given her books by gerontologists, one the same maven who wrote *The Joy of Sex*. He made growing old seem quite manageable. Contrary to myth, he wrote, the elderly don't as a rule lose their memory or other faculties; it merely takes them longer to do those things they did more quickly when young. Like a seventy-year-old secretary who gets all her work done, but more slowly. That, Hannah would gladly settle for.

Her own pace had never slackened. She walked as fast, the bounce in her step just as high. Well, almost. Shopped for all her own groceries (somehow ending up with five boxes of oatmeal and a dozen rolls of toilet paper). Cleaned the apartment just as energetically the day before the cleaning lady came. And yet, there was this . . . this . . .

There! It escaped her, the word she sought. On the tip of her tongue, the word never made it out of her mouth. Talking to Sandra or Josh or what'shername on the phone, Hannah would report the whatchamacallit in the kitchen was no good. Did she mean the refrigerator? stove? toaster oven? No, none of them. And then agitation would take hold. If she wouldn't get so excited, they said, the right word would come. Naturally. Just like that. But the opposite was true. Hannah's inability to say the right word was making her, previously so articulate, *mashuga*.

Said the children: What's the big deal? So what if you have to search for a word or two? Even if it can't be found. Don't you think that happens to us? Nobody is as young as he or she used to be. Neither are we. Not to worry, Mom. Just forget it.

Hannah would think to herself. That's just it. I *am* forgetting. That's the problem. The biggest of deals. No, not forgetting, exactly. The words were lurking someplace inside her. Hearing them spoken—as when Josh finally said, "You mean the fluorescent light in the kitchen?"—she recognized them instantly. But to fish them out of her brain and draw them out of her mouth was sometimes an effort, and becoming worse.

Or was it just crankiness? For twenty-five years she had complained of deteriorating eyesight; yet her eyes were better than her children's and grandchildren's, and the eye doctor never changed her reading glasses' prescription. Good cheer Hannah always had, but that other thing was becoming more and more like the whatchamacallit in a broken thing that told you whether or not you were running a fever. The more she gave chase, the more swiftly it dodged her. Shit! (Where did *that* word come from? A word she never used, not even when taking it several times a day from what'shisname. And if that sprang so easily from her tongue, why not all the *other* words, the *nice* ones?)

Then, there were the rabbi's sermons, which she always loved discussing afterwards. Now lost their thread. Of no comfort were fellow congregants, who said they didn't hear all of the sermons either. Comedians and sitcoms weren't as funny as before, nor the news shows on TV as newsy. Old-ageitis, friends called this condition. Accept it.

Not Hannah. But the ENT doctor she consulted said her a hearing was pretty good. In a few years she'd need a hearing aid, but not yet.

Before, her eyes skimmed sentences like skis on snow; now, they plodded along, every word a snowbank. And forgetting people's names, phone numbers. A series of humiliations, this getting old promised to be. That book should have been called *The Oy of Age*.

Sometimes Hannah would wake in the middle of the night feeling lonely. For the person she used to be. What had become of that woman? Mornings she forced herself to do what had always been done automatically, without a moment's thought. She made the bed. Until now not considered an achievement.

Still, no complaints. And what was the use? Other people were worse off. Wherever one looked there was plenty of *tzuris*. If everyone opened up his or her bundle of troubles for all to see, everyone would pick up his or her own and skip away content. So whenever the children asked, as they did every day when calling, how she was, Hannah always replied, "Perfect." Sometimes what she felt was perfectly awful, but at her age that was to be expected, thanks to rainy weather and arthritis and the woes of the world. The price one paid for living so long. But so long as there's hope, the ancient rabbis said, there is life.

And Hannah still had her beloved painting. Even though that had become a chore, what with shlepping her supplies all the way to West 57th Street, then all the way back. But the box seemed so much heavier, as if the paints were now loaded with solid lead. Mixing them of late, she was inventing the oddest colors. The paintings themselves were darker, hotter, burning, a little scary, surging out of the canvas. They were more . . . more . . . *something*. As for washing the brushes afterwards, she wouldn't wish that killing work on Israel's worst enemies. Well, on them, yes, you bet.

Still, *abi gezunt*. What did it matter? She had her health. And Sandra reconciled with Charlie. Josh finally happily married, his second novel a success. Lovable Laurel graciously agreeing to their having a baby by a surrogate who must be a saint. (Or a lunatic). Zack and Debbie also getting married someday soon, continuing the line and maintaining the links between past and future, God and Israel. Though her own mother had never lived to see even one grandchild, Hannah might yet see a *great*-grandchild! Who could pray for more?

The prayers she loved most sanctified the ordinary. Arising each morning, digesting food, going to the bathroom, standing up, seeing. All miracles renewed daily. Alas, ones no longer granted Leo, now hospitalized in New England Sholom for a disease so bad, the children never named it. She wanted to visit him, but neither one would take her to Boston, and flying there alone was too much for her now.

Still, to Hannah God had been good. Yes, He had, most certainly. Rejoice in the present, she told herself, every day is a gift. And think not of what may lie ahead. God never burdens us with more than a human being can bear, she prayed.

20

*T*HE diagnosis stunned Sandra and Josh, who had brought Mom in for a simple annual checkup. By a gerontologist this time instead of her regular physician. Made sense, now that she was eighty years old. Soon, Sandra had joked, she herself would be in need of a specialist in aging. Better make his acquaintance now, get in on the ground floor.

"*Aphasia?*"

But nothing suspicious had happened that year. Mom's forgetting names of things were merely lapses, weren't they? Her eating and cooking by color just an eccentricity. Well, at the Passover seder she did make mistakes for the first time in reading Hebrew from the Haggadah, but Debbie's date made twice as many reading English. As for Mom's stocking up five cans of coffee and six boxes of oatmeal and a dozen rolls of toilet paper, they'd all been on sale. True, names had been giving her difficulty. Not the people themselves, however; personal histories, residences and illnesses she still rattled off with ease. Lately, she engaged in circumlocutions, but always with a little laugh that indicated she was only being cute. (Instead of bank, she'd say the place which some crooks steal from and other crooks put their money.)

Possibly, painting had become too much for her—all that undue pressure. She just didn't know how to do anything without all her heart and soul and might. Everyone else in art class took a break for a smoke, snack, shmooze, flirting. Not Mom. Every canvas she went at fiercely till exhausted. Even in Central Park, she'd paint continuously without a word to onlookers. Only to the trees and flowers and bushes and lake and Great Lawn did she speak: "Don't move! Stay put! Don't go 'way now!"

Why attack every canvas as if it were her last? And it was affecting her work. The latest had a confrontational quality. Full of feeling, but tougher now, muscular, churning, brooding, almost menacing, like the last works of Van Gogh. Yet Mom herself was buoyant, her radiant smile undimmed.

It took Dr. Ray just ten minutes of simply listening to Mom to diagnose her condition. A milder version of what had rendered Tante Miriam speechless. Yes, aphasia.

"But my brother and I would have *noticed*," Sandra exclaimed. "Not a day goes by without our speaking with Mom. Sometimes several times. And our visits every single week. We talk to her all the time, and we understand her *clearly*. Don't we, Josh?"

"Yes, indeed. And *she* understands *us*. Well, sometimes—"

Patiently, Dr. Ray said, "Knowing the aphasic so well—being on the same wave length—family members fill in words unspoken. So it takes time to realize something's amiss." He scheduled a CAT scan and an appointment with a psychologist.

That gave Sandra and Josh a week to figure out when Mom had been stricken. Alzheimer's? God, no! Without either mentioning the dread disease to the other, each researched it on his own, after studying the symptoms, concluded gratefully she had been spared. But if not that, what?

For the first test, the psychologist drew several pictures of objects which she asked Mom to identify. She couldn't, but Josh also had difficulty with the crude drawings. Mom was an artist, with an aversion to abstract art. Why not show her *pictures?*

"Are you *questioning* my technique? my methodology? my proficiency?"

No, just your intelligence, as well as coming forty-five minutes late and unprepared and disorganized in a hippy get-up, Josh restrained himself from saying.

The psychologist did eventually locate some photographs, after sending him out of the office. These, Josh overheard, Mom identified more easily. But some of the names she couldn't say until given a choice of three. The conclusion after hours of tests: apparently, Mom had suffered a stroke, which accounted for her difficulties in speaking, comprehension, reading and writing.

A *stroke?!* (The same as Tante Miriam!)

The CAT scan corroborated it. Dr. Ray showed Sandra and Josh the report. A massive stroke, or series of strokes, had damaged the left frontal lobe of Mom's brain, its language center. Hence, aphasia. (But no paralysis.)

In the interim having read up on the usual effects of stroke—anger, depression, crying jags—Josh protested. "But Mom's personality. There's been no change at all. The other day I slapped her hand—she was piling food on my plate, and I'm only a dozen pounds over-weight. Well, the next day I asked if she had told my sister I'd smacked her. Quick as a flash, Mom said, 'Are you kidding? You think I want Sandra to learn from you?' "

Dr. Ray smiled, but there was no disputing the CAT scan. "A sense of humor is a good indication of mental health. But nobody knows which part or parts of the brain that involves. What's amazing is your mother's having functioned so well on her own despite this massive stroke or strokes."

"What can we do to help her?"

"Good question. I'm constantly amazed by adult children who see in an aged parent's loss of power only their own lost childhood. Instead of helping out, they bemoan her condition, simply endure it. Your mother needs a therapist to work with her on speech and comprehension."

"Did Mom suspect something was wrong with her?"

"That's why she consulted ear and eye doctors."

"*What?* She never told us."

"Didn't want to burden you, she said."

"Doctor? Let's not burden *her*, okay?" Sandra said. "Call it a burst blood vessel or something. Her dearest sister had a stroke, you see, and I don't want Mom thinking of that now—"

Just then, Mom emerged from the examining room. "When I took off my bra before," she said to Dr. Ray, "well, I certainly hope you don't think I do that all the time for just *anybody*."

The doctor chuckled, Josh laughed much too hard, and Sandra turned away and burst into tears.

The smile on Mom's face flickered. "Is it really that bad, dear? My little joke, I mean."

She insisted afterwards on taking Sandra and Josh to Tavern on the Green. Only, it took five minutes to figure out which restaurant. Finally, "Where we ate when I came home from . . . the land of our fathers . . . and our mothers."

Once there, she exclaimed over the restaurant's gardens, as she had done that first time a decade earlier. Only, this time instead of naming all the flowers, she just pointed. Then, "Don't look like that, children. Please don't. Breaks my heart. What the doctor said made me happy."

"Happy?"

"Yes. Before, it was much worse. I was beginning to think my mind was—well, better not say. At least now I understand why so many of my words stick up here in my . . . And never come down to my . . . So that's *good* news. Believe me."

She was trying to cheer *them* up!

Sandra explained. "It's called retrieval. You haven't forgotten the words, Dr. Ray says. You still know them, Mom, but you have to work at pulling them from the language center of your brain. Because . . . of a blood vessel that burst. T.I.A., that's what it's called. You've had a transient ischemic attack."

"Watch yourself," said Mom. "Such big, hard words can break your . . . whatchamacallits, God forbid."

Josh dug his teeth into his lower lip. Before he could stop himself, "Don't you wonder, Why *you*?"

She reached out and touched his hand. "I did that a lot the last few weeks. Asked myself, Why me? Until I came up with the answer.

Why *not* me? Children, no one is— . . . No person can– . . ."
When the words wouldn't come in English, she took refuge in her
first language. ". . . *beshitzt fin alle kronkeit*, . . . *avekfleehin.*"

What did that mean? Mom couldn't explain. Sandra and Josh
made guesses, none right. So *frustrating.* They felt cut off. Angry,
even at her.

She continued. "Anyway, look at the happy side. I have twice as
many words to draw on. Yiddish as well as . . . Let's just hope I
haven't forgotten the same words in both languages."

A Lincoln Plaza neighbor translated, "No person is *immune.* No
one *escapes.*"

Nodding, Mom said, "But Yiddish makes that sound so much
more comforting. Well, after all, it's *mamaloshen*, the mother tongue."

Of course, she could no longer live alone. That was obvious to
everyone but her. Could still manage on her own. Would not be
budged. Definitely not. Case closed.

"Let *me* try," said Laurel, who told Mom to have a live-in companion wasn't for *her* benefit, but for Sandra's and Josh's. "Want
them worrying about you twenty-four hours a day?

Mom yielded at once. "Well, under those . . . in that case. Okay.
Very important to a mind, peace."

Josh still could not fathom the lack of change in Mom's personality.
A marked difference in the patient's behavior was the tip-off. Bad
temper. Irascibility. Rage. Tears.

Not always, said Dr. Ray. "Strokes strip their victims bare. No
more masks. One sees people as they really are. Everything is
revealed. There's been no change in your mother because this is what
she's always been, what she truly is. Without pretense."

Now to find a companion for Mom. Sandra asked employment
agencies for a Jewish woman, but was sent a Pole who spoke frac-
tured English, a Brazilian with a thick accent, a Jamaican much too
young to have much in common with an octogenarian. The agencies
wouldn't honor requests for someone Jewish, it being unlawful to
discriminate. Though Sandra repeatedly explained that someone
speech-impaired needed a companion easy to understand and to talk
to, each time the response was the same.

"Sorry about your poor old mother. But you want us to get fined?"
Until Sandra finally thought of asking for an American citizen of

any religion whatsoever, or none, who was fluent in Yiddish. Soon
Mom engaged Pearl, a fiftyish, simpatica, talkative woman with a
lilting laugh, granddaughter of a rabbi.

It couldn't have been easy for a woman as fiercely independent as
Mom to share her apartment. But she made the best of it, giving Pearl
plenty of leeway, but never relinquishing control. When the companion said, "My last lady and I got along wonderfully well; everything I told her she did", Mom politely responded, "My dear, I am
not paying you good money to be my boss. Do hope you understand."

Finding a language/speech therapist was no less difficult. Some
refused to be auditioned. One's dangling, clanging jewelry drowned
out her words whenever she moved. Another was efficient but chilly,
still another displayed her diplomas in the bathroom. Finally, Sandra
asked whether choosy Josh was seeking a therapist for Mom or a
mistress for himself.

"I just want somebody like Mom."

"Terrific. And how many years did it take you to find Laurel?"

Within five minutes of meeting Shoshana Kisch, however, Josh
knew she was the one. Sunny, warm, a pretty if portly, fortyish
redhead with a generous sprinkling of freckles. She offered Josh her
own cup of coffee and half a Danish.

"I consider a stroke a detour, not the end of the road," she began.
"My job is to encourage your mother, despite the occasional awk-
wardness, to do as she wishes. To say, I will, I insist on doing.
Improvements, no matter how slight, keep the spirit from being
crushed. Keep hope alive."

A routine was devised. On Shabbas, the companion's day off, Josh
and Laurel would take Mom to shul, after lunch for a walk in Central
Park. To her, nature had always been one proof of the existence of
God. One corner's trees, shrubs, flowers she used to check on
regularly; with her tapwater she had watered a few bushes one
rainless summer. Their locations she still knew, but not their names.

"Isn't that a terrible thing, forgetting?" she'd say.

"Not at all," Laurel would reply. "What's important to you, really
important, will never leave you. You'll always remember. Quick!
Name your two favorite children."

Mom would chuckle.

"Now, which child-in-law do you like better?" Josh would ask. "Charlie or Laurel."

Mom would laugh. "That's too easy. Ask me a harder question."

Once a week Sandra came to shop with Mom—salespeople always treated her better when accompanied by Mom—and to take her to a matinee or evening performance at Carnegie Hall or Lincoln Center. Twice a week Mom worked with the language/speech therapist, twice a week went to museums with her companion Pearl. The weekly visits to the chronic diseases hospital, however, had to end.

"But my friends there will think I deserted them."

"They know better. That you've earned yourself a vacation. For the time being."

Wistfully, Mom said. "The person that was, will I ever be again?"

It tore at their hearts, that question. However, recalling that Mom never oppressed the hospital patients with her own emotions, the children never let on. "You'll get better," each assured her.

"*All* better? Or is that asking for the—?" Gracefully, she extended her right arm upward toward the heavens.

21

RE: Hannah Trilling

I, Shoshana Kisch, was interviewed today! By Mrs. Trilling's son. (Never mentioned his bestsellers, so neither did I.) Wants just the right speech/language therapist for his mother. Not only highly qualified, but a twenty-four-karat mensch. (For a moment, thought he was going to whip out a Rorschach and test me.)

Son instructs me never to say Mrs. Trilling has suffered a stroke. Afraid it would devastate her.

Far more frightening for Mrs. Trilling, I explain, to remain ignorant of her condition. She may be thinking herself senile, or a victim of Alzheimer's, even mentally unbalanced. Son adamant, says he's described in detail what happened inside her brain, just never used that word *stroke*.

Rejects outright my recommendation that Mrs. Trilling join a support group, where stroke victims see how others cope with the same affliction and all vent their feelings, share the distress. But, he claims, just seeing handicapped strangers on the street pains his empathetic mother, overwhelms her with feelings of pity. And seeing herself now among those handicapped would wipe her out.

Common to stroke victims are depression and crying spells. No, none of these telltale signs. His mother's disposition is, except those times her arthritis flares up, invariably sunny. And if she did feel depressed, she would hide it.

March

Hannah Trilling, age "God knows" (her reply), is vigorous, friendly, very pretty, immaculately groomed. No physical effects of stroke. Moves gracefully, dignified bearing. Voice musical.

She presents moderate to severe fluent aphasia affecting both receptive and expressive language abilities. Her speech is characterized by semantic and phonemic paraphasia, word-retrieval difficulties, and poor self-awareness. Although her speech is frequently fluent, as in her use of social idioms, it lacks content. Has difficulty with such automatic tasks as naming days of the week. Orientation to person, place and time is poor. Has difficulty labeling items presented or pointing to items on request. Exhibits mild perseveration. Switches to Yiddish when English fails her.

Mrs. Trilling expresses great eagerness to improve. Asks me several times to help her. Am I a mother? When I nod, she says then I should understand, her hating to be trouble to her children.

What about trouble to herself?

"Or to myself," she says. "Thank you so much for reminding me."

Very hospitable, she asks me several times to stay for lunch. When I decline, she thrusts some Danish pastries on me to take along. (Coals to Newcastle.)

April

Focus today is on person, place and time. I have Mrs. Trilling write her name and address in notebook, then copy it again and again. Does so very conscientiously. Handwriting is à la the old Palmer Method, but very shaky.

Practices saying her address. Then: Where is Lincoln Plaza? In which city? In which state? In which country? When offered a choice of three, selects the right one.

Make out flash cards for days of the week to practice reading. Then have her say them by heart. Mixes up order of days or skips, but never the Sabbath. Needs constant reinforcement drill by companion and/or children.

Kashruth is very important to Mrs. Trilling. Shows me the dishes and silverware for meat, then those for dairy. Never confuses the two even when I try to mix her up. Her morning and evening prayers she can recite by heart, as well as blessings over bread and wine—all in Hebrew.

Her companion reports Mrs. Trilling weeping while watching *Showboat* on TV: "Those two girls had such unhappy lives." That means she was able to follow the movie. *Good.*

Session starts off poorly. Mrs. Trilling's arthritis bothering her. When her companion brings us two big dishes of ice cream, Mrs. Trilling orders her to take them away at once. Lesson continuing when all of a sudden Mrs. Trilling bursts into tears. What's the matter? She won't answer.

I offer her three choices: 1) She doesn't like interruptions, or 2) Doesn't like her companion, or 3) Doesn't like ice cream.

None of the above. Still in tears, Mrs. Trilling apologizes for hurting my feelings! How so? By withholding the ice cream because I'm "a little too heavy." Wasn't considerate to remind me. But being "a little to heavy" (only 75 lbs. worth) is bad for my health, which she worries about. Can I forgive her for embarrassing me?

That settled, we work on contextual and phonemic cuing. (Wash your_____. Hang up your_____. I talk on the tele_____. Put the milk in the refri_____.) She responds well. Pleased to see herself progressing. Mrs. Trilling typically exhibits improvement during the course of every session.

May

Reviewed address, date, days of the week, months of the year, which Mrs. Trilling can now rattle off. Companion and children report how conscientiously she does her homework, writing for hours in her notebook with the same intensity she once brought to her painting.

We print three dozen opposite-cards: up-down, boy-girl, day-night, etc. Some difficulty, confusion complying with requests. (e.g., May I have a glass of water?) Also, some inappropriate behavior (e.g., wiping her eye with plastic wrap, or choosing a spoon to cut an orange).

To relieve the pressure, ease her discomfort when not being able to express herself fully or follow conversations entirely, I suggest Mrs. Trilling tell people she's had a T.I.A. (the term her children use). But she refuses to do so. (Out of a sense of embarrassment? Pride? Or because, as her children say, she's never unloaded a problem of hers on others.)

Mrs. Trilling herself says: "No excuses for me. I am what I am."

We look at a family photo album. Few problems recognizing everyone, but can't name people. Disturbs her, naturally. Explaining, I describe the effects of her stroke (without using that word).

"Why didn't anyone tell me that before?" she asks.

June

Mrs. Trilling had company today. As soon as I walk in, the woman jumps up, pulls a few dollar bills from her purse, stuffs them in my hand. "My sister raves about you." To Mrs. Trilling: "You're mistaken. I never lived with you. Well, maybe two *weeks*." And she's gone.

The lesson goes so poorly, Mrs. Trilling gives up—for the first time. "No memory anymore! I was sure Tessie had lived with me two *years*. But you heard . . ." She rushes from the room, distraught.

Fearful she's suffered another stroke, I phone her son.

"Of course *two years*. Tessie slept in *my* room. After her annulment, my mother couldn't bear the thought of Tessie's living in a rooming house, with a hot plate, sharing a toilet with strangers. And though Mom made my aunt's wedding, Tessie denies my mother even attended."

Why would his aunt lie?

"When you figure out human nature, kindly clue me in." He asked to speak to his mother.

The lesson goes smoothly afterwards. I reassure Mrs. Trilling her memory isn't that bad.

"Not good. Else I'd have remembered the kind of person my beautiful baby turned into. There's a Yiddish saying: When she was a puppy, I fed her—and when she became a dog, she bit me."

June

We go over parts of the body and articles of clothing. Asked where she wears a hat, she points to her head, then laughs as if to say she realizes she's been caught in the act of evading my question. A moment later, out comes *head*, and she's very much relieved. (So am I!)

When I praise her for naming something correctly, she says, "It's about time. You know how old I am?"

How old is she?

"Don't ask. You count years when there's nothing else to count."

Sometimes Mrs. Trilling gets impatient with her companion, who can be bossy. But a minute later, she says in a voice loud enough to carry to the next room, "She's really a very nice lady. Works hard. I like her so much. She cooks for me, you know," she says. "Me, I paint—used to. And one day I'll paint again. I will."

July

Mrs. Trilling greets and sends me away with kisses, has adopted me. Yet still can't remember my name, it being something that had to be learned new (after her stroke). Not something known before that can be retrieved. She calls me *Royta* (Redhead) or *Sheinkeit* (Beauty).

Occasionally, she mentions once having lost almost 20 lbs. "Yes, it can be done if a person really tries hard." (One guess who that person is.)

There are noticeable increments in her production of language and comprehension. When asked, she's good at making her feelings known, yet unfailingly polite and well-mannered. Those she likes or loves, she talks about; as for the others, mum's the word. Wants me to tell her about my own family.

On her time we should talk only of what's important to *her*.

Mrs. Trilling: "*You* are important to me." As usual, she escorts me to the elevator. "Please don't tell my children," she says.

{267}

Tell them what?

"I don't want them to know I have what my sister Miriam had."

July

Today devoted to a discussion of strokes, the many different kinds, the importance of never comparing one to the other. No two exactly alike, each one affects a different part of the brain. Mrs. Trilling's stroke is nothing like that of her sister. Vital for Mrs. Trilling to understand that. Does she?

"I think so."

Doesn't she *know* so?

"Yes. Miriam and me—we're not the same. Miriam didn't have you, *Sheinkeit*."

Miriam had somebody better.

"Better? Impossible. Who?"

She had Hannah.

". . . Am I improving?"

Well, what does *she* think?

"Little by little, yes." She thanks God. In the next breath, me as well.

We work on numbers. She's good at that. Make change of a dollar. A little harder, but it's coming back. We play rummy.

Asks several times how I feel. Why? Just interested. (Something tells me she's worrying about my weight.)

Outside the apartment, we encounter some neighbors. Considering her handicap, Mrs. Trilling's social amenities are remarkable. Still retains all the niceties of dealing with people. Asks about this one's sick husband, that one's grandchildren. Introducing everyone, albeit without using names, she carries it all off. (How many of the neighbors realize she's had a stroke?)

"All the good luck," she calls after me as the elevator door closes. "I love you."

August

The entire session we work on stimulating functional communication via participation in activities of daily living. Setting the table for the Sabbath, preparing the Shabbas meal.

{268}

She's delighted to hear about my diet.

It's going to be a long haul. (75 lbs. drop off speedily only when removed surgically.) Yet quicker than most diets, mine, because—

Should never have gone into specifics. Mrs. Trilling starts worrying about me all over again. I should beware of starving myself to death. (Fat chance!)

September

Mrs. Trilling's son called to ask about my health. His mother is very upset. I explained my so-called starvation diet. Now Son starts worrying I'll be popping off any minute from a potassium deficiency.

I show Mrs. Trilling literature to convince her my liquid diet is perfectly safe. Done under strict medical supervision. Mrs. Trilling asks for my doctor's name and phone number—she wants to call him up herself to check!

Not much accomplished today because all of the talk about my diet. So I refuse that session's fee. She insists. So do I. (Big argument, but pleasant.)

I've explained to both her children that following Mrs. Trilling's initial spurt of progress, the goal of treatment has been to provide stimulation to deter further deterioration of communications abilities. The limitations of such maintenance therapy has also been explained.

Daughter seems to be more realistic about Mrs. Trilling's condition and prognosis than Son. He tells of long discussions with his mother. What he quotes her as saying sounds entirely in character. He sees her as the same person as before the stroke. Like someone with a broken leg that hasn't set properly. She herself, her essence, has not changed in the slightest.

Sometimes, though, Mrs. Trilling does express discouragement: "Maybe it's time for me to go bye-bye." However, Son is always able to talk her out of it. Or make her laugh, as she does him.

Question: Does Son actually succeed in talking her out of it? Or is Mrs. Trilling just pretending to spare his feelings? Pretending so hard, does she convince herself?

Me, I don't recall ever seeing Mrs. Trilling without that lovely face wreathed in a smile.

December

Mrs. Trilling continues to compliment me on my steady loss of weight. We do that a lot, encourage each other. On occasion, she gets annoyed with herself, but remains optimistic.

We make a big salad today. She nearly empties all of the refrigerator's contents on the kitchen table. I tell her to put back everything that's not suitable for a salad. Does so with a little help, but keeps the red horseradish. "Such a pretty color," she says.

Does she miss painting?

"Oh, yes! Sometimes I go around the house, looking at the . . . these things on the . . . and ask myself, Know who did all this? Me, myself and I. Someday I'll do it again . . ." Her face lights up. "There! I got the right word, 'paint.' Words are so like colors? Give life. Mothers, all of them, words are. Fathers also, of course. Shouldn't forget fathers. My Sandra and Josh had a nice father. He gave me them."

January

Invited Mrs. Trilling over for dinner to meet my husband, children, and my mother, visiting from Chicago. Four other friends there. Mrs. Trilling took such pleasure in meeting those closest to me, praising me to the skies.

Throughout the evening she handles herself so well, my mother never realizes Mrs. Trilling had a stroke. When I tell her so, she gives me a big wink. "I try hard to fool myself too."

February

Mrs. Trilling's performance inconsistent today, it being affected by her physical/emotional condition on any given day. Today she was worrying again about my weight. That I'm losing too quickly for my own good. So tough maintaining both my diet and an even keel at the same time, I must have snapped at her. Got upset, understandably, and I apologized at once.

"Don't be foolish," she says. "I already forgot what you said."

Though Mrs. Trilling often gets annoyed at herself because of difficulties encountered in all areas, she is invariably cheerful and cooperative, eager to work and to succeed.

If only a strong will and fierce determination were all!

August

After my vacation in Israel, Mrs. Trilling's welcome couldn't have been warmer if I'd just returned from the dead. The incidence of inappropriate behavior remains consistent, indicating no further deterioration of cognitive functioning. That's the good news. The other: she didn't make any progress. Chances are, she isn't going to get much better than she is right now.

Yet her spirits remain high. Her children credit me (though other stroke patients of mine aren't half as responsive). Asked to account for her good nature and optimism, Mrs. Trilling says, "God. I believe in God."

Mrs. Trilling presents me with a present, a lovely white silk blouse. "It's a ten, Shoshana. Just like you."

Can't tell which moves me more. The size or the Shoshana. This is the first time Mrs. Trilling has called me by name. How hard she must have worked to get it right! All that endless writing, reading, saying, memorizing.

After I thank her and kiss her, she says, "Such a beautiful name, Shoshana. I'm so sorry it took me this long to learn. But now I'll never forget it. And if you can lose—was it 71 lbs.?—I can learn to do just like before. Right? And to see my grandchildren married." She chuckles. "I do that a lot. Make bargains with God to keep me till something wonderful happens, and when it does, I ask for something more. Now it's Jewish great-grandchildren. Tell me the truth, Shoshana. You think I give God too hard a time?"

22

*I*NSPIRED by Bernard Baruch, who made millions in the stock market by always selling too soon, Zack had opted to pull out of the sexual revolution. There was only so much even an inventive fellow could do before repeating himself. The awful predictability of each first date, recounting still again one's life story, then enduring hers. And at evening's end this era's good night kiss, bed.

It was hard to concentrate on a career while plunging into affairs or withdrawing. Constant time-consuming search and seduction could impede one's climb up the corporate ladder to partnership, R.J. intimated. Someone pushing thirty needed a home base for recharging batteries. There were enough pressures and challenges in the business jungle. After the daily fray, Zack wanted constancy and comfort, simple adoration.

Enter Sarah, a posh Wall Street restaurant's knockout hostess whom all the male clientele were after. A woman in her position had to be clever to turn them off, while keeping their business, done with utmost finesse. And a man had to be truly superior to triumph over all the other bidders. As yet, the family knew nothing about Sarah.

(Zack hated subway riders looking over his shoulder while he was reading a newspaper.)

Some flack was to be expected from Mother and Dad, his being a negative personality—hers positive. Positive she was always in the goddam right. They were sure to come around, however, once they met Sarah. Everyone adored the green-eyed strawberry blonde with the dynamite body born for pleasuring. An old-fashioned girl—like Grandma—she lived to please Zack. Unlike those demanding JAPs whose idea of civil rights began with the right to first and last orgasm amid credit cards galore. From Sarah none of the standard women's lib line that classified men as the enemy who wanted only one thing from a woman—her scalp—and to whom was owed one thing only— the back of a hand. Sweeter than sugar, Sarah appreciated how hard 'Zack worked, how much he'd achieved, his likes and dislikes, wisdom. And unlike most women, she wasn't the least bit rigid: she might even convert to Judaism one day.

What was needed, before introducing a gentile fiancée, were allies, his parents having been programmed from birth to consider inter-marriage an evil state. First-generation Americans, they still thought like newly arrived immigrants to the shores of the twentieth century. Their closest brush with America's great melting pot was cheese fondue.

First, Zack felt out Uncle Josh, but without his knowledge. During lunch one day, Zack mentioned this friend of his who wanted to marry out. What should Zack tell him?

"Is the woman willing to convert?"

"Well, not right now."

"Then how do your friends plan to raise their children? As Jews? Christians?"

"Well, they don't want to *impose* any religion."

"What about table manners? Will your friends refrain from im-posing *them?*"

"Well, then, perhaps an admixture of the two religions. So neither one is rejected. That way their children can be *both*. Or decide for themselves later on."

"And sexual preference. Will your friends raise their children as both, then let them choose for themselves at puberty ?"

"Hey! Uncle Josh. Trying to score off me, you've lost sight of the most important point of all."

"What's that?"

"This man and this woman really love each other. Passionately. Have you never experienced passion?"

"Passion?" he said, as if it were a Third World country whose location he couldn't quite pinpoint. "Isn't that what dies within a year of the wedding day? To be replaced, if you're fortunate, by perpetual caring."

"*That* you can buy from any *cemetery*, for crying out loud!"

Uncle Josh shrugged. "You asked my advice, but you meant my approval. Me, I think intermarriage is the freeloader's way out of loneliness. Having one's children pay the price for parental passion."

"What price? Have two heritages to draw on. Enriching."

"Think now, Zack. How can a child take pride in one parent's religion, whose New Testament labels the other's co-religionists Christ-killers? Or in the other parent's, which regards a man-God as blasphemy? " A college friend of Uncle Josh's, the Catholic-raised son of a Jewish father, would date only Protestants, so much did he hate his parents for screwing up his identity, relegating him forever to no-man's land.

Just then Zack's beeper sounded, activated by himself to end the pointless conversation. Anyone who didn't realize that Zack had been talking about himself for eighty-five minutes couldn't be very smart.

Support aplenty was found among Zack's friends, many inter-married or inter-shacked up, who lived broader lives than those envisioned by his family. Let Mother and Dad categorize people as either Jewish or un- and segregate themselves accordingly. They still wondered aloud which people in the news and on TV were members of the tribe. Tallied how many of each year's Nobel and Pulitzer and Miss America winners were Jews. In short, provincials.

Sarah's family, in contrast, welcomed Zack like king of the Jews. No prejudice shown even by grandparents who had immigrated from Poland the very same year as the Brody family. Nothing to make him feel the least bit uncomfortable. The first Sunday brunch they served him lox and bagels and cream cheese and pastrami and corned beef: chosen food. On the wall over their TV set was a rectangle lighter than the surrounding area where till the night before, Sarah confided, a portrait of Jesus had hung. When Zack mentioned Grandma's own copy of Rouault's *Jesus*, everyone laughed—and back up went the painting.

Zack wanted to tell all that to Dad when he sought him out at work, but never got the chance. Though he was never as attached to Judaism as Mother, the news about Sarah enraged Dad. "Make your choice, Zack! That gentile girl or your father." And out he stormed, forgetting the office was his.

Zack not being forgiving of tantrums not his own, that worked in Sarah's favor. A contest between Dad, who always criticized, and Sarah, who never found fault, was no contest. Always supportive, enveloping, the woman was all womb.

So unlike picky, picky, picky Mother. "A convert is as much a Jew as Moses. No problem . . . No? At least if your *children* are raised Jewish—"

"Well . . . there's Sarah's family. Sarah wouldn't want to hurt their feelings."

"Very commendable." Then—air sharply inhaled, cheeks caving in—"But what of *your* family? The family of Jews dating back 4,000 years? We have no feelings? no memory? no—" She sputtered like a tea kettle at full boil.

"Hey! Don't you think you're overdoing it, Mother? It isn't as if I were marrying a man, you know."

"Was that the only other option available, Zack?"

"Wait till you meet Sarah. Here, you've always disparaged me as being materialistic, money-mad. Won't you give me any credit now for not choosing a rich girl?"

"You want a medal, Zack, I'll give you a medal. The Order of Benedict Arnold. You were raised in the Jewish religion. Nurtured you, made you in great part what you are today. No person comes out of himself. So there's a responsibility to maintain the inheritance received and bequeath it. Don't you owe the Jewish people *something?*"

"What, my *life?* I'm proud to be a Jew, of course, but—"

"Proud. Like those Jewish entertainers who say so all the time

{275}

while fathering battalions of gentile children. You'd deliberately junk thousands of years of Jewish history, millions of Jews who lived, even died to produce you?"

"Thousands! Millions! Cut the melodrama, Mother. And think of just two people very much in love, one of them your very own son."

"You expect to build a happy marriage on betrayal?"

"We may very well raise our children Jewish, after all. It's a distinct possibility."

"May! May!"

"It isn't as if Sarah is pregnant. We have plenty of time to deal with the religion thing—"

"Tell me something, Zack. How come you never dated a fat girl?"

"What's that got to do with—?

"Answer the question."

"Obesity repels me. Why—?"

"Yet every fat girl is a slender girl *potentially*. Just as your future children are *possible* Jews. Tell me, Zack, would you propose to a girl who might *consider* dropping 100 lbs.?"

"Look, Mother. If we can't discuss this with some degree of intelligence—"

"Would you have looked at this Sarah twice if her nose were half an inch longer? Or her bust three inches flatter? Or her backside five inches bigger? Why isn't the religion of your people, their sacrifices to remain Jews, sometime martyrdom, their future existence on this planet at least as important to you as a nose, breasts, fanny?"

Incredible!

"Know how many Jews are left in the entire world? Twelve million. We're the only people never to have recovered from the Holocaust. Of America's six millions Jews, one out of every three now intermarries. Ever read the wedding announcements in the Sunday *New York Times?* Every week a new casualty list. What the Holocaust started, Zack, love is liable to finish. And this time our own children are doing it to us. All in the name of love, sweet love."

There really was no talking with the woman, who wanted to impale him on her will. Well, Zack would dance to nobody else's tune. His definition of a man was someone no longer in need of the approval of mommy and daddy. The child Zack was dead, long live the adult!

Yet, he wanted approbation. Besides, how would it look to friends and colleagues, a parental boycott? "My parents think nobody should marry gentiles except gentiles and other creatures from outer space."

Perhaps his kid sister would help out. Too late to make it in the theater, even for one so talented, Debbie was now in medical school which Zack, the good brother, had warned her against. What potential husband would put up with a medical student's grind, followed by residency in pediatrics (the least financially rewarding specialty)?

"What do you say, Debbie?"

She replied, "You think Sarah is the only woman in the world? Only one Juliet for each Romeo?"

"I've searched everywhere. For years and years."

"On the ski slopes of Colorado and Switzerland? Snorkeling in Acapulco Bay? Vacations in Paris and Peru? Is that where New Yorkers seek suitable brides these days? And those weekends you flew to San Francisco because, you confided, girls there were hungry, *real* hungry."

"Why are you all against me! Siding with Mother, who loused up *your* life—"

"Isn't it about time you realized parents aren't *congenitally* wrong? Ninety percent of actors are either unemployed or saying, 'I'm just doing this part for the money.' Why, there's more drama in healing a sick child than—"

"Wait till you meet Sarah. You'll see how wrong Mother is. Besides, now with AIDS on top of herpes . . ."

For the wedding Sarah wanted something small, which her parents could afford, but Zack insisted on underwriting a lavish affair that would show her off. Since he wouldn't have a priest officiate, and Sarah's family might resent a rabbi, they compromised on a judge who was Jewish and a kosher caterer.

There was no appeasing Mother, however. Sooner or later, though, she'd have to come around. The nerve of her to forbid Zack from telling Grandma about his engagement!

That gave him an idea. Grandma often referred to her own mother as a *gute beiter* for her loved ones on earth, a pleader and intercessor up in Heaven. Grandma, the family's most progressive Jew, was the ideal advocate for Zack. Just living so long had taught her not to make crises out of molehills. Hadn't she, the kosherest of Jews, fed Mother pigs' feet? At a time when it was considered scandalous, supported Tessie's decision to leave her husband, even lied on the witness stand about her brother-in-law's saying he didn't want children (the only grounds for divorce in New York in those benighted days). Painted a stark naked man. Approved of surrogate motherhood.

"Right now," Mother was saying, "the stroke is more than enough for Grandma to handle."

Yield to pressure? to extortion? When broad-minded Grandma could easily set this matter entirely aright? "Okay, Mother. I promise not to breathe a word of Grandma about my engagement."

No need to say a word. Meeting Sarah and getting to know her would be enough to sway Grandma, who would then *insist* he marry her. There was nobody in the world who could *not* love Sarah.

23

WHEREVER Laurel looked, there were bellies swelling. Here a maternity dress, there a maternity dress, everywhere maternity clothes. (And on the subway, ads for abortion, a million and a half being performed each year.) Except for the male population and her, it seemed nearly everyone in Manhattan was pregnant, or had been, or could be. Having delayed matrimony and childbearing in favor of a career (why she'd put up with Josh's dawdling), Laurel was now finding it harder not to sympathize with those demented women who kidnapped infants from maternity wards. Well, their fecund mothers could always resume production, couldn't they?

Once having decided on motherhood, while Josh joked about marriage to a nymphomaniac, Laurel went at it like a dog worrying a bone. Deadly serious, their lovemaking, with egg whites substituted for commercial lubricants or saliva, which impeded fertility. All during this time without consequence, Laurel had been infinitely solicitous of the frail male ego. Then tests revealed the one to blame—Josh had forbidden her to use the word—was *Laurel*.

"Nobody is to *blame*," he said repeatedly.

"Perhaps so. But *nobody* is getting pregnant, either." She felt incomplete, not part of what was going on out there. Worst of all, cheated.

Growing up determined to live a life different from her own mother's, with no intellectual outlet or career other than homemaker, Laurel had believed everything possible. In careers that was coming true. But biology still had not budged. Just as Josh imagined marriage an option open till the grave closed over him, Laurel assumed childbearing could be put off until she finished her big book, guaranteeing her chairmanship of the psychology department. To atone for having kept her waiting for matrimony, Josh didn't noodge Laurel about motherhood. Only to discover eventually that whereas infertility strikes only five percent of women 20–24, it was five times that after thirty-five, plus a far greater likelihood of miscarriage. For all their lack of education and sophistication, their grandparents had married and procreated in time. Laurel and Josh had erred in temporizing far too long. Chances now were their Me Generation might never propagate a We Generation. End of the line?

Project Baby was launched. If Laurel and Josh couldn't create one the old-fashioned way, they would spawn it in a petri dish in a lab. For twelve days straight he would shoot her up with drugs to stimulate the ripening of multiple egg-containing follicles, after which came daily blood tests and ultrasound examination. Also headaches, mood swings. But no lovemaking that could deplete Josh's offering. As soon as harvested eggs were fertilized and cell division occurred, the embryo was implanted in Laurel, crazed with hope. Then, to prepare the uterine lining for pregnancy, more injections, of progesterone.

"Sometimes, I think it would be easier," Laurel said, "to fly me to the moon."

Certainly cheaper. A total of $25,000 worth of attempts. Nothing compared to the grief that followed each failure, *her* failure, each one a tiny death. When she could mourn no more, they called it quits. Abrogated, Laurel's right to become pregnant.

Adoption, she resisted for reasons that were less acceptable to herself than to Josh. There was still an outside chance of conceiving normally, wasn't there? Why take into their hearts a complete stranger, the issue of God knows who?

"It's natural to want a baby," Josh argued. "Everyone wants a baby."

"Are you calling me *un*natural?"

"Don't be silly, Laurel."

"So now I'm *silly*. In *addition* to unnatural."

Josh kept at the whys and why nots and becauses until one evening Laurel lashed out at him for prizing her only as a vehicle for satisfying an atavistic male yearning to continue the Trilling dynasty.

Josh laughed and laughed. "That's rich! We don't even have a condo."

"The only condo-less couple in New York. Josh, we are failures."

"Who's a failure? Not yours truly."

"*I'm* the failure, right?" She ran from the kitchen.

Josh came after her and sat her down on the couch in the living room. "Okay, Laurel. My first novel got rejected no less than forty-nine times. Did I ever show you the T-shirt I had printed up at the time? *There is no hope*, it says, *pass it on.*"

"Eventually, you did get published, Josh. Successfully, too. A second time as well."

"And if not? Would you have rejected me? I'd still be a damn good editor. Would you think me a failure? For shepherding the work of others, sometimes from an embryo of an idea, to the time they're sent out into the world. Does that spell failure?"

Only to her mother-in-law did Laurel confess: "To tell the truth, I don't know if I'm *capable* of loving a child not my own."

"A person as lovable as you? Don't be foolish."

"What did you say?" (Laurel wanted to hear it again.)

". . . Of course you can do it," Mom said. "If *I* could—"

But she had raised siblings, her own flesh and blood. Far different from raising a total stranger.

Mom paced the floor, then took several deep breaths, as if preparing for a broad jump. "Tell me, what do you think of the relationship between my children and myself?"

"Quite extraordinary. Highly unneurotic." (A mutual adoration society, really.)

{281}

Hesitantly, Mom continued, "You can't tell which of them is adopted, can you?"

"*Adopted?*" The revelation astounded Laurel. "Josh never breathed a word!"

"Of course not. I never told him. Or Sandra."

"What? *Why*—?"

"My oldest sister was the daughter of my father and his first wife, who died in childbirth. I never told anyone she was a half-sister. But she told her children. A mistake. Because they were always estranged from the rest of the family, feeling they weren't full-fledged members. So . . ."

"You still haven't told me who's the adopted one, Josh or Sandra."

"Never mattered one bit to me. Why should it matter to you?"

Was Mom telling the truth? Considering her vested interest in perpetuating the family bloodline, not to mention the unlikelihood of an adoptee not sensing his or her being a total human transplant, Laurel had doubts. Still, when asked about his oldest aunt, Josh did confirm she was Mom's half-sister (which he accidentally learned just a few years before). At which point Laurel agreed to adopt.

Studiedly casual was Josh's response, "Fine. Go ahead."

He wanted wifely participation, clever guy. And so she did become involved—ever more so as doors were slammed in her face. Astonishing. Now that Laurel was finding it impossible to adopt, she yearned to do so.

Yet when surrogate motherhood became a viable option, Laurel shied away. A baby born of surrogacy's peculiar circumstance might come between her and Josh. Whereas an adopted child would place them on equal footing, the issue of Josh alone might sentence her permanently to left field. Of late she'd been dreaming, face pressed against a nursery window, of watching Josh inside cuddle an infant version of himself.

"Well, Laurel?" Josh said for the umpteenth time.

Still another rebuttal. "Lots of people regard surrogacy as further exploitation of women. They want it outlawed."

"Oh, do they? Abortion, Laurel. How do they feel about that? What about you? In favor?"

"Of course. Exercising control over one's own body is a woman's prerogative."

"Then you'd allow a pregnant woman to withhold life. Yet deny a surrogate the right to *give* life?"

"You don't *understand*," she burst out. "The life isn't *mine!*"

He turned away and spoke without looking at her. "Maybe I do understand, Laurel. More than you realize. So much has been written about women's envy of men. However men too can be envious. Of women's procreative power. But, Laurel. Envy doesn't make someone an awful person. Just a human being."

How dare he call her envious! "Tell me something, Josh. Suppose positions were reversed. Would you agree to *my* being artificially inseminated by a total stranger?"

"Yes, of course."

She didn't believe that for a minute. What kind of man would live with a woman swelling daily with another's seed? Such a man, Laurel herself could never live with. "Tell me the truth, Josh. I'll agree to this if you're honest."

If positions were reversed, he swore up and down, he'd positively let her be impregnated by another.

"Liar! Tell me the truth."

"Typical communist ploy. They get prisoners to confess to imaginary crimes, then have them executed . . . Okay, okay. The only time I'd let you bear someone else's baby would be posthumously."

"*Why* wouldn't you let me, Josh?"

"I love you too much. No, out of male possessiveness—isn't *that* what you want me to say?"

"Well, I love you too much too, Josh. So why should *I* allow *you?*"

"Dammit! All I know is there's something inside me that . . . *hungers* for a child. To leave something *enduring.*"

"In *that* case—" Having reconciled herself before to adopting a strange couple's baby, how could she bar Josh's for being his alone? "—go ahead and make the arrangements."

From applicants submitted by a broker, Josh asked Laurel to select the surrogate mother herself. That called for interviews. Why hold an ovum to less stringent standards than a cleaning lady? Only, she could hardly demand references in this instance. (How many babies have you had with how many other men? What percentage did you give away? Mind if I ask your husband how good a mother you are to the children you've retained?)

Having a baby for the sole purpose of discarding it like toenail clippings certainly wasn't normal. That automatically marked a prospective surrogate mother abnormal. By inheritance, any baby of hers equally so. And how does a mother-that-can't-be relate to a success?

In person the applicants did nothing to allay Laurel's misgivings. One spoke of treating her three children to Disneyland with the $10,000 proceeds, another wanted the money for a divorce. What kind of baby would emerge from women of this sort?

After a while, a long while, Josh mentioned, very delicately, it had taken the College of Cardinals less time to select the latest pope.

"I don't want someone to bear a precious child of yours just for the money."

"What then for? This is not exactly a dating situation, remember. Or maybe you want to kidnap the future baby of some Phi Beta Kappa I'll go out tonight and rape?"

The interviews continued, with no result other than Laurel's being fired by the broker for giving applicants complexes. Now she also had to interview brokers, one of whom matched her up with a thirty-five-year-old mother of two, a pharmacist's wife who wanted nothing for her service.

"Did I understand correctly?"

"That's right. No money at all. For *her*."

That was *really* peculiar. Made the prospective surrogate immediately suspect. Unless she was Mother Teresa living in Rockland County under the pseudonym of Kimberly Levin. Still, Laurel went to meet the high school graduate, who very possibly would produce a baby not college material, but a future salesperson at McDonald's.

Ms. Levin's middle-class home in Nyack had an ill-tended lawn and a living room stocked by Sears, Roebuck and Company, very few books in a large credenza, TV Guide and People magazine on the coffee table, but no paintings on velvet. Yet why so judgmental? After some uncomfortable small talk, Laurel fired the obvious question.

"My two children have made me and my husband so happy," Kimberly replied, "we just want to give some of the same happiness to another couple."

"Of course. I see." (In a pig's eye.)

"Started with my older sister. She couldn't conceive because of a dry womb. Her doctor took secretions from mine and, well, today she has a beautiful baby girl. That made me feel so *good*. Then, these cousins of mine can't have children. They're really hurting. So I thought . . ."

"Giving a baby away. That won't hurt?" Laurel could have bitten off her tongue.

Kimberly thought for a long moment. "I think we're put on this earth, people are, for a reason. If for nothing else, to make life a little less sad for each other."

"Oh . . . !" This woman meant what she said. Not even TV evangelists could fake sincerity so convincingly. That examination of genuinely good people to discover why they differ from the rest, where their goodness comes from, how it was nurtured. She had to complete it now. So what if Kimberly's child wouldn't have an I.Q. that equaled Laurel's or Josh's? No less a genius than Albert Einstein had written: "Goodness and a strong character are better than intelligence and learning."

One of the children awoke, crying for her mother and rousing her brother. When Kimberly went to them, Laurel tagged along. So adorable were they—one two, the other four—smelling of milk and cookies, Laurel had to restrain herself from asking if either of them was available.

"This one's going to Harvard," Kimberly said, smiling, "and this one to Yale."

There was a sure way to subvert Kimberly's offer. One question would do it. What effect, do you suppose, will seeing Mommy give away baby brother or sister have upon these two? "Kimberly, haven't you considered . . ." Laurel hesitated.

"Considered what?"

Aborting that question, she said, "Ten thousand dollars would pay for a large chunk of college tuition. Why turn it down?"

Kimberly's open face clouded over. "I was sure you would *understand*. Why I selected you. Well, evidently not. Would you please excuse me now while I tend to my children?"

Selected? Laurel, back in the living room, wondered about that until the kids quieted down and Kimberly returned.

"You don't think I'd bring into this world a baby I'd hand over to just *anyone*, do you?" She had reviewed dozens of applications and investigated several applicants herself after a fashion. She read Josh's novels and Laurel's articles and audited several of her classes. Josh she followed around during lunch hour, even approached him with an idea for a nonexistent article. He had turned it down with such kindness, mentioning having been repeatedly rejected himself.

"You did that? All that trouble and expense?"

Kimberly shook her head sadly. "You really *don't* understand, do you?" Outside, a car horn sounded several times. "That's your cab, Mrs. Trilling."

"What cab?"

"The one I called to take you back to the bus station."

Laurel was being *dismissed!*

"I wish you luck, Mrs. Trilling. I really do. Elsewhere."

Body chilled, face burning, Laurel picked up her purse and left the house without a word. Failure? No, self-destruction. But why? Was it possible she feared motherhood more than childlessness?

Josh naively supposed all mothers were like his, but Laurel knew better. Many friends reported stormy mother-child relationships. Her own mother had been self-centered. After her death, when Laurel packed up all her belongings, she found not a photograph, not a letter, nothing of children there. As if Laurel and her brother did not exist. Had never been.

Growing up, she had consciously patterned herself after her warmly affectionate father and kind spinster aunt. So hard to break the cycle of unloving. Usually, a caring nature develops during pre-Oedipal infancy from a mother's loving nature, which becomes internalized. The make-or-break power that parents wield! The power to make defenseless children feel good or feel bad about themselves, to love others. Was Laurel fleeing the challenge?

On the walkway leading to the taxi that would take her away from perhaps her last chance at parenthood, she tripped over a toy baby carriage. Stooping to pick it up, she cradled in both hands what she'd never find at home. A moment later, she spun on her heel and ran back into the house.

"I don't want just *any* baby," Laurel said, weeping. "I want a *good* baby. *Your* baby, Kimberly. *Please?*"

Kimberly's selflessness made Laurel completely rethink her study of altruism, after which she jettisoned years of research. Her questionnaires, projective tests, experiments, interviews had all revealed only what respondents *said* but little about how, facing profound moral options, they would *act*. Such theoretical responses naturally favored those deft at lip service. As Josh's mother noted, the German people—long superior in learning, culture, sophistication—perpetrated the Holocaust, whereas the saviors of nearly all their Jews were the Danish, known chiefly for pastry.

Several months after Kimberly, with Josh's offering, conceived, Laurel flew to Denmark to interview a dozen Righteous Gentiles. Among her early findings: those who had risked their lives for Jews were for the most part neither high nor low in social status, education, intelligence, creativity. They were modest rather than clever, common people of uncommon virtues, heroic without being boastful, not intellectual.

Nor did rescuers simply happen on victims to save: they recognized opportunities where others did not, sought out, or created them. Because they cared for fellow human beings, even those they sometimes didn't like. For the rescuers there simply was no choice other than to help. Impelled by their values, they had a sense of personal obligation that did not allow them to do otherwise. Exactly why, Laurel would determine after interviewing scores of other Righteous Gentiles, as well as those who chose *not* to help any Jew.

On her return, Josh announced amiocentesis had indicated the baby was a girl and asked her to select the name.

"We are really going to be parents!" she exclaimed over and over again, never using the word *mother*.

With Josh's baby due the week of his annual NES fundraising speech, Laurel stayed behind in New York. So when the phone rang at seven-thirty that Sunday evening, she bounded from the chair.

But it was Josh, calling from Boston to talk about his mother. On the phone just before, no chuckle in response to his kidding, voice flat and depressed.

"Probably her arthritis."

"I asked if she'd had a good time this morning at the temple breakfast. But she never answered. *Three times* Mom did not answer. Laurel, I have this feeling—"

"It's your eternal stage fright. Stop projecting. You're tying up the line."

Just before midnight a phone call interrupted Laurel's work on what Josh called the Mystery-of-the-Good Book. Kimberly! To report the start of contractions.

Answering, Laurel asked, "How many minutes apart are they?"

But it was Pearl. So loudly, so funny, Mom was snoring. Hadn't she ever snored before? What was strange about that? Heavy, very heavy. Another thing. Some applesauce had dribbled out of the corner of her mouth.

"Why don't you give her a good shake?" (Instead of bothering me at such an hour for no reason.)

"I've done that."

"Suppose you put the phone next to her mouth." Listening, Laurel heard deep, rhythmic snores. "She's sleeping very soundly, that's all."

"But I can't wake her."

Laurel switched on the telephone answering machine and took a taxi to Mom's, ten minutes away. Wearing a brand-new pink nightgown, two pillows under her head, she was lying on her back, face unwrinkled in repose. Always been something spooky about Mom's looks. The woman got prettier and prettier with each passing year, the reverse of the Picture of Dorian Gray.

"It's just a very deep sleep, Pearl."

Leaning over the bed, Laurel took hold of Mom's shoulders and shook them. "Wake up!" Again shook her, harder.

No reaction. Yet rosy-cheeked Mom was breathing regularly. Why on earth couldn't she be roused?

"See, Laurel? It's just like I told you."

A vase on the dresser contained a dozen large yellow chrysanthemums which had not been there the day before. "Who brought the flowers?"

Pearl, watching nervously from the foot of the bed, fidgeted. "Let me make some tea." She hurried from the bedroom.

Laurel followed after. "Why didn't you answer my question?"
"Mrs. Trilling made me promise not to tell." She looked away.
Laurel felt a sinking sensation in the pit of her stomach. "Mom had
a visitor today? Zack?

Pearl nodded. "He took Mrs. Trilling out to lunch."

"Did he say anything about—"

"Zack said *nothing*. Not a word. Neither one of them said a word
about anything."

"Neither?"

Pearl turned away, trembling.

Laurel went at once to the phone and called Sandra—filling her in
on the details, except for Zack's visit.

She'd drive right down from Westchester as soon as she'd contact
Mom's gerontologist. "Hold the fort."

Now Laurel demanded to hear from Pearl everything that had
happened. Yes, Zack had stopped by unexpectedly with Sarah. No,
no mention was made of a wedding. But he'd never brought a girl
over before, and the way they behaved made the situation clear
enough.

"Did Zack *say* anything?"

"He didn't have to. She guessed."

"About the wedding?"

"And about Sarah being a shiksa. She raved so about the Jesus
painting, then asked about that other painting, what the three men
reading the Torah were doing. After Sarah said goodbye—she called
Mrs. Trilling *babushka*, Polish for grandmother—Mrs. Trilling
dropped into the recliner like a stone. I tried talking to her, but it was
no use. She cried. All she said, so many times, was: 'So this is how
it ends.' " Mrs. Trilling made Pearl promise not to say a word to Josh
or to Sandra. Then she tore out a page from her exercise notebook
and wrote something down.

"Let me see."

Pearl went to the desk and took out a sheet of paper. On it was
written the same word on seven lines, misspelled each time:
REMEMBER.

"Remember *what?*"

"She wouldn't say. I asked her to dictate to me. She can't write well, you know. But she's so independent. Said tonight she'd think some more, then write everything down herself in the morning. Not a letter, she said. Something *like* a letter. An addition to what she'd written a few years ago."

She was that exhausted, Pearl had to help Mrs. Trilling get ready for bed. Pearl overheard her saying a few times, "Go ahead, I'm listening." (But to whom?) Several hours later that terrible snoring, and the dribbling. "What will you tell Sandra, Laurel?"

Certainly not the truth. It would poison everyone's life. Not what Sandra and Josh's mother would want. Down the incinerator went Zack's yellow chrysanthemums.

Sandra, on her arrival, said Dr. Ray thought Mom's drugged sleep was a reaction to the new medication. "She has to be watched carefully during the night. Anything else unusual the doctor wants to know at once. Not that he expects anything."

But the unusual had already happened, Mom's intense reaction to Zack's Sarah, and gone unreported. For an hour Sandra held Mom's hand and stroked her hair. When the heavy snores didn't abate, Laurel took a needle and jabbed it into Mom's arms and legs.

Not a quiver.

Something was terribly wrong.

Though it was three o'clock in the morning, Dr. Ray said, "No need to apologize for calling. This is why I'm a doctor." He instructed them to shine a light into Mom's eyes and report whether or not her pupils contracted.

With no flashlight at hand, Sandra lit a Sabbath candle, and with Pearl holding Mom up and Laurel propping her eyelids open, passed the flame back and forth. "The blessing, Mom. Say the blessing," she pleaded. "Please give us the blessing."

There was no more captivating sight than Mom's arms swooping to encircle the Sabbath flames, harvest their light, bring handfuls to her face, then offering up a stream of blessings and prayers. By the time she'd finish, melted wax would be dripping down the silver candlesticks.

"Look!"

Laurel, however, saw no movement.

Dr. Ray held to his original diagnosis. "Keep an eye on your mother. The medication should wear off by eight o'clock. Call me then."

"I'm *sure* Mom's fine," Sandra said. "Look how beautiful she looks." For Laurel she made up the couch in the living room. She herself would spend what remained of the night next to Mom's bed on the floor. Just like olden, golden days, when Sandra was young and the house teemed with overnight guests. "Where'd that come from?" She pointed to a single American Beauty rose in a vase atop the television set.

Laurel, who hadn't noticed the flower before, froze.

"A gift," Pearl said.

"Who from?"

"Some florist on Central Park West."

Forgetting there were no florists on that residential street, Sandra smiled. "Mom will be furious Pearl had us come over. What should we tell her? I know! That we're here to announce the birth of her new grandchild. Laurel, let's just pray your baby cooperates."

In her lower abdomen Laurel experienced a sudden rush of warmth, which radiated through her entire body. Sandra had called the baby *hers*. Laurel's.

24

*T*HE day before the hospital fundraiser, Josh and Laurel had accompanied Mom to Sabbath services. Praying, what was she noodging God about *this* time? First on her list, of course, was their baby-to-be. Did she really believe God was up there somewhere waiting to be begged or flattered into showering His bounties on people below? Could prayer actually change God's mind?

"All I know is that prayer does change those who pray," she said. "So even if prayer doesn't change the world, it can make the world worth saving."

Mom's regular seat was on the temple aisle, where she could reach out to kiss the Torah when it was carried by, adorned with silver crown and breastplate. This Shabbas she pointed toward the *bimah* as the reader, flanked by two other men, chanted from the sacred scroll. "Remind you of something?"

"Always," said Josh.

She looked pleased.

"Your painting come to life."

Walking up the aisle after reading the Haftorah, the congregation's president paused beside Mom. "You're such a beautiful woman, Mrs. Trilling. But today, simply gorgeous."

"It's the hat." As he chuckled, she quickly added, "So's your wife."

Mom listened attentively to the sermon, difficult though it was for her to follow. Hardness of hearing, a speech professor had told Josh, is even more isolating than blindness. But if true art lay in concealing art, perhaps true empathy required tempering it with a smile. (It was only at home after each visit to the chronic diseases hospital, with no patient there to see her recuperating in bed for eighteen hours, that Mom allowed feelings to surface, overwhelm her.) So whenever she asked the chances of her brain's language center being restored in full, Josh would answer, evenly, "Well, not one hundred percent, unfortunately. But who's a hundred percent anymore? Certainly not yours truly. Shoshana does tell me you *are* improving. You can see yourself making progress, isn't that so?"

"Yes, of course," she'd always say, sometimes with more conviction than others.

Rain aborted that afternoon's stroll through Central Park. Anticipating the bad weather, Josh had brought over a cassette of *La Bohème*, but first played Mom's orchestral tape of Yiddish songs. Its initial selection, *A Yiddisher Mamma*, brought tears to her eyes, which surprised him.

"Why are you crying, Mom?"

"I *miss* her. I miss her so much."

"But that was over sixty-five years ago."

"A mother is forever."

On hearing the next song, she brightened, hummed along. "I used to know the words to these songs. Sang them all the time."

Laurel urged her to sing. "These melodies, you know them by heart, don't you?"

"That's right, I do." In her beautiful, still clear high soprano Mom sang out. "Isn't that wonderful! I can still sing." Hearing *Eili, Eili,* she reminisced about being welcomed to America. Her father weeping for his dead wife and the mother left behind. Everyone wondering what the New World held in store, how they'd survive. "Seems like a dream. All a dream."

{ 293 }

"What *kind* of dream, Mom?" *Happy*, Josh desperately wanted to hear her say.

"Kind," she said.

"I asked, *what* kind of dream?"

"Just told you, Josh. A *kind* dream. A dream of *chesed*."

"Lovingkindness? Your own? Or lovingkindness received?"

"Same thing. That's a sign God is alive and well."

"What is?"

"*Chesed*. The beginning and the end of the Torah, you know, is the doing of *chesed*."

When Josh played *La Bohème*, Mom, instantly enchanted and exalted, joined in with each aria. Still intact was her ability to live in the moment. At opera's end, she remarked, "So sad! Poor girl was much too young to die. Life hardly started. If she'd had what I've had, Josh . . ."

"Yes?"

"Well, take the holy days. I always look forward to them. Despite all the work, preparing. When they come, I appreciate every single minute. Still, with all the enjoyment, I'm not all that sorry to see them over. They . . . What they were supposed to do, they did. What they were . . . born for."

Josh chose his words as carefully as Mom had. "Remember the holiday of Succos? Legend has it God so loved being with the Children of Israel on Succos, he asked to have it prolonged twenty-four hours more. And they, loving God's company, accepted His invitation to stick around longer. And were absolutely delighted they did. A regular party they've had ever since on that added holiday of Simchas Torah."

Mom chuckled. "You should be a writer."

Escorting Josh and Laurel to the elevator, so passionately did she wish them a wonderful time at that night's dinner party, nothing else in the whole world seemed to matter more to her. "Enjoy, children, *enjoy!*"

That week's particularly heavy schedule might keep them from seeing Mom till the following Shabbas. Seven days had to be an exceedingly long time to one whose many previous activities were now restricted. For whom time might be hanging heavy.

{294}

"*Whatever* you do, children, *be happy.*"

"Pee happy?" Josh said.

"Well, that's important too."

As the elevator doors closed, she cried with her whole being, "All the good luck! I love you both so much."

Surely, Sandra hadn't heard aright. It wasn't possible! It wasn't *fair!*

The emergency room doctor nodded. "Comatose. Massive cerebral hemorrhage."

That's not my mother."

He pointed. "Isn't this her name?"

"What I meant was . . ." Her voice trailed off. (What *did* she mean?)

Led to a chair in the corner, Sandra just sat there, struck dumb. "Go, Laurel. Josh will be phoning," she said once she found her voice. And made her leave for his office.

Then Sandra fussed with Mom's snow-white hair, combing out the natural waves. An absurd thing to do, but she so wanted to do *something* for the one who always reassured her, praised and encouraged, took such pleasure in her. She kept up a steady patter until rewarded, she could have sworn, with a smile.

Mom would recover! She'd be fine!

No, not a chance. Never. If Mom survived, it would be as someone other than Hannah Brody Trilling. The brain scan showed extensive damage. Irreparable.

Suddenly, Mom's breathing turned rasping. Panicky, Sandra dashed into the hall and grabbed hold of a woman in a white coat with a stethoscope around her neck. "Nurse! Nurse! Help—"

The woman shook herself free. "I am a *physician*," she snapped, striding off.

A young man appeared. "*I'm* a nurse."

The problem was a minor one, it turned out. Adjusting the angle of Mom's head eliminated the rasp. Everything else, however, remained the same. Dire.

Why return to Mom's apartment? Once there, Sandra could not remember what she had come for. Overnight the place had undergone a drastic change of personality. Now so *desolate*, devoid of light and air: no music, spirit fled.

A person had only one set of parents. Nobody would ever love Sandra the way they had. Totally, without qualifications. Who else would always make allowances for her foolishness, her shortcomings? Take such inordinate pride in her?

Sacrifice for her. Convalescing at Sandra's after her heart attack, Mom rose each morning at dawn to clean the kitchen and make the family breakfast. The big fights they had over that. "Can't you understand?" Mom would say. "You do so much for me. I want to do something for you."

By the time her eyes had dried, Sandra remembered she had come for the little bag of Israeli soil to place beneath Mom's head. She also determined what to do while Mom still drew breath. Ensure a graceful exit. Not for her mother what was happening to very ill parents of Sandra's friends. Suffering, disintegration. In *this* case, death would not be kept at bay with delaying actions that made a mockery of living. There would be no extending an existence that only machinery registered as life.

Sandra would so instruct the doctors. One who had lived her entire life with dignity and compassion for all peoples would herself depart with dignity and compassion. Sandra would see to that. On her own. So should anyone object to the bending of some mindless, heartless man-made law, neither Josh nor Debbie could be implicated. Charlie, if need be, would defend her. For the final gift of love from daughter to mother.

It troubled Debbie that she hadn't seen more of Grandma that year, but the residency schedule left her little free time. She did phone regularly. Always, Grandma replied, "I understand. When I was your age, I was very busy myself."

But Debbie should have *made* the time. Ailing elderly grandmothers don't live forever. And Grandma always had time for Debbie as well as everyone else. Still, every month Mother sent her flowers and signed the enclosed card "Debbie."

Hard to pigeonhole, Grandma. She had discouraged Debbie from a career in the theater. Not bad advice. With few American repertory companies, little government support for the arts, Broadway's devotion to music spectaculars, movies made primarily for pubescents, soft-core nudity galore, acting had become a form of self-indulgence for exhibitionists and a sweepstakes for those gambling to win a TV series. But for regurgitating inane lines in a TV soap, Debbie's friend with the six-figure salary despised herself.

Yet when Debbie entered medical school, Grandma got after her to pursue acting in amateur productions, such as community theater. A life needed balance. Poetry as well as prose, the Sabbath as well as workdays, music to overcome clamor.

Invariably on the receiving end of their relationship, Debbie once expressed a desire to repay her debt, and Grandma said, "Don't be foolish. Just pass on whatever you think I've given you. All of us live off the generosity of those who have gone before. I do."

In a way, Debbie was reciprocating now. She had dictated the letter Mother submitted to Grandma's doctor, with instructions never to take heroic measures or resuscitate. And answered all questions about Grandma's condition patiently, what was keeping her alive.

Again and again Mother asked, "How long can this go on?"

"Nobody really knows."

"*Someone* knows. Yes."

And then, all too suddenly, before Debbie could be reconciled to her loss, Grandma was gone. (With Mother's loving help? Debbie refrained from inquiring.)

Before the funeral, Laurel volunteered to go through Mom's papers to see if they contained any last wishes to be honored. So she *said*. Actually, she wanted to check Mom's adoption story, which for some time she half-suspected of being a big white lie told to persuade Laurel to accept another's child as her own. Though both Josh and Sandra claimed never to have experienced jealousy—indeed, reacted with surprise to the question, as if sibling rivalry were a Freudian myth—surely it wasn't possible to raise an adopted child and a natural child together with neither one discerning the gulf separating them, which one was favored.

In Mom's apartment, walls aglow with paintings, Laurel dug up the famed gray metal box buried under a mound of plastic bags in the broom closet. Inside were passports, naturalization papers, Sandra's report cards, reviews of Josh's novels, stocks and bonds, crumbling clippings from the *Chicago Tribune*. (Sport columns?) At the bottom, two envelopes: one marked *Will*, the other *Ethical Will*.

Beneath them—there it was—a cracking, yellowing manila folder marked *Adoption Papers*. Incredible! Mom had told the truth. (And to Laurel alone.)

Which one was the adoptee? Josh? Or Sandra? And how would this revelation affect them all?

Laurel picked up the folder and turned it over and over in her sweating hands until the adoption papers spilled out on the kitchen table . . .

Zack intended to have it out with that Laurel after the funeral. The nerve of her to tell him to keep quiet about his Sunday visit to Grandma, who had taken a shine to Sarah from the start. She loved her biblical name, not, like Mother's, Americanized. Laurel should have seen her stroke Sarah's reddish gold hair.

Thoughtfulness itself, Sarah complimented Grandma's chic outfit, drew her out. Held her by the arm as they walked along Central Park West. They made a lovely couple, passer of the torch and recipient. And the matchmaker was Zack.

Before the approaching High Holidays, a middle-aged Italian flower vendor, on the street, was doing a brisk enough business to keep four assistants hopping. After pausing to admire the flowers and chat with the vendor, Grandma proceeded with Zack and Sarah toward Seventy-second Street. When he came running after them, they were half a block away.

"All of a sudden you disappear on me! Such a pretty lady. Here, I want you should have this." Into Grandma's hand the vendor thrust an American Beauty, and was gone.

"Aren't people sweet!" she said, touching the exquisite long-stemmed rose to her lips. Beauty and the beauty.

Along the way Grandma ran into friends and acquaintances, to whom Zack was introduced with great pride. Each time she got Sarah's name right. "My mother's name," she said wistfully.

Back at the apartment, Sarah exclaimed over the paintings. And she wasn't just putting it on, sincerity being her long suit. She said, *This* one is the finest; no, *this*. Finally selected seven paintings as the very best one. By afternoon's end, Sarah was calling Grandma what she called her own grandmother, *Babushka*.

A terrific time was had by all, one they promised to repeat real soon. A few more such get-togethers, and Grandma would be urging Zack to marry Sarah. So where did Laurel get off trying to make him feel the slightest bit responsible for an act of God!

Josh dreaded the funeral. Thoughts of it brought to mind Mom's words about her own mother: "That such an angel lies in the earth!" To erase that awful image he forced himself to concentrate on her life.

The great editor Maxwell Perkins had written that a book's final purpose doesn't become clear until its very last chapter. Yet Mom's now completed book of life Josh could not fully comprehend. Why so different? rare? Whence such goodness? Lots of clues—but no solution. And how could he nurture altruism in his daughter if he couldn't figure out how it develops, what makes benevolence flourish?

When Laurel shook him awake in the morning, Josh couldn't remember whether or not he had taken a third valium. What he did recall were the words of an associate calling the night before to offer condolences.

". . . But she was old," the follow concluded.

"*Who* was old?"

". . . talking about your mother, aren't we? Wasn't she over eighty?"

At the chapel the funeral director approached Josh and asked him to identify "the body."

Forfeit the last image of Mom, face radiant, dark eyes dancing, insisting he enjoy and be happy? In his ears those last words, I love you so much. "*Never,*" Josh replied.

Laurel said, "Let *me*" and followed the director. The identification of her father she had consigned to a brother; this would be less traumatic. She gritted her teeth, nevertheless, as the lid of the coffin was raised. *"Oh!"* she cried, as a hand from nowhere tugged at her sleeve.

"They told me the wrong time—how do you like that! Been here fifty-five minutes already. Attended another funeral by mistake. For someone from the *Bronx*, of all places . . ."

Still yammering, the intruder was ushered out. On the director's return, Laurel said yes, this was Hannah Trilling, without having taken a look. For Mom was the mother Laurel yearned for as a child. Did still.

"What?" Thoroughly tranquilized, Josh couldn't be sure he was hearing the condolences tendered by some callers. Worse, whether he was voicing the responses bubbling in his brain.

"Just last month I flew back to Miami after visiting my kids here in New York. Now, your mother's funeral. Can't get Supersavers on such short notice, y'know. Had to pay full fare."

Just think of all those Frequent-Flyer credits. Half a dozen more funerals will get you a free trip to Hawaii.

"Did your mother receive all those grapefruit and oranges I sent her two weeks ago? One entire bushel, not just a half. Will you check and let me know?"

You bet. Every orange and grapefruit she ate I'll replace.

"Terrible thing about Hannah, just terrible. I myself was laid up for weeks with the flu. Sick as a dog. Lost seven whole pounds. Look at my face. Wrinkles! And my stomach's still on the blink."

Not to mention your mouth.

"The way *I* look at it, Josh, after all my experiences—someday I'll tell you about them and you'll write another best seller. Death is simply a part of life, that's all. Yes, life is a trip, and death is our destination. The Big End."

No, no. LSD is a trip, and you are the living end.

"You don't have to worry about Cousin Simon. He's taking your mother's death very well."

I'm sure he'll take yours even better.

"Surprised at you, Josh, I really am. For ten whole minutes I'm sitting here and you never came over to say hello. Outrageous, snubbing one of your very closest blood relatives."

Mom never told you? You were adopted. From donkeys.

Laurel, to the rescue, took Josh to the office, where she plied him with coffee.

After the third cup, Josh summoned up the courage to ask, "What did I *say* out there? Have I been talking out of turn?"

"Say? You haven't been talking at *all*. Not a word. Haven't blinked an eye in twelve minutes."

"*Thank God!*"

Back in the family room, Josh, finally sober, was tearfully embraced by his father's brother, five years younger than Mom. "Hannah was like a mother to me. The time I had that car accident. She came running to the hospital all out of breath, crying. The way that woman comforted. Touched me. And taking me home, held me in her arms."

A friend of Mom's: "We were watching the astronauts on TV, and your mother says, 'Those poor fellows, all orphans.' How did she know they're all orphans? 'If those astronauts had mothers,' Hannah says, 'you think they'd let them be shot up into orbit out in space nowhere?' "

In tears, Mom's cousin: "There were five of us children, but we were scattered all around. It was your mother who cared for Mama and Papa till they died in their nineties. As long as I live I'll never forget Hannah."

An elegantly dressed, aristocratic-looking stranger: "Your mother was a great friend. But in talking about her children, a bad liar." Seeing the confused look on Josh's face, she introduced herself. "I am Little Red Riding Hood."

A neighbor from Parkside Avenue: "After my mother died—I was just eight, an only child—my father brought me up all by himself. So when he died—this was twenty-eight years ago—I couldn't stop crying. Could barely look after my two small children. Well, one morning your mother comes in, says my father had appeared to her in a dream the night before. In this dream told her he couldn't rest in peace so long as I kept crying all the time. Declared I had to stop mourning for *his* sake. And so I finally did. Tell me, you think it really happened, that dream? Or did she make it up?"

Then there were all those Mom had helped who could not attend— the infirm, the hospitalized, the dead; they counted too. As did numberless others unknown to her children, for Mom never spoke of her good works. So it hadn't been for nothing, her life. No great void had swallowed Mom up. In memory, still lived.

A fellow congregant from Brooklyn touched Sandra's hand. "You know what the *Shechina* is?"

"The Divine Presence, the Spirit of God."

"Right. Well, that's what I always saw in your mother's face."

Sandra gasped.

"I told that to your mother lots of times. 'The *Shechina* is in your face.' Know what she always said? 'Please don't say that. Maybe your wife won't like it.' "

This was so like the open school days of childhood, teachers praising Sandra and Joel to a beaming Mom. Would that Mom were there now to hear! Had they told her often enough how proud they were of her?

Too soon came the announcement for everyone to move to the chapel.

Looking from Josh to Sandra, then back again, Laurel felt certain that hiding the adoption papers from them without allowing even herself a look had been the right thing to do. What benefit at this late date in uncovering Mom's secret, disclosing what was now *their* secret, Mom's and Laurel's? (Maybe someday, if she ever doubted one's ability to love another's as her own child, Laurel would examine the papers.) Now she prayed Sandra was the adopted one, so that whichever character traits were transmissible could be inherited by Josh's baby and hers.

"We'll name our baby after a Righteous Jew," Laurel announced, as they all entered the chapel. "Hannah."

Not trusting himself to speak, Josh squeezed her hand.

What, Sandra wondered, would Mom's beloved rabbi from Brooklyn say about what used to be called "just a housewife?" No longer heard, that term. It had become archaic, something of an embarrassment, almost a pejorative. Nowadays, with most women in the workplace—their worth, like men's, reckoned in terms of salary and position—even if they wanted to help others as Mom always did, they didn't have the time. Society's loss; life would surely be less kind, less caring for the disappearance of the housewife. Look at all the lives Mom had touched for good, how she'd made a difference. Still, what had been *her* reward?

At first it was hard for Josh to concentrate on the eulogy, for to the rabbi's left was the coffin. Behind it, however, loomed a large picture window, framing trees, bushes and flowers outside. Josh focused on them, visualizing Mom setting up her easel to paint the scene. "Hold it," he murmured, "stay put. Don't go 'way now."

". . . When I think of Hannah Brody Trilling, three words spring immediately to mind," Rabbi Silverstein was saying. "The first word is *Eidelkeit*.

"*Eidelkeit* means refinement, and more. Lovingkindness and tenderness. Goodness and elegance, sweetness and well-mannered politeness. You could see the *Eidelkeit* in Hannah's regal bearing as well as behavior. In that expressive face . . ."

Sandra turned to Josh and found him smiling too. Mom was receiving the testimonial she always deserved. No farewell this. A celebration.

"*Beauty* is the second word. Physical beauty together with a beauty that was spiritual. Or, as I believe, a physical beauty that *reflected* Hannah's beauty of spirit and character. Within each of us is a spark of the Divine. Hannah's showed for all the world to see in that loving countenance . . .

"The third word has to be *purity*, for Hannah never lost hers. A childlike purity. Untarnished, undisillusioned. Those around her felt its effect. Hers was a purity so cleansing, it often made us examine our actions and appearance. In her goodness, simplicity and directness, Hannah Trilling reminded us of a human being's possibilities. Of choices we ourselves can also make, of the mensch we too can become, *if only* . . ."

That last afternoon together, in the middle of *La Bohème*, Mom had exclaimed, "That music! Those voices! From God Himself. Thank you so much, Josh, for bringing me such joy."

"Thank *you* so much, Mom," he had responded.

Now, Mom rested with the *Shechina*. Surely, she would bring Him joy too. Lucky God!

25

Dear Children,

Just before getting married, I started what I planned would be a running journal (enclosed). Never did keep it up, though—not enough hours in the day. So much for good intentions.

This here is something else—my ethical will. I wrote one when your father was terminally ill and I didn't expect to survive him. But that farewell address got lost during my move from Brooklyn. So this is a new, improved one—after all, I am a good ten years wiser!

Things do look different now. The older I get the more I think of life as a painting. Seen up close, one may miss its essence. Beauty is discovered when one stands some distance away. Who, for example, would dream that weekly visits to a beloved sister written up in a novel groggily described on a TV show seen by a couple in Boston would play a part in founding a great hospital!

But I'm stalling. It's not easy to say goodbye. I hardly know where to begin or how.

Perhaps as I've done in years gone by at the end of a beautiful evening, after a gathering of family and friends, just as I start for home.

Anyway, here goes.

I've had a wonderful time with you. It's been a genuine treat, being together all this time, getting to know you more and more, better and better. Relished it with my whole being. Even feel I've accomplished a thing or two.

No person, I think, can ever be too grateful for what he or she achieves and receives, or express it too often. Accepting gifts without acknowledging the givers is, to my mind, a form of thievery. So in place of prayers for those I appeal for every week over the Shabbas candles, here's a list, a partial one, of those I want to thank now with all my heart:

1. God, first of all, for creating this wonderous world, granting me life and sustaining my every breath, especially these last ten years which have been happier than I had any right to expect. For creating all peoples in His image, as well as initiating the Covenant with the Children of Israel. (Of course, if they hadn't chosen to be chosen, there never would have been any deal. And like most others, it's been a marriage of tremendous ups and downs.)

2. My golden-haired mother, for her love, which I feel even as I write. (The reason God created mothers, they say, is because He couldn't be everywhere.) I was always a little disappointed I didn't look like Mother, which would have started off each day with her reflection in my mirror. Hers was the glow of a pure and shining light, my undying source of affection and encouragement and consolation.

3. My father, for uprooting himself and relocating the family to America. Not for money or anything material—Papa made a very good living in Galicia—but to keep us faithful Jews. Who else will preserve Judaism and transmit it? Despite what became of him here in America—a small-time shopkeeper working twelve-hour days who never mastered English—the man never complained. His reward: all of us escaped the Holocaust, which killed just about all the Jews who remained in Galicia.

4 America, for welcoming us, as well as so many others, and for giving us freedom and opportunity undreamed-of in Europe. I doubt native-born Americans can appreciate this golden land as much as we immigrants do. Today, half a century after failing to rescue Jews

from certain death, the United States has become a growing haven for the oppressed—Koreans, Hungarians, Vietnamese, Latin Americans, Lebanese, Russian Jews. Some consolation.

5. The Righteous Gentiles, who let neither bigotry nor circumstances dictate to them. They restore one's faith in humanity, replenish the soul, gladden God Himself. Sometimes I wonder why there were so few Righteous Gentiles. Other times, considering the extraordinary sacrifices they made, I marvel there were so many. On account of such people, I am convinced, the world still abides and humanity deserves to triumph.

6. Israel, for rescuing the tattered remnants of European Jewry from the death camps and the 600,000 driven out of Arab lands in 1948. In a way the birth of the state of Israel that year meant more to me than your birth days. I'm sure you understand why. Both my children had a mother and a father, Israel took in hundreds of thousands of orphans.

7. My husband, for being unfailingly respectful to my father and so good to my sisters and brothers, and for two wonderful children and dozens of happy years. In my mind's eye I can see that nice young man, so gentlemanly and understanding, come to call in his navy blue suit and sky blue silk shirt. His love letters I still know by heart. If there was a change later, much later on, I think I now realize its cause. A stroke so silent nobody knew about it. Not even poor Rupert. Or maybe he did know and, to spare me, never told.

8. My children, for their devotion and support and encouragement and good humor. For noodging me with daily phone calls, constant visits and invitations, worrying about me. For being proud of me, as I am of them. And how! God knows I tried with my whole being to be a good mother. Whether I succeeded, I don't know. That's for them to say.

9. My grandchildren, for the warmth of our attachment and for maintaining our tradition. I trust they will marry within the faith, preserve the Covenant and transmit it. They should always care for others, not just for themselves alone. From them should come more good Jews who are good to everyone. I should love them to be examples for all peoples to follow.

10. Dr. Litvak, for saving Rupert's life repeatedly and being the

best of friends. That good man should never be forgotten. Since he left no children to say kaddish *for him, would you kindly recite it on the anniversary of his death each year? Also for Eleanor Roosevelt, friend to the whole world.*

11. Sheldon, for giving me a big lift just when I really needed one. It bothers me, not doing right by him, though what I did was right for myself. All the more reason to be pleased he got married eight months after our disengagement. (I checked.)

12. Leo, for always giving me a laugh. He never meant anyone any harm. If everyone was a Leo, the world wouldn't be a better place—but neither would it be any worse. Me, I can't help feeling grateful to anyone who proposes to me. (Like Mike, the young man I didn't marry.)

That was the easy part. The following is harder to put into words. A person doesn't know just how deeply she loves till faced by separation. Happily, though, I am not just going away. I am also going toward. So please do me a big favor, children, don't grieve. You know me by now. Wherever I go, I always enjoy myself.

As you read these words, I have already rejoined Eili, Eili. Know I have gone in perfect peace. I do not believe death is the end. Only something else, something different. Though my journey from the Old World to the New World put me through the most terrible storm, I did reach a country more wonderful than I ever imagined. Now—with no such tzuris, I hope—another journey will take me from This-World to the World-to-Come. Since life is so full of surprises, I see no reason why death shouldn't have even more wonderful ones in store.

Just as people are not born out of nothing, I feel certain they do not disintegrate into nothing. Sugar dissolved in tea, nobody sees, but the taste is there. Remains even after swallowed, the taste clinging to the tongue. I believe with Henrietta Szold: "In the life of the Spirit, there is no ending that is not a new beginning."

Death I think of as a reunion of sorts. It's a great mystery where we come from, an even greater mystery where we go. Probably to something like a star unseen by day that materializes only when night falls. Yes, I do believe: "The dust returns to the earth, but the Spirit returns to God who gave it." Lives that are lived with faith can end with this trust. Just as lives lived serving others—and all of us need help—do end with a sense of fulfillment.

Know one thing, dear children. I'll be your *gute beiter* in the World-to-Come, pleading your case with the Almighty at all times. If you think I've pestered God too much in This-World—well, just wait! He might have second thoughts about taking me to Him. Maybe even send me back in a big hurry!

Know another thing. I have no intention of ever leaving you. I'll always be with you, so long as that is your wish. A person never dies whose values remain, whose work is continued. So please serve God with joy and treat people, all people, with chesed. And a smile.

Me, I've always thought of God as just that, a heart-gladdening, soulwarming smile. No face, no body, no gender, of course. Just pure smiling radiance. Alternating with tears. Oh, so many, many tears! For life's tragedies over which He has little control (why Tattenyu *also needs our help*) and from lamenting all those terrible things some people do to others.

Know what counts in the end is not the successes of life or the failures, not the fortune or the fame. (I can't imagine anyone on a deathbed regretting not having a larger estate to leave or a bigger pile of newspaper clippings.) What counts then, as ever, is the loving-kindness we have extended to others day by day.

Of course, if you're too good in this world, some people think you naive. Or just plain stupid. But that doesn't matter, provided you don't think you're stupid. As for me, I have no regrets. None. Some of the nice things I've done were for people who weren't very nice at all. But who cares! I've always had my own standards, set down in the Torah, and all my life I've tried to live up to them. That's kept me happy, knowing I was doing the right thing, however difficult.

Actually, not at all difficult. Let me tell you a secret: No matter what you may think, I've never sacrificed myself for anyone or anything. You see, when a person wants to do something with all her heart, it's no sacrifice. It's joy, pure and simple. Said a famous writer: "Happiness is a kind of genius." But me, I think of happiness as a form of gratitude.

As I began with God, let me conclude with Him. Thank Him once more—this time in advance—for taking me to His bosom before, I pray, I overstay my welcome on earth and become a burden to my cherished ones.

Into Thy hands I now return my Spirit. May my death be an atonement for whatever sins and errors and wrongdoing I have committed. In Thy mercy grant me the goodness that awaits the righteous, and bring me to eternal life . . . Father of the orphans, Protector of the widows, protect my loved ones with whom my soul is forever bound.

All the good luck, my dearest ones! I love you all so much! Pass it on!

Mother

TAR   **Tarr, Herbert.**

        A woman of spirit

$18.95

DATE			